THE
BABY
THIEF

Books by L.J. Sellers

The Detective Jackson Series
The Sex Club
Secrets to Die For
Thrilled to Death
Passions of the Dead
Dying for Justice
Liars, Cheaters & Thieves
Rules of Crime

The Lethal Effect
(Previously published as *The Suicide Effect*)
The Baby Thief
The Gauntlet Assassin

THE BABY THIEF

L.J. SELLERS

THOMAS & MERCER

Printed in the United States of America.

Published by Thomas & Mercer
P.O. Box 400818
Las Vegas, NV 89140

ISBN-13: 9781612186238
ISBN-10: 1612186238
Library of Congress Control Number: 2012911787

Cast of Characters

Jenna McClure: restaurant manger/kidnapping victim
Eric Troutman: freelance journalist/Pulitzer winner
Elizabeth DeMauer: geneticist/fertility specialist/David's lover
David Carmichael: OB-GYN/religious cult leader/Liz's lover
Zeke: Carmichael's handyman/ex-con
Rachel: cult member/compound nurse
Sarah: teenage cult member
Tamara: Sarah's mother/cult member/David's lover
Darcie: pregnant teenager/left the cult
Wade Jackson: violent crimes detective
Joe Pikerton: newspaper reporter
Gerald Akron: head of R&D at JB Pharma
Daniel Potter: adoption lawyer
Patty McClure: Jenna's legal mother
Katrice: bartender/Jenna's friend

Chapter 1

Elizabeth stared at the file on her desk, heart pounding with indecision. *Say it!* Her forehead went damp and she reached for a tissue, avoiding her patient's gaze. Ms. McClure sat calmly, waiting for her to speak. The patient had come to the Assisted Reproduction Clinic in good faith. How could Elizabeth violate that trust? She was a doctor!

The thought of Dr. Gybbs, her chief of staff, discovering her deception horrified her more than anything. She owed him so much. He'd promoted her to director of genetic science her third year with the hospital, passing over several male associates. Then Columbia had honored her with its Scientific Excellence Award just last year. To risk all that—

Just say it!

McClure shifted in her chair. Elizabeth glanced at the file again and took a deep breath. "The test results show you have the genetic marker associated with cystic fibrosis."

There, she'd done it. She'd told the lie that set the plan in motion.

Her patient's eyes widened, then filled with despair. Elizabeth knew how she felt. Hearing that you couldn't or shouldn't have a baby was the most devastating news a woman could receive.

She wanted to reach out and comfort the woman. Instead, she leaned back and spoke casually. "Don't be too alarmed. One out of twenty-two Caucasians is a carrier. But unless the father is also a carrier, your chances of having a healthy child are still good."

"What does that mean?" McClure's light-brown eyes flickered with anger.

Elizabeth understood the anger too. But she couldn't let herself feel kinship with this woman. McClure had something she wanted, something she was entitled to. She had to be strong to take it from her.

"In practical terms, it means before you have yourself artificially inseminated, the donor should also be screened for the cystic fibrosis marker." *Damn!* She was making it sound too easy. Elizabeth didn't want her coming back to the clinic any time soon. So she continued, "The test is more difficult with the limited amount of DNA in sperm, thus more expensive. If you wait until you're pregnant, then have an amniocentesis, you're faced with the decision of either giving birth to a diseased child or aborting it. Perhaps you should take some time to read up on CF. You may decide to consider other options."

"Like what?"

"Adoption." Just saying the word made the old bitterness rise in her throat. Elizabeth swallowed hard to keep it down. "The joy of children isn't limited to genetic offspring."

If only that were true.

The summer of her tenth birthday crashed on her consciousness like a tidal wave. Standing by her mother's grave, watching the casket being lowered, Elizabeth had wanted to throw herself in and let the earth swallow her too. But her grief then was only the beginning. The whispering of relatives at the funeral was followed by the sudden crushing knowledge that she'd been adopted, that her beloved mother was not really hers.

Elizabeth had never considered adopting a child, even when she learned her ovaries were worthless, damaged—so she believed—by pelvic infections she'd suffered as a child. Before she could compose herself, another memory engulfed her. The drunken sweaty face of Ralph, her adoptive father, grimacing in a strange blend of pain and joy as he forced himself on her.

Elizabeth felt the tremors starting, the buried rage fighting to surface. She'd never been to a counselor, never spoken of it to anyone. Even after learning she was sterile, she'd kept her silence. But the rage never diminished. It surfaced less often now, but with the same intensity.

Her patient's voice, hauntingly familiar, broke through the anguish. "Do you have any literature about cystic fibrosis that I could take with me?"

"I'm sorry, I don't," Elizabeth snapped.

She had to get this woman out of her office. Just looking at her weakened Elizabeth's resolve. McClure had the same wide cheekbones and stubborn chin, the same wavy hair. "Here's the name of an organization you can call for information. They can also put you in touch with a support group."

Elizabeth stood and handed McClure a card, willing her to leave. She didn't want to see her again until she was unconscious on the operating table. Elizabeth wished there was another way, but the laparoscopy was a simple procedure and wouldn't hurt her at all.

What about afterward? she asked herself for the hundredth time. The drugs would wipe out McClure's memory, but what if the oocytes didn't fertilize? What if the transfer failed? Could they keep her until she ovulated again?

Don't think about it, she told herself. David was a great embryologist. If anyone could make her pregnant, he could.

"Thanks," McClure said quietly, tucking the card in her purse. She squared her shoulders and wiped mascara from under her eyes before turning to leave.

Elizabeth admired her composure, her refusal to cry or complain as so many did at the first sign of trouble. She was a sturdy woman physically too. An inch or so taller than Elizabeth and meatier all over. Not overweight; just robust, healthy. Elizabeth felt a pang of jealousy. She had always been pale and thin from spending long hours in the lab and skipping meals.

"Good luck." Elizabeth bit the inside of her cheek. She had a sudden urge to call her back. Maybe they could become friends and eventually she could ask…

No. She couldn't take the risk.

The woman was gone and Elizabeth was alone again. Collapsing back in her chair, she started to tremble. It had begun. In her whole life, she had never been so frightened, or so excited. Suddenly she had to see the slides again.

She jumped up and walked briskly down the corridor to the lab. Her assistant, a young woman with one eye glued to a microscope, ignored Elizabeth as she passed. She unlocked the lab door and hurried to the drawer where she kept enlarged film of DNA slides. From the back, she pulled a special file marked only by initials, then inserted two enlargements into a projector.

There they were. Those single-stranded DNA probes lined up like matching bar codes from the supermarket. Elizabeth had noticed McClure's facial similarities the first time she'd come into the clinic. She had compared their DNA on a whim. Elizabeth stared, checking for inconsistencies, then smiled when she didn't find any.

There was no doubt. McClure was her sister.

Chapter 2

The restaurant's double doors burst open as Jenna reached for her keys. *Damn!* Sixty seconds too late. Even though technically the place was closed, Jenna forced herself to smile. When she looked up, a short, heavy man, face covered by a bandanna, thrust out a gun and said, "Piss me off and I'll kill you."

Jenna's heart skipped a beat, then pounded frantically as a startled cry burst from her throat.

"Where's the money?" A second man stepped forward. He was tall and scrawny, a kid with a ponytail. Black and red paint covered his face but didn't hide a large boil on the side of his nose. Without the gun he would have seemed comical.

Jenna wasn't laughing. She knew she had to respond, but her brain scampered from one thought to another and couldn't form a sentence.

"Listen, bitch." The skinny kid grabbed her hair and pressed his gun, a big gray semiautomatic, under her chin. "Tell me where the money is or I'll kill you and anybody else in—"

"Everyone on the floor, now!" the short guy screamed as he pivoted toward the sudden murmuring in the lounge. A bourbon fog filled the air where his voice had been.

He's drunk, Jenna realized. Panic surged through her body, making her feel weak and confused. She didn't know if she was supposed to lie down or get the money. The kid dug his fingers into her scalp and dragged her across the narrow lobby into the darkened lounge. She bit the inside of her cheek to keep from screaming. Stale cigarette smoke and alcohol permeated the air.

The kid's lips curled in a sick sort of smile as three guests, the bartender, and a waitress dropped to the floor. Jenna tried to mentally count how many others were in the building. Two or three guests still in the dining area, plus Antonio, the broiler cook, Evin, a new dishwasher, and three, maybe four food servers.

The short guy seemed to read her mind. "Check the back," he shouted suddenly. "Get everyone in here so I can see 'em."

The pleased look disappeared as the kid let go of Jenna's hair. He scurried through the bar, high-stepping over the middle-aged men in suits on the floor. Jenna wished she could lie down too; her legs shook so badly she thought they'd collapse. But she stayed upright, afraid to move.

"About the money." The short guy lifted the small dark gun to her temple.

"In the till, behind the bar." Jenna forced the words through clenched teeth.

"Open it for me." His eyes darted nervously between Jenna and the men bunched together on the stained blue carpet. The top of his head was bald but straggly dark curls covered the back of his neck. Even with the bandanna, he looked like a creepy dishwasher she'd worked with in Seattle when she was still a waitress.

"You! Outta there first," he shouted over the counter. Jenna held her breath. Nate, her bartender, spent his free time writing letters to the editor and arguing philosophy for sport. But he crawled out from behind the bar without a word. Jenna let out some air. Thank god he'd kept his mouth shut.

As she stepped toward the register, an older waitress, who'd been with Geronimo's since it opened, hurried into the lounge. She was waving a bill. "Anybody got change for a twenty?" Carmen stopped short when she spotted the men in suits on the floor.

"I'll take that," the short, creepy guy said, stepping away from Jenna to reach for Carmen's twenty. "And anything else you've got in your pockets."

Jenna winced. Most of the evening's receipts were walking around with the servers, who acted as cashiers. As soon as the short guy and the skinny kid realized it, they'd turn their guns on her crew. Fear snaked through her gut. They could be killed. It happened all the time. People gunned down during robberies for no apparent reason. She thought about Nate's five-year-old twin boys and Carmen's three teenage daughters. Those kids would be devastated if these people didn't come home.

Jenna fumbled for her key to the till, hoping to distract the short guy with a drawer full of cash. The rest of the crew shuffled in, hands above their heads, eyes darting between Jenna and the short gunman. The kid had a grip on Tami, an eighteen-year-old waitress who sucked back tears with little gulping noises. "Get on the floor, all of you."

As her employees dropped down, the restaurant was silent. Even the roar of the dishwasher had stopped. Jenna knew there were still guests on the other side of the partial wall that separated the lounge from the main dining area, but no one made a peep.

Then the register drawer popped open with a loud ping. Startled, the kid jerked and fired a round, shattering the mirror behind the bar.

Tami screamed as shards peppered the liquor bottles and stuck in her hair. Jenna's knees buckled but she held on. Ears ringing, she refused to collapse or cry out as she so badly wanted to do. Even though some of the crew were older, she was in charge here; everyone counted on her. Jenna desperately wanted to believe that if she kept herself together no one would get hurt.

Jenna snatched up the cash in the till, her fingers fumbling to hold the stack of bills. She passed it all to the short guy, who grabbed it with one hand and stuffed it into his half-zipped jacket. Tami started to whimper.

"Shut up!" the kid shrieked. "Or I'll shoot your stupid mouth off." He kicked Tami to make his point. Tami let out a brief cry. Nate started to speak up, but Jenna gave him a look. Be quiet, please, Jenna silently pleaded. You have little boys. Don't get yourself killed. She wanted to say something, to turn the two men's attention to herself. As badly as she'd always wanted children, she hadn't been lucky enough to have them yet. She didn't have a husband either—or brothers and sisters. There was no one to miss her if she didn't come home. But her throat wouldn't cooperate, except to swallow meekly.

One of the guests from the main dining room suddenly bolted for the front. As he reached the door, he turned and looked back. The short guy fired twice into the lobby. Jenna heard a shout and the soft thump of a body hitting the carpet. Then her legs finally buckled and she went down. The bar tile was wet and cold under her knees, yet Jenna wanted nothing more than to press her body against the floor, close her eyes, and wait for it to be over.

"Nobody moves for at least five minutes!" the short guy bellowed, jerking his gun from one person to another. The kid started to say something, but the short guy cut him off. "We're outta here." He stepped back toward the lobby.

"But we're supposed to lock 'em in the freezer." The kid hadn't moved.

"Forget it, let's go!"

The kid looked over at Nate, shrugged, then kicked him in the face before running out. Not until the front doors slammed did Jenna's body relax. She fought the urge to cry great gulping sobs at the sheer relief of being alive. After many deep breaths, she willed herself to get up and call 911.

The guest, a small man in his early forties, had been shot in the right side of his chest. Except for the blood oozing from the hole where his pocket had been, he was perfectly still. Jenna knelt next to him and checked for a pulse or a breath. Nothing.

She cursed softly, hot tears still pressing the back of her eyes. She couldn't remember a thing she'd learned in the mandatory CPR class she'd taken just eight months ago.

Carmen had followed her up front, then vomited after one look at the wound. Nate, the only other person who would have been helpful, was bleeding profusely from his nose. *How do you stop bleeding in the chest?*

"Somebody bring me some towels."

The man wasn't breathing. Four minutes. The number popped into her head. The brain could only survive four minutes without oxygen. She had to get his heart pumping. She leaned over him and began chest compressions.

"I brought towels," a gentle, unfamiliar voice said. Jenna looked up. The man had a camera hanging from his neck.

"Press them against his wound, please."

For six long minutes, they worked together over him, their faces inches apart. Jenna became aware the stranger had a nice face and smelled like mint. His presence gave her comfort and she didn't know why.

Finally, the paramedics arrived.

Chapter 3 >—

Eric Troutman had quietly taken a few pictures of Jenna as she gave compressions to the wounded man. He still had guilt about observing and recording other people's trauma. But this was the best story he'd ever witnessed, and he couldn't let it go without at least a couple of shots. He'd almost bolted when she asked him to help. The sight of blood sometimes made him queasy. But she had been so determined, so fearless; how could he not do his part?

Jenna McClure. He'd learned her name from one of the restaurant staff. Eric was impressed. She was more than just good copy. She was someone he wanted to know. He'd stopped by the hospital long enough to find out the shooting victim, Arthur Brentwood, had died, and he now headed downtown to the police station, hoping to find Jenna—with visions of an in-depth interview and a front-page story in the *Oregonian*. Maybe even a second piece, a personality profile, for *Northwest Lifestyle*. His career needed a good jolt.

He'd been freelancing since being laid off the newspaper a year ago. He had a lot less money now, but he liked the features he was writing a lot more. After ten years on the crime beat, the stories all started to sound the same. No one ever told the whole truth anyway, not the cops, the criminals, or the victims. He'd become desensitized to people's traumas and had hated himself for it.

He was happier now, but sometimes he missed the excitement, the adrenaline rush of being a half step ahead of a big breaking news story. The year he'd won the Pulitzer had been the best and worst of his life. His series on abusive foster parents and the Children's Services personnel who looked the other way generated the largest response the paper ever had. Before the ruckus died down, the Children's Services director was replaced and a citizen review board established. But the children still haunted him.

Eric shuddered and reached for the radio, needing to shake off the images of the battered children. The gaping hole in the dashboard reminded him the radio had been stolen a few weeks back. Still wanting to brighten his mood, he sang the chorus of *I Feel Good*, an old James Brown song.

It was his own fault the radio had been ripped off. After he sold his police scanner and CB radio, he'd quit locking his car, figuring no one would bother a '72 Firebird. If they did, he wanted to make it easy. Used radios were cheap and easy to come by; windows were not. He could afford a nicer car, but he couldn't bring himself to spend the money. Not yet anyway. His Firebird still ran fine and had a good working heater. Besides, he liked old cars. Today's designs didn't compare to the classics.

The downtown streets were deserted at one o'clock in the morning except for an occasional party car, the occupants oblivious to everything but their own music. Eric ignored the speed-limit signs. After working the crime beat for years he knew most of the cops and could probably talk himself out of a ticket. He was determined to get to the police station before they finished questioning Jenna. He had to see her tonight. The compulsion was overwhelming, and Eric never ignored his instincts. It was more than just a story. Jenna was too special to let her slip away, unexplored.

Eric was surprised by Jenna's attractiveness when he saw her pass through the open security door and walk into the police-department lobby. He hadn't noticed it during the chaos. He'd been aware of the overall package, her athletic build and sun-kissed complexion, but hadn't really taken in the caramel-colored eyes and sensuous, unpainted lips. She'd let her hair down now, a thick mass of curls that matched her eyes and seemed slightly out of control.

Eric shook his head. He'd sworn never to get hung up on a woman's looks again. The gorgeous ones were always trouble. Fortunately, she wasn't really his type. The executive-style matching skirt and jacket were a turnoff. Eric hated suits on anybody, male or female. They intimidated him, made him feel instinctively rebellious. But as she stood there, eyes blinking, Jenna looked so tired and vulnerable that Eric wanted to put his arms around her. Instead he offered his hand.

"Eric Troutman, freelance journalist."

She hesitated, then leaned forward and gave his hand a quick, powerful squeeze.

"Jenna McClure. Thanks for helping back at the restaurant. What do you want?"

"To buy you a cup of coffee. Hear your story." He smiled his best you're-gonna-love-me smile.

"You were there. There's not much more to tell."

"I was in the dining room and missed most of the action." Eric kept smiling. "I want to hear your backstory too."

"I have to go home and get some sleep." She turned away.

"Tomorrow?" Eric couldn't let her get away. He had to see her again. "I'll buy you lunch. Anywhere you like."

Jenna turned back, lips pressed tightly together. Little flecks of dark brown glinted against the lighter shade of her irises. "I just spent two hours with the police, going through the whole ugly thing over and over. I really don't want to talk about it anymore. I'm sorry, but I have to go now."

Eric reached for her arm, but Jenna jerked away. Eric wanted to kick himself. The poor woman had just been robbed at gunpoint. The last thing she needed was some stranger grabbing her. "I'm very sorry, ma'am. I shouldn't have done that."

Why had he called her *ma'am*? Women under fifty hated that. He tried again. "You've had a rough night. Do you have a ride home?"

"I can call a cab." She walked toward the exit.

Eric called after her. "Sooner or later you'll talk to someone from the press just to get them off your back. I'd be honored if you'd let it be me."

Jenna stopped. "Why you?"

Her expression was stern, but her eyes smiled. He was getting through. Or maybe she liked his perseverance.

"Because I was there. Because I won't ask you stupid questions like, 'How did it feel to have that gun at your head?' Because"— Eric paused for dramatic effect—"I know what a hero you are, and I have an obligation to share that triumph with a public starved for some good news amid all the chaos and fear."

Jenna threw back her head and laughed, an uninhibited roar. The front-desk officer looked up and smiled.

"What a load of crap," she said finally. "You're gonna make a buck off someone's misfortune just like everybody else in the news business." She half smiled. "I'll think about it. In the meantime, I'll take that ride if it's still offered."

* * *

Jenna had never felt so tired in all her life, not even after the first time she'd done a full hour on the stair stepper at Court Sports. At least a heavy-duty workout made her feel stronger, more worthwhile. Standing in the shabby lobby of the police station at one in the morning made her feel diminished.

But the reporter seemed to vibrate with energy. And that grin, what was that about? Jenna chewed the inside of her cheek as they headed outside. He was attractive and charming in his own way, but she wished she hadn't accepted his offer of a ride. She would have to do the interview now as a payback. Where would they meet? The idea of sitting in a public restaurant made her uneasy. Maybe she could cancel at the last minute, tell him she got called in to work. The thought of going back in to Geronimo's also filled her with dread. Jenna shivered.

"Are you all right?" The concern in his voice warmed her heart, but the trembling in her arms and legs wouldn't stop.

"No, not really."

He moved in closer and put his arm lightly around her shoulder. "Let me buy you a drink. If anybody ever needed one, you do."

Jenna let him guide her across the empty downtown street to an older, slightly beat-up car. She had no idea what make it was and didn't care. It was big and comfortable, and Eric opened the door for her, which seemed amazingly sweet.

They drove in silence for a few minutes, Jenna thinking that under any other circumstances she would never get into a car with a man she didn't know. Yet after what she'd been through, Eric felt as safe and comfortable as a cup of hot chocolate.

A green station wagon with a glowing yellow taxi light passed them. In an hour, when the bars closed, there would be a little surge of traffic, but now the streets were empty. Even with a population of 160,000 and more than its share of world-class runners, Eugene was still a small town.

"How long have you lived here?" Eric wanted to know, as if reading her mind.

"Five years. Up until tonight, I couldn't imagine ever wanting to move."

"Where are you from?"

"I moved here from Seattle, but I was born and raised in Astoria." Jenna shuddered as the memory of the robber's voice and the pressure of the gun played in her head. She'd left Seattle to get away from an escalating crime rate. Eugene had been her first choice because it was close to her mother, who lived in Florence, a small town sixty miles away, on the coast.

"A real native. By the way, where are we going?"

"Riverside Apartments, just past Valley River Center."

"I was going to buy you a drink, remember?" Eric glanced over with a look she couldn't read.

"I think I'd better go home. I'm starting to feel shaky."

"You're entitled. I couldn't see what was happening from my chickenshit place on the floor, but it sounded rough in there."

Jenna was silent. Every response she came up with sounded trite. Earlier, the police detective had referred to the robbers as "the clown and the cowboy." It bothered her that the men had nicknames, as if it were all a game not to be taken too seriously. She might not ever be able to talk about this night, she realized.

Jenna shivered again. The heat of an Indian summer day was long gone, replaced with the chill of an October night. She wanted desperately to be home.

"Should I turn on the heat?"

"Please."

"They'll get these guys. I have a good friend in the department who never gives up."

"What if they do catch them? I'll have to testify. I'll have to sit in the same courtroom with those assholes." She fought for control, but her fear gathered strength and poured out in an angry stream. "There's only a fifty-fifty chance they'll ever go to jail, and if they do, they'll be out again in a few years. Our justice system is insane."

"I know how you feel."

"I'm not sure you do."

Jenna didn't think she would ever feel safe again. Nobody was ever safe anywhere. The papers proved it every morning. Innocent people gunned down by some lunatic having a bad day.

The car slowed, and she realized they were almost there. They turned into the complex and Jenna pointed to the left, her throat too dry and tight to speak. Suddenly the thought of being alone in her apartment terrified her. What if someone had broken in while she was gone? What if he was hiding and waiting? Jenna knew she was being ridiculous, but she couldn't get the image out of her mind.

She swallowed hard. "Will you walk me up please? Maybe take a look around my apartment. I'm not ready to be alone just yet."

"Of course." Eric pulled into a visitor's space and shut off the engine. He reached over and found her hand. "I'll stay as long as you need me to. Scout's honor, and I mean that in the most gentlemanly way."

* * *

She smiled when he said that, and Eric was pleased that she trusted him. He tried to imagine how vulnerable she must feel and failed. He hadn't been physically threatened since his big growth spurt at age twelve and didn't know what it was like to be afraid for his life.

This woman needed him to make her feel safe. It would be tough not to take her beautiful face in his hands and press his mouth against those luscious, trembling lips, but he wouldn't violate her tender trust in him no matter how badly he wanted her.

Jenna's hands shook so much she couldn't get the key in the lock. Eric gently took her keys and opened the door.

"I'll check everything out first." He opened the closet door in the foyer and stuck his head in to demonstrate his intentions. A blanket on the shelf caught his eye, so he brought it to Jenna and encouraged her to sit on the couch.

He watched her for a moment, then methodically went through her apartment. He could have cheated, feeling quite confident that no one was in her apartment, but he didn't. Jenna had asked him to make her feel safe and he wouldn't let her down.

Her bedroom was a little messy, with books and clothes scattered around. But that was all right; superficial clutter he could deal with. The bathroom sparkled with a recent cleaning, and Eric was relieved. He couldn't stand a crusty bathroom or kitchen. The most surprising thing about her apartment was the sparseness, the lack of knickknacks, the wide-open wall spaces. It looked as if she hadn't lived there long.

In the kitchen, he poured two glasses of wine and carried them to where Jenna sat, wrapped in a big comforter.

"I see you found the bottle of white zin that's been in my fridge forever." Her smile was gone and she sounded far away. "I don't usually drink much."

"Me either, but it sounds good right now." Eric stood for a moment trying to decide if he should sit next to her on the couch or in the rocking chair by the window. He wanted to be comforting, but without making her uneasy.

"Come sit down, you're making me nervous."

Eric eased himself down on the couch, leaving a large space between them. *Now what?* he wondered. *Do I make small talk? Or do I encourage her to talk about the robbery?* Eric suddenly felt inadequate. He picked up his wine and drank it down. He noticed Jenna had already finished hers. "Can I get you another glass?"

"No thanks."

"Do you want to talk about it? I'm a good listener."

She shook her head. Her eyes misted over and her lips pressed together in a tight line. Eric realized what she really needed was another woman, a good friend who would let Jenna cry on her shoulder. He could do that; he could be there for her. Eric eased over and gently draped his arm around Jenna. Her body relaxed.

"Tomorrow will be better. I promise."

* * *

Jenna leaned against him, instinctively knowing she could trust this man. In a moment she started to cry. She was too exhausted to be embarrassed. She gave in to the sobs, purging herself of the day's poisons. Eric stroked her hair and whispered soothing sounds. His kindness made her cry harder.

How long had it been since she'd felt someone's arms around her? The warmth of Eric's body, the softness of his flannel shirt, the faint scent of aftershave. It seemed so natural, so necessary. How long had she lived alone without the simple touch of another person? What if today had been her last?

Jenna kissed him on the cheek.

"Thank you," she whispered, hoping he would not misunderstand, yet wishing with all her heart he would stay.

"My pleasure." He tried to sound casual, but his voice betrayed him. His eyes searched hers for understanding.

She kissed his mouth this time, with only the slightest touch, feeling her lips tremble as they met his. His body tensed, and her heart began to hammer. Eric's lips swelled against hers with a heat that made her light-headed. He held back, giving her a chance to change her mind. Jenna couldn't have stopped herself if she wanted to. It felt too right. Her other choice was to let him leave, and that she couldn't bear. She pressed her mouth against his, letting him know the depth of her need.

Eric responded with equal passion, his big hands pressing her into the circle of his strength. Slowly and gently, he melted the tension from her body with his touch. In time, everything around her disappeared, including the horror of the day. Jenna's only awareness was Eric, his strength, his passion, his tenderness.

Her joy came as a surprise, bringing tears to her eyes. Jenna would have been content to simply not be alone.

Chapter 4 >—

Wednesday, October 25

"Let us have a moment of silent prayer." Reverend David Carmichael lowered his voice to the softness of a caress. Moments earlier he'd been shouting, caught up in his sermon about unconditional faith. But his mind was on money. The church was broke, few donations were coming in, and Carmichael was worried. They'd been in financial binds before, but never like this one. He clenched his hands together and begged God for a miracle. The women and children kneeling before him were his family. They counted on him, and he couldn't let them down.

When the children got restless, Carmichael looked up. "Who among us has a special need for prayer?" He scanned the room, stopping to make eye contact with Tamara, who'd been withdrawn lately. Tamara, along with Rachel and Marilynn and a few others, had a special place in his heart. They'd been with him from the beginning, when the church was meeting in rented basements and sharing Bibles. But the dozens who'd joined over the years had been welcomed with open arms. The more the merrier, as his mother always said. His family had grown from within too. Women were blessed with the gift of life.

Carmichael sighed when Sarah raised her hand. He knew verbatim what she would say.

"Please pray the Lord will purge my mind and body of desire so that I may serve him with a pure heart." Sarah was a very sweet sixteen, but the issue of her overactive hormones was becoming tiresome. Carmichael had been tempted more than once to initiate her in the joys of the flesh. But he had resisted. Sex between unmarried adults was not a sin in his church, and few of his followers would condemn him for it. But Tamara would never forgive him if he slept with her daughter.

Carmichael kept it brief. "Dear Lord, watch over and guide Sarah so that she serves you in every thought and deed." He gave the girl a quick nod, then looked around. "Anyone else in need of prayer?"

Silence. Heads bowing to avoid his gaze.

"Surely you are not all so perfect that you have no need for the Lord's guidance?" Carmichael softened his words with a small smile.

A few of the women giggled; others took him literally and blushed with shame. Several spoke at once.

"I've been selfish with my Sisters, Reverend."

"Please ask the Lord to bless my growing child."

One by one, Carmichael prayed for his Sisters in Christ.

Their transgressions were inconsequential, everyday human failings, unlike deeds in his own past that he could never atone for. He pushed the memories away. Wallowing in the past was pointless. What mattered was the work he was doing now, keeping his congregation spiritually sound as well as reproductively healthy. God had given him several talents, and it was his duty to use those skills to serve the Lord.

Carmichael dismissed the women with kind words from the Apostle Paul and retreated from the makeshift chapel through a back entrance used only by him. The short hallway led to his private quarters, as austere as any eighteenth-century monk's, except for the iMac. The computer and satellite phone/internet service were the church's only link to the outside world. The rugged survivalists who'd built the compound hadn't needed cable TV, and Carmichael believed his family was better off without worldly influence as well.

Twenty-five miles from the nearest town, nestled in a horseshoe canyon at the foot of the Cascades, his church was an isolated fortress against the evils of modern civilization. Fewer than a dozen people outside its walls knew the location, and most of them were still in jail on illegal firearms charges. Leah Johnson, mother of the militia's founder, had donated the land to the church to keep the state from claiming it for back taxes. Just one of the many blessings he'd received after forsaking the secular world and dedicating his life to God.

Carmichael slipped outside, using the secret panel in the back of his closet that opened to the west side of the compound. The sun was moving toward the horizon, leaving behind a pink glow that would slip into twilight. He loved this hour of day and rarely missed an evening walk on the grounds, seeing the property in its best light. So much of his time was spent in the lab that his skin had become almost translucent. His golfing buddies from the old days at North McKenzie Hospital would hardly recognize him now. Carmichael smiled, imagining their expressions if they could see him. He might have lost his tan, but he'd gained fifteen pounds and a ponytail. They would be even more shocked to discover his self-imposed isolation. When he'd decided to leave the hospital, amid rumors and allegations, Northup and Rubison had tried to talk him out of it. They couldn't believe he'd give up his career so easily. But he hadn't left it for long.

Soon after moving to the compound, he'd borrowed money to transform the basement—originally built as a bomb shelter— into an OB clinic. He'd delivered Marilynn's baby in the new clinic a few months later. Then Tamara had begged him to leave the condom off and let her get pregnant. Carmichael had refused. After what he'd done to his only child, he could never let himself be a father again. But out of compassion for Tamara, he'd convinced Elizabeth—his longtime colleague, friend, and lover—to appropriate some sperm from the Assisted Reproduction Clinic.

The insemination was successful, and soon other Sisters clamored for babies without the complications of men and sex. God had shown his approval with a second financial blessing. Liz's stepfather died, leaving her a small fortune that she had planned to donate to child-abuse prevention. Carmichael had persuaded her to give him the money to equip an embryo lab instead. He'd always been fascinated with in vitro fertilization and had seized the opportunity to pursue new techniques without bothersome restrictions.

His first petri dish embryo had given him a thrill that neither sex, nor money, nor drugs could replicate. He'd become obsessed with creating life that was predestined to flourish. His clinic was basic, but his success rate was excellent, partly because of his skill and partly because his patients didn't have fertility problems. Eventually, he borrowed money to purchase a DNA thermal cycler so he could biopsy the embryos and determine which were female. The Sisters seemed to prefer baby girls. The males, and any other abnormal embryos, were studied and discarded.

All of that was at risk now. Elizabeth had asked him to do a bizarre and dangerous thing and, God forgive him, he'd had no choice but to agree. Elizabeth had kept him from losing his medical license and going to jail after "the accident," and then she had funded the clinic. He owed her everything.

Carmichael rounded the corner of the compound and slipped quietly onto a bench near the children's playground. The swings and slides were rough, homemade from timbers and tires. But the kids didn't care. Their jabbering, squealing frenzy of activity was strangely soothing to his troubled heart. One by one, he recalled each of their names, forgetting only a boy of about ten swinging by himself.

The boy seemed out of place among the girls gathered around the swings. It reminded him of his own childhood in rural Illinois, surrounded by seven giggling, chatty sisters. He remembered the thrill of the chase as he ran careening through the house clutching a doll or purse as two or more sisters pursued him, shrieking and threatening bodily harm. Their mother had hated the noise and occasional destruction, and usually sent them to their rooms to memorize Bible verses.

But his father had been unpredictable, laughing and joking one minute, shouting and slapping the next. Those delicate doctor's hands that never touched a chore could pinch harder than those of any school bully.

The piercing cry of a blackbird shattered the images. Carmichael eased himself off the bench and watched the creature disappear into a Douglas fir. He thanked God again for the beauty around him. If not for the majestic pines on the hill and the lush gardens, the compound would be as ugly and austere as any gray-brick prison. In a way, it was a self-imposed prison for the church members. The women were free to leave any time, but they had lived in the secular world and found it lacking. Here, at the Church of the Reborn, he provided them with fresh-grown food, spiritual guidance, a safe place to raise children, and the best ob-gyn in the state. Even those who left, usually seeking romance, often returned.

But what would happen when he brought Elizabeth's sister to the compound? She would have to be drugged and restrained. Could he keep her presence a secret? More important, would God forgive him? Carmichael stopped to say a silent prayer.

A moment later, he walked past the greenhouses, where the tangy scent of tomatoes lingered in the cooling air, then on past the chicken coops and pigpens. Carmichael said a quick thank-you to God for Brother Ezekiel, a jack-of-all-trades who patched up old plumbing and butchered livestock with equal dexterity. He'd met Zeke at an AA meeting years before and witnessed his transformation from an aimless, troubled soul into a dependable man of God. When the church moved out to the compound, Zeke was one of three male members to follow and the only one to stay.

Carmichael felt guilty about the pitifully small salary he paid Zeke to keep everything running. Zeke was the first close male friend he'd had since grade school, and Carmichael depended on him more and more every year. There were still a few young boys in the compound to help with heavy chores, but they would leave as soon as they cut their apron strings. Carmichael sighed. Women had always loved him; men did not.

"Reverend." Out of nowhere came Zeke's voice, as if thinking about him had made him appear.

Carmichael turned back and fought to control his irritation. He hated to be disturbed during his evening walk. "What is it?"

"The bank." The handyman's tight voice gave nothing away. He was lean, brown, and muscular and looked like a balding rancher. "I thought you should know about it right away." He handed Carmichael a folded, single-page letter.

"Tell me." Without glancing at the letter, Carmichael started toward the compound. Zeke fell in step beside him.

"Either we make a payment right away, or they'll start the process to assume ownership of the property."

Even though he'd known it was coming, hearing it was like a punch to the belly. He should have paid better attention to finances. With all the donations coming in and payments going out, Carmichael couldn't keep track of it by himself. Zeke handled the everyday bookkeeping, while he did most of the fundraising, even though it degraded him—a doctor and a man of God—to beg for money.

"Can we make a partial payment?"

Zeke shook his head. "We don't have enough cash to meet next month's overhead. The donation we were expecting from the United Christian Foundation fell through."

Carmichael fought the urge to swear out loud. He was sick of worrying about money. He pressed his lips together and walked in silence. They reached the compound and entered the huge kitchen through the attached greenhouse. The five women preparing the evening meal called out to them simultaneously.

"Good evening, Reverend. We're fixing your favorite meal."

"Fried chicken and mashed potatoes."

A burst of giggling. Chicken and potatoes were almost daily features on the menu. For a while, the Sisters held a contest to see who could create the best new recipe with chicken and potatoes. Carmichael had finally made them stop, unable to eat some of the bizarre concoctions they'd come up with.

"Good evening, ladies. Glad to see we're back to basics. Don't forget the corn on the cob." He grinned to show he was teasing, but he knew they would send a couple of kids scampering out to the fields to pick what was left of the crop. Even if no one else had any, there would be corn on his plate. "Thank you for preparing our evening's nourishment and enjoying the work the Lord has given you. See you at supper."

They left the kitchen and moved quickly down the narrow stone hallway into Zeke's office. Once the door was closed, Carmichael said, "What do you suggest?"

"We're out of options, Reverend. Except that idea I have you don't like."

"I asked you not to bring that up again. Show me the books, and I'll see if I can come up with anything."

After an hour of going through every expense, every expected donation, they were no closer to a solution. Carmichael's jaw began to ache from grinding his teeth. He couldn't let the bank take his land. Nor would he let Zeke see how worried he was.

"Let's pray together, Ezekiel. The Lord will provide." Together they went to the chapel where Carmichael humbly begged God to send him a pile of cash.

He'd just returned to his living quarters when his satellite phone rang. Smiling, he hurried to answer it. Only a few outside people had his private number. God was working quickly. He picked up the phone. "Hello, Mr. Akron."

"No, David, it's Elizabeth. The donor is going to ovulate sometime around the fifth of next month. You need to pick her up this weekend and get her on hormones immediately."

Chapter 5 >—

"Hey, those aren't the right words," the little boy in the white hospital bed protested. "You're skipping stuff."

"Sorry, pal." Eric glanced at the boy, whose name he'd temporarily misplaced. "I've got a lot on my mind today." He hadn't stopped thinking about Jenna since he'd left her apartment that morning. She'd been sound asleep, so he'd left a note asking her to meet him that afternoon. He'd called twice to confirm, but she hadn't answered. His feelings for her were a kaleidoscope of worry, awe, affection, and lust.

"Eric?"

"Here we go." Feeling guilty, he flipped back to the beginning of the book and started over. The story about a wimpy dragon was so familiar he could almost recite it from memory. But Matt—how could he have forgotten his name?—knew it even better. Eric had read it to him ten times over the last three months.

Matt's chemotherapy wasn't working. Eric had spent enough time in children's cancer wards to know, starting with his little brother Chris, who'd died of leukemia when he was five and Eric was sixteen. He knew what it felt like for a parent to lose a child. Eric had practically raised Chris, feeding him bottles, changing diapers, and walking him while he cried with the pain of teething. In fact, taking care of everything whenever his mother and her current husband were drinking. He'd also helped with his half-brothers, Nick and Trevor, when they were babies, but not as much as with Chris. By the time Chris was born, his mother had been so burned out, she'd practically handed him to Eric and said, "Here, you do this one."

Losing Chris had been more than he could bear. He'd left home soon after, hitchhiking to Oregon with seventeen dollars in his pocket, and hadn't set foot in Illinois again. He kept in touch with everyone by phone a couple of times a year, but he couldn't bring himself to go back.

Eric smiled at Matt over the top of the book, but the boy's eyes were closed. He kept reading, forcing himself to put some enthusiasm into the litany of words. Jenna popped into his brain again, this time wearing a tight white nurse's uniform, leaning over the bed, stroking the boy's forehead. Then those wonderful, kissable lips parted slightly as she looked up at him and said—

"No sleeping on the job, Troutman." Eric's eyes flew open. Dr. Clark shook his head. "That book finally put you to sleep too?"

"I wasn't sleeping." Eric's cheeks flushed hot.

"Matt is, so why don't you get out of here for today?" Dr. Clark picked up the clipboard hanging from the bed and flipped through it.

Eric started to ask about Matt's condition, then stopped. It was better not to know. The first year he'd visited kids with cancer he'd asked a million questions. Knowing every detail had overwhelmed him in the long run and made their deaths harder to take. Now he just tried to be their friend and leave the disease to the doctors.

"See you next week." He stood and picked up his coat. His mind was on Jenna again. He would see her in a few hours. If she showed up. Eric's pulse quickened, and his legs followed suit. If he hurried, he'd have time for a quick shower. He wished he'd gotten his hair cut the week before, as he'd planned. He wondered if he had time to pick up a new shirt. He'd asked her to meet him at Full City, a coffee shop downtown, so maybe he looked all right. Then again, he hadn't bought a decent shirt since his last Christmas banquet at the paper. Maybe it was time. When Eric reached the parking lot, he was running.

* * *

Jenna was on her second cup of coffee by the time noon rolled around. She hadn't planned on showing up at all, then at the last minute had rushed out of the apartment and arrived early. Her phone had rung all morning, and she'd finally unplugged it, not wanting to talk to anyone but Eric. But then she'd been too upset to talk to him either. She was embarrassed by her display of emotions the night before, first crying, then throwing herself at him like a nympho. What must he think? Jenna was unnerved by how much his opinion mattered.

He'd asked her to meet him so he must want to see her again, she rationalized while sipping her coffee and trying not to watch the door. What if he just wanted an interview so he could write the story? The thought of Eric dumping her made Jenna's chest tighten. Liking someone this much so soon was scary. Maybe she should get up and leave. Walk away before she got hurt.

She stayed put.

Eric rushed in a few minutes later, breathless and wet from a shower. "Am I late?" He slipped into a chair across from her, banging his recorder on the table.

Jenna's shoulders went rigid. He'd brought a recorder. He expected an interview. How could he after last night? Despite her professional appearance and hard-earned slimness, she suddenly felt like an overweight, small-town girl who'd grown up without a father or boyfriend and would never be taken seriously by men.

"I shouldn't have come. I'm not sure I want to do an interview." She started to get up.

Eric reached across the table and touched her hand. When his blue-gray eyes caught hers, Jenna's heart tap-danced. "Forget the recorder. I carry it out of habit. I'm here to see you. I tried calling you a couple of times today."

"I took the phone off the hook."

"Why?"

"I don't know."

An awkward silence followed. Eric said, "I'm going to grab a coffee. Don't go away." He was back in a moment with a cup of house blend. "How are you feeling today?" he asked. "You were pretty upset last night."

"I don't know. I think I'm still numb." Jenna had trouble expressing her anxiety. "It almost seems like one of those vivid dreams where you wake up shaky, exhausted, and not sure what really happened."

"I've had a few of those." Eric held her hand. "Do you have someone you can stay with for a while?"

"I'm fine." Jenna wished she had the courage to pull her hand away. As much as she liked the attention, she couldn't let herself believe it was sincere. As soon as he got his interview, he'd be out of here, and she'd never see him again. She might as well get it over with.

"You were fantastic, you know." His cheeks flushed. "I mean at the restaurant. Saving that man's life." His color deepened. "You were great later too." He cleared his throat and slumped down in the booth. "I need to shut up now. Tell me about yourself."

"What do you want to know?"

"When and where you were born, what your childhood was like, everything."

Jenna's chest tightened, then she blurted out, "September seventeenth, Astoria, Oregon. Single mom, only child, overweight and unhappy."

"Why unhappy?"

"I just told you. No father, no siblings. I felt empty and lonely as far back as I can remember. I tried filling the void with food, which made me fat, which meant I didn't have many friends either. It's a pathetic but unoriginal story."

"What was your mom like?"

"She did the best she could."

"Is she still in Astoria?"

"Florence."

"Do you see her?"

"Once a month or so. That's why I chose Eugene." Jenna shifted uncomfortably. She and her mother had never been close and she didn't know why. "You're giving me the third degree."

"I know. It's a habit." Eric sat back in his chair. "I still plan to write a story about the robbery. I hope you're okay with that."

Jenna shrugged, not sure how she felt.

He gave her a sly smile. "Why don't you want to talk about your mother?"

"Now you sound like a shrink. 'Why don't you tell me about your childhood and the terrible things your mother did to you.'"

The smile went out of Eric's eyes. "I never had a real father either, and I've been mad at my mom for most of my life." He stared down at his coffee for a few seconds, then looked up. "But I had a whole truckload of little brothers to love and hate and horse around with, so in that sense I'm lucky."

"You are lucky. I hated being an only child. It was so lonely and boring. I have to be careful about saying that because so many people only have one child these days. I can understand why, but I feel sorry for the kids. It's the pits."

"I'll have to take your word for it. Being the oldest, I often wished I didn't have any brothers. I spent most of my tender years as an unpaid babysitter." Eric drained his coffee. "By the way, where did you learn CPR?"

"At the restaurant." Jenna cleared her throat and reminded herself not to think about Arthur and the wet, sucking hole in his chest. "Public-service employees have to take CPR classes every three years. I used to think it was excessive, but after last night, I don't think it's often enough. I swear I forgot everything I learned, and I've taken the class at least three times."

"You looked like you knew exactly what you were doing: calm, confident, in control."

"I fake it well." Jenna laughed. "I have to. The restaurant is crazy busy every Friday and Saturday night. Someone has to be calm in the midst of the chaos."

"I couldn't handle it. I'm patient with kids, but with adults…" Eric paused and shook his head. "I expect them to have it together or stay away from me."

"Doesn't the newspaper business drive you crazy then?"

"It did. The layoff was really a blessing. I now have minimal exposure to the public and its criminally ugly side."

"I think I'm getting to that point myself." Surprised by the intensity of her feeling, Jenna wondered how long she'd been resenting her job. In a moment she knew—since she'd decided to have a baby. Subconsciously, she'd known her manager's hours would take up too much of her time and personal energy for her to be a good mother to a newborn. The robbery had been the final straw. She wanted out. "I think I'm going to quit my job."

"Seriously?" Eric frowned. "Maybe you should take some time off first, see how it feels. Go lie on the beach and soak up sun for a while."

"I might do that. But in the long run, I have to find a way to make money at home so I can be a good parent." Oh dear, why had she said that?

Eric's forehead furrowed. "What haven't you told me? Are you married? Do you have kids I don't know about?"

Jenna tried not to laugh. "Of course not. But don't you think you should have asked me that last night?"

"I should have, but you didn't give me much of an opportunity."

Her cheeks were suddenly warm. "I'm not usually like that."

"That's good. We didn't use any protection, and I feel kind of uncomfortable about that."

It was not typical of her either. Jenna was more concerned about AIDS than getting pregnant, but she suspected Eric was talking about birth control. She respected his willingness to talk about it and decided to be completely honest with him.

"I wouldn't mind being pregnant."

Eric looked confused, then angry. Jenna realized what he must be thinking and held up her hands. "That's not what last night was all about. You have to believe me. I just decided to tell you—" Jenna stopped and took a deep breath. This was harder than she thought it would be, but if they were going to have any kind of relationship, he needed to know up front.

"I want to have a baby. I'm thirty-two and can't see any reason to wait. In fact, I'm thinking about being artificially inseminated, but I have to wait for another blood test to come back." She didn't like to think about the first one that said she carried a marker for cystic fibrosis. It had to be a mistake. She'd gone to an independent lab in Portland to have another test done.

Eric looked a bit stunned. "You get more amazing by the minute."

"You mean crazy."

"No. In fact, I admire your determination. I wish I had the same options you do."

"You mean you want kids?"

"Very much."

Was Eric just saying what he thought she wanted to hear? "So what kind of dad would you be?" She smiled to let him know he didn't have to take it too seriously.

"I'm not sure, but I know I'd be there. No working late at night or stopping at the bar for a few hours on the way home." Eric's voice trembled. "Why have a kid if you're not willing to be a big part of his life?"

"I know what you mean." Jenna wanted to jump up and hug him. He was either completely full of shit or one in a million. They were both quiet for a minute. Jenna's cheeks blazed as she thought of the possibilities. Physically he seemed perfect: six two, not much body fat, lots of hair, and good-looking. He was kind and sensitive, a generous lover, and even had a sexy little mole near his jaw.

It had been a long time since she'd been really attracted to someone. She'd had lots of dates and a few short-term relationships, but something was always wrong. Lack of common interests or annoying little habits. No matter what seemed wrong, the real problem was always lack of spark.

Now the sparks were flying. Jenna's stomach tightened. She'd probably never see him again. He was just toying with her, trying to get as much material as he could for his story. Oh god, he wouldn't put all that personal stuff about her in the paper, would he?

They both started to speak at once, then stopped and smiled. Eric motioned for her to go ahead, but a food server stopped at the booth and asked if they wanted a pastry. Jenna waited while he ordered a cinnamon roll.

After the food server left, Eric grimaced. "I'm sorry. Did you want one too?"

"No thanks. I lost twenty pounds last year and have no intention of gaining it back." *Damn!* What was wrong with her? Was she trying to scare him off? *Why not just show him her high-school picture and be done with it?*

"I think that's great. Did you join a diet group?"

"I joined a gym, but it wasn't enough. I finally had to give up all the crap in my diet, the stuff I love the most, like chocolate and potato chips and cream cheese."

"I don't think I could." Eric suddenly looked sheepish. "Here comes my order. Should I send it back? I feel bad about eating it in front of you."

Jenna smiled. Eric was pretty decent for a guy. "It's okay. But thanks for asking."

The food server came and went, and Eric dug into his roll. "How often do you work out?" he asked, his mouth full.

"Every day."

Eric raised his eyebrows. "That's impressive." He put down the pastry and licked frosting off his thumb. Jenna's heart skipped a beat. It took her a moment to realize he was talking again. "What motivated you? I mean, to do it on your own?"

Jenna hesitated. Why should it be hard to admit she was looking for a husband? Especially after telling him she wanted a baby.

His eyes pleaded with her to trust him and she let out her breath. "The truth is, I've wanted a family for a long time. I originally planned to do it right, you know, with a husband and all. But I was getting older and the dates were getting fewer, so it was time for drastic measures. Making myself more attractive seemed like a necessity."

Eric leaned across the table, took her chin in his hand, and kissed her full on the mouth. Jenna's heart stopped. She closed her eyes and everything disappeared but the feel of Eric's lips on hers. He was so tender, yet so gloriously male. Where had he come from? When Jenna opened her eyes, Eric was looking at her with an expression bordering on reverence.

"You're the most attractive woman I've ever met."

The man was either a first-class bullshitter or certifiably nuts. Either way, she had to be careful, or she'd fall in love with him the next time he kissed her.

"I have to go now." Jenna grabbed her purse, ready to bolt. She had to get out of here. Eric was too intense, too good to be true. He had to be hiding a really major flaw, and she didn't want to discover it after it was too late.

"Why so soon?"

"I run every Wednesday with a friend of mine. We're training for the River Run."

"Oh no." Eric rolled his eyes in mock horror. "You're one of those running fanatics this town breeds like rabbits. More than two hundred people showed up for the event last year!"

"What's wrong with that?"

"You make the rest of us look bad." Eric shook his head, laughing. "What is it with you people? I know exercise is supposed to be good for you, but thirteen miles? Why?"

"It's fun."

"Fun is winning seventy-five bucks in a poker game."

Jenna shrugged. "I like being in good shape, knowing I could hike thirty miles out of the woods or run fifteen miles if my life depended on it."

"Hey, don't be offended. I'm jealous. I've always wanted to be athletic, but I don't seem to have the motivation. I admire you more all the time."

She blushed and got to her feet. "Like I said, I have to go."

"When can I see you again?"

"Good question. I work most weekend nights. Call me."

Jenna almost ran from the restaurant. She felt bad about leaving Eric hanging like that, but she wasn't prepared for the way she felt. Or the way he felt, or claimed to feel. It was too much, happening too soon. She didn't trust herself right now. The robbery had upset her more than she realized and she wasn't herself yet. This was not a good week to start a serious relationship.

Jenna unlocked her bike and pedaled furiously toward home. The wind stung her face, making her eyes water. She missed him already.

Chapter 6

Saturday, October 28

Jenna woke with a sense of dread. She'd been having bad dreams all week, but this one was the worst. A man with a gun had chased her into a dark tunnel, pushing her deeper and deeper into a maze until she was lost, trapped by sheer rock walls. Jenna forced herself to block out the lingering images and concentrate on the day ahead—the River Run, an event she'd been excited about for weeks. The thought failed to brighten her mood. She rolled over and looked out the window. Early dawn, dishwater-gray sky. Depressed, she lay in bed until 8:30, getting up at the last minute to dress for the event.

Jenna's anxiety escalated as she made coffee. It would probably rain the whole thirteen miles. Or worse yet, one of her knees would go out and she'd be crippled, unable to run for weeks. She could picture hundreds of people hanging around the park: runners, spectators, street people, and who else? Jenna tried to shake it off. There wouldn't be any armed men in the park, she told herself. Who would want to rob a bunch of skinny fanatics in neon spandex?

Jenna stepped outside and retrieved the newspaper. Since the robbery, she'd had a tough time leaving the apartment. Martin Stoltz, Geronimo's owner, had told her to take a few days off, but almost a week had passed and she still hadn't been back to the restaurant. She hadn't really been anywhere since meeting Eric at the coffee shop, except once to the gym. For the first time in her life, Jenna now carried a little can of pepper spray her apartment manager had pressed on her. As a tall, muscular woman, Jenna had never worried much about being attacked. Now she felt like a victim and she hated it.

She hadn't figured out what to do about Eric either. For now, she'd asked him not to call her, claiming she needed time to herself. The truth was, she was scared. Loving and losing someone like Eric would be more than she could take. Jenna felt paralyzed. She was afraid to let their relationship move forward, yet she couldn't let Eric go.

Going through the motions, Jenna grabbed a blueberry bagel out of the fridge and sat down at the table with the newspaper. She stared at the front page for five minutes without comprehending a word. Her head was a mess and her brain jumped from one negative thought to another.

She pushed the paper aside and poured herself a cup of coffee. It was only after she'd taken her first sip she realized she'd already eaten her bagel. Food had lost its importance over the last year, and eating fast was against the rules. Today she didn't care. She'd probably drop two pounds during the run. Even that didn't cheer her.

As she drank her second cup of Italian brew, her phone rang. Jenna jumped to answer it. As soon as she picked it up, she regretted it. This would be bad news.

"Jenna, it's Katrice. I know you'll be disappointed, but I can't run with you today."

"Don't say that."

"I'm sorry. I can't help it. I twisted my ankle playing basketball yesterday."

"Why didn't you call me last night?" Jenna tried not to sound upset. Katrice, a bartender at Geronimo's, had been her best friend since she moved to Eugene. It wasn't right to make her feel bad about something she couldn't help.

"I was afraid you'd decide not to run if I called last night. I know you're dressed and ready now and drinking that killer coffee, so you'll go anyway."

"You know me too well."

"I'm sorry. You sound so down."

"Don't worry. I was bummed before you called."

"What about?" Katrice sounded surprised. "It's not like you to get depressed."

"Nothing. Everything. I woke up feeling weird." Jenna started to tell her about the dream, then changed her mind. Katrice was superstitious, even mystical about such things. "I haven't been myself since the robbery, but I'll bounce back, don't worry. I'd better go. Since you're not picking me up, I have to catch the next bus."

"You don't have to ride the bus."

"Yes, I do. I can't rationalize driving such a short distance by myself, and I'm not leaving my bike in the park for three hours even if it is locked. I paid too much for it to let some junkie with bolt cutters have it."

"You're a bit much sometimes, you know?" Katrice was half-serious. Like everyone else, she thought Jenna's commitment to environmental issues was excessive. "This is about that guy, isn't it?" Katrice was friendly now, teasing her. "The reporter you told me about."

"That's a big part of it."

"Go out with him and see what happens. What if he's your soul mate and you let him get away? You think you're unhappy now?"

"I don't know."

"Just do it. It'll make you feel better, I guarantee." Advice from a person who believed in lucky stars.

"I'll see you later." Jenna hung up, not giving her friend a chance to protest.

She finished her coffee and headed out the door before she could change her mind. She'd promised herself she would do this and she would, but it had seemed like a better idea at the time.

* * *

Eric couldn't find a parking place within three blocks of Skinner Butte Park. Jogging from his car to the registration table had made his heart hammer like a set of cylinders in the Indy 500. He had second and third thoughts about finding Jenna and attempting to run thirteen miles with her. It seemed feasible the night before, when the inspiration hit him during the eleven o'clock news. They'd shown clips from last year's run—little old ladies and heavy middle-aged men crossing the finish line with big smiles. Eric had been deceived into thinking it would be, if not easy, at least possible.

He parted with the fifteen dollars anyway. It was a lot to pay for a T-shirt, but maybe Jenna would admire him for trying. If he could find her in the crowd. The women all looked the same in their neon running gear and pulled-back hair. Fortunately, the participants were grouping into categories based on how long it would take to run the course. The serious runners were up front to race against the clock, amateur athletes in the middle, and misfits bringing up the rear.

He found Jenna toward the tail end of the women's amateur group. Even in a black T-shirt with no makeup, she was gorgeous. Eric wondered how this woman had made it to thirty-two without some guy snatching her up. Did she have some really bizarre quirk that hadn't surfaced yet?

"Hey there," he said casually as if he'd just happened to bump into her. Jenna jumped, looking frightened.

"Eric." She shivered. "You startled me."

"Sorry." Eric touched her shoulder. "How have you been?"

"All right. What are you doing here?"

"You know, I've had all morning to come up with a good cover story. Yet the fact is, I just wanted to see you and maybe impress you with my new dedication to physical fitness." Eric rolled his eyes in mock disgust. "But five minutes into this run you'll hear my heart pounding so hard it'll scare you, so why pretend?" Jenna chuckled politely but Eric could tell something was wrong. "You seem upset. Is it because I'm here? I know you asked me to give you some space, but it's been three days."

"I'm feeling a little apprehensive." Jenna chewed on her lower lip. "This is only the third time I've left the house since the robbery."

"Have you been back to the restaurant yet?"

"No." She looked away, then bent down to stretch her quads.

"Maybe you should join one of those victims' groups, get some support. I don't know how you feel because I've never had a gun to my head, but I can imagine it has some long-term effects. You should talk to a counselor."

A loud whistle blew, signaling the runners to get ready. Jenna turned away without answering. A woman with a bullhorn made an announcement Eric didn't hear. The crowd of bodies moved forward, a thundering herd of feet hitting the asphalt. Eric had no choice but to move with them. He'd planned to back out at the last minute, telling Jenna he'd meet her at the finish line. But she seemed so vulnerable—so unlike the confident woman in the restaurant who'd tried to save a man's life—Eric decided to stay with her all thirteen miles, even if it killed him. He laughed out loud.

"What's so funny?"

"I was just thinking that if I had a heart attack, you'd be able to save me."

"Don't count on it. I plan to finish this run in two hours and that doesn't leave any time for first aid along the way."

"Two hours? Get real. We have to slow down, or I'll never make it." Eric was already sucking wind.

She slowed her pace a bit, and Eric was grateful. Even if he walked the thirteen miles, he'd have to wait a week to ask her out because he wouldn't be able to move again for that long. He hadn't done anything this foolish for a woman since high school, when he'd stolen a bottle of Boone's Farm apple wine from the corner store just because Cindy Miller really wanted some.

After ten minutes Eric experienced a strange floating sensation, as if his body weighed only a few pounds and he could run forever. He took advantage of it while it lasted. Later he knew he wouldn't be able to speak. "So what else do you do for fun?"

"Skate, dance, ride my bike." Jenna smiled. "Anything that keeps me moving."

"No, I mean for fun."

"Exercise is fun."

"No. Seriously. I'm talking about hobbies, like knitting or chess or watching old movies."

"I am serious. I don't knit, play chess, or watch old movies. But I do like new movies, and I think I might like poker." She didn't even sound winded, as if running and talking at the same time were effortless.

"This is disappointing," Eric joked. "I was hoping we could get together, you know, do stuff, maybe even date." He paused, waiting to see what she would say. Jenna didn't respond, so he kept up his nervous chatter. "I've exercised more in the last twenty minutes than I normally do in a month. Except for softball season, which is over now."

"I play softball."

Eric grinned. "We have something in common."

He was grateful the bike path along the river was flat. The euphoria was gone, and his lungs and legs ached so badly he had to clamp his jaw shut to keep from moaning. "How far have we gone?"

"About three miles."

Eric cursed silently to himself. He hadn't even made it halfway. Jenna would just have to like him the way he was—or not. This was torture and he couldn't do it anymore. Fortunately, the route crossed over the river at the last pedestrian bridge, then looped back. He could cut across before that and walk for a while, letting Jenna catch up with him for the last mile of the run.

"How are you holding up?" Jenna finally asked.

"I'm in agony, but you're worth it." Eric's heart felt like it was going to explode. It was now or never. "Can I buy you dinner tonight? Restaurant of your choice?"

She hesitated, then gave him a shy smile. "All right."

"Pick you up at seven?" Eric grabbed Jenna's arm so she would look at him again. "I have to stop now. I'll cross the bridge up here at the university and walk until you pick me up on the other side. I'm sorry, it's the best I can do."

She laughed. "I never thought you'd make it this far. It's not particularly healthy to overdo it your first time."

"Now you tell me." Eric stopped running. "See you in an hour."

Jenna waved and picked up her pace. Eric's legs almost buckled in relief. He started up the path to the bridge, hoping he wouldn't collapse. The hammering in his heart finally tapered off, but he felt light-headed, almost giddy. It was either oxygen deprivation or love. Eric wasn't sure, but he figured he'd have to get used to it either way.

Jenna picked him up on the other side of the river, a mile from the park. The pain was worse the second time. Eric promised himself he would never run again. Knowing it would be over in ten minutes didn't help. It seemed like an eternity before they crossed the finish line and someone called out, "Two hours, eight minutes."

"Sorry about slowing you down," Eric gasped, fighting the urge to fall face-first into the grass. Jenna was still moving, not running, but not stopping either. Eric hurried after her to catch what she was saying.

"It doesn't matter." She looked relaxed for the first time that day. "Thanks for keeping me company. You're a good sport."

"Can we stop any time soon?"

"Go ahead. I need to keep moving for a minute."

"Why?"

"So my legs don't get cramps."

Eric didn't care what happened to him. He had to stop. Involuntarily he bent over and sucked in air. When his heart rate stabilized, he began to walk slowly, looking around for Jenna. Runners and spectators were everywhere, stretching out, gulping down bottled water, taking pictures, and talking excitedly about their race time. Eric didn't see Jenna anywhere, so he went to the registration booth and picked up his T-shirt. It was white with green trees, blue sky, and a rainbow. Typical Eugene life-is-a-picnic artwork. He'd never wear it.

Eric walked down the bike path in the direction Jenna had gone, passing wooden tables and kids swinging in the playground. He didn't see her and finally turned around. The path branched out all over the five-acre park, and she could have taken almost any route and circled back already. The crowd had thinned out by the time Eric got to the registration area. In a few seconds, he realized Jenna wasn't there. Eric went to the booth, currently being dismantled by the woman with the bullhorn and two men in running gear.

"Can you tell me if Jenna McClure picked up her shirt?" he asked.

"Why?" The muscular woman eyed him suspiciously.

"I just want to know if she already left, or if I should wait longer."

"Just a sec." She picked up a clipboard and flipped through several pages. "Yep, she did."

"Thanks." Puzzled, Eric headed for his car. It seemed strange Jenna would leave without saying anything, especially after making a date for that evening. Maybe they'd missed each other and she thought he'd left. Eric decided to call her when he got home, make sure everything was still set for that evening.

Halfway to his car, he saw Jenna two blocks away, waiting at a bus stop. He paused, uncertain, then hurried toward her. She wasn't close enough to hear him if he called out. Before Eric reached the first cross street, a big gray van stopped in front of the bus stop. A man in a suit, sporting a short ponytail, hopped out and spoke briefly to Jenna, then showed her a piece of paper. He moved beside her and put his arm around her waist. Eric couldn't see Jenna's expression, but her body seemed to go rigid.

Eric started to run.

A second man stepped out of the van just as Jenna relaxed. Eric shouted her name, but the three of them got into the vehicle and drove off. He stopped mid-stride and stared at the slowly disappearing back doors.

What in the heck had just happened? If he didn't know better, he'd swear Jenna had just been kidnapped.

Chapter 7

Zeke glanced in the rearview mirror at the guy in blue sweats. He'd stopped running and stood staring after the van. Was he memorizing the license number? Fuck and doublefuck. Zeke pressed the gas pedal, then cut in front of a white sedan, blocking the plate from the guy's view. Zeke hadn't even seen the guy until he heard him shout at the woman. Did he know her or was he just some busybody passing by? Had he shouted her name? *Shit.* He hated not knowing, hated having to worry about the cops. It had looked like a perfect snatch. No struggle, no witnesses, no purse or coat or car left behind. Then, out of nowhere, this jogger comes running up the street.

"Relax, Zeke. He was too far away to see us or the license number."

Carmichael's voice cut into his thoughts. The Reverend sounded calm and confident as usual. Zeke eased up on the gas. It wouldn't be smart to get stopped for speeding right now. Their passenger was unconscious and hidden from sight, but Zeke tended to sweat and stutter every time he talked to a cop. Or at least he used to. When he was a kid, before he took the long time-out, he'd been arrested so often he'd lost count. Only convicted twice, but brought in and harassed regularly because he couldn't keep his cool when facing the pricks in uniform.

Zeke couldn't believe he'd let the Reverend talk him into this bullshit. If he got picked up for kidnapping...No. He couldn't think like that. He wasn't going back inside. Not after what happened last time. He'd rather be dead than on a bus heading for Pendleton State Penitentiary.

But if he was careful, nothing bad would happen. He almost had enough money salted away now to move to Florida, live on a boat, and spend his days fishing. It was a dream that kept him going through a lot of dark days. And it was coming true thanks to the Reverend and his flaky little church. It wasn't that Carmichael paid him enough to save any. He spent that little pittance going into town every once in a while. Zeke had embezzled sizable chunks of cash from the donations over the years, and Carmichael never knew. The man was a decent preacher, a great twat doctor, and quite the ladies' man, but a real dingbat when it came to money. He'd put Zeke in charge of bookkeeping when they'd moved out to the compound so the Reverend could play God in his embryo lab. Zeke never had any formal training as an accountant, but compared to Carmichael, he was a natural. Other people's money had always come easy to him.

Zeke crossed the bridge into Springfield, wishing they were out of town already. He looked over at the Reverend, who seemed to be praying. Zeke wouldn't be able to relax until they reached the compound. Life in the compound had been all right for the first few years. Nice, actually, compared to jail or the crappy foster homes he'd grown up in. The church women were not exactly his type, with their baggy skirts and plain faces, but after doing without for thirteen years, pussy was pussy. And the isolation had kept him away from booze and out of jail. But now the boredom was wearing him down, making him have crazy thoughts about robbing the bar in Blue River just to feel the adrenaline rush. That kind of thinking could get him in trouble faster than anything. Except maybe kidnapping. This was serious shit.

The Reverend had given him some song and dance about the woman's rich parents and how they wanted her off heroin so badly they were willing to pay fifty thousand to have her picked up and forced into detox. The fifty grand had caught his interest. If he could filch the whole fifty, add it to the $46,932 he already had in the bank, he'd have enough to buy himself a nice boat. He could be in Florida before the Reverend even knew the money was gone. What could he do about it? Call the police? Zeke didn't think so.

Picking up this woman changed everything. She'd seen both of them. Even though Carmichael swore on his Bible that the drugs would mess up her memory, Zeke was skeptical. An eye-witness was a ticket to the slammer. He'd learned that the hard way. Zeke had never killed anybody during a robbery, but he wished he had. It would have saved him thirteen years of hell. He couldn't let this witness walk away. The thought of killing her revolted him, but she was a threat to his freedom, the dream he'd worked and waited a lifetime for. There was no turning back. He'd already traded her life for fifty grand.

* * *

Drowning. She'd always known it would be the worst way to die. Exhausted, Jenna struggled against a ton of water that crushed and filled her lungs. The ache was unbearable. She was losing, she knew, fading in and out as her oxygen supply dwindled. Despite years of childhood lessons, she'd never been a good swimmer and had a tenacious dread of getting into water over her head. Now she was drowning, taking her last breath in black liquid hell. A soft light above the surface beckoned and she floated upward, no longer struggling, at peace with her destiny.

For a few minutes, she floated in and out of consciousness, then finally opened her eyes and blinked at the hard metallic gray above her. The earth rolled and she braced herself to keep from falling. A sharp pain behind her eyes brought clarity. She was in the back of a moving van, not dead or drowned but alive and headed who knew where with a couple of psychopaths. For a moment Jenna longed for the serenity of darkness. Drowning was not so bad. Not compared to the images that popped into her mind with vivid, horrifying detail.

She would be raped, tortured, and killed. Why else would they take her? There was no ransom money available, no political points to be gained. Jenna's eyes darted around frantically, but her head, which seemed to be squeezed in a vice grip, would not move. Her heart and lungs kicked into gear, pumping oxygen to her paralyzed limbs. She cringed at the merciless hammering of her heart, hundreds of bruising blows against tender ribs. Small mewling sounds escaped her throat and hot tears built up behind her eyes. Jenna had read of people dying of fright, and now she understood. Her heart would soon explode from the pressure of being all worked up with nowhere to go.

Jenna closed her eyes and thought of her mother, whose secrets she would never know, including the identity of the man who'd fathered her. There would be no future McClures to worry about the family tree and missing branches on one side.

The sound of her own whimpering disgusted Jenna and she fought for control. She held her breath as long as she could, then let it out slowly. She repeated the action over and over until her heart slowed and she could think somewhat rationally. The drug they'd hit her with was still in her system and Jenna had trouble focusing. She tried to move her arms and legs but couldn't. She pressed her head slightly forward and glanced down the length of her body. Completely covered with a brown plaid blanket, Jenna couldn't tell if she was tightly restrained or paralyzed from the drug. She willed herself to be patient, to start with her fingers and wiggle them until they responded. She'd rather die trying to save her own life than give them the satisfaction of taking it from her.

The tingling began in her lower left calf, just above an old tendon injury. Excited, she wiggled all her toes until the stinging sensation surged up through her quads. Her fingers and arms had been tingling for a few minutes, but Jenna hadn't tried to use them yet. The pain she could handle. Discovering she was tightly bound would be devastating.

She waited until her fingers felt almost normal, then began flexing them until they lost that stiff, first-thing-in-the-morning feel. She felt around and discovered she was strapped to a homemade plywood gurney. The three straps crisscrossing her body seemed designed to stabilize rather than restrain her, and they came unbuckled easily. She moved slowly under the blanket, afraid to attract the attention of her captors.

She could hear their voices now that the buzzing in her head had cleared some. They were arguing in very controlled, almost deferential tones. A shiver ran up the back of her neck. Jenna recognized the voice of the man in the passenger seat as the one who'd shown her the map and asked for directions right before sticking her with something sharp. The driver, whom she'd barely seen before she blacked out, mumbled, "I really think you ought to get back there and secure the package."

"Relax, Zeke, the ketamine will keep her unconscious until we reach the compound and carry her down to the clinic."

Jenna scrunched forward as far as she could without lifting her head above the backseat and unbuckled the last strap. Pushing the blanket off, she scooted toward the back door. She knew it would be foolish to jump out while the van was cruising at what she guessed to be around fifty miles an hour, but she wanted to be ready. The route they were taking seemed to wind slowly uphill, and she hoped the van would slow down at some point for a sharp curve. Jenna suspected they were heading out Highway 126 toward Blue River, but they could have been on any one of a dozen back roads.

"What could it hurt to spend a minute tying her hands together?" the driver argued. "Drugs don't have the same effect on everybody. We've seen that enough times to know better."

The other man laughed. "I've never had to restrain a woman before. They usually do what I expect without argument, but I suppose you're right. This one is different."

Jenna heard a soft crackle of plastic and the rustle of fabric on the move. He was coming. It was now or never. She grabbed the handle and leaned against the door.

Nothing happened.

Damn! It was locked. Jenna pushed to her knees and instantly felt dizzy. Groping blindly, she searched for the lock as the van braked and slowed for a sharp corner. She spotted a red strip near the handle and hoped it was the lock.

Suddenly his hands were on her, pulling her back. Jenna struggled pointlessly for a moment, then lunged for the back door, pressing the red knob and the handle at the same time. The door popped open just as the van curved sharply left. Jenna fell sideways and out the back, dragging the man, who still had a grip on her shirt, with her.

The pavement jerked up and smashed into Jenna's shoulder, an agonizing blow that left her blinking in and out of consciousness as she rolled off the road and into a drainage ditch. The chill of mountain water trickling under her back and the jagged four-inch rock pressing into her left buttock kept her from passing out. Slowly, Jenna shifted sideways. Her arms and legs were numb, and her shoulders felt as if they'd been nailed to the ground. Even the air she pulled into her lungs was heavy. The silence was overwhelming, as if time had stopped.

Slowly, Jenna eased herself into a sitting position. The blood seemed to rush from her brain, and the trees above her swayed. She let her shoulders fall forward, easing the nausea for a moment. Then she opened her eyes and noticed the blood oozing from her black Lycra running pants, which were ripped open from her hip to her knee along one side. After a few deep breaths, Jenna pushed the material aside and examined the wound, relieved to discover it was only the worst case of road rash she'd ever had. Her shoulder felt dislocated, but her legs looked okay, no bones sticking out that she could see. Jenna looked up for the first time, blinking her eyes against the bright sun that had come out of nowhere while she was unconscious in the van.

The van—oh shit—where was it?

The world around her suddenly kicked back into life. A cool breeze licked Jenna's face, and the sound of a roaring engine filled her ears. Frantically, Jenna looked around for her assailant, hoping against all odds he'd been seriously injured in his fall from the vehicle. It was her only chance of escape. Even being an experienced runner, with a bum shoulder she'd need a good head start to get away. She pushed herself to her knees. The sun disappeared, leaving a cool shadow on her back. Jenna looked up, and there he was.

Overcoming her fear, Jenna lurched to her feet, prepared to fight for her life. The man was a stranger, strikingly handsome, and dressed in gray slacks with a pink button-up shirt. Except for the tear in his shirt and the small smear of blood on his cheek, he looked more like an advertising executive than a psycho kidnapper. Jenna stepped back, suddenly unsure of where she was or what had happened to her.

"Don't be frightened," he said quietly, his gray eyes probing her mind and sensing her confusion. "I'm a doctor. Let me help you." The man eased toward her.

"Don't come any closer," Jenna shouted, panic returning full force. "I don't know who you are or what you want, but if you touch me again I'll kick your balls so hard you'll wish you were dead."

He smiled and gently shook his head. "That won't be necessary, Jenna. I don't intend to hurt you, nor do I intend to let you hurt me. Let's get back in the van and get you the medical attention you need."

He knew her name. That frightened her more than anything she'd experienced yet. Jenna bolted. The searing pain in her shoulder knocked her off balance with a force equal to a hearty shove. She stumbled on her injured leg and went down with a painful thud.

The man was on her instantly, jabbing a needle into her upper arm. Jenna managed to roll over just in time to see him smile before the world went dark again.

Chapter 8 >—

Elizabeth hummed softly to herself as she tossed a small vial of sperm in the trash. The sample had DNA markers for muscular dystrophy. No need to test it further.

She tried not to think about the dozen things that could have gone wrong with the kidnapping. There had to be a problem, or David would have called as he'd promised to do as soon as he got back to the compound. Had he and Zeke been arrested?

No. She refused to even consider it.

Elizabeth forced herself to concentrate on her work. If she didn't find a suitable donor soon, the whole plan would be jeopardized. Fortunately, using polymerase chain reaction and a DNA thermal cycler, she could test potential fathers for chromosomal abnormalities and single-gene defects in a matter of hours. The sperm had already been screened by the clinic for AIDS and other infectious diseases, then categorized by physical description and abilities. Elizabeth was limiting her search to donors who were blue-eyed, artistic, and intelligent. She was determined to find the perfect father, genetically superior in every way. Her only limitation was time. She had only a week left.

Why hadn't David called? She should have heard from him hours ago. Had they been delayed? Were they still following McClure and waiting for a better opportunity?

Elizabeth got up from the counter and headed for her office, the acid in her empty stomach churning into a fiery knot. *David better have a damn good reason for not letting her know what was going on*, she thought for the hundredth time. He knew how important this was to her. She opened the freezer unit and reached for a vial of sperm. It was the last of the batch she'd recently smuggled out of the Assisted Reproduction Clinic, an extension of the hospital, where she acted as a consultant two mornings a week in addition to her position as director of genetic science.

It was ridiculous to be this anxious this early in the process, she chided herself. Even after McClure was secured and sedated in the compound, Elizabeth still had to get through a week of waiting for her sister to ovulate. That was the easy part. The two weeks following the egg transfer would be the worst, when she would be crossing her fingers and hoping her pregnancy test was positive. If the transfer didn't take, the entire perilous endeavor would have been for nothing. She had to relax or her nerves wouldn't make it.

Elizabeth shook her head at the irony. She'd never been really relaxed in her whole life, not since she was a child, before her mother died. Even her marriage had been stressful, with John pressuring her to put her career on hold and get pregnant right away. Then months of trying and not being able to conceive, followed by the devastating discovery that she couldn't.

Her life had been one heartache after another, with only work in between for company, but Elizabeth hadn't felt sorry for herself in a long time. Her work was exciting, and the prestige of being recognized as a brilliant geneticist had distracted her from the emptiness.

In a single instant, everything had changed. Elizabeth smiled at the memory. Seeing those familiar DNA patterns and discovering the existence of her sister had opened a door she thought was closed forever. All her research, the long hours in the lab, had real meaning now that she could use her expertise to create the perfect child for herself. *If David had successfully picked up McClure and if everything else went well.*

Elizabeth returned to her bench and began the methodical separation process. She reminded herself that it was foolish to get her hopes up. Creating embryos outside the uterus was a delicate process with a high failure rate. Even though David had become a highly skilled embryologist, the real difficulty of any IVF cycle was getting the embryos to implant in the endometrium. The uterine environment at the time of transfer was critical, yet difficult to assess. And with her iatrogenic ovarian damage, it could be tricky.

Oh dear god. What if her sister was sterile too? Elizabeth's fingers tightened on the vial. After all, McClure had gone to the Assisted Reproduction Clinic to be artificially inseminated. Had she been trying to conceive on her own? Would she even know if she was fertile?

Elizabeth began to tremble as Dr. Avery's questions came back to haunt her. The fertility specialist said he'd never seen such severe scarring around the ovaries. He'd asked politely about uterine infections and whether her mother had taken DES. Elizabeth hadn't been able to answer. She'd left his office in a blind rage, cursing her adoptive father with every possible profanity. His repeated sexual assaults had given her countless pelvic infections as a teenager. It had been so easy to blame him for the scarring that made her sterile, but what if her mother had taken DES? What if McClure's ovaries were as damaged as hers were?

Elizabeth stepped back from the table and sank into a lab chair. She had to get a grip on herself, even though her assistant had gone home and there was no one to see her fall apart. She massaged her temples and reminded herself that it was just speculation. Her sister's ovaries were probably fine. She regretted not finding out first. To have taken such a risk for nothing...

The tiny tinkle of a phone cut into her thoughts. Finally! She grabbed her cell phone from her lab-coat pocket and forced herself to sound calm and professional. "Dr. Demauer."

"Hello, Elizabeth."

"David! What happened? Why didn't you call?"

"It's a long story, and I need to see you right away."

"Damn it, David! Just tell me what's wrong."

"Not over the phone. Why don't you come out here? I don't think I should leave the compound right now."

"What's going on? Is McClure okay?"

"Just come now, Elizabeth."

The phone clicked in her ear. Sharp pinpoints of pain danced behind her eyes. What could be happening? Had the patient been harmed in some way? Or was David just being dramatic and manipulative? Suppressing her anger, Elizabeth moved into action, putting the vial back in the deep freeze and locking every cabinet before stepping out of the office and locking it too.

The research section of the hospital was almost always quiet, and on weekends it was virtually empty. Elizabeth hurried through the corridors without encountering a soul. Her dark-gray Lexus was one of three cars left on the fifth floor of the garage. She was so preoccupied, she failed to follow her usual precautions of keeping her mace in hand and staying in the lighted center.

She wanted to stop at home and change into something comfortable, but the indulgence would set her back almost an hour. Her home was in an exclusive riverside community with a gate and a guard, the first enclosed development in Eugene. Elizabeth had gladly paid the price for the comfort of security. The crime rate in Eugene had risen dramatically in the last few years, and she had slept easier knowing she wouldn't be burglarized or raped in her own home. She would have to forgo that luxury for now. The drive to the compound would take almost two hours, and she wanted to get there before dark.

She swore out loud just thinking about the last five-mile stretch of road and what it would do to her car. David was doing this to her just because he could—because for once, she was in his debt. Elizabeth lit a cigarette and willed herself to be calm. She took a right on Franklin and headed toward Highway 126.

She limited herself to three cigarettes on the drive out, listening to jazz on the radio and pushing the Lexus to seventy-five on all the straight stretches. As worried as she was about McClure and what had gone wrong, it was David she kept thinking about. In some ways, he was like a spoiled little boy who expected to get exactly what he wanted, when he wanted it. Yet he could be so tender and loving, it made her heart ache to remember.

They'd met in medical school, Elizabeth being the youngest student at twenty, and David one of the oldest at thirty. He'd noticed her right away and pursued her with a tenacity she had to admire. He'd been so handsome and attractive, gentle and never crude like other men. She'd fallen in love the first time he seduced her. Until she'd met David, Elizabeth thought of herself as damaged goods. Her few sexual experiences as an adult had been painful and frustrating. With David, she experienced her first orgasm, changing the way she felt about men, about herself.

Elizabeth rounded the last corner and pulled into the clearing in front of the compound. The sun was slipping below the horizon, casting an eerie light over the stone building. God, she hated this place. She would help David fix whatever his little problem was and be on the road. She wouldn't stay overnight even if he begged. David needed to know she was angry with him for not calling, for making her drive out here. Reflexively, Elizabeth checked her face in the rearview mirror before getting out. It was too dark to notice anything except the fact that her lipstick was long gone. Fortunately, David liked the natural look.

She could hear singing as she entered the front double doors and breathed a sigh of relief. They were all in church, and she wouldn't have to see or talk to anyone. David's followers were sickeningly sweet and naive. Elizabeth couldn't stand their simple homespun chatter and open adoration of David. In fact, she believed religion was nonsense, and David had learned not to discuss it with her.

She went directly to his office to wait. Her presence had already been reported, as she knew from past visits, and David would be along soon. Elizabeth tried to get comfortable, but the room was barren, dark—even with the light on—and cold. She lit a cigarette, knowing it would irritate David, and began to pace.

He surprised her by coming up his private stairs from the clinic instead of from the chapel. The sight of his handsome, worried face made Elizabeth set aside her anger for the moment and reach out to him. Without a word, they embraced. Their relationship, free of social expectations, had been forged over the years from respect, passion, and isolation.

Elizabeth had never known anyone like David. Not even the man she'd married had touched her as deeply. But she had things on her mind. She pulled away and demanded, "What went wrong? Why did you wait so long to call me?"

"Patience, Elizabeth. Everything's fine now. Let me kiss you. It's been so long." He reached for her, but she shook him loose.

"Damn it, David. Tell me why I'm here." Elizabeth wished she could ask for a glass of wine, but it would be a waste of time. Nobody in the church drank. Not because they couldn't, but because David didn't.

"I needed to see you." David shrugged, discomfort creeping into his eyes. "Today was difficult for me. I had to remind myself why I went through with this dangerous thing." Elizabeth stiffened, but he gently stroked her neck. "Your sister is a fighter, just like you." David paused to kiss her neck. Elizabeth chewed the inside of her lip. She was still upset that he'd tricked her into coming, but pleased that he wanted her in his time of need instead of one of his groupies. She wouldn't give him the satisfaction of begging for details. He would tell her the whole story eventually anyway.

"She almost got away from me on the trip to the compound," David finally said. "Apparently I didn't give her large enough doses of ketamine and Versed. But I grabbed her again. She's been adequately sedated and secured now. I've done a thorough examination and her ovaries seem healthy."

Elizabeth's shoulders slumped with relief. McClure didn't have the same ovarian scarring that she did. Her sister would ovulate on schedule, and everything would be fine. Elizabeth's muscles began to relax under David's steady caress. She leaned against him. His erection pressed into the small of her back, sending shivers through her. Elizabeth turned and embraced him. One touch and she lost control. She could go for months and not look at another man or think about sex. With David, she became a giant, pulsating need. He slid his hand under her skirt and squeezed her gently. Elizabeth groaned and spread her legs. She had learned not to be ashamed of her response, to take what fleeting pleasure she could. Nothing good lasted long enough to matter.

* * *

Carmichael hadn't stopped thinking about money even during their lovemaking, except for those few minutes at the end when his body felt as if it were about to take flight.

"You were wonderful, David." That was her cue for him to move away. He untangled himself and eased over. Elizabeth was the only woman he'd ever been with who didn't like to cuddle after sex—or any time, for that matter. She claimed it was a mild case of claustrophobia, but Carmichael knew it was a basic fear of intimacy, probably a result of some childhood trauma. He'd never pressed the issue because he liked things the way they were. Elizabeth's refusal to cling to him was one of her main attractions. Her intelligence and restrained beauty had caught his attention, but it was her rare combination of sexual submissiveness and emotional distance that kept him coming back, even while they were both married to other people.

Carmichael knew he had to ask now or her moment of softness would pass. "Liz, I need your help. The church is out of money, and I can't keep the clinic going without funds."

"You son of a bitch." She sat up, grabbing the sheet to cover herself. "How dare you?" Liz turned and stared incredulously. "I gave you a half-million-dollar inheritance! You didn't have to spend every dime of it on the clinic."

"Liz, we've been through this. You know how expensive in vitro equipment is." He reached for her shoulders. "You know I wouldn't ask if I wasn't desperate."

She shook him loose with a violent jerk. "Whatever happened to the yearly donation that was supposed to end all your financial trouble?" Her dark eyes blazed as she held the sheet tightly over her breasts.

"It fell through. Apparently the United Christian Foundation got wind of our nontraditional doctrine about sex and procreation. Now I'm in a bind over a loan, and the bank wants to repossess my land."

"Oh, David." Elizabeth closed her eyes for a moment as if that would make him go away. "Why do you keep buying equipment you can't pay for? I understand the obsessive nature of research, but we all have to work within our budgets. I'm not bailing you out again." She bolted out of bed and started pulling on clothes. Carmichael kept quiet, soaking up the pleasure of watching Liz, sleek and beautiful in her black slip, brushing angrily at her short bronze hair with crisp strokes.

When she stopped, he said softly, "What price would you have paid for an adoption? Fifteen thousand? Twenty?" Carmichael scooted to the edge of the bed and reached for his pants. "What about two or three failed IVF cycles? Thirty grand, easy. I'm only asking for ten. Just enough to make a couple of loan payments to keep us going until I can work something out with the pharmaceutical company." He didn't mention the money he had promised Zeke for helping him grab Jenna.

Elizabeth whirled around. "Don't you dare put a price on my child! You owe me this favor." She moved toward him and pointed an accusing finger. Her whole body was shaking. "I lied to the police to keep you out of jail when you lost your family. I gave you my inheritance so you could pursue your research ambitions. And I've supplied you with stolen sperm for years so you could impregnate your little groupies. You owe me!"

Carmichael fought to stay calm. Elizabeth hadn't wanted her stepfather's money, so he harbored no guilt there, but she knew that any mention of his first family was excruciating to him. He had to believe she was beside herself with anxiety. The impact of what they'd done, what they still planned to do, overwhelmed him at times too. He said the words out loud for the first time, reminding Elizabeth of the enormity of what she'd asked of him.

"I kidnapped your sister and I'm holding her hostage in the sanctity of my church. In time, I'll harvest her eggs, fertilize them, and transfer the embryos to your body. That more than makes up for you getting me off the hook after the accident." Carmichael grabbed Elizabeth by the shoulders. "I think I've paid my debt. If you want your donor to have the hormones and medical treatment she needs, you'll write me a check for a lousy ten grand."

Carmichael kissed her hard on the mouth before she could respond. He was tired of fighting, tired of worrying about money. Liz would come through for him, he was confident. Right now he wanted to enjoy her slender body again while he had the chance. She resisted for a moment, pushing against his chest with her hands, but opening her mouth to his kiss at the same time. Carmichael slid his hands off her shoulders and began to massage her sweet breasts through the black silk. In a few seconds, she began making tiny moaning sounds and he knew he had her. Perhaps he could talk her out of fifteen thousand. Lord knew, he could use every penny.

* * *

Zeke stood just inside Carmichael's office, too stunned to retreat and too furious to care about the grunts and groans coming through the partly open door. He'd come looking for the Reverend to let him know he was headed for town in the morning and he'd gotten an earful instead.

The Reverend had lied to him about the woman they'd picked up. There were no rich parents, no money was in the works. He'd been suckered, conned into kidnapping someone so Carmichael's skinny bitch of a girlfriend could steal a baby from her.

Zeke couldn't believe he'd been so gullible. Just because he and Carmichael had been friends, had lived and worked together for ten years, didn't mean he had to believe everything the man said. He should have asked more questions, done a little investigation. But when he'd heard fifty thousand, his head had zeroed in on the money, and it had clouded his thinking. Fuck and double-fuck. He'd probably never even see the five thousand Carmichael had promised him, unless the ice doctor came through with the money Carmichael was trying to hump out of her. Zeke had only met Liz twice but he hated her on sight. She was a blast of cold air. Now that the Reverend had done her dirty work, the church wasn't likely to get another dime out of her.

Zeke slipped out of the office, leaving the door open as it was when he came in. The kidnapping and egg-stealing thing would blow up in their faces, sure as the sun would come up tomorrow. He needed to get as far away as he could as soon as he could. It was risky enough when he thought he was kidnapping a heroin addict who would probably not go to the police or be able to identify him if she did. Stealing someone's baby right out of her body was something else entirely. It was worse than anything he'd ever done.

He felt sorry for the woman in the basement, and he wished like hell he'd left her at the bus stop. She didn't deserve all the shit that was happening to her, but Zeke couldn't do anything about it now. What was done was done. It was her life or his at this point.

If he let her live, she'd put the finger on him and he'd go back to prison, which was the same as dying. He wasn't ready to think about how he would take care of the problem yet. It would take a few days just to get used to the idea. On the other hand, Zeke thought squeezing the life out of Carmichael for getting him into this mess would be a pleasure.

Zeke headed for the church office and the computer he used for bookkeeping. There had to be some money he could get hold of quickly. He thought about blackmailing the ice doctor, but that would be more work than he had in mind. If only one of their contributors would make another large donation. It was so easy to steal from the church.

Zeke didn't worry about the compound going broke, the way Carmichael did. The women and kids would never go hungry; they had at least six months' worth of food stored up. They also had a year's supply of gas for the generator. The only thing that would suffer if the money ran out was the Reverend's little embryo clinic, and Zeke didn't give a rat's ass about that.

His personal bank account was another matter. He'd been worried for a while that the cash flow was drying up. The drug company hadn't sent a check in five months, and the big United Christian donation had been canceled. Zeke was bitterly disappointed. He'd expected to skim a chunk off the top, putting him close to his goal of fifty or sixty grand. That was why he'd let Carmichael talk him into the kidnapping. He needed the cash to get on with his plan.

All he wanted was to buy an old boat he could live on and fish from. He'd been thinking about Florida ever since he read a John MacDonald mystery his second year in prison. Zeke hoped he'd have enough cash left over after he bought his boat to send a nice little nest egg to his sister. Give Elsie a little security for once in her life. He'd been sending money once or twice a year since he'd joined the church, but never more than a couple hundred at once. He hoped he could do better for her.

Zeke called up the complete databank of cash donations, then sorted it for one-time donors. He was looking for a name he would recognize, someone he could lean on. Another fifteen thousand and he would be on his way. Zeke didn't even think of it as stealing. Carmichael hadn't done anything to earn the money people sent him, and Zeke figured if someone was foolish enough to send their money to a flaky church like the Reborn, they deserved to have it end up in the wrong hands.

Zeke grinned at the thought. All he planned to do was buy a boat and be a bum. Carmichael, on the other hand, used their money to make babies in glass tubes, picking out the females to stick into his unmarried followers, then experimenting with the rejects like they were lab rats. Wouldn't those little old ladies who sent their hundred-dollar checks shit bricks if they ever found out.

"Oh, it's you." Rachel, one of the longtime Sisters, stepped into the office. "Where's Reverend Carmichael?"

"He's busy humping his guest." Zeke was being cruel and didn't care. Rachel, like all the women, had a crush on Carmichael.

"Oh." Rachel looked upset, as expected. She turned to leave.

"Say, Rachel."

She spun back.

"Do you or anyone else ever hear from Darcie?"

She looked surprised. "No." After a moment, she shrugged and walked away.

Zeke stared at the list of names on the computer screen but couldn't concentrate. One baby sold on the black market was worth a lot of cash, and he knew just the baby he wanted. Teach that little slut a lesson.

An image of Darcie standing by the highway with her cute little butt and thumb out burned in Zeke's mind. She'd seemed as fresh and sweet and juicy as the first peach he'd eaten after thirteen years in the pen. The girl had flirted with him shamelessly, seducing him with her adoring looks and soft laughter.

They'd spent a couple of days in town together while Zeke picked up supplies and took care of church business. She'd let him kiss and fondle her luscious little body parts until he'd been insane with lust. But Darcie had held out on him and, for reasons he still didn't understand, Zeke hadn't forced himself on her. Instead he'd fallen hard for the little vixen. He'd talked her into coming with him to the compound, thinking he'd be able to win her over. The little bitch had taken one look at Carmichael and closed her legs to Zeke forever. As far as he knew, the Reverend had never screwed her, but it made no difference. Darcie had burned him, and it was time to even the score.

She'd left the compound months ago, but Zeke would bet his boat money she hadn't gone far. If she was in Eugene or Springfield, he could find her. All he had to do was check the places a pregnant girl could get free doctor's care. He'd tried to talk the Reverend into helping him, but Carmichael wouldn't go for it. Kidnapping someone so his girlfriend could have a baby was somehow all right, but snatching Darcie's baby—which wasn't really even hers—to make some quick cash was not.

Zeke shrugged. Everybody had his own idea of right and wrong. In the long run, only God would be the judge. He knew he'd already blown it with the big guy and ruined his chance at heaven, so he figured he might as well make the most of his short time on earth.

Darcie was due any day. He'd checked her records when they got that nasty letter from the bank demanding a payment. All he had to do was find her, wait for the baby to be born, then grab it. By then, Carmichael would be done with the kidnapped woman in the basement, and Zeke could quietly take care of her and be on his way.

Chapter 9 >

Sunday, October 29

"Can I use the gym a few times, check it out before I sign a contract?" Eric asked the very muscular and surprisingly attractive young woman behind the counter.

"Sure." She flashed him a capped-teeth smile. "Just fill out this application and we'll give you a week's free membership."

Eric reached for the papers, unable to take his eyes off her bulging upper arms. How did a cute twenty-year-old girl get arms like that? *Damn!* She looked better than he did in a tank top. He was ashamed of how he'd let his body go over the years, had been stewing about it since the day before, when he failed to impress Jenna by running a few miles.

He felt a frown pinch together on his brow. Every time he thought about watching her get into that van his blood pressure escalated. It was inexplicable. He still did not know what he'd witnessed. Eric hated when things didn't make sense. He'd quit watching David Copperfield because he went nuts trying to figure out how he did his magic. Which is probably why he ended up an investigative reporter. He had a compulsion to analyze and set things straight. This mystery with Jenna was personal as well as puzzling, and he couldn't let it go.

He'd called Jenna's number all afternoon, never gotten an answer, then arrived at her place as they'd discussed. She hadn't been home—no surprise at that point—nor had she shown up during the thirty minutes he'd waited in front of the apartment. He'd called again several times during the evening, his attitude altering between disgust with himself for chasing a woman who wasn't interested and concern that she might not have entered the van willingly. The mental flip-flopping was still going on, and Eric had convinced himself a good workout would help put his mind at ease.

So here he was on Sunday morning at Court Sports thinking about spending fifty dollars a month for the next year. Eric didn't know if he was ready to sign, but he filled out the application anyway. He had nothing to lose by trying it out for a week. The idea of getting back in shape excited him. He'd liked the way he'd felt in college, being a wrestler and lifting weights four days a week. The thought of being able to take off his shirt in public and be proud of his upper body—and flat stomach, if things went according to plan—would be worth every penny. But working out would take time away from his short stories and the remodeling project he was supposed to finish before he rented out the other half of his duplex.

Eric headed for the locker room to change into the shorts and tank top he'd stashed in an old gym bag. The bag had been dug out of the back of his closet, where it had been collecting dust since his short infatuation with racquetball years ago during his engagement to Kori. Eric shuddered involuntarily. Kori had dumped him, thank god, even though at the time he hadn't felt quite that way about it. Her sister's husband, a homicide detective Eric had stayed friends with, kept him updated on Kori's troubled marriage. Even though he was glad to have escaped that fate, he still wanted to find the right woman and settle down. For a brief few days, he entertained the idea that Jenna might be that woman. Now he didn't know what to think.

Eric left the locker room and went upstairs to the cardio room. He decided to start on a stationary bicycle, which seemed simple enough for a novice. The computerized program choices were easy to follow, and he set himself a twenty-minute course of short hills. From his location, he could see in the window of the aerobics room. As heads bounced up and into view, he checked carefully for long, honey-colored hair. Jenna wasn't there. Nor was she using any of the weight machines. During his twenty minutes of short-hills hell, he didn't see her come out of the tanning room or in the front door either. Eric finally admitted to himself that was the real reason he'd come to the gym.

As the pedals came to a stop, he decided Jenna was either a flake—and he could forget her—or she was in some kind of trouble. If it was trouble of her own doing, he wanted no part of it. If she was an innocent victim, he had to do whatever he could to help. Which meant he had to call Jackson. Relieved to have finally settled on a course of action, Eric headed for the showers.

Later at the police department, Eric plopped himself on the empty desk next to the detective's. "Hey, Jackson, how come you're working on Sunday?"

"I had to get out of the house for a while. Katie has some friends over, and I can only take so much giggling and squeal-ing, if you know what I mean." Jackson rolled his eyes, and Eric laughed at the thought of his macho friend trapped in a house with a bunch of fourteen-year-old girls. He also knew Jackson was a workaholic and didn't need an excuse to be at the department.

Although a little older, the detective was in better shape than Eric. Taller, leaner, darker, and more muscular too. Eric recommitted himself to working out. Their friendship, which had started when he was on the crime beat at the paper, was based on a shared quest for the truth about the sometimes dreadful things that happened in Eugene. Their shared passion for vintage muscle cars always gave them something to talk about.

"You've got that look again, Troutman." Jackson put down his pen and squinted at Eric. "Another crusade to save the innocents?" His tone was a blend of teasing and respect.

"Maybe." Eric still owed the detective for his help with the Pulitzer story about abusive foster homes. Now he needed another favor. Eric wished he had something to offer in return.

"Just tell me what's on your mind," Jackson said. "You're one of the few civilians I really respect. I promise not to laugh."

"Thanks." Eric gave him a sarcastic smile.

"You're welcome." Jackson leaned back, put his feet on the desk and his hands behind his head.

"Remember the robbery at Geronimo's last Tuesday?"

"Sure, the clown and the cowboy. Are you following this one?"

"I just happened to be there. Remember the restaurant manager, Jenna McClure?"

"She gave the victim CPR?"

"That's her."

"Admirable woman. What about her?"

"I gave her a ride home that night, then saw her again at the River Run yesterday. We made a date for last night, then she disappeared. When I was leaving the park, I saw her get into a van with two guys, then she stood me up and I haven't been able to reach her by phone since."

"So?" Jackson let out a small laugh. "Women treat you like that all the time. I keep telling you, Troutman, you've got to toughen up. Women love bad boys." The detective grinned. "And men in uniform."

Eric had expected to take a certain amount of crap about his experience with Jenna, but he also expected Jackson to understand his gut feeling that something was wrong. He tried to explain. "It wasn't as if she'd been hanging out with these guys and they all left together. It was strange." He jumped up and began to pace back and forth between the empty desks.

"She was standing on the corner by herself at a bus stop, and a gray van pulls up. This guy in a gray suit jumps out and starts talking to her. Then a second guy, a skinny cowboy type, hops out and puts his arm around Jenna. I think I see her tense up, but I'm not sure, because I'm a block away. So I start to run toward them. Then she seems to relax, and they all get in the van and drive off. Meanwhile, I'm standing there with my mouth hanging open, wondering: Did this woman just get kidnapped or have I been reading too much crime fiction?"

"I don't know." Jackson rubbed his chin. "Maybe you miss your newspaper job and are creating a crime story to track down."

Eric began to doubt himself. "How could I witness a simple event like that and not know what really happened? I'm supposed to be a reporter."

"Don't beat yourself up over it. I'm sure she's fine. No one has reported her missing. How well do you know her anyway?"

"I don't, really." Eric sat back down, suddenly deflated. "I only met her the night of the robbery, then saw her briefly the next day for coffee. I did get to know her a little yesterday when we were running, and she seemed stable, very down-to-earth."

"You ran in the River Run?" Jackson laughed out loud. "I thought you meant you were there as a reporter. You must have it bad for this woman."

"Maybe."

"Crap." Jackson reached for the tall cup of coffee that was always present on his desk. "Have you lost your objectivity?"

"Maybe."

"Most adults who are reported missing turn up shortly after. The rest don't want to be found."

They sat in silence for a few minutes. Eric thought about the two women who had disappeared last spring. They hadn't turned up later. Jackson must have remembered them as well because he finally said, "If she doesn't show up in the next twenty-four hours, I'll investigate."

Eric stood to leave. "Meanwhile, I'll keep looking around."

"You're a good man."

Eric drove mindlessly for a while, thinking it was time for lunch, and ended up at Geronimo's. His presence in the restaurant the night of the robbery had been a fluke, a last-minute meeting with a magazine editor who was staying at a nearby motel. He rarely spent money eating out, but here he was ordering an expensive prime rib sandwich and asking if Jenna McClure was around.

"I'm sorry, she's on leave of absence."

"When do you expect her back?"

"I don't know." The young woman smiled brightly. "Do you want anything else with that?"

"No thanks." Eric handed her the menu, wondering what the waitress knew that she wasn't telling. He'd learned to read people over the years, and this young lady was keeping a secret. Had Jenna been fired? Or had she just gone to sit on the beach as he'd suggested? She had talked about quitting her job, but he'd thought it was just a case of victim jitters. Now he wasn't sure.

The waitress came back with salad and black coffee. "Is Jenna a friend of yours?" she asked quietly.

"I just recently met her, but I'd like to think of her as a friend. Why?"

The girl shrugged. "Just curious."

She darted off before Eric could think of a subtle way of asking if anyone had seen or heard from Jenna. He ate his salad, then pulled out the small notepad he always kept in his pocket and began to doodle. The restaurant didn't seem busy, just a few tables with middle-aged men and women in business suits. The walls were paneled in pine halfway up and had a pale-adobe look around the top. Rounded archways separated the three dining rooms, and the furnishings had a distinctive southwestern look, done mostly in greenish-blue and brownish-red. That was his best guess anyway. Somewhat colorblind, Eric was never sure. He preferred the comfort of vinyl booths and formica tabletops in places that served breakfast twenty-four hours a day. He hoped the prime rib sandwich would be thick and pink and juicy with a big pile of fries on the side, because he was starved, as usual.

When the waitress brought his sandwich, which almost lived up to his expectations, she said, "My name's Stacey if you need anything else." She didn't look at him, but she didn't leave either. Eric decided to press for information.

"I need to contact Jenna McClure. Can you help me?"

"It's against restaurant policy to give out information about another employee." Her tone was firm, but her expression was playful. Stacey wanted to trade dirt, Eric could tell.

He leaned toward her and whispered, "Tell me where she is, and I'll tell you why I'm looking for her."

Stacey whispered back, "Tell me who you are and why you're looking for her, and I'll decide whether I can tell you anything."

"My name's Eric Troutman, I'm a freelance journalist, and I think I'm in love with her."

Stacey grinned. "Show me your ID."

Eric dug out his driver's license and press card and handed them to her.

"How do I know you're not some irritating reporter who won't leave her alone?" Stacey handed the cards back.

"I've already interviewed the lady, and I know where she lives. She's just never there."

"Then I can't help you." Stacey shrugged. She was going through all the motions before she broke the rules. Stacey wanted to help him, he could tell.

"I've called her twenty times since Saturday—no answer."

"Maybe she went to Florence to see her mom, that's all I can think of. I gotta get back to work now. Good luck. Jenna's a great person."

Stacey scooted off, and Eric wolfed down his huge, but now somewhat cold, sandwich. The Riverside Apartments where Jenna lived were less than a mile away. He decided to stop by and talk to the manager, find out if Jenna had been home in the last few days. Stacey's suggestion that Jenna had gone out of town to see her mom made sense. Eric suddenly felt foolish for telling Jackson he thought Jenna had been kidnapped. There were so many other explanations for her behavior. Maybe the guys in the van were brothers or relatives. Maybe her mother was sick or in the hospital, and Jenna had to leave town in a hurry and forgot about their date. Eric remembered a few times he'd bolted off on a story lead without telling anyone but his senior editor.

Once he got out of the mall traffic, the drive to Jenna's apartment complex took only two minutes. Eric would have bet money she either biked or walked to work. It felt good to know that about her, to counter the nagging feeling he'd become obsessed with a total stranger. He pulled into the wide circular driveway and parked in front of the office.

Because it was a spur-of-the-moment idea, Eric hadn't had much time to figure out how he wanted to handle the manager. He considered claiming to be Jenna's brother in town for a visit, but at the last minute decided on the truth. He sized up the chunky little woman behind the counter as the cheerful, busybody type who wouldn't be able to resist the lure of a mysterious disappearance. The new office with its tasteful art and "everything at the touch of a computer" didn't compensate for the basic boredom of her job.

"Good afternoon, ma'am." Eric often wished he had a hat to tip with his southern gentleman's routine.

"Hello," she gushed. "What can I do for you?"

"You can help me find my Cinderella. She disappeared before we had a chance to get back together, and I can't let her go without making a gentleman's effort to win the lady over."

"You're giving me goose bumps, young man." The manager shivered with delight. "You do have a way with words. What's your name?"

"Eric Troutman, freelance journalist."

"I'm Dottie." She extended a plump little hand. "Who's the lucky lady? Does she live here at Riverside?"

"Jenna McClure. Do you know her?"

Dottie brought her hands together. "Of course I know her. She's a wonderful person." Suddenly, her delight vanished. "What do you mean, disappeared? Has something else happened to that poor girl?"

"What do you mean 'something else'?"

"Didn't you hear? The restaurant was robbed last week. Jenna could have been killed." The little manager's eyes blinked rapidly. "They put a gun to her head."

Eric nodded. "I was there. That's when we met."

He told her the whole story, keeping back only the fact they'd slept together. Their lovemaking had been the most intimate and tender experience of his life, and he didn't want to share it with anyone.

Eric paused for a moment to let the manager absorb it all, then said tentatively, "What I'd like you to do is open her mailbox and see if she's picked up her mail in the last few days." He really wanted to get inside her apartment. He'd know in a glance if Jenna had been home recently. But he didn't want to push for that yet.

"I don't know if I'm supposed to, but I don't like the sound of this." Dottie looked distressed. "I've never seen Jenna with anybody that drives a gray van. Most of the people she hangs out with are from the restaurant."

"Does she have any family around here?" Eric asked as he followed Dottie out to the dozens of silver mail units in front of the complex.

"Not that I know of. I've heard her mention visiting her mother at the coast, but not recently."

Their conversation in the coffeehouse came back to him. Jenna said she'd grown up with only her mother. So much for his theory that the guys in the van were relatives. "Did she say anything about leaving town?"

"No. I haven't seen her much lately. I think the robbery shook her up pretty badly." Dottie picked through a bundle of keys that was bigger than her fist, finally selecting one and opening a mailbox on the lower left corner of the unit. It was crammed full. Dottie pulled out the pile and quickly sorted through it. "There's nothing personal here. Just an electric bill and a bunch of junk mail. Now what?"

"Will you open her apartment for me? Let me glance inside to see if she's been home in the last few days?" Eric crossed his mental fingers.

"I can't do that." Dottie looked more upset by the minute. "I don't believe she'd go off for more than a few days without telling me. Besides, it's in the rental contract that tenants have to notify me of any prolonged absence. Jenna just isn't like that. She's a responsible person."

"You can look inside yourself," Eric pleaded. "I'm sure it would be all right. It's your duty as a manager."

"I should call Geronimo's to see if she's been at work."

"I was just there. One of the waitresses told me Jenna was on a leave of absence, whatever that means."

"Oh dear." Dottie looked about to cry. "She could have moved out and not told me. That happens sometimes."

"Only one way to find out."

"You're right." The little manager abruptly turned and marched down the circular sidewalk surrounding the common green. Eric followed.

Jenna's apartment was as Eric remembered, a collection of contradictions. The living room was perfectly clean and uncluttered while her bedroom had clothes and books scattered everywhere. The kitchen had every imaginable countertop appliance, but the living room didn't even have a TV. Eric checked the bathroom and kitchen sinks. Both were bone-dry. Nobody had used any water in the apartment recently. A quick look in the hall closet revealed Jenna had left without her matching set of luggage. Neither Eric nor the manager knew enough about Jenna's wardrobe to determine if clothes were missing, but they agreed that if Jenna had gone somewhere, she'd packed lightly.

The bathroom bothered them the most. Toothbrush, deodorant, shampoo, everything a person would use on a daily basis, was there on the countertop. A magazine was open on the floor.

"I think we should call the police," Dottie said as she bent down to see what Jenna had been reading.

"I've talked to a detective. He's a friend of mine." Eric picked up the deodorant. It was a generic, unscented brand. "He seemed to think I was overreacting." The soap by the sink was the clear, see-through kind. He picked it up and sniffed; also unscented.

You could learn a lot about a person in their bathroom, he decided. Jenna didn't seem to have any curlers, blow-dryers, or other hair gizmos, meaning her curly hair was probably natural. The amount of makeup seemed minimal too. Eric realized Dottie had been talking to him.

"What if she was kidnapped? Did you file a missing-persons report?"

"Not yet. Do you have her mother's name or address in her rental application?"

"Only if she used her for a reference." Dottie twisted her hands nervously. "Should we look through her address book for it?"

"Maybe we won't have to." Eric headed back to the kitchen where he'd seen a cordless phone. Next to it was a list of names and numbers with *Mom* right on top. Eric picked up the phone and started to dial.

"Wait!" Dottie grabbed his hand. "You can't just call her up and say, 'I think your daughter's missing, have you seen her?' If Jenna's not there, her poor mother will worry herself to death, and we don't know anything for sure."

"You're right." Eric set the phone down. He hadn't thought about how Mrs. McClure might react. He could get around that. The survey ploy usually worked. "I have an idea." He dialed the number again. A woman's voice answered on the second ring. The voice was high-pitched and uptight, completely unlike Jenna's warm, friendly alto.

Eric jumped right into his spiel. "Hello. This is Michael Fish with KVAL. We're conducting a survey to find out what your favorite programs are. Do you have a minute?"

"I don't watch KVAL. That guy that does the weather is a weirdo." Mrs. McClure seemed irritated.

"What station do you watch?"

"I like the Discovery Channel. Most of that other stuff is garbage."

"Are there any other viewers in your household?"

"Nope."

"What about guests? Will anyone in your household be watching one of the three major networks tonight?" Eric remembered Jenna didn't have a TV and might not watch even if she was at her mother's.

"Well..." Mrs. McClure pretended to consider the question. "I'd have to say no. I'm going out to play bingo, and the cats haven't figured out how to turn the TV on."

The dial tone buzzed in Eric's ear. He turned to Dottie. "I don't think Jenna's at her mother's."

"Are you going to file a missing-persons report or should I?" Dottie twisted the rings on her fat little fingers and blinked back tears.

"I will." Eric wanted to say something kind, but couldn't think of anything that sounded sincere. He was just as worried as Dottie. "I'm going to copy some of these names and numbers. The police might want them for their investigation."

"Do it quickly, please. I want to get out of here. It feels creepy to be in the apartment with Jenna gone."

Eric wanted to snoop more, but he pulled out his notebook and copied the list, skipping entries like *Tsunami Books* and *Dr. Lovell (dentist)*. He did another quick tour of the spacious apartment, hoping to see something obvious he'd missed, like airline tickets or travel brochures. Nothing caught his eye except a large collection of plants in a front bay window. "Will you water the plants if she doesn't show up?"

"Sure."

They stepped out of the apartment and Dottie locked the door as the wind blew rain under the covered upper balcony. Eric zipped his jacket and hurried down the stairs behind the manager. He wanted to get downtown and file a missing-persons report. It was possible Jenna had gone AWOL, but he didn't think so. The fear in his gut was real now, a physical presence that didn't go away when he tried to think about something else.

He and Dottie exchanged phone numbers and promised to call each other if they heard anything. Just as Eric stepped out of the office, the sky opened up and the rain exploded in a downpour, the first of the season. He ran for his Firebird, the only car in the lot that hadn't been made in the last decade. The engine fired right up, as it always did. He wondered how Jenna felt about his car. She hadn't said anything when she rode in it. He wondered what kind of car she drove, if she even had one. He wanted to know everything about her. Starting, of course, with where in the hell she was.

Jackson was on the phone when Eric entered the Violent Crimes Unit, so Eric wandered over to Rob Schakowski's desk and read over his shoulder as the detective keyed in an assault report with thick fingers. His crew cut and barrel chest made him seem out of place in front of a computer.

"Hey, I thought you weren't into this crime stuff anymore," Schak said without looking up. It was after three, and Eric knew from experience that the detective was pushing to get this paperwork done before the four-to-midnight crew came on duty.

"It seems to be following me around." Eric noticed that the people in Schak's report all had the same last name. "Domestic violence or family squabble?"

"Both." Schakowski grunted, then said, "The guy was beating on his wife, and his brother tried to stop him. So the guys get into it, and it's still a fistfight at this point. Then the wife attacks the brother with a knife and puts him in the hospital. Now the kids are at grandma's, and she's an alcoholic."

"Sorry I asked."

Eric walked over and slouched in a chair next to Jackson's desk. In a moment, Jackson hung up the phone and looked over at Eric. "Tell me you found the woman and everything is okay."

"No." Eric sat up. "I went to her apartment, and she hasn't been there. It doesn't look like she packed anything to take with her either."

Jackson let out a big sigh. "Women always do this to you, my friend. Haven't you figured that out yet?"

"What are you talking about?"

"Remember Amber? She got so in touch with herself after knowing you, she ran off to Reno to be a blackjack dealer. And Suzan? She moved to Alaska."

"Her mother was sick."

"What about Kori?"

"What about her?"

"Never mind." Jackson rubbed his forehead. "Tell me about the apartment." He looked up suddenly. "By the way, how did you get into the apartment?"

"The manager."

"Some ridiculous story about being a long-lost brother?"

"I didn't have to lie. The truth of this situation is enough to alarm a normal person."

"Tell me all of it."

Eric summed it up. "Jenna hasn't been to work, and I don't think they've heard from her. She isn't at her mother's, and that's the only family she has. She hasn't been in her apartment and didn't take anything with her. All that stuff women usually drag around with them is still there—makeup, lotion, hair stuff, all of it. Her luggage is still in the closet, and her drawers are full of clothes."

Jackson said, "She could be staying with a friend, another woman who has all that stuff."

"Maybe." Eric felt deflated. "Call the restaurant. Tell them you need to question her again. I'll bet they have no idea where she is."

"What's the number?"

Eric rattled it off. He'd called there a few times recently. Jackson asked for the manager, then held his hand over the mouthpiece. "Go get us some coffee, please. Bobbie always brews some of the good stuff about this time of day."

Eric knew the front-desk clerk well. He'd spent a lot of time on the phone with her over the years. She always brought her own fresh-ground coffee to work and charged fifty cents a cup for it.

"Hey, Eric, good to see you." Bobbie filled two ceramic mugs with coffee.

"Thanks, Bobbie. You remembered how much I hate styrofoam."

"It hasn't been that long. Besides, you're the only one who brings my mugs back." Her phone rang, so he headed back to the violent-crimes area.

Jackson was keying information into his computer. "You're right. They haven't seen or heard from her."

"What now?"

"You should fill out a missing-persons report, but don't get your hopes up. We're understaffed and underfunded as usual." Jackson looked up. "People do a lot of strange things after they've been victimized. It's called stress disorder. Why don't you ask around some more, talk to her friends? I'll bet she's hiding somewhere, licking her wounds."

"What if I'm right? She could be dead before you decide to do anything." Eric was almost shouting now.

Jackson looked a little hurt. "We'll do what we can. But what's the motive? Is her mother rich? Has there been a ransom demand?"

"People get kidnapped for other reasons than money."

Neither of them wanted to speak about such horrors out loud.

Finally, Jackson said, "File a missing-persons report. I'll ask to be assigned the case."

The phone rang, and the detective picked it up. He listened for a moment, then responded in an excited voice. "What's the address again?" Jackson scribbled something, then slammed down the phone. "Let's go, Schak! I've got a lead on the clown and the cowboy."

Schakowski jumped up and grabbed his jacket all in one motion. The two detectives bolted from the room. Eric decided to follow in his car. The clown and the cowboy had robbed Jenna. Maybe they had kidnapped her too.

Chapter 10 >—

Monday, October 30

Reverend Carmichael kept his morning service short. He had more important things on his mind today than leading his congregation. He figured by setting a good example and providing an ideal environment, he made it possible for them to live a spiritual life without heavy-handed guidance. For the next week or so they would be in God's hands while he kept a close watch on Jenna. As anxious as he was to get down to the clinic, Carmichael felt compelled to stick to his morning routine so he wouldn't arouse any curiosity.

Usually he was up at six, followed by an hour of Bible reading and prayer. Then breakfast at seven in the dining hall crowded with rough wooden picnic tables, amid the women and children who gathered around to ask questions, present him with homemade gifts, or simply enjoy his company for the few minutes that they could. Morning service was held at eight in the chapel. Attendance was not required, but few ever missed it. He had noticed Rebecca's absence for the second day in a row and decided to make time to see her. Perhaps her pregnancy was giving her morning difficulties. Some women seemed to suffer horribly while carrying out the Lord's work, and others never had a sick day. It was the one aspect of pregnancy he had never been able to diagnose or properly control.

Morning chores were next. A rotation chart was posted in the main hallway and, even though his name was not on it, Carmichael always did his share. Today he went with Faith and the crew into the fields to pick the last of the second potato crop. Anyone who wanted to eat had to help gather and prepare food. It was the way he was raised. There were no exceptions. Even his father, who never did a single other household chore, would slice vegetables or grate cheese if his mother couldn't locate one of the girls to help. His father, after the first or second martini, was amenable to most things. After three or four, he became unpredictable, sometimes giddy and rambunctious to the point of embarrassment, and other times short-tempered and abusive. When they were teenagers, he'd encouraged his children to drink with him. And they had. Three out of six of his kids had become alcoholics before they were old enough to drink legally.

Carmichael pushed his father out of his mind, not wanting to be distracted by old emotions. He had stopped abusing his body with drugs and alcohol long ago when he renewed his faith in God, but by then his life had been shattered, and it was no one's fault but his own. He would not let himself think of the accident, not even to ask forgiveness, not today.

Carmichael put down his potato digger and stood, stretching his hands toward the crisp blue sky. "Praise God for this day!" he shouted.

"Praise God!" the women sang out after him.

"Keep me in your heart. I'll see you at the noon meal."

He hurried through the greenhouse and into the kitchen to drop off the fruits of his labor. His lab and the greatest challenge of his medical career awaited him.

* * *

Jenna tried to swallow, but her tongue felt as hot and dry as August. Imagining a tall, cold glass of water brought tears to her eyes. She eased her shoulders forward and glanced at the room again. Her head felt heavy and wobbly, as if a big rock were rolling around in her skull. She wanted to drift back into never-never land, but she was awake now, or at least she thought she was awake. The previous few days seemed like a bad dream that had gone from disturbing to nightmarish.

The tiny room was lined with smooth, gray tiles. The walls, floor, and ceiling were all the same, the blankness broken only by a single door and a strange dark window that she was sure did not lead outside. The bed seemed like standard hospital issue, the monitors and assorted equipment, vaguely familiar. If not for the lack of a television, it could have been a room in a hospital. Except it wasn't.

The silence frightened her almost as much as the wide leather straps pinning down her arms and legs. Occasionally Jenna would hear a small thump or scrape above her, but there seemed to be no life outside the walls. She almost wished her captors would come back, do whatever they planned, and get it over with. The waiting and not knowing was an agony unlike anything she had ever experienced.

What do they want? Why me? The questions echoed in her mind over and over. None of it made sense. How had she ended up here? She had a fleeting image of a dark-haired man in a suit, but the image blurred and slipped away before she could focus on it. Was the man in the suit a doctor? Why did she think that?

Jenna had trouble thinking clearly. She assumed the IV line in her right arm, which she could hardly bear to look at, had to be pumping her with a drug that dulled her senses as well as the pain along her left side that came and went. What had they done to her? A thin gray blanket covered her body, so she couldn't see her injuries. Her shoulder hurt the worst, as if it were broken, but all she could see when she twisted her head to the side was the white of bandages. Had they dropped her or beat her when she was unconscious? Blurry images of a wet ditch floated in and out. Had she been in a car wreck? It seemed as if a doctor had come to help. Had it all been a dream? What if she'd been raped? Jenna didn't feel violated, but she didn't trust her perceptions.

The last thing she remembered clearly was running with Eric. They'd made a date, then something had happened to her. Eric must have thought she stood him up. Jenna fought back tears. He was the sweetest guy she'd ever met, and he probably thought she was a complete nutcase. But what did it matter now? She was drugged, injured, and restrained, and couldn't remember how any of it happened. Despair washed over her. How in the hell would she ever get out?

Except for her IV stand, the monitors, and a small wooden stool, the room was barren. Even if she did manage to get free of the straps, Jenna expected to find the door locked. That strange dark window was probably plexiglas or something unbreakable. She could almost picture faces behind it, old men with cold, hard eyes, watching, waiting. Jenna shivered. She could feel their eyes on her skin. She was a bug under a microscope, and she would die in this room.

Silent tears rolled down her temples and pooled in the pockets of her ears. She was helpless to wipe them away or stop the flow. Would anyone even miss her? Her mother, of course, would worry for a while, then get back to her own busy life. Katrice would try to contact her through the psychic world, then get sidetracked and forget her. Otherwise, Jenna figured her disappearance would go largely unnoticed. Would anyone even report her missing? She'd acted so strangely after the robbery, talking about quitting her job and moving, people might think she'd just taken off.

Jenna groaned out loud. In July she'd left on vacation without telling anyone where she was going or when she'd be back. Except for Dottie. Jenna had asked her to water the petunias and geraniums on her patio. Would Dottie notice the dying flowers this time? Probably not. It was late October, and her flowers had only a few good weeks left anyway.

Why, why, why? The words bounced around in her brain like an echo. Jenna thought it would be easier to accept her fate if she understood it. Then again, knowing might be more than she could bear. What if they planned to keep her for a long time? Treat her like a rat in a lab experiment, infecting her with a little of this and a little of that? Jenna shuddered. She'd rather die than be degraded or tortured. She'd find a way to kill herself before she let them use her.

Then it hit her, what they wanted and why: organs. They wanted her kidneys or lungs or, god no, maybe even her heart would be cut out and given to someone else. Her body would be violated and left to die so that some rich stranger could live. Was it the bald, skinny guy with the beat-up face who needed the new heart? Who was he anyway?

The image disappeared as quickly as it came. The idea that they would cut out her heart lingered. She couldn't stop thinking about some bastard walking around with her heart. Jenna trembled with rage. Action-packed scenes played in her mind. Getting free from her straps and leaping on the doctor when he entered the room. Rising up from the operating table, seizing the scalpel and stabbing them both. Given a chance, she would fight for her life. Even if it meant her own death. She would not let them take little pieces of her for themselves.

It was impossible to stay angry. The drug made her mind float from one thought to another. She drifted off for a while, then was suddenly awake again. Hours seemed to have passed. Why weren't they coming to check on her? How long had it really been?

Time seemed to have stopped. With only horror for company, each minute seemed like an eternity. The painkiller made it worse, slowing her brain so that each thought was a struggle. How long had she been awake? How long had she been in the room? What day was it by now? The drug was also a blessing. Without it, the confinement of her arms and legs would have been unbearable. She would have driven herself crazy struggling against the bindings.

Jenna closed her eyes, unable to look at the blank grayness of the room any longer. She pictured herself on a beach somewhere with a brilliant blue sky, a warm sun, and a cool breeze. She listened for the rhythm of the ocean, the call of a seagull, the rumble of a fishing boat leaving the bay. Her body relaxed, and the afternoon stretched out in a gentle daydream.

"How are you feeling?" The voice was soft, but the suddenness of it startled her. Jenna's eyes flew open. A dark-haired man wearing a surgical mask was at her bedside. All she could see of his face were gray eyes, which seemed surprisingly kind. He wore a cream-colored sweater and black wool pants and did not match her image of a kidnapper.

Confused and afraid to trust her perceptions, Jenna demanded, "Who are you?" Her voice betrayed her. It was scratchy and weak and still desperate for water.

"It's better for both of us if you don't know." He set down a tray and patted the back of her hand. Jenna flinched, unable to pull away. "Please don't be afraid." His eyes pleaded with her to believe him. "I'm a man of God as well as a doctor."

"I need water."

"Ask and you shall receive." He smiled and turned to pour from a pitcher beside the bed. His reference to God failed to comfort her. The Son of Sam claimed God spoke to him through a dog. In fact, God was pretty popular with psychos.

"What do you want with me?" The water could wait; she had to know.

"It is not I who wants something of you. God has given us all a purpose in life, and now he calls upon you to do his work. Can you sit up to drink this?" He held the water over her chest, eyes twinkling with amusement.

In that instant Jenna hated him. Hated his power over her— that she should need his help with a simple sip of water. She wouldn't let pride get in the way. She wanted that cool liquid. She needed it to live.

She eased her head forward, letting the queasiness pass in stages, then opened her lips. He gently poured little sips into her mouth until she'd swallowed the whole glass. Jenna cleared her throat and asked again, "Why am I here? What do you want?"

He seemed uncertain. "I've debated at length about how much to tell you. First, let me put your mind at ease. I don't intend to harm you in any way. Second, if things go according to plan, you won't remember anything about your stay here, which should be a relief to you. For now, let's just say I plan to borrow some tissue."

Jenna sucked in a breath. "You're going to cut me open?"

* * *

"Not really. It's a very small amount of tissue, and it won't be painful." Carmichael used his most soothing voice. He'd meant to ease her fears, not escalate them. He'd forgotten how easily non-medical people were alarmed by invasive procedures. His church members had such faith in him he rarely had to worry about bedside manners.

"Don't bullshit me!" Spit flew out of the woman's mouth.

Stunned by her vehemence, Carmichael was speechless. She should have been more sedated. He would have to increase her dosage of Versed. He tried again, more firmly this time. "As long as you're in my care, you will not be harmed. The best thing you can do for yourself is stay calm and let your wounds heal."

He reached for the apple butter sandwich he'd brought and held it to her lips. "You need to eat to keep up your strength and fight infection."

"I'd rather die." She turned her head away.

What a feisty one, he thought with grudging admiration. She reminded him of his wife, Anne. She'd been a spitfire too, the only woman he'd never been able to dominate.

"I won't let that happen," Carmichael said, gently stroking her chin. "I'll just add a nutritional supplement to your IV line, if necessary. You might as well eat and enjoy what pleasure you can."

"Why? Why me?" Jenna cried out, her face red with fury.

Carmichael realized the poor woman must be terrified under all that anger. He wished he could explain to her why she'd been chosen; it would probably make her feel safer. He'd promised Elizabeth that Jenna would never know she had a sister. The less she knew, the safer it would be to let her go.

The memory-impairing drugs were not foolproof, and Jenna seemed to have a high tolerance for them. She had already surprised him by coming out from under the ketamine much sooner than he'd expected, and now she was more alert and hostile than she should be. The fall from the back of the van had given him a sprained forearm and two bruised knees. Only the fact that he'd landed on Jenna had kept him from serious injury. Carmichael had no intention of underestimating this patient again.

"Do you want the sandwich or not?" he asked softly. After a few seconds, Jenna turned back. She's beautiful, Carmichael realized. Although Elizabeth was attractive, Jenna, with almost the same features, was stunning. He reached to touch her hair, its long honey-colored waves forming a halo around her face.

"What is it?" she asked, pulling her head away.

At first Carmichael didn't know what she meant, it had taken her so long to respond. Then he realized she was asking about the sandwich. He found it amusing that it mattered to her.

"Homemade apple butter and bread. The simple and nutritious food the good Lord meant for us to eat." He held the offering to her mouth again. Jenna leaned forward and tore off a hunk, chewing slowly at first, eyes narrowed suspiciously, then ravenously reaching for another bite when she realized it was exactly what he claimed it to be.

Carmichael watched her with pleasure. Her skin glowed with the pinkish tan of outdoor exercise and her eyes danced with life despite the drugs and the injuries. He admired her muscle tone and vitality. What a great baby maker she would be. Too bad Elizabeth insisted on carrying the child herself. Jenna seemed so much sturdier, so much more likely to have a healthy ten-pounder than Liz.

"Water." Jenna grunted around a mouthful of bread.

He lifted the glass and let her drink, but decided he would have to teach her some manners if she wanted him to be her friend. "You should say *please*."

Jenna let out a short, harsh laugh, causing her to choke and cough repeatedly. Carmichael watched her silently, unable to help. Finally the spasm passed. When she spoke, her words were slurred from the drugs, but the hostility was clear. "Put me back where you found me, and I'll say *thank you*. Until then, you can go fuck yourself."

The words stung. Carmichael thought they had reached an understanding. Earlier in his life, he would have slapped Jenna for her disrespect. But the need to punish women physically had faded in the years since he'd given up drugs and alcohol. He'd promised God never to hurt anyone again. But he couldn't let the insult go. He had treated her civilly and expected the same in return. There were many ways to alter behavior and win someone's respect.

"I'll be back in a few minutes." He ignored her curses and strode out of the small room. Some women were so noisy during labor that he'd designed a small, soundproof room in the underground clinic just for that purpose. Zeke had changed the knob to a lock-and-key system the day before they picked up Jenna.

Carmichael moved quickly across the combination birth/surgery area to a supply cabinet where an assortment of painkillers, antibiotics, anesthesia, and synthetic hormones was kept. He intended to give her some Valium, then try to feed her again. It was important that Jenna eat. Sometimes when women didn't eat properly their bodies didn't ovulate. He also needed to give her another injection of clomophergonal, a powerful follicle-stimulating hormone that hadn't been approved yet by the FDA. Every extra egg Jenna produced would increase Elizabeth's chance of becoming pregnant. If Jenna produced extra oocytes. There was a possibility she would have a bad reaction to the fertility drug and need to be taken off it. Clomophergonal was the most powerful synthetic hormone he'd ever tested. But the chance seemed unlikely considering Jenna's tolerance for depressants.

The girl was silent when he reentered the room, but as soon as he reached for the IV bag she started shouting questions. "What is that? Why are you drugging me? How do you know I'm not allergic to it?"

"Relax, dear." Carmichael emptied the Valium into the IV line. "It's only a mild tranquilizer. I know you're not allergic to it because I've given you plenty already. Without this drug, you'd be going crazy in here. I want you to be as comfortable as possible."

"Ha!" It was more of a grunt than a word. "If you want me to be comfortable"—her eyes started to swim—"let me keep my tissue"—her voice got woozy—"and go home."

Carmichael smiled. He'd thought Anne was one in a million, but Jenna was so much like her it made him ache. Jenna hadn't once begged for mercy or complained about pain, yet he knew her collarbone still hurt, even with the drugs. What pride. He lifted her gown and rolled Jenna up on one side. With practiced fingers, Carmichael dabbed her with isopropyl alcohol, plunged the hormone hypodermic into her smooth white buttock, and rolled her back. Her eyes flickered wildly.

"Just an antibiotic to keep you from getting infections," Carmichael said, trying to ignore the rush of blood to his groin produced by his glimpse of Jenna's muscular glutes. She looked away, refusing to meet his eyes.

"I understand you're angry." He stood and let the emotion flow through his voice. "But being abusive will not help. I have no intention of harming you in any way. The only reason you're hurt now is because of your own foolishness. I'd like to make your stay here as comfortable as possible, but in the future I will not tolerate profanity." He picked up the water glass and plate and turned to leave.

"Wait."

Carmichael suppressed a smile and turned back. "Yes?"

"How did I get hurt?" She seemed suddenly frightened and needy.

"You don't remember?"

"Not really. Did we have an accident?"

He was pleased. The ketamine/Versed combination had wiped out her memory of the abduction and ride to the compound. But he had to be careful with the ketamine. Too much of the powerful paralyzing drug could kill her. He didn't plan to use it again until the oocyte retrieval. For now he would only give her Versed to keep her sedated, but if the drug lived up to its reputation for short-term memory loss, he would feel safe about letting Jenna go when it was all over.

He decided it wouldn't hurt to tell her. "You leapt out of a moving vehicle, taking me with you." Carmichael smiled warmly. "But I'm not seriously hurt, so I forgive you. You, on the other hand, have a broken collarbone and multiple abrasions. So I don't recommend further heroics." Tomorrow, he would quiz her on the details to see how much she remembered.

Jenna was silent for a moment, then said, "You're never going to let me go, are you?"

"Of course I am. I'm a doctor and a man of God. When you have fulfilled your destiny here, you will return to your life as if nothing happened. In the meantime, you are safe in my care."

"What do you plan to do with me?"

"You've forgotten already, haven't you?"

She tried to glare at him, but her eyes blinked back tears.

Pleased, Carmichael smiled brightly. "Don't worry about it. You'll be fine. Rachel will be in later to give you a bath and check your catheter."

Chapter 11

Eric found himself eating at Geronimo's for the third time in a week. This time he sat in the lounge, not wanting to take up a table during a busy dinner hour. Yesterday had been a total waste. He'd sat down to write a few times and accomplished nothing. The story he was working on for *Modern Man*, about men taking maternity leave, was not fleshing out the way he'd hoped. Perhaps it was a lack of attention.

First, he'd gone chasing after Jackson to witness the arrest of Jason Reinhart and Leo Manfred, aka the clown and the cowboy. Eric had taken several decent pictures of the armed robbers, which he'd sold to the *Willamette News*, but that was it. Jackson had agreed to question the men about Jenna's disappearance, which they vehemently denied knowing anything about. The detective later admitted that questioning Reinhart, who was only eighteen, about the kidnapping had frightened the kid so badly he'd readily agreed to accept a plea bargain on the robbery and murder charges in exchange for his testimony against Manfred.

Eric was no closer to knowing what really happened to Jenna. He couldn't move forward with his life until he found out. His reporter's obsession with an unfinished story, combined with an intense attraction to Jenna, made it impossible to think about anything else.

He sighed and pushed his plate away, leaving the baby carrots and rice untouched. The bartender, a woman in her late thirties named Katrice, had been near the top of Jenna's phone list, and Eric intended to pump her for all he could. He'd introduced himself earlier, but she'd been too busy to talk to him.

Eric watched as she poured another beer for a man at the other end of the bar. The woman moved with an elegant grace, despite the hustle around her, never spilling a drop of the brew served in tall, slender glasses. Her dark hair grew to her waist and gave her a gypsy look. Eric suspected that she would eventually tell him more than he wanted to know.

After a few minutes, Katrice motioned him to come sit at the middle of the bar. "That way we can talk while I wash this pile of glasses," she said. Eric liked the way she talked out of the side of her mouth with a southwestern accent. *New Mexico*, he thought.

"Can you believe this place doesn't have a dishwasher behind the bar?" Katrice snorted. "Two twenty-inch color televisions and they can't afford one little dishwasher. Ha!"

"You mean being friends with the manager doesn't pull any weight around here?"

"Works against me, more likely." Katrice wrinkled her nose in a funny smile. "How can you say no to a friend when she calls you on your day off and begs you to come in? Especially when she already knows you have no plans." The bartender was suddenly serious. "By the way, have you seen our mutual acquaintance lately?"

Eric's heart sank. He had hoped Katrice would know something, anything. "Not since Saturday. Have you?"

"No, damn." Katrice yanked her hands out of the sudsy water and grabbed a small bar towel. "Why would Jenna take off like this again when she knows how it upsets me?" Her anger dissipated rapidly, replaced by a worried frown, as she absent-mindedly rubbed her hands.

"She's done this before?" Sounded like good news to Eric.

"In July." Katrice shook her head. "Jenna took a week's vacation and left without telling anyone where she was going. Of course, Stoltz knew when she'd be back at work, but that was it."

"Stoltz?"

"The owner."

Eric nodded, relieved. "Where did Jenna go?"

"You're not going to believe this." Katrice's expression dared him to guess.

Eric was not in the mood. "Tell me."

"Disneyland."

"Disneyland?"

"Yep. She said she always wanted to go as a kid but never could, and if she didn't do it now, she'd be too old to enjoy it." Katrice leaned forward and lowered her voice. "I never quite believed it though. I mean, Jenna is so straight-laced, so serious about everything. I just can't see her in Disneyland. I personally think she had some kind of elective surgery she didn't want to talk about, you know, like having fat sucked out of her ass or something. She lost a lot of weight, you know." Katrice looked worried again, as if she'd said too much or thought of something unpleasant.

"Where do you think she is now?"

"I feel a little uncomfortable discussing this with you. Even though Jenna told me about your date." She arched her eyebrows.

"And I can tell she likes you a lot, even though she wouldn't come right out and say it. This seems too personal to discuss with a relative stranger."

"What's personal?" Eric forced himself to stay focused on the conversation. Inside he was singing, *Jenna likes me*. To Katrice, he said, "You mean the weight loss? She told me about that."

Katrice looked away. "There's more to it. I think I might know what she's up to."

"You mean the artificial insemination?"

Katrice's head snapped back. "She told you?"

"We met for coffee and she told me all about wanting a family and not being willing to wait any longer."

"She must really like you. No one else in the restaurant knows but me."

"You think that's why she's missing now?" Eric was doubtful. It didn't feel right. If their night together meant even half as much to Jenna as it did to him, then she would postpone her pregnancy plans long enough to give their relationship a chance. He had to believe that. "I thought she was waiting for blood test results from a lab in Portland."

"What if she got them back, then rushed off to get pregnant before something else went wrong?"

"What else has gone wrong?" Trouble comes in threes, his mother's voice echoed in his head.

Katrice hesitated. Finally she said, "Jenna's blood analysis indicated she was a cystic fibrosis carrier. At first, she was pretty depressed, then she called her mom. I guess no one in her family has ever had CF, so I advised her to get a second test." The bartender scowled. "I neither like nor trust doctors."

"Where would she go for the insemination?" It was hard for him to think about Jenna getting pregnant by someone else, even in a clinical way.

"Good question. She liked most of the staff at the Reproduction Clinic, so I assumed she would go back there. Even if she went to Portland instead," Katrice squinted as if trying to see something far away, "I don't see why she would be gone almost a week. It's not like an operation."

"It doesn't explain the two guys in the van either."

"What guys?"

The printer at the service bar jumped to life, rattling off a list of drinks to be made. "Don't go away," Katrice instructed, reluctantly moving to pick up the order.

Eric drained his coffee and made a trip to the restroom. The carpet in the lobby was new, the bloodstains from the night of the robbery whisked away—back to business as usual. Jenna couldn't have been the only one affected by the crime, Eric mused. Maybe he should interview other staff members who were in the restaurant that night. Maybe there was a bigger story.

When he returned to the lounge, Katrice was chatting with one of the waiters. Eric waited patiently. He didn't want to be anywhere else. Geronimo's was starting to seem like home. It made him feel close to Jenna to be in the restaurant where she worked, where he'd first seen her. As if she might come waltzing in any moment with a good reason for standing him up last Saturday night.

The young woman who'd waited on him the day before spotted him at the bar and came over to say hello. Eric tried desperately to remember her name.

"Did you ever figure out what Jenna is up to?" she asked quietly.

Eric shook his head. "I'm still open to suggestions."

"Ask Katrice. She and Jenna are good friends."

"Ask me what?" Katrice leaned into the conversation, elbows on the bar, chin in hand.

"The same question I've been asking for days: Where in the hell is Jenna McClure?" Eric felt suddenly deflated. He hadn't slept well since Saturday, and the coffee could no longer mask his exhaustion.

"By the way, what did you mean by 'two guys in a van'?"

How many times had he told this story? "Saturday, after the River Run, I saw Jenna get into a gray van with two guys. I was a block and a half away and couldn't tell if she went voluntarily or not. I talked to a friend in the police department, but he thinks I'm overreacting. He thinks Jenna just went off to recover from the trauma of the robbery."

Katrice scowled again. "I was supposed to run with her. I called that morning and canceled. She sounded a little depressed, but not traumatized." She began to pace. "I can't think of anyone she knows who drives a gray van. I should have been there. I should have seen it." She turned back. "What did these guys look like?"

"One was dark-haired with a ponytail and well dressed. The other was semi-bald and shabby."

"They sound like a couple of creeps."

"Maybe they're friends or relatives," the waitress offered tentatively. "You know, like they showed up unexpectedly."

"Jenna doesn't have any family except her mom." Katrice suddenly brightened. "Have you tried calling her mother?"

"Yes, but I didn't come right out and ask about Jenna because I didn't want to worry her." Eric wished he had waited and simply told Jenna's mother the truth. "I don't think Jenna is there, but I can't swear to it."

The young waitress—Stacey, he remembered a moment too late—wished him luck and went back to work. Katrice offered to call Mrs. McClure again and find out what she could. Eric thanked her and started to leave, but Katrice grabbed his arm. "Do you have something of hers I could borrow?"

"What do you mean?"

"Something that belongs to Jenna, like a book or a piece of clothing."

"No, why?" Eric was baffled.

"My group will need something to handle. I have some of Jenna's clothes, but they've been in my apartment a long time and, of course, I've worn them all several times." She paused, deep in thought. "I don't think we could get Jenna's psychic vibrations from them. We need something she's worn or touched in the last few weeks."

"Psychic vibrations?"

"Sure." Katrice shrugged casually. "Everybody has their own energy patterns. They rub off on things, sort of like a fingerprint of the soul. Maybe someone in our group can find her. We found Julie's wedding ring." Her eyes clouded. "We found Eva's dog too, but he was dead."

Eric didn't know what to say. He personally had never experienced anything that science couldn't explain, but he also had his own superstitions. He never swore at his car, he never wished bad things on other people, and he never said anything negative about God or any other entity possibly greater than himself. Being a practical man, Eric didn't believe in anything he couldn't touch, see, taste, or smell—but he didn't burn his bridges either.

"You're skeptical, I can tell." Katrice ruffled his hair as she would a silly child. "My Aunt Sylvie and I have been communicating telepathically for years."

Eric tried to be open-minded. "Is Sylvie alive?"

"Of course." Katrice laughed lightly in the same way she moved, as if keeping in tune with music only she could hear. "You think I'm some spook who talks to dead people?"

That's exactly what he'd thought, but he liked this gypsy lady too much to hurt her feelings. "I think Jenna is lucky to have you for a friend. Let me know if you find out anything." He dug out a business card and handed it to her.

"Hey, you too." Katrice's aqua eyes seemed to have lost their sparkle.

"Don't worry. She'll turn up."

"Sure."

Chapter 12

Elizabeth stepped outside, shivering against the chill, and lit a cigarette. Her nerves were already shot, and now that she had a moment to make the phone call, she wanted to be as steady as possible. Quitting smoking was such a bitch. She had to be off nicotine completely before she got pregnant. Elizabeth intended to be the best mother a child could want, and smoking just wasn't in the picture.

She inhaled deeply, trying to take in as much as she could as quickly as she could. An old habit. She hadn't had a relaxing indoor smoke in years. In fact, David was the only person who knew she still smoked. Her colleagues at the hospital shook their heads in disgust at patients and nurses who wouldn't quit. Doctors who smoked were considered more foolish and self-indulgent than their civilian counterparts.

She stubbed out the last third of the butt and hurried back to her office. On Tuesdays and Thursdays, she spent mornings in the Assisted Reproduction Clinic doing pre-implantation embryo diagnosis, which had become more satisfying than her search for a genetic marker for ovarian cancer. But this morning she couldn't concentrate. All she could think about was her sister. And her sister's mother. Wouldn't Mrs. McClure also have to be her mother? Elizabeth shivered.

Finding her real mother had been a lifelong dream, abandoned only when her adoptive father threatened to cut off her funds for medical school if she continued to search. Now Ralph was dead, the phone number was in her hands, and it was time to discover everything she could about her biological heritage. Especially now that she could never be close to McClure. It was heartbreaking to think she would live in the same town as her sister and wouldn't be able to see or contact her. Elizabeth had made her choice. She would have a daughter instead, and maybe discover the woman who had given birth to her.

The thought that she might speak to her real mother for the first time made her knees weak. She held the paper with Mrs. McClure's number and tried to prepare for the possibilities. The woman would hang up on her. Mrs. McClure was Jenna's stepparent. Their real mother had died, or disappeared, or was in a mental institution somewhere.

Elizabeth took a deep breath and dialed the number. As it rang, she rehearsed the speech she'd been preparing for days. As a doctor and a scientist, she was always confident. But this was about family, the part of her life that always failed her.

"Hello?" The voice was high-pitched and abrupt.

Elizabeth's heart sank. "Patricia McClure?"

"Yes?"

"This is Dr. Meyers at North McKenzie Hospital in Eugene. I'm with the genetic-science department."

"What can I do for you?"

"You have a daughter named Jenna McClure?"

"Yes, why?" Panic pitched her voice even higher. "Is something wrong?"

"No. I'm sorry if I alarmed you. We're conducting a study of families with genetic markers for cystic fibrosis. Do you—"

"I can't help you," Mrs. McClure cut in. "As I told Jenna, I don't know anything about her father's family, and there's never been any history of the disease in mine."

"What about your other children? Has any—"

"I told you, I can't help you!"

The woman was frightened and hiding something. Elizabeth knew she wouldn't get another chance if Mrs. McClure hung up.

"I don't mean to cause you any discomfort," Elizabeth said, struggling to sound soothing. She didn't understand how anyone could refuse to cooperate with medical research. "Our intention is to find a cure for the disease so that people like your daughter can become pregnant without worrying about the health of their child. If we knew her father's name and whereabouts, we could get the information from him directly."

"His name is Jack McClure, but I don't know where he is." Mrs. McClure's voice stiffened with old indignities. "Why don't you just forget it? That's what I told Jenna when she told me about the blood test. If she wants to get knocked up by some guy she never met, she'll just have to take her chances."

"You disapprove of artificial insemination?" Elizabeth began to hope this abrupt and selfish woman was not her mother.

"Doesn't matter." She sniffed. "Jenna does what she wants."

"What about your grandchild? What if he or she is born with cystic fibrosis? Wouldn't you like to help us find a cure?"

In the silence that followed, Elizabeth could hear her soften, could hear her searching for a way to help without revealing her secrets. Elizabeth had a small pang of guilt about making up the CF condition.

"Can you tell me your maiden name at least?" Elizabeth asked gently, after a long time. "Perhaps we can trace your family medical history for you."

Another long silence.

"There's no point in asking about my family. Jenna's adopted."

Elizabeth was stunned. She hadn't prepared herself for the possibility. It was her turn to be silent.

"Are you there?"

"Yes, sorry. This is surprising. Jenna never mentioned it during any of her interviews, nor in any of the paperwork she filled out." Elizabeth's mind whirled. How could McClure—it hurt too much to think of her as Jenna—not tell the clinic she was adopted? More important, what did it mean for the child Elizabeth planned to have with her sister's oocytes?

"Jenna doesn't know."

Elizabeth's mouth fell open in disbelief. "You never told your daughter she was adopted?" The shock and grief she'd felt at discovering her own adoption surfaced with intensity. Her heart went out to McClure. "She's thirty-two years old and planning a family. How could you not tell her?"

"I know I should have, but the older she got, the harder it seemed. Then it was too late. If I told her now, she'd never forgive me."

Elizabeth's guilt about lying to the woman vanished completely. "You have to tell her."

"What difference does it make?" Mrs. McClure was defensive now.

"Knowing who you really are is the most important thing in the world." Elizabeth fought to control the emotion in her voice. "For a woman who wants to have her own child, it's even more significant. As a geneticist and a reproductive consultant, I guarantee you, biological heritage is everything!"

After a long silence, Patricia McClure said softly, "I love my daughter, you know."

"I'm sure you do," Elizabeth said without really believing it. "That's why you have to help her by telling me about her family."

"I can't. I don't know who her parents are." The woman sounded distraught. Elizabeth didn't know if it was because she wanted to help and couldn't, or if she was frightened that her daughter would discover her deception.

"Tell me where the adoption took place and the name of the lawyer who handled it for you."

"Promise me you won't tell Jenna. Let me tell her myself."

"Fine. Where was she adopted?"

"In Astoria. Daniel Potter handled it for me, but the adoption agency was in Portland. You don't really think they're going to tell you anything?"

"It's worth a try. Thanks for your help." Elizabeth hung up. She felt emotionally drained. Her sister's childhood had been painful too, she could tell. The woman who raised her was a selfish coward. Now that Elizabeth knew where to look, their biological mother should be easy to find. Maybe Daniel Potter would have all the answers, and she wouldn't have to bother the adoption agency at all. Either way, if she presented herself as Jenna McClure, they would have to tell her what she wanted to know. And someday, when this was over, she would find a way to let Jenna know who her real mother was. She deserved that, at least.

Chapter 13 >———

Sarah couldn't decide if she should ignore Jessie's tantrum, or send her to the time-out corner. By the time she decided that at age five Jessie should know better, the little girl had calmed down and moved on to another toy. Sarah let it go. She handed the doll back to Lindsey and gave her a quick hug. The three-year-old smiled, put down the doll, and toddled off in search of something new.

Sarah wished her life could be that simple again, but she was sixteen now and everything had changed. Reverend Carmichael had come to her the day before and told her it was time for her first physical. Sarah had been unable to think about anything else since. Her mother had explained, in rather embarrassing detail, what the exam would be like, making Sarah even more nervous. Excited too, she had to admit. Reverend Carmichael was going to touch her body. He would look inside her private place. Her stomach tingled in anticipation. It was as close as she would ever get to having sex if she stayed in the compound.

That was the real dilemma. Should she stay or should she go? It had been on her mind for months now. Ever since Darcie had come to the church and filled her head with thoughts of boys and sex and movies and shopping malls. Darcie was gone, but the images stayed. Especially the ones about sex. Sarah prayed for God to take her desires away, but she suspected he didn't want to make things too easy for her.

"Sarah? It's snack time. I could use some help." Marilynn spoke softly, but the reproach was there.

"Sorry." She jumped up and hurried over to the long, low picnic table. The kids had heard Marilynn say "snack time" and began to converge, many of them with hands out. She and Marilynn cut slices of homemade bread and passed them out to the twenty or so toddlers in the daycare room in the largest bunker house. Their mothers were all busy with their own chores elsewhere in the compound. Canning tomatoes and quilting blankets were both enjoyable, but Sarah liked working in the daycare best of all, especially with the babies.

The most exciting thing about turning sixteen was that she could have a baby of her own now. Sarah had wanted her own baby since she was eleven and her little sister Delilah was born. The first time those tiny little fingers curled around her thumb, Sarah was hooked. Babies were the most precious things in the world. She was glad the Reverend, smart and wonderful man that he was, had found a way for the Sisters to have babies without a husband. Most of the Sisters seemed to think men weren't much use, except for sex. If you prayed hard enough or went without it long enough, you could learn to live without sex. Or so she'd heard.

But most of the Sisters had experienced sex before they joined the church. Sarah was still a virgin and could expect to remain one if she stayed at the compound. Reverend Carmichael and Zeke were the only men left. Sarah shuddered at the thought of having sex with Zeke. The Reverend was different. She could imagine him as a gentle but passionate lover. He would…

"Sarah, where is your mind today?" This time Marilynn made no attempt to conceal her disapproval. Sarah looked up in surprise at the chaos around her. Jessie had taken Lindsey's bread and eaten it, leaving Lindsey sobbing, while Mia tore her snack into shreds and fed it to a stuffed bear.

"I'm sorry." Sarah quickly cut Lindsey another piece of bread. She hoped Marilynn would forgive her. She longed for someone she could talk to about her life, her future. There were a few other girls in the compound her age, but after Darcie they all seemed naive and boring. Oh, how she missed Darcie. The longing for her friend was so intense it was painful.

Sarah made a decision. When Darcie wrote and told her where she was living, Sarah would go see her—and the world—before she made a commitment to the church. The decision frightened her more than the rapidly approaching physical exam. She'd been eight when she and her mother moved to the compound and she hadn't left it since. Sarah remembered very little of her life before joining the church. She had brief memories of first grade and vague memories of early birthday parties, but she didn't remember her father at all. Her mother claimed he had their address and could write or send presents, but he never did.

Sarah shut down any thoughts about her father. It was too confusing to feel such strong emotions about someone she didn't know. She began helping the kids put on sweaters to go outside. Sarah loved the outdoors and took the toddlers out at least once a day regardless of the weather. And she spent most of her free time walking in the forest. After eight years, Sarah knew the land like the back of her hand.

The air outside was crisp and cool, the sky a murky blue-gray. The kids ran screaming for the playground and Sarah followed. After ten minutes of pushing Katie and Kelly on the tire swing, Sarah made them get off and give her a turn. She pumped her legs hard, working the swing higher and higher. The cold air stung her cheeks and floated her skirt out like a parachute. Joyously, Sarah pumped higher and higher, oblivious to the children watching below. For a moment, she felt as if she could sail out over the trees, drifting gently on the billows of her skirt until she found a soft place to land.

The feeling disappeared as quickly as it came. Sarah brought her legs down and dragged the ground until she came to a stop. She wasn't a kid anymore. Today she would become a woman.

* * *

Carmichael stood in front of the tinted window, watching Jenna sleep. She was so beautiful, so peaceful. He envied her drug-induced oblivion. He hadn't slept well since he'd brought her to the compound. One minute he was worried sick about going to jail for kidnapping Jenna, and the next minute he was trying to figure out a way to keep her. Which was equally worrisome. Carmichael had to assume his attraction for Jenna was rooted in her physical resemblance to Elizabeth—or her spirited similarity to Anne.

Yet his feelings for Liz were waning. He resented her for putting them all in a precarious situation. Carmichael didn't believe Jenna would be capable of such behavior. She had a purity of spirit. Their shared DNA made both women intelligent, beautiful, and strong willed, but Elizabeth was flawed, lacking wholeness in a way Carmichael had never understood.

He forced himself to turn away from the window. He would visit Jenna later. Right now he had to prepare for Sarah's first gynecological exam. Rachel would actually set up the front room with gloves and swabs and such, then stay through the pelvic to make Sarah more comfortable. What he needed to prepare for was the pre-exam talk. Carmichael knew all too well the influence Darcie had exerted on Sarah, the natural curiosity and rebellious-ness all kids felt at her age. This was a crucial point in Sarah's life. Carmichael knew if he didn't handle this well today, he would lose her. On the other hand, if he convinced Sarah to have a child, she would likely stay in the compound for years, where she was safe and supported.

Carmichael took a moment to pray, asking God to guide his thoughts and words. Bringing new members into the church through procreation was a directive straight from God himself. Carmichael had no doubt the church was the best place for any Christian woman. Especially at Sarah's age, with hormones and curiosity kicking in at the same time that she was becoming unbearably beautiful. In the secular world, men would use her, betray her, infect her with diseases, and probably break her heart. He would spare Sarah all of that if he could.

"Reverend?" Sarah knocked gently before pushing open the door, one hand gripping the knob, the other twisting a strand of long blonde hair.

"Come in, Sarah. Have a seat." Carmichael smiled gently and gestured toward a padded folding chair. His office in the clinic was small, just big enough for the desk, file cabinets, and two chairs. Except for the computer terminals, the furnishings were all used, but sturdy and comfortable. He would have liked a win-dow, but the bomb shelter had been the only available space left in the compound to build the clinic. He'd come to like the privacy and security of the underground layout.

"How is your day?"

"Uh, okay, I guess. I've been a bit distracted."

"I get that way myself sometimes." Carmichael tried to help Sarah relax. "Those toddlers are a handful. I admire and appreciate the work you do with them."

Sarah's fair skin blushed at the compliment. "Oh, it's not really work. I have a lot of fun with them."

"Marilynn tells me you're especially good with the babies."

Sarah blushed a deeper pink.

Carmichael decided to back off for a moment. "Do you want to continue helping in the nursery and daycare? Now that you're sixteen, you have more choices. I've always thought you'd be a great teacher. Perhaps you should think about starting our correspondence course for homeschooling."

"I've thought about it, but I'm not sure." She started to say something else, then stopped.

"What is it, Sarah?"

She stared down at her lap, tracing the pattern in her green print skirt. "I know I want to have a baby someday, but I'm not sure I'm ready now."

"It's normal to be uncertain about something so important." Carmichael paused, as if carefully considering his words. "Have you prayed about this?"

"Oh yes."

"It's not just your decision, you know."

"I know. God has a plan for my life. It's hard not to think about things I want though."

"Do you think it's God's plan for you to have a baby?"

"I hope so." Sarah smiled brightly for the first time.

"I know it is." Carmichael caught Sarah's eyes and held them captive. "You have been in my prayers every day for quite some time. The Lord wants you to be part of this church. To have a child and raise her to be a Sister in Christ." Carmichael touched his chest. "I know this with all my heart."

Sarah sat up straight, lips pressed together. He was certain she wouldn't be able to argue with a directive straight from God. "Would you like to pray with me now?"

The girl nodded.

"Dear Lord," he began, his voice slightly louder, "again I ask you to reach out to Sarah, bring peace to her spirit, clarity to her thoughts, and confidence to the work you have chosen for her. Show Sarah, as you have shown me, that the gift of life is a privilege and responsibility. Bless us both as we endeavor to bring another soul into this church. Thank you for the blessings we have already received. Amen."

"Amen," she whispered.

Carmichael waited, trying to read her expression. A certain reluctance still played in her hazel eyes. A tiny fear perhaps.

"Sarah," he said gently, leaning forward. "I can see you still have doubts. Can you talk to me about them?"

"It's the hormone shots," she blurted out suddenly.

Carmichael was relieved. This he could deal with. "Sarah, you know the needle isn't really going to hurt you; it's very quick. Rachel's feelings would be hurt if she knew you were scared of her." He winked to show he was teasing.

"It's not the needle." She looked up, her voice finding courage. "It's the other stuff, afterward." Her words tumbled out in a rush. "I've heard people complain about hot flashes and headaches and painful cramping."

"I know we've had problems in the past," Carmichael said, using his doctor-knows-best voice. "Some of the hormones have not worked out. But we have a new one now, and so far, I haven't heard one complaint." He felt a tiny twinge of guilt. There was no new hormone, but he was pushing JB Pharma to send him one, and if they did so soon enough, Sarah would be the first to use it.

"Why are the shots necessary?"

Carmichael reminded himself to be patient. "The hormones help your ovaries produce more than one egg for me to work with. The more eggs I harvest, the better chance I have of selecting a healthy baby for you."

"Why can't I just have your baby?"

As many times as he'd heard the question, it surprised him to hear it from Sarah. Her mother, the lovely Tamara, had been the first of the Sisters to ask him many years ago. The anguish of losing his son had still been an open wound then. And the guilt would never go away. He had caused the boy's death and would never let himself father another child.

"It is not God's will."

"Why not?" Sarah squirmed in her seat. "What if I had a boyfriend and wanted to have a baby? Would I still be welcome here?"

"Of course." Carmichael smiled in spite of his worry. "The church is your home. You and any children you may have will always be welcome."

Sarah was silent for a moment.

He decided it was time for his pitch. "Having a baby shouldn't be left to chance. The babies I create in the clinic are special. The semen has been carefully screened for diseases and defects, and your eggs are carefully harvested. Once the eggs are fertilized, I select the most perfect embryo to transfer to your uterus. You can even choose the sex of your child." Carmichael paused and lowered his voice. "A boyfriend can't do that for you. Only I can."

"Do I have to decide right away?"

"Of course not."

Her body seemed to relax a bit.

"But your prime childbearing years are between now and twenty. That doesn't mean you can't have children after that," he quickly added, because many women in the compound had done just that. "It's just easier on your body now. You'll have an easier labor and recover your health and figure faster."

"Should we skip the exam today?" she asked timidly. "Since I don't know if I'm ready for a baby?"

"Sarah, a pelvic exam is something every woman should have once a year just to make sure she's healthy. To make sure she can have a baby. You do want to find out if everything is in working order, don't you?"

Sarah nodded, lips pressed together again.

"Don't be nervous. Rachel will be in the room, and it only takes ten minutes." Carmichael was disappointed by Sarah's hesitation, even though he half expected it. Darcie's influence on the girl had been profound. But in the long run he would win her over, he was confident.

"Why don't you go back to the exam room, get undressed, and wait for me?" When she stood to go, he added, "Please think about what I've said. Getting pregnant the old-fashioned way is quick and easy, but a child is forever."

Back in her room, actually a small corner of a larger room partitioned off with blankets, Sarah lay on her bed and cried. She didn't really understand why. Nothing bad had happened to her. The Reverend had been very gentle, very kind. He hadn't pressured her about having a baby either. She had disappointed him, Sarah knew, and it made her feel guilty.

He had always been kind to her, to everyone, and she loved him like a father. Sarah couldn't believe what she'd said about having his baby. She didn't even know why she'd said it. It just popped out.

Maybe she'd meant it as a test. Or thought he might tell her why he wouldn't get any of the Sisters pregnant with his own sperm. She knew he had sex with her mother sometimes, and Sarah suspected he slept with Rachel too. But none of the kids were his.

Maybe he couldn't have kids, Sarah thought with sudden horror. She'd probably hurt his feelings by asking. Sarah wished she could disappear. How could she face him again? After today, he must think the worst of her.

Sarah cried even harder, angry with herself for the way she'd handled everything today. She'd told the Reverend she wasn't ready, yet when Rachel had stepped up with the needle to give her a hormone injection, she hadn't said a word.

Sarah told herself it would be okay. Nothing serious would happen. Other women had survived the injections and so would she. It didn't mean she had to have her eggs harvested either, Sarah decided. Just because her body would be producing extra eggs didn't mean she had to give them up for anything. All she had to do was say no. The Reverend would never force her, she was sure of it.

The tears kept coming. Sarah was ashamed to be so emotional about routine stuff. She wondered if it was the hormone kicking in already. She hadn't heard anyone else complain about being depressed after the injections.

"What's the matter, Sarah?" Her little sister, Delilah, stood by the bed with a worried expression. It was such a grown-up look for such a tiny girl, Sarah had to smile.

"Nothing really. I was just missing Darcie."

"I miss her too sometimes."

"She was lots of fun wasn't she?"

Delilah shrugged, her expression still serious. "You're fun too, when you're not sad." Her little sister was dark-haired and delicate, unlike herself. At six, Delilah was like a miniature woman, poised, sensitive, and flawless. Sarah loved her so much it hurt sometimes, like now, when she was being so sweet.

"Thanks for saying so." Sarah sat up. "I'm not really too sad. It's just been a funny kind of day for me." She thought of that morning on the playground, wanting to be a child again and knowing she could never go back.

"Do you want to play checkers? That might make you feel better."

"Sure." Sarah's heart ached even more. If she left the compound, even for a while, she would miss Delilah and her mother terribly. If she met a boy and fell in love, which deep in her heart she wanted more than anything, Sarah knew she would not come back. Either way, she was bound to be unhappy.

Sarah tried to push it all out of her mind and focus on Delilah. Her sister needed her right now, and it was selfish to dwell on her own problems so much. She reminded herself how lucky she was to have a home, a family, and someone as special as the Reverend to take care of her.

Chapter 14

"Look, if you have another priority right now, I can assign the story to someone else." Tom Warren, associate editor for *Modern Man*, spoke in the clipped tones of someone who is pissed off but wanted to be able to deny it later.

Eric resented the threat. He tried to keep his voice amicable. "Give me two more weeks. I've done all the research and most of the interviews. I just need to write the thing, and you know how fast I work when I have to. I've never let you down."

"You've never been a week late either."

"Give me a break." Eric was irritated now. He'd always suspected Tom was a control freak but had never experienced it first-hand. He would have told him to shove the story up his ass if he hadn't already spent so much time on it. He needed to finish the piece and get paid. "Everybody needs some slack at least once in their lifetime."

"That's true." Tom's voice softened slightly. "But I want to run the story in January alongside the tax article on how to get the most benefit out of your dependents."

"Now there's a heartwarming story."

"Don't knock it. If you had any kids yourself, you'd know how expensive they are. If you don't start planning and saving for college from the moment they're born, you'll never be able to afford it."

"But if you raise them to be resourceful, they'll make it on their own," Eric countered. He'd paid his own way since he was fifteen, including five years of college.

Tom was silent for a moment, then abruptly changed the subject. "All right, two weeks. Don't screw me on this. January is a big issue. Almost half our renewals come in the first of the year."

"It'll be on your desk November fifteenth, I promise."

"Good."

The phone buzzed in Eric's ear. Tom had moved on to the next item on his list. Eric reminded himself that freelancing was better than the alternative, dealing with someone like Tom every day. Worse yet, becoming someone like Tom.

He turned back to the blank computer screen, determined to make this draft work. He'd abandoned his first two efforts, both of which were mushy and melodramatic. Obviously, his feelings for Jenna had taken hold of his entire life, even affecting his ability to write objectively on the subject of families. His yearning to be a father had never been greater. In fairness, he knew he had to give more voice to the employer's position in the "Men and Maternity Leave" article.

After a few minutes of staring at the screen, Eric decided to read through his notes again.

An hour later, he started making phone calls to clarify insurance policies.

When he'd run out of sources to call, he went to the kitchen and made himself a peanut butter and banana sandwich, which he ate standing in the kitchen, drinking milk straight from the jug.

Another forty-five minutes in front of a blank screen and he was back in the kitchen. Eric stood with the refrigerator door open, staring at a loaf of bread and a bag of broccoli he would never eat. He'd bought it on a whim last weekend, thinking he would start eating healthier. There it sat, getting soft and brown. He pushed the door closed.

Time to get out of the house. No point in sitting in front of a computer all day gaining nothing but girth around the waist.

It occurred to him—as he stared down at the worn brown carpet while putting on his shoes—that he could go next door and start one of the dozen projects he needed to complete before renting out the other half of the aging duplex, thus making the property a profitable enterprise, as intended. Eric rejected the idea just as quickly. Fixing up one side so he could live in it had wiped out what was left of his savings account. Spending any real money on the other half before he finished the *Modern Man* piece would be foolish.

Eric grabbed his rain jacket, then headed out to the Firebird. Feeling guilty about not writing, he planned to visit his hospital kids to ease his conscience. He drove in a downtown direction but ended up parked under city hall, home of Eugene's public-safety officers.

Eric sat for a minute, disgusted with himself and what he was about to do. After he'd talked with Katrice—who was even nuttier than Jenna—he had decided, or so he thought, to stop wasting his time looking for her. Yet here he was, about to take a little more grief from Jackson, because apparently he couldn't accomplish anything else, including a good night's sleep, until he had resolved the mystery of Jenna McClure's disappearance.

On his way upstairs, scenes from the movie *Vanished* played in his mind. What he remembered most was how Kiefer Sutherland became so obsessed with his girlfriend's disappearance it took over his life. Eric refused to think about the fate of the girl in the movie. To believe for a second that Jenna might be dead took his breath away. She was alive, he knew; he just had to find her.

Jackson was not in his office. Eric was relieved and irritated at the same time. He'd expected the detective to humor his request, but not without more teasing. The sketch artist was another story. Without Jackson's authority, he might not be willing to spend the time. Eric decided to risk it and ask anyway. He went back out to the reception area. Bobbie, his sweetie, was not around. A middle-aged cop named Rick Wetzel was at the front desk.

"Hey, Rick, who's doing sketches these days?"

"Officers Rice and Burchly. Why?"

"I need a favor."

"Still looking for that girl?"

"Yep." Eric grinned, trying not to feel foolish.

"You must really have it bad."

"Yep."

"Rice is in the data room. Good luck."

"Thanks."

Officer Rice had quads that threatened to burst out the seams of her pants and blonde hair cut short enough to make the Marines happy. Eric had spoken with her a few times during his stint as a crime reporter and found her to be courteous but not very friendly. He'd heard enough about her to know that charm and bullshit would work against him. He opted for the direct approach.

"Officer Rice?"

"Yes?" She looked up from her computer terminal and reflexively squared her shoulders.

"I need a couple of sketches done. Do you have time?"

She pushed back from the desk and stared at him. Eric tried and failed to read her expression.

"Is this police business?"

"A woman has disappeared, possibly kidnapped. I've filed a missing-persons report and need someone to draw sketches of the men I saw her with."

"You were the last person to see her?" She was curious now; Eric could see the flicker in her eyes.

"I believe so. I've talked to her employer, her friends, even her mother. No one has seen her since Saturday."

"Tell me what happened."

Eric told the story yet again, keeping it brief. He resisted the urge to add his own impressions of the events. Rice listened without interruption, her pale-blue eyes in rapt attention, filing away the details.

"Did you ask the people you talked to"—Rice used her fingers to count them off—"her employer, her friends, her mother, if they knew either of these men?"

"Yes. They have no idea who they could be."

"How far away were you?"

"A block and a half."

"Two hundred yards?"

"I guess."

"Don't guess. Tell me."

"Less. At the time I didn't think I saw them very clearly. But I have watched the scene over and over in my mind so many times these guys have faces now. I don't know if my subconscious has made up the details or remembered them, but I'd like to try to get it on paper before it fades again."

"I'll see what I can do." Rice stood. Eric had to respect the work that went into shoulders like hers. "Come this way."

Each sketch took about forty minutes, and Eric felt drained when he left. The likenesses turned out well, and Rice had let him make photocopies. He stopped in the missing-persons office and Detective Zapata told him an investigation was under way. When Eric tried to learn specific information, Zapata brushed him off.

It was time to put his own plan into action. Eric left the department and drove out to Chad Drive. He hated that the paper had moved from the downtown area out to the suburbs. It felt like the paper was no longer in the heart of the city. No matter how many years he'd worked in the new building, he still missed the old office with the giant, old-style lettering across the front. Someday, he would miss having the morning paper delivered to his door. A new era was coming, whether the newspaper industry admitted it or not.

Eric headed across the half-empty parking lot, his shoulders tense. He hadn't been back since his layoff, and that had been a stressful day.

The longtime receptionist was gone too, and a classified salesperson was behind the front desk. Beva Woods, the city-section editor, passed through the lobby and did a double take. "Eric Troutman! I don't believe it. You slimy dog." The big woman threw her arms around him in a bear hug before he could maneuver out of it. "Why haven't you been in to see me?

"I've been busy."

"No excuse."

"I know." Eric started moving away. "I'm going up to see Joe. Nice seeing you."

The second-floor newsroom was surprisingly deserted for a Thursday afternoon. Eric was relieved to only have to make a minimum of small talk with old acquaintances as he crossed the room. He was anxious to see Joe and make the four o'clock deadline.

Joe Pikerton, his six-foot-five lanky frame perched on a chair too small for him, was reading copy on his monitor and chewing gum in a steady, rhythmic frenzy. "Be with you in a sec," Joe said without looking up. "I have to cut two inches out of this story or the Dutchman won't even look at it."

"How is it with Hoogstad as your boss?"

"They're all the same. I try not to take it personally." Joe leaned back and grinned, his narrow face and beak nose making him look rather birdlike. "By the way, where have you been for a week? You missed the poker game Monday night, and without your unfailingly bad luck, I actually lost money."

Eric had to laugh. Joe was always broke between paydays, but he was a skilled poker player who regularly went home with most of the cash. "I'm surprised BJ didn't call me to say thanks. How much did he take off you?"

"What was that favor you wanted?" Joe stood and began moving toward the hallway.

Eric followed. "Where are we going?"

"Out for a smoke."

"Oh joy."

"You're the one who needs a favor." Joe didn't look back. "I'm not usually in a good mood unless I have a cigarette in my hand."

"In that case, have several."

They went outside to a small foyer behind the building. The chairs and table were made of green plastic, and there was little cover from the weather. Eric was relieved it was not raining. Joe had a cigarette going before Eric sat down. His face relaxed immediately. "Ahh, that's better. Maybe you should have one too. You look like shit."

"Thanks."

"Seriously, pal, you look pretty stressed. What's going on and how can I help?"

Eric summed it up as briefly as he could. "I met this wonderful woman, fell in love, then she disappeared. Possibly kidnapped right in front of my face by these guys." Eric slid the composite pictures out of the manila envelope and handed them to Joe. "I need you to run these in tomorrow's paper, along with a picture of Jenna and a story about her disappearance."

"Whoa." Joe set the pictures on the metal table. "How come you never told me about the woman?"

"I haven't known her long."

"But you're in love?"

Eric hesitated. He'd thought he was being flippant when he said "fell in love," but it had to be true. He'd never felt this way before. "I must be. I can't seem to think about anything else."

"Who are these guys and how do they fit in?" Joe, being a reporter, would not be satisfied until he had the full account. Eric told his story in short bits, as his friend interrupted repeatedly to ask questions.

"You think these are good likenesses?" Joe reached for the pictures.

"I can only hope. Will you run the story?"

"The Dutchman won't like it." Joe seemed worried. "You're talking about three pictures. That's a lot of space. Something big would have to be dumped and a whole page rearranged." Joe lit a second cigarette. "It's so iffy. What if these guys turn out to be her brothers or something? We'll look like idiots and Hoogstad will lay me off next."

"She doesn't have any brothers, and no one has seen or heard from her since."

His friend popped up and began to pace. Eric took it as a good sign.

"You've been to the police?" Joe paused.

"Of course."

"Are they investigating?"

"Sort of."

"Meaning, they don't have the time or money, and adults disappear on purpose all the time, so don't expect much."

"Exactly. No sign of foul play except a biased reporter's gut feeling something is wrong."

Joe began pacing again, and Eric was silent. Just because he would've done anything to find Jenna didn't mean he had a right to pressure his friends. Finally, Joe turned and said, "If the story pans out, Hoogstad will love me for getting a jump on it. If it slaps us in the face, I'm history."

"You'll be history soon anyway."

Joe gave him a look. "Spell this chick's name for me and let me get back to work."

"Jenna McClure. Little *c*, big *C*, just like it sounds."

Joe stubbed out his second cigarette. "I hope she appreciates you, unlike your past girlfriends."

Chapter 15 ⟩

Jenna had become aware of her escalating heartbeat earlier, but attributed it to her frantic efforts to loosen the bindings. But even after nodding off and sleeping for a while—she had no real sense of time—her heart rate was still up. In the high eighties, she figured. She could feel the pulsing in her toes, her groin, and occasionally her temples. The pounding seemed to be steadily increasing in intensity as well as frequency. For the first time in her life, Jenna feared she would have a heart attack.

She tried to calm herself by meditating as best she knew how. What little she knew, she'd learned from a group session with a hypnotist in one of her many attempts at dieting. She remembered being told to get into her subconscious mind by imagining herself walking down a set of stairs that kept going down farther, deeper and deeper. But her descending pace kept picking up to match her heartbeat until she imagined herself running down the stairs at breakneck speed.

She tried holding her breath for counts of twenty, but it didn't seem to help. She tried telling herself eighty beats a minute was normal, lots of people had heart rates that fast, to relax and she would get used to it. Just because her usual resting pulse was around fifty didn't mean eighty or ninety would kill her.

Then the hot flashes started. Searing heat that inflamed her uterus, then spread through her chest like a fire out of control. She wanted desperately to throw off the thin white blanket and expose her body to the cool air. But her legs and arms were strapped down and she was unable to even touch her own skin. What was happening with her body? What had they done to her?

Jenna's rage quickly gave way to tears. Why didn't they just get it over with, whatever it was? Her hope of escape had dissipated with the passage of time. She had spent what seemed like hours rubbing the soft leather bindings against the edge of the metal bed. Her wrists were raw, but the leather was intact.

Escape was all she thought about when she was coherent, except when she let herself think about Eric. As the hours and days merged into a foggy blur, her time with Eric began to seem like a pleasant but fading dream. Jenna forced herself to focus on the present, but the possibilities were so limited. She had come to accept that she would never get out on her own, no matter how smart, how strong, or how defiant she was. Deceit and trickery were her only options. Neither of which she was practiced at.

As she tried to form a plan, another hot flash hit her, taking her breath away with its intensity. By the time the inferno passed, she couldn't remember what her idea had been. That happened frequently, thoughts and hours disappearing as if they never existed. They were messing up her mind, and it pissed her off even more than the confinement and their plans for her body.

Sometimes Jenna thought she would go mad and kill her captors if she ever got the chance.

"Hello, Jenna. My name's Rachel, in case you've forgotten again. I've been taking care of you."

A tiny woman with a long, dark braid paused in the doorway just long enough for Jenna to get her first peek outside the confines of her room. She tried to process what she'd seen. Stainless-steel cabinets with rows of drawers and a white table. More IV stands? Another hospital room?

"Jenna? Can you hear me?" The nurse stood next to her bed, a concerned look on her face. A small red birthmark under her left eye was her most distinctive feature. Jenna guessed they were about the same age.

The image beyond the door faded, and Jenna turned to the woman, who seemed to think they'd met before. "Where am I?"

"You're in God's church, and that's all I can tell you. Please don't be frightened."

"Why not?" Jenna cried out. "Why shouldn't I be frightened?" She desperately wanted Rachel to say it was all a mistake, that she would be released soon. Just having a woman walk into the room had raised her hopes.

Rachel's eyes filled with adoration. "Because Reverend Carmichael is a wonderful man. He's trying to save you, and someday you'll be thankful."

"Save me from what?" Jenna's hopes were sliding. "Who is Reverend Carmichael? Who are you?"

"We are both God's humble servants. I've already said more than I should. Just trust me. The Reverend would never hurt you. He's a peaceful, loving man." She turned and reached for the IV bag.

"If he's such a nice guy, why is my heart racing so fast? Why do I have hot flashes that make me feel like I'm being microwaved? What the hell are you putting in the goddamn IV line?" Jenna's voice escalated to a shout, causing Rachel to recoil.

"Don't take the Lord's name in vain if you expect me to care for you," Rachel said with false bravado, as she set the empty syringe down. Jenna squeezed her hands into fists, relaxed them, them squeezed again. It was a new technique she'd developed to calm herself.

"I'm sorry," she said after a moment. "I really am worried about my heart. It's beating twice as fast as it should. I think I need attention."

"Reverend Carmichael is a fine doctor." Rachel seemed slightly indignant. "And I'm a trained nurse. You're in excellent medical care."

"Then why do I feel so—" Jenna stopped herself from another outburst. She didn't want to alienate the nurse. Rachel could be the one to help her out of here. Under different circumstances, Rachel would be easy to manipulate, easy to overpower physically as well. Drugged and confined, Jenna had to go slow, win Rachel's trust. She started over. "Perhaps I'm having an allergic reaction to a drug that usually doesn't bother other people. Check my heart rate. See for yourself."

"I plan to take your pulse, temperature, and blood pressure, but not until I bathe you." Rachel looked at her strangely, as if Jenna had deliberately let herself go.

"I'll pass." She didn't want a bath, didn't want to get prettied up for the pigs who kidnapped her. If she smelled bad enough, it might keep them from raping her.

"Please cooperate with me. You'll feel better about yourself when you're clean."

Jenna snorted in disgust. Cooperate? Like she really had a choice. Rachel was as kooky as this whole setup. "Cleanliness is next to godliness, right?" she said with muted sarcasm.

Rachel laughed. "You're catching on."

The goodwill Jenna had begun to feel for Rachel after the nurse removed her catheter was quickly obliterated by the enema and the sharp sting of a needle that followed.

"What are you giving me?" Jenna was alarmed by the multitude of substances being forced into her body.

"It's an antibiotic to keep you from getting an infection." Rachel unbuttoned the top of Jenna's nightgown and began to wash her underarms. It was a strange sensation. Jenna distracted herself by watching carefully as Rachel adjusted her bindings one side at a time, allowing Jenna to roll and expose her backside for washing. The flexibility gave her renewed hope of escape. If Rachel could be distracted while one of the bindings was loose...

She lost track of the thought as the fresh dose of sedatives took effect. Jenna closed her eyes and let her mind float while Rachel brushed her hair. Jenna was vaguely aware of Rachel singing softly, a catchy little tune about the "blood of the lamb."

Obviously she was in the hands of religious fanatics who also ran some bizarre hospital. It was the last thought she had before drifting off again.

Chapter 16

Carmichael flopped back on the bed, heart pounding. He knew he should say something to Tamara but couldn't find the words. Earlier, watching Rachel bathe Jenna, he'd become inflamed with desire. For a second he'd fantasized about running Rachel out of the room and forcing himself on Jenna, conscious or not. He wanted her that badly. Keeping her prisoner was as seductive as it was frightening. Jenna's contempt—her refusal to be intimidated by his authority and power over her life—excited him.

Carmichael had fought for self-control. Raping Jenna would be shameful in the eyes of God. He'd never had to coerce a woman into having sex. They were always willing. So instead, he'd summoned Tamara from her quilting and penetrated her forcefully, without thought for her pleasure. His behavior shamed him. He was normally a sensitive lover who enjoyed pleasing his partner.

"Did I hurt you?"

"No," she lied.

"Forgive me, Tamara. I don't know what came over me. If I wasn't so upset, I'd make it up to you right now."

"It's all right." Tamara suddenly rolled up and out of bed, grabbing blindly for her clothes. The room was dark; even in late afternoon, the only light came from a single bulb. Pale skin flashed in the shadow, then disappeared as Tamara jerkily pulled on her sweater. Carmichael was excited by her anger. He began to get hard again.

"Don't go."

He scrambled across the bed and playfully grabbed Tamara around the waist. She didn't respond. But she didn't struggle either. Carmichael began to massage her breasts.

The shrill ringing of the phone startled them both.

"Get your clothes off and get back in bed," he whispered. "I'll just be a minute." Carmichael received few calls, but they were all too important to miss.

He hurried to the desk, scooping his shirt off the floor on the way. Except for the kitchen, the rooms in the compound were always cool, heated only by centrally located furnaces in each building. The phone rang twice more while he struggled into the long sleeves.

"David Carmichael speaking."

"Mr. Carmichael, it's Walt Frunmeyer with First Pacific Continental Bank. We need to meet sometime this week to talk about your loans."

"Is there a problem?"

"I'd rather not discuss this over the phone."

"It's not convenient for me to see you this week." Carmichael thought of Jenna and how long she would be in the clinic. "Next week is hectic too. What about later in the month?"

"It can't wait." Frunmeyer's voice lost its well-trained civility. "You're eight months behind on your payment schedule. We've granted every extension possible. You have thirty days to get current on your loan, or we'll repossess both the property you used as collateral and the equipment you bought with the loan. Good day."

The dial tone buzzed in his ear. Stunned, Carmichael stood for a moment, phone in hand, penis shriveling.

"Is everything all right, David?"

"Fine." He slammed the phone down. That arrogant son of a bitch! They would never get his DNA cycler or his Olympus microscope. Never!

Carmichael moved quickly to find his pants. Finances had reached emergency status, and he had to do something immediately. His options were limited and mostly unpleasant, but he couldn't risk having the local sheriff show up to run him off the property. Not right now with Jenna in the clinic.

"David?" Tamara sat up, a quilt pressed against her breasts.

"I have work to do now. I'm sorry. Will you please get dressed and leave?" He sounded cold despite his effort not to, and Tamara was hurt. He could feel her distress like a presence in the room. He didn't have time to deal with her. "Let it go, Tamara. You know I love you."

They dressed in silence. Carmichael moved to his desk and clicked on a light, waiting for Tamara to leave before he picked up the phone.

A polite female voice answered in the middle of the second ring. "JB Pharmaceuticals, can you hold, please?"

"No, I need—"

Canned music cut him off. He closed his eyes and tried to relax. He had to stay calm. His past dealings with the Seattle drug company had not been a complete success. Getting a check out of them in the next thirty days would require patience, charm, and a certain amount of butt kissing. Carmichael set the phone down for a moment and stretched, letting the anger flow out his fingertips. He'd picked up the technique in rehab long ago, when he'd learned how to live without drugs and alcohol.

"Yes, can I help you?"

"I need to speak with Gerald Akron. Tell him it's David Carmichael, and it's urgent."

"One moment, please."

The canned music came back, an upbeat instrumental version of a song from the late sixties called *Windy*. Carmichael set the phone down for another stretch. He could still hear the music, but it was so faint it seemed comical. After a few minutes, Akron came on the line.

Carmichael snatched up the phone. "Thanks for taking my call, Gerald. How have you been?"

"Great, thanks. Now cut to the chase. What's so urgent?"

"Money, of course."

"I can't help you."

"Why not? I know you're developing new fertility hormones, and I've got the perfect group of women to test them on."

"We don't have anything ready for human testing right now."

"But you're close, right?" Carmichael's stomach tightened. A few of the Sisters had developed bad reactions to the experimental hormones he'd tested for JB Pharma.

"Yes, we're close, but not close enough. Even if the hormone was ready, I wouldn't pay you to test it again. You know what I'm talking about."

Carmichael sucked it up and said what the man wanted to hear. "I'll stick to the recommended doses this time, I promise. And I'll document everything. Give me another chance. I need twenty thousand by the end of the month."

Akron laughed. "You're a dreamer, but you've got balls. Or audacity anyway."

Carmichael's fist clenched around the phone. "I'm willing to negotiate."

Akron laughed again. "Be in my office tomorrow morning at ten. We'll talk then."

"I can't leave the church right—"

The line went dead. He'd been hung up on for the second time in half an hour. Carmichael's temples pounded. He wanted to smash Akron's and Frunmeyer's heads together. He wanted to burn down the bank and everyone in it. More than anything, he wanted a double shot of Wild Turkey, neat. God was testing him to see how much he could handle.

Carmichael fell to his knees in prayer, reciting the first half of Psalm 128: *Blessed is every one that feareth the Lord; that walketh in his ways. For thou shalt eat the labor of thine hands: happy shalt thou be, and it shall be well with thee. Thy wife shall be as a fruitful vine by the sides of thine house: thy children like olive plants round about thy table. Behold, thus shall the man be blessed that feareth the Lord.*

Carmichael's knees cried in agony before he felt calm enough to get up. He limped stiffly to his reading chair and opened his Bible to Job. The familiar plight of God's most faithful servant failed to make him feel better. He was too worried about the church, about what would happen to his followers if the bank took his land or he went to jail for kidnapping. The Sisters were not like Elizabeth. They would not survive on their own, not as a community anyway.

He had no choice but to go to Seattle and convince Akron to give him some money. If there was a chance to save the church he had to take it. Creating a safe place for women to bear and raise healthy children was the work that God had chosen for him. He had been given the skills and the financial means to create heaven on earth for his followers. Carmichael wouldn't throw it all away because of a greedy bank and its petty rules. He had to have faith. God would take care of the church while he was away for one day. With Zeke and Rachel's assistance, nothing would go wrong with Jenna while he was in Seattle. What could happen in twenty-four hours?

He bought a ticket online for a flight that evening, then went to look for Zeke.

* * *

Zeke was reading the latest issue of *Boating* when Carmichael knocked on his door. He quickly stuffed the magazine into his top drawer. He had no reason to hide the publication—the Reverend knew of his interest in boats—but Zeke was secretive and impulsive by nature. Those impulses sometimes landed him in trouble, but they often saved his ass too. Either way, he was powerless to control them.

"Just a sec." Zeke glanced around his stark quarters before moving the few steps to the door. Carmichael had been in his room several times before to pray, and it always made Zeke uncomfortable. He opened the door slightly. "What's up, Reverend?"

"We need to talk. Will you come to my office?"

"Sure." Zeke stepped out, locking the door behind him.

The hallway was busy with females of all ages moving from one activity to another. Classes and chores were over for the afternoon, but a steady downpour kept everyone inside. Almost every door they passed was open. It amazed Zeke that even in their living quarters where the women went to read or sleep, the doors were rarely closed. The Reverend passed the central spiral staircase leading up to the lookout tower and headed toward the back of the compound. Zeke had thought Carmichael meant his main office near the chapel, but instead he started down the stairs to the clinic. This would have something to do with that woman they'd kidnapped, Zeke realized. Now that he knew what was really going on, there was no way Carmichael could talk him into doing anything foolish. He hadn't confronted the Reverend yet, but if Carmichael pushed him too far, he would lay it all out. Zeke wanted nothing to do with this patient until it was time to get rid of her. The less he saw of her, the easier it would be.

When they entered his office, Carmichael went straight to the window and stared intently into Jenna's room. Finally he turned to Zeke, with a peculiar, almost painful expression lingering on his face. "I'm catching a plane for Seattle tonight. I have a meeting with JB Pharma in the morning. I need you to keep an eye on Jenna while I'm gone."

Even though he expected it, Zeke resented the request. "Forget it. This is your game, whatever it is, and I already risked too much helping you snatch her. You're on your own with her."

"Zeke, I'm disappointed. Rachel will do all the real work. All you have to do is make sure no one else sees her." The Reverend was staring at him in that way he did sometimes, his eyes all soft and seeming to generate their own gravitational pull. Zeke looked away.

"When will you be back?"

"Tomorrow night. Or the next morning. Depending on the flight schedule. Can I count on you?"

Zeke planned to monitor the woman while the Reverend was gone whether he agreed to verbally or not. Making sure she didn't escape was in his best interest. He decided to test Carmichael. "I want to know who she is and why she's here. I don't buy the heroin-addict bullshit."

Unfazed, Carmichael said, "All right." He sat down and gestured with an open palm that Zeke should do the same.

Zeke sat stiffly, now putting on a show of resentfulness. He was curious to see what Carmichael would say. Another clever lie, or the truth? Zeke would never trust him again, that was for sure.

"Her name is Jenna McClure. I have not kidnapped her for my own purposes as you might have suspected. She is to be an egg donor for a very good friend of mine, to whom I am extremely indebted."

"Why didn't you tell me that in the first place?"

"I don't know, Zeke." Carmichael twisted his hands together in his lap.

Zeke didn't buy it.

Carmichael continued. "I think I was afraid you'd say no, and I desperately needed your help. I'm sorry."

Zeke was silent. Their friendship no longer mattered. In a week or two he'd be gone for good. Yet he was curious about the whole egg-transfer process and how they planned to get away with it. He had only a vague idea of what the Reverend did to make all those women pregnant without actually fucking them. Carmichael had talked about it plenty, but Zeke had only half listened. After a long silence, he said, "What exactly are you going to do with her?"

Carmichael took a long, slow breath.

"Keep it simple," Zeke said, trying not to feel stupid.

"I'm going to take one of Jenna's eggs, fertilize it, and implant the embryo"—Carmichael paused before adding—"in my friend's uterus."

"What's so special about this woman's eggs? Why not get an egg from one of the Sisters?" Zeke had heard Carmichael refer to Jenna as "your sister" when he was talking to Elizabeth, but all the church women were called Sisters, and he hadn't taken it seriously.

"Genetically, Jenna is very similar to the recipient."

So the kidnapped woman really was Elizabeth's sister. The ice doctor was even colder than he'd thought. "You mean your doctor friend that was here the other day."

"Yes."

"She must be pretty special for you to kidnap this woman and steal a baby from her." Zeke knew exactly who Dr. Elizabeth Demauer was and why Carmichael was in her debt. Zeke knew all Carmichael's dirty little secrets. Before, when they were friends, he hadn't thought of using Carmichael's troubles against him. Now, with what he knew, he wouldn't hesitate to blackmail the man if the opportunity presented itself.

"She is very special. I'm also extremely indebted to her."

"Wouldn't it have been easier to pay her off?"

The Reverend suddenly seemed agitated. "It's not just about money. Liz wants a baby more than anything. A genetically related baby. This is my chance to make her happy, to make up for the family I destroyed."

It was only the second time the Reverend had ever mentioned his family. Zeke had heard the whole story after an emotional AA meeting long ago. Carmichael had wept openly, and Zeke had been moved by the man's grief. That seemed like another life. "So what happens to the sister when you're done?"

"Nothing. Once Liz is pregnant, we let Jenna go." Carmichael smiled slyly. "I'm giving her a drug that makes her forget things almost as fast as they happen. I figure we'll drop her off near the McKinley Mental Institution outside of Portland. She'll have no idea where she's been or what happened to her. Just like a person with amnesia."

"What about us? Will she remember what we look like?" Zeke was skeptical. Anything that sounded too good to be true usually was.

"Of course not." The Reverend's expression wasn't as confident as his words. "It's actually a combination of two drugs, ketamine and Versed. Even if she goes to the police, she'll never be able to describe either of us well enough to be helpful to them."

"My picture's in a mug book, remember?"

"You haven't committed a crime in twenty-some years." The Reverend reached over and touched Zeke's arm. "Relax, Zeke. Even if something goes wrong and the police question us, I'll take responsibility. I'll tell them you weren't involved. Even on the one-in-a-million chance I do go to jail, I need you to stay here and look after the church. I've given this a lot of thought."

Zeke wanted to laugh. With his record, no matter what the Reverend told the cops, he'd get put away for the rest of his life. If by some streak of unnaturally good luck he managed to avoid arrest, Zeke sure as hell didn't plan to hang around and babysit the church. If he had enough money, he'd be gone right now.

"How long is she going to be here?" he asked.

"Another week at the most."

"Why so long?"

"These things take time."

"It seems like a lot of trouble for—"

Rachel came through the door just then. "You wanted to see me, Reverend?"

"Yes. Here, take my chair." Carmichael moved next to the window again. The tiny room seemed suddenly crowded. Zeke started to get up.

"Please stay, Zeke," Carmichael said without taking his eyes off the window. "This will only take a moment, but it concerns both of you."

Rachel shot a sideways glance at Zeke. They had slept together years ago when they first met but, in time, had come to dislike and distrust each other. Zeke had kept both facts from the Reverend and, as far as he knew, so had Rachel.

"As you've heard, Zeke, I'll be gone for a day or so." Carmichael turned slowly toward them, as if resisting a great pull. "Rachel, I'm counting on you to take good care of our patient while I'm gone."

The nurse seemed to stiffen. "I'll do my best, Reverend, but I'm worried about Jenna. She claims to have horrible hot flashes and her pulse seems high."

"How high?"

"Around ninety."

"That's in the normal range, Rachel," Carmichael said with a touch of impatience.

"But her legs are so muscular. In fact, her whole body is quite—" Rachel paused, blushing. Zeke wondered, not for the first time, just how many Sisters were lesbians.

"She looks like an athlete," Rachel said, gaining confidence. "I don't think a pulse of ninety is normal for her."

"Believe me, she is not an athlete." Carmichael looked down at his hands. "I appreciate your concern, Rachel, and I will look in on her before I go. Keep in mind that she is a heroin addict. Withdrawals from long-term drug abuse can cause erratic heart-beats, hot flashes, and a host of other unpleasant reactions. That is why she is with us."

"Of course." Rachel looked like she wanted to say more, but pressed her lips in silence.

"I'm holding you both responsible for Jenna's welfare. Any decision that needs to be made, you should make together. Understood?"

Zeke nodded. If push came to shove, he would call the shots. Rachel would stay the hell out of his way if she knew what was good for her.

Rachel fidgeted for a moment, then said, "Why can't I talk to her about why she's here? She seems so confused and frightened. I think it would help her if she knew that her family loves her enough to go to such extremes to save her from her addiction."

Zeke tried not to laugh. Women were so gullible. Rachel had been told the same line of hogwash he had, only she believed that in a few weeks Jenna would walk out of the compound into the loving arms of her parents to begin her new drug-free, spiritual life. How the Reverend planned to explain Jenna's upcoming surgery, Zeke didn't know. He had every confidence Carmichael could make it sound plausible. The man could charm the skirt off a nun.

"Perhaps later, Rachel. I know you mean well, but Jenna's too hostile right now to appreciate her family's efforts."

"She's a lucky woman. So many drug addicts are abandoned by their families." Rachel's expression seemed suddenly forlorn. "What, specifically, are my medical instructions for her?"

"Just continue as before with the specially marked syringes of methadone in her IV every eight hours, two injections of the specially marked antibiotics per day, and a pulse, temperature, and blood-pressure check every three hours." As he spoke, Carmichael turned back to the window. "If, God forbid, she should arrest"—he paused and swallowed hard before continuing—"do everything medically possible to save her."

"She'll be fine, Reverend. I pray for her health and her soul every day."

"Bless you, Rachel. Now, if you'll excuse us, I need another word with Zeke."

After Rachel left, it occurred to Zeke that with Carmichael gone, he could sneak in and suffocate Jenna, eliminating the risk that she would ever identify him. He didn't give a shit if Liz had a baby or not. He had only two basic concerns. One was to stay out of prison. The other was to keep his life as simple as possible.

"I need you to do me a favor." Carmichael was looking at him with those hypnotic eyes again.

"What is it?"

"Fix that old rocking chair in the storage area and give it to Tamara. If you could clean it up and make it look nice, I'd appreciate it."

"Sure." Zeke wondered if the two of them had a fight, but he kept his mouth shut. He didn't mind doing something extra for Tamara. She was a fine woman who'd always been decent to him. He hoped Carmichael was treating her right. Zeke stood to leave. "I'd better get back to work."

Carmichael was watching Jenna through the glass again.

Zeke's legs felt heavy as he climbed the stairs out of the basement. Killing the woman just to silence her would be the most shameful thing he'd ever done, but he couldn't trust Carmichael's drugs to keep her quiet. Some of the drugs Carmichael had given the Sisters hadn't worked out that well. If Jenna ever looked at his mug shot and recognized him, it was all over. He could kiss his dreams good-bye and say hello to a huge man in prison named Mookie, who would kill him in the most painful way Zeke could imagine.

Jenna had to die instead. He would make sure she didn't suffer.

Chapter 17

Jenna flinched when she heard the door open. It was only the nurse, not the crazy preacher/doctor who made her skin crawl. She relaxed and let out her breath, then drew it back in just as quickly. She remembered parts of the previous day. It wasn't just a blur of spaced-out dreams. She actually remembered Rachel bathing her and giving her an injection. She could picture a well-dressed man in a surgical mask holding her hand and talking about God. Frightened as she was, Jenna felt a timid joy at her mental breakthrough. If she could stay coherent, maybe she could escape. Maybe Rachel could be talked into—

"Good evening, Jenna. Are you feeling any better now?" Rachel's concern was sincere. Jenna couldn't hate her even though she wanted to. She suspected Rachel was only a pawn in the doctor/preacher's game, whatever it was.

"Not really."

"I'm sorry to hear that. Reverend Carmichael says it'll get better with time." Rachel sat next to the bed and smiled warmly. "I brought you something to eat."

"What is it?" Jenna filed the name Carmichael away, hoping she would remember it. She didn't feel hungry, but decided to eat anyway to keep up her strength. When the opportunity to escape presented itself, she had to be ready.

"Apple pie with a slice of cheddar cheese." Rachel, still grinning, held up the plate for her to see. "But first we have to take care of business."

What now? Panic rose in Jenna's throat.

"Don't look so scared. It's just your medication. You've had two injections a day since you've been here. Don't you remember?" The pie had disappeared and Rachel's hands held a hypodermic needle. She looked puzzled.

Before Jenna could respond, a searing pain started in her chest, then spread through her arms and face, burning with a new intensity. Unable to clutch her heart, Jenna thrashed back and forth, making small grunting sounds in an effort to control the pain.

"What is it?" Rachel cried out.

"My heart." It was painful to speak, to even breathe. "It's on fire."

Rachel's lower lip trembled, and her eyes filled with confusion. Jenna saw her opportunity.

She thrashed harder, rolling her eyes back in her head. Rachel called out her name, but Jenna didn't respond. Instead, she brought her knees up in short, repetitive jerking motions, making strange gagging sounds at the same time. Being bound at the wrists and ankles limited her performance, but she gave it all she had. The pain in her chest continued to burn and Jenna let herself go, crying out as if in agony.

Rachel, who was now near tears, bent over and fiddled with something near the floor, then grabbed the IV stand and pushed against the bed. Jenna's bed rolled toward the door.

Yes! It was hard not to shout out loud with jubilation. She was leaving the little gray room. Even if she couldn't escape, she would at least see some other part of the building. Maybe figure out where she was. Prepare for her next attempt.

Rachel let go of the bed and ran to the door. She pulled it open, propping the door with one foot while she reached back for the end of the bed. Grunting with effort, Rachel tugged until she had wheeled Jenna into the next room.

The searing pain in her heart began to subside, but Jenna continued to thrash and roll her eyes. The show she was putting on made it difficult to take in the exact details of her surroundings, but she did get a general feel for the room. Long lines of stainless-steel cabinets and counters and—her heart skipped a beat—what looked like an operating table. For a moment, she had second thoughts about her faked emergency. What if it made them speed up their plans?

Jenna relaxed her eyes and looked around for Rachel. The nurse immediately clamped a mask over Jenna's mouth and nose. She tried to slow her breathing but soon became light-headed from the excess oxygen, making it difficult to concentrate. From what she could tell, Rachel was shouting into a handheld communicator for someone named Marilynn.

Jenna sat up slightly to better see the room. She had to memorize escape possibilities. There was a double set of swinging doors, with glass in the upper half, leading out into a hallway. A single swinging door with a small peep window led into an adjacent room. The wall next to the operating table also contained a foot-square pass-bar leading into the next room. Nowhere did she see a window to the outside.

Rachel pushed her bed through the double doors and turned right. At the end of the hall was a wide set of stone stairs.

She was underground! Jenna had thought so at times because of the solid walls and eerie silence, but where? And why?

Rachel pushed her shoulders down. "Relax, sweetie, you'll be fine. I'm taking you to an emergency room."

Did she mean a real ER with real doctors? *Please let it be true.* Jenna was afraid to hope. These crazy people probably had their own little trauma unit where they would sedate her with elephant tranquilizer and do exploratory surgery for fun.

Another woman's voice called out, "What's going on?"

Jenna eased her head forward to see a stout redhead appear at the bottom of the stairs.

"I don't know. She's having some kind of seizure," Rachel said.

Jenna realized she had stopped faking the convulsions. Except for the oxygen mask she probably looked fine. She rolled her eyes back and began to jerk her head in a rhythmic pattern.

"Who is she?"

"She's a friend of the Reverend, that's all I can say. Help me get her onto a gurney."

"Why is she strapped down?" the other woman asked.

"For her own protection. Please don't ask any more questions, Marilynn. Just help me get her up to the truck." Rachel began to loosen Jenna's wrist bindings. After a moment, Marilynn reached for her ankle straps.

Jenna's heart hammered with adrenaline. She was loose! All she had to do was get up and run for her life. But then what? How many others were out there? How easily would they catch her? She hadn't used her legs in days, maybe weeks. Jenna had no idea how long she'd been lying in bed. Could she even run, or would her legs buckle like a couple of noodles?

Marilynn moved to the head of the bed and reached her strong arm under Jenna's shoulders. Rachel grabbed her feet and the two of them lifted her off the bed, then eased her down onto a canvas gurney similar to the type paramedics used.

This was her chance.

No. Jenna changed her mind just as quickly. Running now was foolish. She had no idea where she was. If they caught her, they would take her straight back to the gray room. She might not get another opportunity. She had to wait until she was outside. But what if she never made it outside? What if they were only taking her to another part of the building?

Rachel reached across Jenna's chest and pulled a canvas strap into place. *Oh shit.* They were buckling her in again. Jenna resisted the urge to knock Rachel out of the way and charge up the stairs. She forced herself to be patient, to keep faking convulsions. The gurney straps were loose and could be wiggled out of later. She would wait and see where they were taking her. They could be on their way to a real hospital. She couldn't blow her one chance of being saved.

Jenna thrashed around to keep up the act while the women carried her upstairs. She had much greater movement now, but her legs felt like dead weight. How would she run when she got the chance? Was that why they'd kept her drugged and prone? What kind of psycho freaks was she dealing with here?

As they cleared the top of the stairs, a man stepped into the hallway and blocked the open doorway at the end. The two women froze. The thin man rushed toward them, boots clomping and the smell of pig shit coming with him. Jenna's skin went cold.

"What in the hell is going on?" he shouted. "The Reverend has only been gone for ten minutes!"

"She went into convulsions." Rachel stammered like a kid caught sneaking out. "I'm afraid she'll die. We need to take her to a hospital, Zeke."

Jenna's heart leapt. A real hospital!

A callused hand came out of nowhere and yanked off the oxygen mask. Before Jenna could flinch, Zeke slapped her with a force that loosened her teeth. Tears filled her eyes, but she was too stunned to cry out.

"See? She was faking it." His mouth grinned, but his eyes looked right through her. Jenna could feel the heat of his breath and smell the cigarette he had smoked recently. This man frightened her in a way that no one else in this crazy place had yet.

"What are you waiting for? Get her back down there. Now!"

Jenna clamped her jaws together to keep from screaming obscenities. The bastard had blown her one chance.

Zeke grabbed Rachel's end of the gurney and started moving toward the stairs. Marilynn had to walk backward and almost tripped on the first step. A few minutes later Jenna was back in her little gray room. The right side of her face was hot with the sting of a new welt, and her ears were filled with warm tears.

"Get her situated, and I'll be back in a minute." Zeke grabbed Marilynn by the elbow and half dragged her from the room.

Rachel flitted nervously around the bed, checking Jenna's straps and putting up a fresh IV bag. She wrapped a blood-pressure sleeve around Jenna's upper arm. "I'm sorry he hit you. I feel terrible about that. He's not at peace with God or himself."

"Who is he?"

"Brother Zeke. Reverend Carmichael says we'd be lost without him, but I'm not so sure." Rachel removed the stethoscope from her ears. "Your blood pressure is a little high, but after what just happened, I think that can be expected."

Jenna was suddenly aware of her heart, which, despite all the excitement, was slowing down. So was her brain. The sedative was in her system again, and it was always bad at first. In time she would adjust to it.

"What did you say?"

Rachel looked hurt, but determined. "I want to know if you were faking the whole thing."

Jenna gave her the same hurt look back. "How can you say that?" Instantly, she was angry. "I'm tied to a bed, my heart races all the time, I have horrible hot flashes, and I can't remember anything from one minute to the next." Jenna had to stop and think about what her point was. She couldn't remember. She had never felt such despair. "I'm going to die here!"

Rachel started to speak, then stopped. She stood, poised to leave. Finally she blurted out, "Your family loves you very much," and rushed toward the door.

Jenna called after her, but Rachel kept moving.

What family? All she had was her mother, who couldn't possibly have anything to do with this. What was Rachel talking about? Maybe the nurse didn't really know why she was here. Sometimes Rachel seemed as confused as she was. That man, Zeke, he'd been quite sure of himself. For a moment, she'd thought he was going to kill her.

Jenna closed her eyes, suddenly exhausted. The steady beat of her heart was reassuring. Maybe she wasn't going to have a heart attack after all. Instead she would be alive and well for whatever they had planned.

"Hey, pretty girl."

Jenna's eyes flew open. Zeke was looking down at her with a gentle, curious expression. Her body went cold with fear.

"Don't be afraid. I just want to ask you something."

Jenna swallowed hard.

"Do you remember me from before?"

She stared, unblinking, afraid to answer. Before when? What was the right answer? She couldn't think straight. Would he be mad if she said no?

"You do. I can tell." The idea seemed to make him sad. She noticed the web of lines around his eyes and the brown spots on his skin. He did seem vaguely familiar, as if she'd dreamed about him or someone like him.

"Who are you?"

He laughed. "I can't tell you that, but I will tell you something else." Zeke pulled up the chair and sat down. "I'm going to tell you why you're here. It's not your fault, and I figure you have a right to know what this is all about before you die."

Jenna's heart seemed to stop. They were going to kill her! The crazy preacher/doctor had lied.

"The good doctor plans to take one of your eggs." Zeke frowned. "Maybe more than one." He shrugged, as if it didn't matter. "Anyway, they're going to fertilize your egg with sperm from some guy you never met and put it inside another woman's body."

What was he talking about? Jenna felt foggy. Why would anyone want her eggs?

"Guess who the woman is?"

Jenna had no clue.

"Your sister." Zeke leaned back and grinned. "She's a cold bitch, isn't she?"

"I don't have"—Jenna could barely talk—"a sister."

"They seem to think you do. I just thought you might like to know your kid is gonna make it out of here even if you don't."

Her kid?

Zeke jumped up and left the room before Jenna could make her mouth form the question.

Chapter 18 >—

Elizabeth had called the hospital earlier and said she'd be late. Now she sat in front of the phone working up the nerve to call Daniel Potter, the lawyer who had handled Jenna McClure's adoption. He would know where to find her birth mother. All she had to do was ask, so why not? All the missing pieces of her life were suddenly out there, tangible, just waiting to be claimed. Elizabeth felt like throwing up. She could feel another migraine coming on. It was too much all at once. First a sister, and now a mother. Both of them monumental risks. She went to the bathroom and rinsed her face with cold water. When she came back, Elizabeth picked up the phone and dialed the number before she could change her mind.

The man on the other end of the phone sounded older than God. "Daniel Potter, attorney at law. Who is calling?"

Elizabeth swallowed hard. "Jenna McClure."

"Patty McClure's little girl?"

"Yep." Elizabeth could hardly breathe. She fought the urge to hang up.

"How is your mother? I haven't seen her in decades."

"She's great. Thanks for asking."

There was a short silence. "What can I do for you, young lady?"

"Tell me about an adoption you handled thirty-two years ago," Elizabeth blurted out, surprising herself. "A baby girl adopted by a woman named Patricia McClure."

The old man cleared his throat. His voice seemed stronger. "Why now? What difference does it make? Patty McClure did right by you. You should be grateful."

Elizabeth stiffened. She'd encountered this attitude when she had searched for her mother in Chicago. What did he know about being adopted?

"I am grateful." She grabbed her purse and searched for an extra-strength Excedrin. "I love my mother dearly, but I have a right to know. Especially now that I want to get pregnant." Elizabeth had rehearsed this speech over and over, but for some reason she started crying. "I just found out I'm a carrier for cystic fibrosis, and a research team wants to study my family genetics. How can they if I don't know my own family?"

"Oh dear." Potter sounded distressed. "Please don't cry."

Elizabeth found the medicine and also a tissue to blot her eyes. What was wrong with her? Was it nicotine withdrawal? She hadn't had a cigarette since last night.

"I'm not sure I can help much. I don't remember your birth mother's name, and all my early files were destroyed in the flood of 1973." Potter was fumbling now. "The adoption agency was run by the All Saints Catholic Church in Portland. Perhaps they can help."

Elizabeth's heart sank. "Do you think they will?"

"Certainly." The old man tried to sound perky. "You call me if they give you any trouble, and I'll put the pressure on. I may be mostly retired, and the doctors tell me I've got less than a year with this liver cancer, but I'm still a force to be reckoned with."

"Thanks." Elizabeth started to hang up, then decided to take one more risk. "Would you call me if you remember anything else?"

"Certainly. Give me your number."

She could hear David in her head lecturing her about how foolish this was, but Elizabeth gave Potter her cell number anyway. "Thank you, sir, I hope to hear from you." She started to hang up again.

"Wait, Miss McClure." Potter's weak voice called her back. Elizabeth put the phone to her ear. "I just remembered something. There were two little girls. The other one was adopted by a couple from Chicago. You have a fraternal twin sister out there somewhere."

Fraternal twins. Elizabeth closed the phone and started to cry again. Even if they hadn't come from the same oocyte, she and McClure had been conceived around the same time and brought into the world together. They were more than siblings. They were partners, womb mates. Elizabeth wept for the sister she would never know, for the love she would never be able to share.

Chapter 19

Eric woke early, anxious to see the day's edition of the *Willamette News*. Jenna's picture and the sketch drawings of the two men were on page three of the city section. The picture of Jenna didn't do her justice. It was one he'd taken after the robbery and she looked grim. Joe had done a good job with the story, listing Eric's name and phone number as well as the missing-persons office at the police department.

It had to work. It was his only hope.

The phone rang before he finished reading the paper. A quivering old voice said, "He's my nephew, Clarence Bisbow. The ugly, bald one, I mean. He's been nothin' but trouble his whole life."

"Who is this?"

"Beverly Mayfield. What difference does it make who I am? I thought you wanted to know about the guys in the paper."

"I do." Eric forced himself to be polite. "Thank you for calling." The cantankerous old woman was probably crazy, but it wouldn't hurt to humor her. "Do you know where to locate Mr. Bisbow?"

"I don't know why you're calling him 'Mister.' He's a no-good crook." Beverly cleared her throat. "Last I heard, he was living on Q Street over in Springfield, still dealing drugs at his age. It's shameful the way he treated my sister all these years. Why she puts up with it, I'll never know. I wish the cops would—"

Eric cut in. "Spell his last name for me, please."

"Just like it sounds, B-i-s-b-o-w."

"When is his birthday and what kind of car does he drive?" Detective Jackson would need all the information he could get to help narrow down the computer search. Especially if the suspects were using aliases.

"June third, 1955." The old lady snorted. "Old enough to know better. I don't know about a car. He lost his license a time or two."

"Thanks for your help. Will you leave me your number in case I need to ask you more questions?"

"It's 346-2015. Don't call after nine. That's my bedtime."

"All right. Bye now." Eric hung up. Instinct told him the old lady was probably just lonely and bored, but he called missing persons anyway. The line was busy.

He grabbed a second cup of coffee, wolfed down a stale doughnut, then called again.

"Detective Zapata speaking."

"It's Eric Troutman. Did you just get a call from Beverly Mayfield?"

"So she called you first. I'm hurt. She's one of our regulars."

"I was afraid of that. Is the nephew even real?"

"Oh yeah. But he's been in prison since 1988, and he won't be getting out any time soon either."

"Any legitimate calls yet?"

"Nope. Sorry. Check back this afternoon."

"Thanks."

Eric refused to be discouraged. It was still early. Lots of people didn't read the paper until after work. He made sure the answering machine on his landline was still on, then headed for the shower.

Freshly shaved and dressed, Eric decided to listen to the recording he'd made the day he and Jenna met for coffee. It had been an interview of sorts, and at that point, he had still planned to write a profile about her. Now he didn't think he could. He just wanted to hear her voice. To see if there was anything she'd said that would give him a clue, something he missed the first time he played the tape.

He sat in his favorite chair, an old leather-covered recliner, plugged earphones into the recorder and slipped them on. Jenna's voice seemed more intimate that way. She was so open, so painfully honest. He'd never met anyone like her before. He wished he'd known her longer.

The intrusion of his own voice bothered him. Eric backed up to the beginning of the file and recorded the silence of the apartment over his speaking parts. Then he retrieved a second recorder from his bedroom and retaped Jenna's voice, editing out the silent gaps.

He leaned back in the chair and played the new version, hearing with a fresh ear the pain in her voice when she talked about her lonely childhood and a lack of closeness to her mother. What really caught his attention this time was the shift in her voice when she said, "I'm going to get artificially inseminated, but first I have to wait for another blood test to come back."

Was it anger? Frustration? Why another blood test? Was something wrong with the first one? Where did she have it done? The Assisted Reproduction Clinic next to the old North McKenzie Hospital seemed the most likely place.

Eric shut the recorder off, excited by the possibility of a new lead. As a hospital volunteer, he was well enough known by the staff that he might be able to sneak a peek at clinic records. It couldn't hurt to try.

Before leaving, he checked his answering machine. Another woman had called. This one sounded younger. She claimed Jenna was her sister, a prostitute who often ran off with older men to make porn movies. Disgusted, Eric reset the machine. Jackson had often complained about crackpots who called the police with bizarre tips or confessed to crimes they knew nothing about. Eric never realized how excessive it was. These people obviously needed attention, but he didn't have time for nonsense. He was glad to be getting out of the house. It would be easier to screen the legitimate calls from the wackos with the answering machine.

He entered the hospital just before noon. The timing couldn't have been better if he'd planned it. Most of the nurses were busy serving lunch or rotating lunch breaks. Doctors were seldom visible in the middle of the day. They did their rounds early in the morning and again in late afternoon. Mid-day was reserved for surgery, paperwork, golf, or naps. And now that North McKenzie had built a new hospital in the Gateway area, the University District hospital was pretty quiet.

Eric knew just the computer terminal he'd use. It was on the second floor, in a little cubby adjacent to the pediatrics admitting desk. It was a small office, shared by several doctors who worked part-time for the hospital and had their private practices elsewhere. He circled through the medical-surgery ward and approached from the south side so he wouldn't have to pass the admitting desk. He stopped once to talk with a nurse named Susan whom he'd dated briefly and said a passing hello to several others. No one questioned his presence, even though Friday was not his usual visiting day.

Eric slipped into the little office and sat down. The computer was slightly to the left of the door, so he would not be seen unless someone came into the room. He wouldn't see someone coming in until the last second either. His palms were suddenly sweaty, but he was grinning. He hadn't had a decent adrenaline rush since the last time he thumbed through Jackson's weekly report on the sly.

He'd talked with enough admitting-desk nurses while they operated the system to bluff his way into patient files. A search for Jenna McClure produced nothing. Eric swore softly. He'd assumed the Assisted Reproduction Clinic, as an extension of the hospital, would have overlapping files. Maybe it didn't. Maybe Jenna hadn't had her blood test done locally.

Eric searched quickly, trying a dozen different requests until the screen finally lit up with a catalogue of files. He moved the cursor to ARC and pressed RETURN. The unit asked for his access code. *Damn.* He tried Clark, a pediatrician he was friendly with. No access. He tried Gybbs, the chief of staff. No access. Eric went back to the list of files, scrolling until he saw a heading for access codes.

Shaking his head at the lack of security, he hit ENTER and punched up a complete list of everyone using the system, their department, and their code. Eric memorized several that listed their department as the ARC, then went back to that heading. Once he was in the secondary system, he typed in Jenna's name and waited.

Voices! Right outside the door. Eric's heart lurched against his rib cage. *Shit!* He reached to click it off, then his hand stopped in midair as Jenna's name came up on the monitor. He quickly scanned the screen. Address, phone, insurance information. Nothing significant. Then toward the bottom it read, *blood test for artificial insemination followed by consultation with Dr. Demauer.*

There was more, but Eric didn't have time. Someone was moving through the doorway. He quickly shut off the machine and put his head down on the desk.

"Hey, are you all right?" Toni Norris, an intern he knew casually, peeked over the top of the monitor.

Eric lifted his head a little. "I just needed to be alone for a minute." He rubbed his temples, squeezing his eyes closed in what he hoped looked like a painful grimace. Thank god it was someone who knew him. Someone young, female, and nurturing.

"Do you want to talk?" She shifted nervously, apparently not wanting to leave him alone in the office.

"Thanks, Toni, but I should just go home." Eric pushed back from the desk. "I'm not doing the kids any good today."

"We all have our bad days." Toni patted his shoulder and shuffled away.

His heart was racing, more with excitement than fear. Sneaking into confidential files gave him such a rush, and he now knew the name of a doctor Jenna had seen.

Demauer.

Eric stopped in front of the elevator. He'd heard the name—she was a research bigwig—but they'd never met. The lab types had a tendency to stick to themselves. Why had Jenna consulted with a geneticist anyway? Eric's instinct was to head for the research department and simply ask Demauer. He knew his chances of getting a straight answer were slim because of doctor/patient confidentiality rules. It was still worth a shot. Eric had never been shy about asking questions.

He hopped on the elevator and rode up two floors, then turned left and headed for the south wing. Once he stepped through the double doors into the research part of the building, the hum of human activity was replaced with silence. Eric's footsteps echoed in the empty hallway as he passed closed offices. He was stopped by a security guard before he got very far. The guard wasn't someone he'd met before.

"Do you have business here?"

"I'd like to see Dr. Demauer."

"Do you have an appointment?"

Eric hesitated. If he said no, that would be it. Then again, if he lied…"No, but this will only take a minute."

"Dr. Demauer isn't in today. Call and make an appointment."

"Good idea." Eric grinned at the man.

The guard, a thin man of fifty, didn't smile back. Eric turned and walked out. He'd call Demauer and try again later, but it was probably a waste of time. What could a blood test have to do with her disappearance?

Eric left the parking lot, and a Burger King on Franklin waved him down as he passed. He pulled into the drive-in and ordered two cheeseburgers and a large Coke.

"Wait," Eric yelled into the speaker after the girl told him to pull forward. He had heard Jenna's voice in his head say, *Are you trying to kill yourself?*

"Make that one burger, no cheese, and a grilled chicken sandwich."

"Do you still want the Coke?"

"Sure, thanks."

Eric let out a sigh. Sooner or later everyone had to watch his diet. He'd already put it off as long as possible.

He ate the chicken sandwich first, thinking it would taste better if he was still ravenously hungry. It wasn't bad. The traffic was thick and, after losing a pickle in his lap, Eric decided to stop at Skinner Butte Park to eat his burger. He took his time, barely missing the cheese.

With his hunger abated, he noticed the fog had lifted and blue sky covered the park. He watched a small group of homeless men shuffle up the path from under the bridge, passing a cigarette between them. Abruptly, he thought of Buster, a drug dealer and small-time pimp, who hung out at a five-booth café on Blair Street.

Eric had met him when he covered the murder of four homeless men in the Whittaker district. Buster had been paid well for his interviews, and Eric had gone back to him for information a few times. That was three years ago. Even if he found Buster, the odds of him recognizing either of the men in the sketches were slim. Eugene was still a small town in many ways, and ex-cons had a tendency to know each other. Eric started up the Firebird and eased out of the park. What could it hurt to stop by the café on his way home?

Buster wasn't in his usual booth by the window. Eric bought coffee to go and left. Instead of getting back in his car, he walked around the corner and strolled slowly down Blair Street, looking for Buster. The prostitutes and drug dealers stared back, sizing up the stranger in their neighborhood.

He found him three blocks over, at a picnic table in front of the Holistic Bakery. Buster looked better than Eric remembered. Not as skinny or pale, but still dressed in dirty, oversize clothes.

"Hey, Buster," Eric said softly, sliding onto the bench across from him.

"Hey, man." Buster smiled slowly. "Where you been?"

"Working at home. How's life?"

"Good." Buster shrugged. "And bad. I'm off the meth, which is good. But I'm broke, and it's the shits."

"Maybe we can help each other out again."

"What do you want to know?"

Eric pulled the photocopied drawings out of his pocket and unfolded them in front of Buster. "Do you recognize either of these guys?"

Buster squinted at the pictures. "What are they wanted for?"

"Maybe kidnapping."

"No shit! That's heavy." Buster picked up the picture of the man with the ponytail and studied it closely. "You know, this looks kinda like an older, more kick-back version of a guy who used to buy cocaine from my ex."

"What's his name?"

"Don't know." Buster shrugged. "It was a long time ago."

"Would your girlfriend know his name?"

"Ex-girlfriend. Who knows? She's so fucked up. Well, she might be straight now. She's doing eighteen months up in Salem."

"Drug charge?"

"What else?" Buster leaned forward. "What's all this worth to you?"

Eric pulled out his wallet. "I'll give you ten bucks if you save me the trouble of looking for your ex-girlfriend's name."

Buster shook his head. "Still a tightwad, I see. Make it twenty, and I'll tell you all three of her names."

"Deal."

"Her real name is Ellen Parks, but she goes by either Rose Harper or Camilla Paris."

"She likes flowers, eh?"

Buster shrugged. "If you say so."

Eric handed him a twenty and a business card. "Call me if you remember anything else about this guy."

"I only saw him a few times. He used to stop by in the middle of the night when no one else was around. He always dressed real nice too, like a lawyer or something. But he…" Buster shrugged.

"It's probably not the same guy. If it is, Rosie will remember. She had the hots for him."

"Thanks."

Eric headed back to his car, humming softly to himself. Visiting Rose in the Women's Correctional Facility would not be pleasant, but he had a feeling it might be worthwhile.

Chapter 20

Sarah pushed against the stirrups, bearing down on the huge lump in her belly. The room was dark and she could hear Reverend Carmichael's voice coming through a speaker, coaching her, guiding her, yet she was alone. Alone in the birthing room with thick walls and no windows. Where no one could hear her scream. She pushed harder, squeezing her stomach muscles until the baby burst out between her legs. Sarah sat up to peek at the child and froze in terror. Its head was enormous and its mouth full of teeth. Dark hair covered the genitals, obscuring its gender.

Sarah screamed and woke herself up.

She threw back the covers and sat forward, anxious to lose the dream.

"Sarah, what's wrong?" Delilah's little voice called out in the darkness.

"Nothing. I'm fine. Just a strange dream. Go back to sleep."

Sarah waited a few minutes for Delilah to drift back off, then climbed out of bed. Her skin felt hot and tender, as if she'd been in the sun too long. She wanted a cold glass of water in the worst way. She pulled on her robe, grabbed the flashlight she kept by the bed, and scurried across the covered walkway to the main building.

The lights in the kitchen and dining room were on a timer and would not come on in the middle of the night unless someone reset the system. She could have gone to the shower room, which had a night-light, but it was her habit to head for the kitchen to have milk and crackers when she couldn't sleep. The thought of food made her nauseous. She stopped and leaned against the wall until the feeling passed.

Still not feeling right, Sarah quickly got her drink and went back to bed. Sleep eluded her. The thought of having a deformed or diseased baby had never occurred to her before. None of the babies born at the compound ever had anything wrong with them. She'd heard some wild birthing stories, but things had always turned out okay. Reverend Carmichael was the best, everyone agreed.

Maybe God sent the nightmare as a way of telling her not to get pregnant. God might be calling her to do his work elsewhere. Sarah let out a deep sigh. Reverend Carmichael seemed so certain. Sarah prayed for another sign. Her heart beat rapidly, and sleep came slowly.

She woke with the sun as usual. Her skin felt warm, her stomach felt queasy, and her heart was full of uncertainty. Sarah dressed quickly without turning on the light. Conserving resources was part of their religion. She pulled on cotton leggings, a T-shirt, thick wool skirt, socks, and a sweater. The chapel was always cold for morning service.

She woke Delilah first, then quickly shook Tamara's shoulder. Her mother didn't respond. Sarah would have liked to talk with her about the momentous decision she faced, but Tamara, who was prone to depression, had become more and more withdrawn the past week. Sarah shook her shoulder again.

"Leave me be," Tamara mumbled.

Sarah turned away. She'd been through this before, and there was nothing anyone could do but wait for it to pass.

After chapel Sarah headed for the kitchen, where she was posted for canning duty. Faith, who got up at five every day to bake something wonderful, was already hard at work.

"Aren't you having breakfast today?" Gray-haired and plump, Faith pretended to be gruff, but always had time to talk and often slipped her an extra goodie of some kind.

"My stomach's bothering me a little. I think I'll get started with the canning and see if I feel like having something later."

"Suit yourself." Faith shrugged. "Apple muffins are never quite as good as when they're right out of the oven."

Sarah could smell the hot fruit and nutmeg permeating the kitchen, but her stomach said no. She washed her hands and got to work cleaning tomatoes for canning.

The morning passed slowly. She couldn't stop worrying about whether she was ready for a baby, and the nausea came and went, getting worse each time. Sarah thought about going down to the clinic, but she didn't want to see the Reverend just yet. After finishing up in the kitchen, she headed for the daycare, thinking she would go back to her room and lie down later if she didn't feel better.

The arrival of the weekly mail, which was picked up every Friday afternoon by Ellie when she went to Blue River for groceries, momentarily distracted Sarah. Ellie delivered the letter from Darcie to the daycare personally. Sarah could hardly contain her excitement, and Marilynn finally excused her. Sarah skipped back to her family's unit. A letter from Darcie! Finally. She had waited so long.

Stretched out on her cot, Sarah began to read.

Dearest Sarah,

I know I promised I'd write every week and it's been forever…but things have been a little crazy for me.

This won't be good news, Sarah, but you have to believe me. I'm pregnant. The freaky thing is, I haven't had sex in over a year. Try explaining that to a stuffy, middle-aged health worker!! I never slept with Zeke or David, honest. And I never consented to having one of the Reverend's "special babies." How could I be pregnant?

He must have put it in me during one of his pelvic exams. You know how obsessed he is with making babies. Sorry to burst your bubble. I know you think he's the next best thing to God, but I know better, and I'm worried for you. I should have told you sooner, but I didn't think you'd believe me. Then I remembered your birthday was last week and you're 16 now. Don't let him ruin your life, Sarah. Come stay with me. My baby is due any day and I'm scared. I could use a friend right now. My address is 835 W. Monroe, #6, Eugene. I don't have a phone, so just show up. I'm always here. I'm too huge to go anywhere except to the store and the doctor.

Love, Darcie

Sarah reread the letter. She didn't believe it. As much as she loved Darcie, she didn't believe everything she said. Some of the stories she told were too wild!

She eased back on the bed and closed her eyes. God was surely testing her faith today. First the nightmare, now the letter from Darcie. The poor girl must really be lonely to make up something so ridiculous just to get her to visit. All at once, Sarah realized what God wanted her to do. He wanted her to stay with

Darcie while she had her baby. Then she could see for herself if she was ready to have a child of her own.

Sarah began to pack a bag. She would leave right away, before she changed her mind. She would tell Delilah, but no one else. Sarah had never hitchhiked before, but Darcie had made it sound easy. Especially for pretty young girls. If men were as eager to stop as Darcie said, she would be in Eugene before dark.

The first cramp hit her before she finished packing. A second and third cramp had her doubled over with pain in the hallway outside the schoolroom where she hoped to find Delilah. They were not like any menstrual cramps she'd ever had. The intensity of the fourth cramp made her vomit. Sarah lay on the floor, inches from her own mess, and prayed for someone to find her. The pain was paralyzing. She couldn't move or call for help.

The next cramp was so bad she blacked out.

* * *

Rachel was taking a sample of Jenna's urine, as the Reverend had instructed, when she heard Marilynn and Ellie yelling and running down the clinic stairs. She dropped the catheter bag and rushed from the labor room into the main surgery area to see what the commotion was about.

They were carrying Sarah, dragging her really, one under each armpit. The girl was unconscious but vomited as soon as Marilynn and Ellie heaved her up on one of the examining tables.

Rachel quickly twisted Sarah's head to one side so she wouldn't gag. "What happened?"

"I don't know," Ellie said, gulping for air. "I was delivering mail and found her like this in the hall."

A wave of fear washed over Rachel. She'd assisted in dozens of egg retrievals, embryo transfers, and live births, including a few that required C-sections. But her only training had come from Reverend Carmichael, and it didn't include emergency experience. She felt inadequate to handle anything that didn't involve the uterus, except for simple things like stitches and sprains. She could tell by the color and feel of Sarah's skin that something was seriously wrong.

Rachel forced herself to go through the motions, first examining Sarah's body for external damage. When she found none, she checked her blood pressure and heart rate, both of which were abnormally high. Sarah's condition seemed very similar to Jenna's attack the night before. What was going on? And why now? The Reverend hadn't even been gone twenty-four hours and this was her second emergency.

"Where's Tamara? Does she know what's happened?" Rachel didn't expect Sarah's mother to be much help, but she had an obligation to keep her informed.

"I sent Ruth to look for her." Ellie's tone was neutral, but her expression was critical. Tamara's weakness, combined with her beauty, made her unpopular with many of the women.

Rachel checked Sarah's blood pressure again: 152/98. It was going up. Rachel wanted to cry. She couldn't let anything happen to sweet little Sarah. "I'm taking her to the hospital." She hadn't realized she'd made a decision.

"I'll go with you." Ellie, forty and overweight, was still winded from carrying Sarah down to the clinic.

"Wait a minute." Rachel racked her brain for a way to stabilize Sarah for the trip to the hospital, but she was afraid to make her condition worse. Rachel suspected the hormone injections Sarah had been given were the underlying cause. What about Jenna? Why would heroin withdrawals produce a similar reaction to that of fertility hormones? Confused and frightened, Rachel had no idea what to do.

"All right, let's go!" She grabbed Sarah by an arm and a leg. The girl's eyes fluttered, but she didn't wake up. "Marilynn, help Ellie with her side."

As they lifted Sarah onto a stretcher, Zeke burst into the clinic. "What the hell is going on now, Rachel?"

"Sarah needs a doctor, and I'm taking her in." The defiance in her voice surprised her.

"Why is that door open?"

All three women turned and stared through the open door of the labor room where Zeke was pointing. Fury twisted his face.

"I was in there when they brought Sarah—"

Zeke wasn't listening. He rushed to the door, slammed it, and locked it. "Nobody's going anywhere! Ellie, Marilynn, get out. I need to talk to Rachel."

The two women scooted away without looking back. Rachel sucked in a deep breath, prepared to fight for Sarah's life.

"What's wrong with you?" Zeke crossed the short distance and grabbed Rachel's arm in a painful squeeze. "How could you leave that door open? The Reverend is going to be furious."

"I'm sorry." Rachel spoke through clenched teeth. "Right now this girl needs a doctor, so get out of my way. The Reverend will be even angrier if Sarah dies. You know how he feels about Sarah."

Uncertainty flashed in Zeke's eyes. Rachel moved toward Sarah.

"What if she saw who's in that room?" Zeke hissed, grabbing Rachel's arm again.

"She's unconscious!"

"Her eyes are open."

"She's out of it, damn you. And her blood pressure's escalating. Please let me go. I'm taking her to the hospital."

Zeke let go, but moved to block the doors leading into the hall. "If Sarah saw something she shouldn't have and flaps her lips about it, we're all in big trouble."

"She didn't and she won't. Now help me get her up to the supply truck."

"Not me. It's your situation all the way." Abruptly, Zeke turned and trotted out of the medical unit.

Marilynn and Ellie slipped back down the steps while Rachel dug a blanket out of the supply cabinet. Together they carried Sarah up the steps and out of the compound.

Chapter 21 ⟩—

Eric had been on the phone since he got home, trying to arrange an immediate visit with Ellen Parks (alias Rose Harper) at the Women's Correctional Facility just outside Salem. Even with his newspaper and police connections, it wasn't happening fast enough. He felt desperate enough to ask for Jackson's help. Nothing mattered but finding Jenna.

Instead of fading, as he expected, his feelings for her had intensified. The need to find her, to know that she was all right had become a compulsion, an overriding desire that put the rest of his life on hold. He couldn't write, couldn't work on the duplex, hadn't cleaned his kitchen in a week, and barely remembered to eat. It was starting to wear him down.

The phone rang. Startled, Eric almost knocked it off the counter. "Hello."

"Hi, my name's Helen. I'm calling about the story in the paper this morning. The woman who might have been kidnapped."

"Yes?" His first two phone calls that morning had taught him not to get his hopes up.

"I think I saw one of those guys at the Dairy Mart this morning."

"Which Dairy Mart?"

"The one in Veneta."

She sounded sane, articulate. Eric was cautiously optimistic.

"What was he driving?"

"I couldn't say for sure. I was still in the store when he walked out. But a minute later, a van pulled out of the parking lot."

Eric's pulse picked up. "Describe him."

"Late fifties, skinny, gray receding hair. He was wearing dirty jeans and a black jacket and was kind of stoop shouldered."

Damn! He sounded just like the second man to get out of the gray van, although Eric had seen him only briefly. He still had to rule out the possibility this woman was another nutcase with a vendetta against someone she knew.

"Do you know who the man is?"

"Never saw him before in my life, but I think I've seen the van on Lake Drive several times. Do you know where that is?"

"No."

"It's off Perkins Road just after it crosses the creek. I'd be happy to show you."

Eric hesitated. The one message left on his machine while he was out was as nutty as the first two. But this woman sounded sane. Veneta was only a twenty-minute drive from this side of town. "How many times have you seen the van?"

"Three, including today." Her voice seemed to lose some of its patience.

"When was the first time?"

"Monday, then again later in the week. Wednesday, I think. Look, I have to go. I've told you everything I can."

"Wait, Helen. Are you still willing to show me where you've seen the van parked?"

"Sure. Meet me at the Dairy Mart at three thirty. I'll be wearing a purple jacket. See you then." She hung up.

Eric forced himself to remain calm, even though it felt like he finally had a legitimate lead. The kidnappers could be keeping Jenna hostage in a rural cabin or farmhouse. He refused to think about the reasons or the conditions of Jenna's existence, if that were true.

Eric had time to kill before taking off, so he called the hospital's public-relations department. After being kept on hold for ten minutes, he finally got to launch into his spiel. "Hello, this is Eric Troutman. I'm a journalist working on a story about successful women in the medical profession. I'd like to set up an interview with Dr. Mary Atwood, cardiac surgeon, and Dr. E. Demauer, your director of genetic science."

"Why does your name sound familiar?" The question was suspicious rather than friendly.

"I'm a hospital volunteer, but I don't think we've met. If you've lived in Eugene for any length of time, you've probably seen my byline. I was a reporter for the *Willamette News* for ten years and still occasionally write for them. I've also been published in national magazines." Eric resisted the urge to mention his Pulitzer.

"Oh yeah, the series on abusive foster homes."

"Thanks for remembering. Can you help me with those interviews?"

"I'll do my best. Dr. Atwood will probably be okay with it, but Dr. Demauer is rather reclusive. The publicity would be good for the hospital though. Maybe I can get Dr. Gybbs to pressure her. What magazine is this for?"

"*Working Women.*" *Liar!*

"You sound like an interesting person."

Eric suddenly felt like shit. "I'm just trying to make a living. I'll call back in a day or so and see what you've got for me. Thanks again." He hung up before she could make him feel worse.

He paced around the cluttered living room trying to come up with a way to see Demauer. It couldn't be that tough. She was just a genetics researcher, not the president. Then it occurred to him to call the elusive Dr. Demauer at home. It took twenty minutes to find the phone book under a pile of newspapers on the kitchen table. He vowed to clean the place that weekend.

Dr. E. Demauer was not listed. He tried finding her online, but only came up with numbers for the clinic and hospital. It was time to see the lady in a purple jacket at a Dairy Mart in Veneta.

Helen was late. Eric had already checked inside the store, then returned to his car to wait. It rained so hard for a few minutes he couldn't see out the window. He heard a truck pull in and shut off its motor. Then the voices of two men cursing the weather. When the deluge let up a little, Eric trotted back inside the store to make sure he hadn't missed Helen during the downpour.

Nobody in a purple jacket. Just two guys in jeans and scruffy, down-filled vests. Eric bought a pack of gum and went back out to the Firebird. He noticed a new car parked on the side of the store. The woman in it was watching him. She had a thin face and short, dark hair. Her coat was dark, but he couldn't tell if it was blue or black or purple. Being partially color-blind was convenient when buying clothes or getting dressed because he didn't worry about making things match, but sometimes it messed things up with other people, who could be really fussy about getting colors right.

Eric trotted over to her Volvo, which was definitely yellow.

"Are you Helen?" he asked as she rolled down her window.

"Who wants to know?"

"I'm Eric Troutman. I'm the one looking for Jenna McClure."

"Get in the car, it's starting to rain."

Eric hesitated. *What the hell, I've come this far.* He climbed into her car.

Helen looked him over with a peculiar scrutiny. "Are you wired?"

"What?" At first he thought she was talking about drugs, then he realized she meant a microphone. His heart sank. Another whack job. Eric reached for the door handle.

"Let's roll." Helen started the Volvo and shoved it in reverse.

"Wait!" He threw the door open as the car lurched backward. Helen didn't slow down. She slammed the car into drive, cranked the wheel, and gunned it. Eric heaved himself out, landing on his chest with such force it knocked the wind out of him. The Volvo screeched out into the street. He curled up in a ball and waited for the pain in his chest to subside.

Two women stepped out of a Honda and stared. Eric forced himself to his feet. It hurt to stand up straight. Hunched over, he stumbled to his car and flopped in. The women continued to stare, walking slowly into the store, but looking back over their shoulders. Eric didn't care. All women were crazy. At least today they were. Maybe the moon was having some sort of gravitational effect on female-hormone levels or something. Helen needed to be locked up, that was for sure. Eric headed for home and a cold bottle of Miller.

The message light on his answering machine was blinking when he got there, but he ignored it. The only person he wanted to hear from—Jenna—had not likely called his house phone. He was glad he'd kept his landline to give out as a contact number. He would hate for the crazies to have his cell-phone number. He flopped in his recliner and closed his eyes. Taking a short snooze usually helped him relax. But his stomach complained so loudly, he grudgingly got up and went to the kitchen. He hadn't been shopping in a week, so he settled for a couple of PB and Js dipped in microwave-warm tomato soup. Comfort food that reminded him of long-ago Saturday afternoons, when he fixed lunch for the grubbers, while Mom slept off another all-nighter.

The warm memory quickly darkened into a bout of homesickness. Eric felt more alone than he ever had in his life. An image of himself as an old man, sitting at the same table, eating dinner alone, pushed into his consciousness and hovered, pulling him down, deeper into the dumps.

Eric pushed back. His threw his bowl at the pile of dishes in the sink and bolted from the room. He grabbed his coat, locked up, and left the house while he still had the energy. Keep moving, he told himself. Help someone whose problems are bigger than your own. Work until you're too tired to think—a proven strategy.

He drove aimlessly for a few minutes, then instinctively headed for North McKenzie. If nothing else, he would get back into the computer and read the rest of Jenna's file. Maybe even try another visit with Dr. Demauer.

The hospital was crowded with visitors, lots of little family groups with worried expressions. Eric headed straight for the second floor and the computer he'd used that morning.

Two nurses stood talking in front of the little office, so Eric passed the pediatrics admitting desk and caught the next elevator up to the research wing. An attractive woman with short, wavy dark-blonde hair stepped out of the lounge across from the elevator. A younger woman in a matching lab coat followed her. Eric moved toward them just in time to hear the younger woman say, "Good night, Dr. Demauer."

An unexpected rush of excitement propelled him forward. "Dr. Demauer?"

The woman turned and he saw her clearly for the first time. Her face seemed very familiar. Eric figured he must have seen her in the hospital before.

"Yes?" Her voice was curt, but quiet.

"Can I talk to you for a minute?"

"That depends." She tried to calculate who he was and what he wanted.

"My name's Eric Troutman. I'm a hospital volunteer. Can we go sit down in the lounge and be comfortable?"

"I have work to do. Just tell me what you want."

"A friend of mine named Jenna McClure has disappeared. I know she had a blood test done at the Assisted Reproduction Clinic, followed by a consultation with you. I was hoping you might be able to tell me something about her condition. Something that might help me find her."

Demauer's eyes widened for a split second, then she seemed to drift. Eric waited patiently, giving her a chance to respond. He noticed the doctor's skin was unnaturally pale, and she seemed to have a slight tremor in her hands. "I realized you're probably—"

"You don't realize anything." Demauer's voice was shrill and loud. "How dare you even ask me? A patient's confidentiality is sacred. Perhaps your friend is just trying to get away from your overbearing personality. If you have no other business on the research floor, I suggest you leave. I see the security guard coming now. Should I alert him?"

"That won't be necessary." Eric spun around and strode to the elevator. It was the same security guard he'd encountered that morning, and he didn't want the man to see him. He bounced on his feet and kept his face turned away. The elevator door opened and Eric rushed in. When he turned back to face the doors, Demauer was standing in the same place, watching him. *What a hostile woman*, he thought. Seriously lacking in social skills.

Riding down, he felt jittery and almost talked himself out of a second try at the computer. This day had been so frustrating, so full of dead ends, that he felt compelled to take one more opportunity to find a breakthrough.

The nursing staff was mostly out of sight when he exited on the second floor. Only one desk clerk was in the area of the cubby office, and Eric slipped in unnoticed. He accessed Jenna's file quickly this time and scanned past the first page. Then a voice boomed out, "Step away from the computer."

Shit! It was the security guard from the research department. He must have followed him down. "Listen, I can explain. I'm a hospital volunteer, and everyone on the pediatric staff will vouch for me."

"Save it for the police."

"Call Big Al, head of security. He knows me. He'll tell you I'm just a nosy reporter looking at my girlfriend's file."

"Stand up."

Eric realized the guard was wearing a gun, but he hadn't drawn it. *What was with the people on the research floor?*

"Turn around, put your hands on the wall, and spread your legs."

Eric was frisked for the first time in his life. It made him feel sleazy. Shameful. In a moment, they were headed to the security office on the first floor.

Albert Hoskins, head of security, was not in the building but insisted on coming in to handle the problem himself. Eric was forced to wait almost an hour in a tiny, dingy room that stank of sweat. Big Al was not impressed with his story of investigating a kidnapping. He lectured Eric about the abuse of privilege and friendship, then decided he would release him without pressing charges. Relief flooded over the shame.

"Don't come back," Hoskins warned with a sad face. "You're done here permanently. It's too bad for the kids, Troutman. They'll miss you."

"I know. I can't tell you how much I regret this already."

"I hope you find your girlfriend."

"Me too."

Eric had serious doubts. If today was any indication of the way things would turn out, he was in serious trouble. He couldn't think of a worse day. Except when Chris died.

Chapter 22 ⟩—

Carmichael stepped out of the cab and got drenched in a sudden downpour. Welcome to Seattle. Deciding it would take longer to dig out his umbrella than reach the cover of the building, he sprinted toward the glass door marked *JB Pharmaceuticals*.

Once inside, Carmichael checked his watch. Fifteen minutes before ten. After passing through the security checkpoint, he would have just enough time to scoot into a men's room and see how much damage the rain had done.

The bathroom, with its pink-and-gray marbled counter and twenty-foot-long mirror, was a long way from the primitive furnishings at the compound. He reminded himself that material things were not important.

After quickly combing his hair and drying his loafers as best as he could with paper towels, Carmichael grabbed the elevator and rode to the tenth floor. Gerald Akron's secretary, a large, plain-looking woman packed into a small dress, stared at him suspiciously when he walked in.

"Can I help you?"

"I'm David Carmichael. I have an appointment with Gerald Akron."

"You're not in the appointment book." She continued to stare, her expression vacillating between disapproval and curiosity. *It was probably the ponytail*, Carmichael thought. Most women liked it, but some found it out of place on a well-dressed man.

"Tell him I'm here, please." Carmichael smiled politely, but didn't waste any charm on the woman. He was too preoccupied to play the game.

She turned away slightly to speak into her headphone, then turned back after a moment. "Have a seat then."

Carmichael waited patiently, using the time to go over his prepared answers. During the flight, he'd tried to anticipate Akron's conditions. He would only compromise so far. He needed the money more than ever, but would never risk the Sisters' health just to keep the clinic going. The irony of it almost made him smile.

"Mr. Akron will see you now."

Carmichael resisted the urge to smirk as he walked briskly back to the inner door. He might, God forbid, be back here again someday.

Akron's office wasn't particularly large, but it had a spectacular view of the bay. Carmichael refused to comment. He was not impressed with Akron or his half-million-a-year desk job. The man's face was huge and square, with a nasty dimple in his chin. Akron was also overweight, with a pink blush over pale, moist skin. High blood pressure, possibly coronary disease. The man probably wouldn't collect much of his pension.

"Have a seat, Carmichael." Akron's tone was that of a superior talking to a subordinate. Carmichael bristled, but held himself in check. He never let pride get in the way of a contribution. God had taught him to be humble when necessary.

"Thanks." He plopped in the chair, leaned back, and crossed his legs—the look of a relaxed man.

"Let's cut to the chase, shall we?"

"Certainly."

"We're not pleased with the way you've handled things in the past." Akron held up a hand and used his fingers to list grievances. "Altering dosages at random. Sloppy documentation, if any at all. Discontinuing injections before the subject ovulates. And failing to set clinical end points."

"I've reorganized—"

"Save it." Akron reached back and grabbed a large, dark box, which he set to one side of the desk. "When you take our money, you do our research our way. Each subject gets her own special dosage, the same dosage every day. Everything is premeasured, color coded, and labeled just to make it easy for a guy like you. With me so far?" Akron paused, but Carmichael couldn't bring himself to speak. He nodded slightly.

"For example, Subject A gets injected with the needles in the red packages every day until she ovulates, then the eggs are retrieved, counted, and documented. Subject B gets injected with the pink packages, and only the pink packages, every day until she ovulates. It's too simple to screw up."

"What about side effects? What if the dosage proves to be too much for the individual?" Carmichael sounded whiny even to himself, but his heart was sick. He feared what they expected of him.

"Side effects are to be documented, but they should in no way alter the course of the research." Akron's voice dropped a level.

"The most important aspect of this trial is the rate of implantation. We're trying to develop a hormone that is less irritating to the uterine lining, thus allowing more embryos to implant. The success rates of our fertility clinics are declining. The doctors think the hormones they prescribe to increase egg production might actually work against the transfer rate."

"I concur." Carmichael leaned forward, eager to discuss the subject. "They seem to cause abnormal endometrial maturation, adversely affecting the outer hyperechogenic layer." He'd compared endometrium biopsies of women taking fertility drugs to women who'd been exposed only to natural estrogen levels and found a startling difference.

"Keep your theories to yourself." Akron held up his hand. "When you work for us, you have no mind of your own and no patients. They are subjects in a clinical trial. If you deviate from the program, you ruin the data. Am I making myself clear?"

"Yes." Carmichael wanted to slap the man.

"Good." Akron leaned back and smiled. "Now it's only a question of price. How many subjects this time?"

"Ten or twelve." Carmichael gave him what he thought would be the lowest acceptable number.

Akron grunted. "Almost not worth bothering with. But somebody has to go first, so we can fine-tune the dosage for the real test group." He rotated his chair and opened a safe in a cabinet behind his desk. "Because you only have a dozen subjects and there are twenty sets of injections in there, some of your gals will just have to go through a second cycle. But for fifteen thousand, I'm sure they won't mind." Akron held out a stack of bills, waiting for a response.

The urge to snatch the cash and run was overpowering. Carmichael knew he would never give anyone back-to-back cycles of untested hormones. That was insane. He couldn't just walk away from the cash either. Lord help me, he prayed. There had to be a way.

There was. He could fake the results of the second cycle based on the notes from the first. Akron would never know the difference. As long as everything was all neat and accounted for on paper, the drugmaker would be happy.

Carmichael nodded. "You have a deal."

Akron handed him the cash. Carmichael glanced at it just long enough to make sure it looked right, then slipped the wad into an interior jacket pocket. These trials were not registered with the FDA, and JB Pharma wasn't reckless enough to leave a paper trail.

He couldn't bring himself to look Akron in the eye. It wasn't right to cheat the man. But Akron was a heartless asshole, and Carmichael didn't feel too guilty. "I'll send the results in a few months." He stood, feeling his muscles relax for the first time in days.

"Bring them in person." Akron chuckled softly. "It'll be nice to see you again."

Carmichael's throat was too dry to respond. He nodded, then walked out.

"Asshole." He said it out loud for the first time on the elevator. The word had been playing in his head like a mantra since leaving Akron's office. Carmichael promised himself he wouldn't come back here—ever. Elizabeth would come through with the money she had promised, and he would contact the United Christian Foundation personally to find out why his church had been cut out of the yearly distribution. Everything would work out. He would cut the hormone dosages in half and to hell with Akron. Other fertility specialists might push for big numbers like eight and ten eggs per retrieval, but not him. His success rate was in the high seventies. All he needed were a few extra oocytes each time, so he could be sure to produce at least one female embryo with good metabolic activity for transfer. And, of course, have a few rejects left over to study.

Out on the street, the rain had stopped and the sun streaked through the clouds in patches. A dim rainbow intersected the Fremont Bridge. Carmichael took it as a good sign. He caught a cab to the airport and headed home.

Three hours later he moved briskly through Eugene's small airport, thinking it would take him longer to drive to the compound than it had to fly from Seattle. His one piece of luggage, a travel bag, was slung over his shoulder as he hurried to the overnight parking lot and unlocked the church van. Daylight was fading and the sky was heavy with rain. Carmichael made a quick stop at the bank to deposit the cash, then headed east on Highway 126. He wanted to stop and see Elizabeth about the money she had promised, but his need to be at the compound, to make sure everything was all right with Jenna, was overwhelming.

The feeling that all was not well at the church had nagged him during the flight. His anxiety continued to grow, reaching a state of near panic as Carmichael navigated the winding mountain road in the dark. Wind and rain pounded the van in relentless fury. He pushed the speedometer, taking the corners at reckless speeds. He prayed continuously.

Watch over my congregation, dear Lord. Keep them safe from harm, safe from themselves. Especially Jenna. I know I'll have to answer for what I've done to her, but she's innocent, Lord. Help her through the hormone treatment, please. Liz needs this baby, and I need to give it to her. After that, I'll rededicate my life and my clinic to your service only. Please, Lord, let Jenna be all right. Please.

Carmichael drove to the back of the compound, parking under the long carport next to Zeke's truck. From there he scooted in through his secret panel to avoid backtracking through the downpour.

The muted sounds of women chatting, children laughing, and forks clinking on plates were as soothing as any gospel music. He ignored his growling stomach, changed into a clean shirt, and hurried down to the clinic. The exam room and Rachel's office were both empty.

Carmichael strode back to the small labor room and found it unlocked. A tremor of panic rippled through him. He yanked open the door and breathed a sigh of relief. Jenna was sleeping, her breathing deep and even. She looked even better than he remembered. *Thank you, God.* Color had returned to her cheeks, and she seemed peaceful. He wanted to check her vital signs but hesitated to wake her. He gently placed two fingers on the inside of her wrist, checked his watch, and counted.

Pulse, fifty-eight. He frowned, puzzled. It seemed quite slow for a woman on fertility hormones. He remembered Rachel saying Jenna looked like an athlete. An image of Rachel bathing Jenna flashed in his memory. He reached out and pushed Jenna's blanket aside. The sight of her thick, peach-colored thighs gave him an erection.

Ashamed, he stepped back. Where the hell was Rachel? Why was Jenna's door unlocked? Carmichael retrieved his radio communicator from the office and buzzed Zeke. "Find Rachel and both of you get down to the clinic immediately."

"Sweet Jesus." Carmichael felt sick when he heard the account of Sarah's trauma. "Don't tell me you lost her."

"Oh no." Rachel shook her head. "I took her to North McKenzie Hospital. She's fine now." Rachel twisted her hands as she rushed to explain. "I wanted to stay in town with her, but I figured I should be here since you were gone and no one else has any medical training." Rachel's expression begged him to understand that she'd done her best.

Carmichael fought to stay calm. It's not as bad as it could be, he reminded himself. "So Sarah is a patient at North McKenzie right now?"

"Yes."

Zeke, who had remained expressionless during the exchange, said casually, "I told her not to go, but you know how pigheaded she is."

Carmichael gave him a chilly stare. It didn't matter who said what. They had to get Sarah out of the hospital before some doctor discovered the hormone in her system and started asking questions. The truth was, it was probably too late to prevent the questions, but maybe not too late to keep Sarah from answering. "Get her back. Leave now. Do not answer any questions from the hospital staff. Is that clear?"

Rachel's lips were pressed so tightly they disappeared. "Is it the hormone shot?"

"We'll talk about it later. Just go get her."

Rachel jumped up and started for the door. Suddenly she turned back. "Jenna went into convulsions too. A few hours before Sarah."

"She was faking it!" Zeke slapped the desk in anger.

"No, she wasn't." Rachel turned back to Carmichael. "Are you giving Jenna hormones?"

"No!"

Stunned, Carmichael turned away to collect himself. Jenna had gone into convulsions? Thank god Rachel hadn't taken her to the hospital. What if she had died? The thought frightened him in a very personal way. What was God trying to tell him? He'd been gone twenty-four hours, and all hell had broken loose. He straightened his posture and turned back.

Rachel looked as if she were going to cry again. Carmichael felt bad for shouting at her. None of it was her fault. Still, he didn't want her thinking too seriously about Jenna's medical treatment. He softened his voice. "You did great, Rachel. Now please go get Sarah. Take someone with you if you like."

"Should I go?" Zeke asked.

"No, I need you here."

Neither he, nor Zeke, would leave the compound until the embryo transfer had been completed, Carmichael decided. The last experimental hormone he'd received from JB Pharma was obviously deteriorating and becoming a serious risk. He wondered if he should start Jenna on the new hormone. Or lower her dose of clomophergonal. Jenna had seemed fine when he looked in on her. She only had to take it for a few more days. He would have to trust the Lord to get them all through.

Chapter 23

Elizabeth pulled into Dutch Brothers and ordered a double Americano. It was more coffee than she usually drank, but she hadn't slept well in days and her body ached with exhaustion. Last night had been the worst. Her hands trembled as she reached through the window for the hot container. The young man in the little booth said something perky, but Elizabeth was already rolling up the window. She had no tolerance for irrelevant people today. Her head hurt too badly.

Her first night of sleeplessness had been from excitement, generated by the discovery that Jenna was not just a sister, but a fraternal twin. On a technical level, they were no more genetically similar that any other two siblings, but the idea excited her just the same. Elizabeth had started to think of Jenna as family. She had started to think that in a few years it would be safe to contact her and establish a relationship.

Her euphoria hadn't lasted long. The next evening, that reporter had walked right up to her in the hospital and asked about the disappearance of Jenna McClure. Elizabeth had been so frightened she'd gone completely blank, experiencing her first mental void since childhood. Then she'd overreacted in a verbal barrage that made her look psychotic. Later, after learning he was a reporter, she'd rushed to a bathroom and thrown up. Worried sick and disgusted with the way she'd handled things, Elizabeth hadn't slept much that night either.

She knew it was foolish to be upset. There was nothing to worry about. Jenna was just one of hundreds of women she'd counseled at ARC, and there was no other connection between them. Why the reporter had decided to question her was baffling. She couldn't stop thinking about it. Had Jenna suspected something about the blood-test results and talked to a reporter? Or was Eric Troutman somehow connected to McClure, a boyfriend or brother grasping at straws, desperate to find the woman?

Elizabeth lit a cigarette before pulling into the street. It was her fourth already that day but she didn't care. She was too upset to stay home and too distracted to take on the adoption agency. She eased onto the freeway and headed toward the compound. David would soothe her nerves, convince her everything would turn out fine.

Elizabeth swallowed three Excedrin with a gulp of hot coffee. She'd been taking Luprexia for the last five days to prime her uterus for the transfer, and the blinding headaches and nervous irritability were probably side effects. She would feel better when David examined her and reassured her that the problems were only physical and temporary. She also desperately needed to hear David say that Jenna's short-term memory was seriously impaired and their activities would never be found out. As long as the police were not involved, she consoled herself, they had nothing to worry about. Eric Troutman was just a lovesick reporter who would not be allowed back in the hospital.

Elizabeth lit another cigarette from the one she was smoking and moved into the passing lane.

At first sight of the breathtakingly beautiful canyon, Elizabeth understood the pull that brought people here. The compound itself was too austere, too cold for her to be comfortable in for any length of time. She had grown up with a canopy bed, a walk-in closet full of clothes, and a cleaning lady to pick up after her. Elizabeth would have traded all of it for two loving parents, but she'd never had a choice and couldn't change who she was.

She was greeted in the yard by two young girls who seemed excited to have a visitor. "Welcome to the Church of the Reborn. Reverend Carmichael says you're to come wait in his office." The blonde girl of twelve tried not to giggle.

"Thank you, I know the way." Elizabeth started toward the chapel and the girls followed. Their happy, giggling noises made her angry with David for filling their minds with religious non-sense that would make them weak and complacent. She was also painfully jealous—of their youth, their innocence, and the security they had here at the compound, where they would never be molested or degraded by men. Most of all, they had David. Seven days a week, fifty-two weeks a year.

Elizabeth scoffed at her own ridiculousness. She knew she couldn't handle a full-time relationship. Her short-lived marriage had proved it. She froze mid-stride. What if she felt that way about her baby? What if she couldn't handle being a mother twenty-four hours a day?

"Are you all right?" The girls had stopped in front of David's office.

"Of course. I just remembered something important. You know how it is."

They giggled and opened the door. Elizabeth hurried through.

Minutes later, David burst into the room at his usual break-neck pace. "Liz, what's wrong? It's so unlike you to show up like this."

She stood and stepped toward him, hoping he would embrace her. David sensed her need and put his arms around her. Elizabeth held on to him, gaining strength from his vitality. After a few minutes, he stepped back to look at her, but continued to hold both her hands.

"Tell me what's going on, Liz." David led her to a small, ratty-looking couch. Elizabeth was glad she'd worn a pair of inexpensive pants.

"I'll start with the good news. McClure and I are fraternal twins."

David's eyes narrowed with disbelief.

"It's true. First, I talked with her mother, who told me she was adopted. Then I called—"

"Wait a minute." David pulled away. "You called her mother? Why in the name of God did you do that?"

"Don't swear at me." Elizabeth raised her voice as well. "You know I've always wanted to find my real mother. I didn't give her my name, of course. I just told her I was researching cystic fibrosis and needed a family history."

David's face softened. "I know finding your mother is important to you, but everything is different now. You have to be careful. You have to wait until this is all over before you start digging around in Jenna's past."

Elizabeth was silent. His reaction was disappointing. She'd expected David to be happy for her.

"What is the news about twins? Tell me everything, Liz."

She wasn't sure she should tell him about her phone call to Daniel Potter, then she plunged ahead anyway. "Mrs. McClure told me the name of the adoption lawyer, so I called him. He told me there were two babies and that one had been adopted by a couple from Chicago. That's all I know."

David's eyes narrowed suspiciously. "That's confidential information. Why did he tell you?"

A smile flickered on her face before she could stop it. "I told him I was Jenna McClure."

David jumped like he'd been bitten on the butt.

"What are you trying to do? Get us all put in jail?" He looked around nervously, apparently startled by the loudness of his voice. David plopped back on the couch and growled in Elizabeth's ear. "If I had known you were going to selfishly pursue this obsession with finding your mother while I have your sister held captive in my church, I would have never agreed to help you. I can't believe the risk you took."

"Don't be so melodramatic." Elizabeth sounded more confident than she felt. David's criticism hurt, but she would never let him know. "Potter, the adoption lawyer, lives in Astoria and is probably a hundred years old. He'll never even know McClure was missing. And so what if he does?"

"It's risky, and I don't like it. Promise me you'll let it go." David leaned toward her, his face inches away. "I mean it, Liz. Promise me right now that you will not contact anyone else associated with Jenna."

For a second she hated him. For knowing her so well, for needing to be in control all the time. Still, he was right. "Okay, I'll let it go."

David moved back, apparently still angry with her. She knew she should tell him about the reporter in the hospital, but she couldn't bring herself to. Finally, Elizabeth said, "I want to see her."

"For the love of God, no." David gawked, openmouthed.

"Why not?"

"It's risky. The Versed might not be totally effective. After we let Jenna go, she'll never see me again. If she goes back to the ARC and sees you, it might trigger her memory." David shook his head. "It'll be risky enough during the transfer."

Elizabeth was disappointed but not surprised. "How is she holding up?"

"Good." He shrugged. "She's very healthy."

Great news. Elizabeth couldn't bear the thought of Jenna becoming ill or hurt because of her. "When will she be ready?"

"Sometime in the next forty-eight hours."

"That soon?" Elizabeth swallowed hard. "It's all happening so fast. I get scared sometimes about what kind of mother I'll be. Do you think I'll be a good mother?"

"Of course. Where are you in your cycle? Are you producing heavy mucus?"

"I'm not sure. You know how screwed up my system is. The Luprexia should be working. In fact, I think—"

David cut in. "We can't rely on guesswork. You, of all people, should know that." He began to pace. "Embryo donation from one woman to another is a very delicate process. At the moment of transfer, your endometrium has to be in the exact same developmental stage as if you'd produced the egg yourself." He whirled to face her. "The timing is critical!"

Elizabeth chewed the inside of her cheek. She hated to be lectured, and David knew it. He'd never been so careless with her feelings before. It wasn't like him. She assumed it was the stress of the situation. She didn't feel much like herself either.

David kept pacing and talking. "We need to check your estrogen level today while you're here, compare it to Jenna's, and adjust your Luprexia dosage accordingly. You need to check it again in the morning, then again tomorrow night. This is very important, Liz."

"I know it is, David. This is my life we're talking about, my baby. Which reminds me. I've been having horrible headaches and not sleeping well. Do you think it could be the Luprexia?"

"Of course it's the Luprexia! All fertility drugs have side effects—hot flashes, mood swings, cardiac acceleration. It's menopause and PMS all rolled into one. Haven't you ever talked to any of the women who come into the clinic? Or do you just slide the tissue under a microscope and never think about the people it came from?"

"Why are you being so cruel?"

"I'm sorry. I'm under a lot of stress."

"So am I. I think we should be supportive of each other."

"Speaking of which…" David smiled, but his eyes didn't change. "I need that ten thousand as soon as possible."

Damn him! Elizabeth wished she hadn't come. "David, I know I said I'd let you have it, but I can't."

"Why not?"

"Once the baby is born, I'm going to take a leave of absence. I'll need everything I have in savings to get by until I go back to work."

"You can stay here at the compound. It won't cost you anything."

"You know I can't."

"Not comfy enough for you?"

Elizabeth jumped up and grabbed her coat. "Why are you being such a shit? I came here because I needed you. I wanted to make love, not be insulted." She whirled around and strode toward the door.

David came after her. "I'm sorry, Liz. It's been a rough few days for me."

She stopped and let him put his arms around her. His touch was wonderful and her anger started to subside. After a moment her body defied her and leaned against him.

"We can still make love," he whispered.

* * *

The sex had not been good, a first for him and Liz. Lacking real passion, they'd been selfish and impatient, like addicts needing a fix and not caring where it came from. Carmichael had been distracted as well. More than once he'd thought of Jenna. What she would be like in bed.

Now they were dressed and sitting on the bed, not talking. Carmichael was anxious for Liz to leave. He had very little time to be alone with Jenna. Once the luteinizing hormone was evident in Jenna's urine, Liz would have to be on hand for the egg retrieval and stay in the compound while the embryos developed to an eight-cell stage.

"I love you, Liz. I'm sorry I wasn't a better friend and lover today. I have several stressful situations going right now." Carmichael rubbed her shoulders.

"It's my fault. I shouldn't have asked you to do this for me, but I had to." She sounded bitter and worried.

"It's almost over. Everything will turn out fine. A year from now, you'll be changing diapers and calling me to babysit."

She smiled then, a tiny smirk. It was gone as quick as it came. "David?"

"What is it?"

"A reporter came into the hospital last night and asked about McClure."

Stunned, Carmichael grabbed her arm. "What did he want?"

"He said she was a friend who'd disappeared, and he wondered if I knew anything about her medical condition that would help him find her."

"What did you tell him?" Carmichael had expected the police to investigate Jenna's disappearance eventually, but not a reporter. And he never expected anyone to connect it to him or Liz.

"I told him I couldn't violate a patient's confidence, then asked him to leave." Liz rushed to tell the rest. "The security guard had seen him on the fourth floor earlier that day, so he followed him and caught him looking in her computer files. They said if the reporter ever comes into the hospital again, he'll be arrested. The weird thing is, everyone in pediatrics knows him because he visits the cancer kids once a week. That's how I found out he's a reporter. It scares me. I know it shouldn't, but it does."

It scared Carmichael too. Reporters had ruined his life once already. "Don't worry. He's just digging around. When he doesn't find anything, he'll go away. Relax, dear. It's almost over."

Liz smiled gently. "For me, it's just the beginning."

Carmichael patted her belly. "You'll look great with a few extra pounds."

A loud pounding on the door interrupted them.

"Who is it?" Irritated, Carmichael didn't try to modify his voice. He wasn't supposed to be bothered in his private quarters, and everyone in the compound knew he had company.

"It's Zeke. I have to show you something."

"Can't it wait an hour?" Carmichael moved toward the door.

"I think the lady might like to see it too."

What did that mean? Carmichael glanced back at Liz, who seemed to be retreating into her own world.

"See what?" Carmichael stood next to the door and spoke softly.

"There's pictures of us in the paper next to a picture of Jenna McClure. They're calling us kidnappers."

Oh dear god. Carmichael unlocked the door and jerked it open. Zeke held the newspaper in front of him, his face a little grayer than usual. Carmichael snatched the paper, pulled Zeke into the room, and slammed the door.

Liz jumped up, her eyes frozen open in panic. Carmichael ignored her and sat down at his desk. He spread the newspaper and stared at the pictures. They were composite drawings, and the one of him was startlingly accurate. Zeke's image made him look younger and heavier than he was. Where had these come from? Carmichael scanned the story.

"Oh my god, they have pictures of you." Elizabeth peered over his shoulder, hands covering her mouth.

The headline read, "Have You Seen These People?" The story went on to say that a bystander at the River Run had seen the woman get into a van with two men and that she hadn't been seen since.

"It's that guy I saw coming down the street after we snatched her." Zeke pounded the desk. "I knew he was trouble."

"What's his name?" Elizabeth's voice was a whisper.

Carmichael looked for the byline. "Eric Troutman."

"It's the same reporter." Elizabeth chocked back a sob.

"What reporter?" Zeke grabbed Liz by the shoulders.

"There was a reporter at the hospital asking questions last night." Liz pulled free.

"What kind of questions?" Zeke wanted to know.

Carmichael stared at the drawing of himself, sick with fear.

"Nothing specific." Liz took several long breaths, trying to control herself. "He just wanted to know about her medical condition."

"She has a medical condition?"

"No." Liz shook her head, getting irritated. "She was a patient at the ARC. She wanted to be artificially inseminated and had to have—"

Zeke cut Liz off. "The reporter is obviously covering all the bases and intends to find this woman. I think we should get her out of here."

"No." Liz was vehement. Still looking at Carmichael, she jerked her head toward Zeke. "How much does he know?"

"I had to tell him the truth, Liz. He risked a lot to help us."

"That wasn't our agreement."

"Damn it, Liz. We have bigger things to worry about now."

Carmichael pushed back from the desk and rubbed his temples. This wasn't supposed to be happening. The plan was simple and foolproof. How could their pictures be in the newspaper?

Zeke stepped in front of him, arms folded across his chest. His leathery face was inscrutable. "Jenna has to go. I'm willing to take her wherever you like, but if we don't get her out of here now, I'm moving on."

Carmichael would have traded everything he owned for a single shot of bourbon to calm his nerves. Fortunately, there was no alcohol in the church. Somewhere he found the strength to stay in control. "Ezekiel, please. I understand your concern, but this is almost over. A few more days and everything goes back to normal. We've both been out of circulation for a long time. No one is going to recognize us from those pictures."

Zeke did not move. "What if they do?"

"By the time they figure out where we are and how to get here, she'll be gone."

Zeke dropped his arms to his side. "I want to keep an eye on this Troutman guy."

The hard glint in Zeke's eyes worried Carmichael. He hadn't seen that calculating look since the early days. "What exactly do you mean?"

"Just what I said. Keep an eye on him. See if he's working with the cops. See how much he knows."

"I think that's an excellent idea," Liz voiced.

Zeke turned to her. "What else can you tell me about this reporter?"

"Nothing." Liz didn't bother to hide her contempt for Zeke. "He used to work for the paper, but now he freelances. I don't know what his connection to Jenna is."

Zeke stared at Elizabeth for a moment, then turned to Carmichael. "I'm going into town right now. There's nothing critical I have to do around here."

"That's fine. Call me if you find out anything." Carmichael had a frightening premonition about Zeke's motives. "Ezekiel," he said, staring deep into his friend's eyes, "don't do anything rash. Remember, we are God's servants, and He will watch out for us if we follow His commandments."

Zeke paused, then said, "You're right, as always. Pray for me." He left the room with one last sidelong glance at Liz.

* * *

Zeke's bowels were churning as if he'd eaten a live snake. What scared him the most was that if he hadn't stopped at the Blue Hen that morning for a cup of coffee after picking up chicken feed and sat down in the exact booth where someone had left a newspaper open to exactly that page, he would never have seen the pictures and known the reporter was on to them. That kind of thing had never happened to him before. He couldn't really consider it luck.

A reporter had witnessed the kidnapping and was actively looking for the woman.

Why in the hell had he let the Reverend talk him into this mess? It had to be about the stupidest thing he'd ever done. Except the time he and Stick tried to rob a 7-Eleven store where a cop was working undercover to bust kids buying beer. That was the worst, but this was a close second. He wanted to kick himself in the ass. Zeke's instinct now was to run. Throw his stuff in a duffel bag and be on the road in five minutes.

How far could he run? With his picture in the paper, the cops would come looking for him eventually. How long would his money last? His future looked bleaker by the minute. He had to get his hand on another twenty thousand or so and maybe head for Mexico. The money was out there somewhere. That was one thing he'd learned from Carmichael. You just had to know the right people and the right buttons to push. Zeke had to find Darcie, and quickly. As he headed past the walkway leading to the women's rooms, it occurred to him Sarah might have her address. It was worth a look.

Zeke found Darcie's letter in less than two minutes. Sarah had hidden it in the back of her top dresser drawer, under a small collection of notes and pictures. He memorized the address and put the letter back, covering the pile with socks and underwear the way he found it. Under the wool and white cotton, he spotted a pair of red silk panties. *I'll be damned*, he thought, gently lifting the fabric to his face. The panties still smelled like Darcie. She must have given them to Sarah, who was far too prudish to ever wear them. Zeke slid them into his pocket and turned to leave.

"What are you doing?" Sarah's kid sister stood just inside the door, watching him suspiciously.

With a lifetime of practice, he quickly came up with a good lie. "I was getting ready to go into town, and I thought I'd bring Sarah some clean clothes to wear when she leaves the hospital."

"Oh." The kid relaxed. "You should take her pink leggings and the gray skirt with pink flowers. They're her favorites."

"Why don't you find 'em for me, and I'll stop by later and pick 'em up?"

"All right." The little girl moved toward the wooden clothes rack in the corner, then stopped and asked, "Is Sarah all right?"

She looked so worried, Zeke forced himself to smile. "Sure she is. You'll see her soon enough." He turned and hurried from the room before she could ask more questions.

His next step was to pack everything he owned into a large duffel bag. Two pairs of faded jeans, three gray, stained T-shirts, a plaid flannel shirt, a brown sweatshirt, a braided-leather wallet he'd made in prison, a small burglary kit, a razor, shaving cream, and a nine-inch hunting knife in a worn leather sheath. He left all the stuff the Sisters had made for him over the years. He didn't want anyone to think he might not be coming back. He might have to, but not if things went according to plan.

Chapter 24 >—

"Sarah, I'm Dr. Rubison, a fertility specialist. How are you feeling?" The man in the white coat looked over his glasses in a kindly way.

Sarah sat up, wishing she had on more clothes. "I'm fine." Inside, she was shaking. She knew he would ask her questions about the collapse—questions she couldn't answer. She wished she had left already. But the nurses had been so insistent. And so nice. So here she was, still in bed, still in a gown.

"Sarah, you mumbled something about 'hormone shots' when you first came in. So we did some tests and you have an elevated level of FSH. Why are you taking fertility hormones?"

Sarah's heart pounded in her ears. "I don't take drugs." She wouldn't lie, but she couldn't tell him anything that would get Reverend Carmichael in trouble either. "I'm feeling well enough to leave now."

Rubison shook his head. "You're very young to have that kind of hormone in your system. Whoever gave it to you was irresponsible and shouldn't be allowed to continue the practice. Please tell me who it was."

"I don't know what you're talking about." Sarah turned her head and stared at the wall. Maybe he would give up and go away if she refused to talk. It was her first time in a hospital, her first time away from the compound, away from her family. She felt abandoned.

"Sarah, don't turn away. I'm trying to help. Can't you tell me who your parents are? They must be worried sick."

The nurses had already asked her, and Sarah had told as much of the truth as she could. Keeping her eyes closed, she repeated her statement. "My mother's name is Tamara. She doesn't use a last name, and she doesn't have a phone or a car. She didn't give me any drugs. That's all I can say."

"Dr. Rubison?" An older nurse entered the small white room. "The woman who brought her in yesterday is in the visitor's lounge."

"Bring her in here."

Sarah was so relieved, she almost burst into tears. *Thank you, Lord*, she prayed. *I'm sorry about lying. I didn't know what else to do. Please don't let Rachel get in trouble. Please get me out of here.* Sarah kept her eyes closed, waiting to hear Rachel's voice.

"Who are you?" The doctor's voice was no longer kindly.

"My name's Rachel."

Sarah rolled back over. Rachel stood in the doorway, chewing her nails, her braid a mess.

"Rachel who?"

"I don't need a last name. The Lord is my father, and I'm married to the church."

"Are you the one who gave Sarah a fertility hormone?"

Rachel's face went pale. Sarah's fear rebounded.

"Answer the question."

"No, I didn't." Rachel practically stammered. Sarah felt sorry for her. Rachel wasn't a good liar either.

"Do you know who did?" Rubison's tone was sarcastic.

"I'd like to take her home now."

"Do you know her mother?"

"Of course. We live together."

"I want your full name and address before I release her."

"I gave it to the admitting desk when I brought her in."

"I intend to report this matter to Children's Services."

"It'll be a waste of time." Rachel straightened her shoulders. "No one has ever done anything to harm this girl. She had an allergic reaction to something she ate, and you're making too much of it. Someone on your lab staff made a serious mistake, and you should be questioning them, not me. Sarah, get dressed. We're leaving."

Sarah put her feet on the floor, ready to run with Rachel before Rubison could call anyone. She still had an IV in her left arm. "Please take this out. I'm not a child. I turned eighteen in July, and you can't make me stay here."

Rubison seemed uncertain for the first time. He shuffled his feet, eyes darting between Sarah and Rachel. "I'm calling Children's Services. Alice, don't touch that IV." Rubison bolted from the room.

Rachel stepped forward and quickly removed the short needle from Sarah's inner elbow. She bent Sarah's arm up to stop the bleeding, then turned to the nurse. "Where are her clothes?"

"I can't help you." The nurse looked like she wished she'd stayed home.

"Come on, Sarah. I have clothes in the truck."

They rushed through the hospital, down the elevator, and out the lobby, collecting stares and a few smiles. Sarah kept praying.

It was freezing outside, but she didn't care. It was such a relief to be heading away from the hospital.

Inside the truck, Sarah pulled on the wool skirt and T-shirt as Rachel lurched out into traffic. As she reached for the sweater, she caught her first sight of the city. More buildings than she had ever imagined. Many of them old-fashioned, like she'd seen in the history books. Some were bright and beautiful. Others were gray and worn, with chairs and bicycles on the front porch.

"Are you all right?" Rachel seemed to have aged overnight.

"I think so." Sarah quickly pulled on the rest of her clothes and continued to stare out the window. A distant memory circled the edge of her consciousness.

"I'm sorry, Sarah. I feel terrible. We've had a few mild reactions to the hormone shots, but never anything like this. You must be allergic."

"Why was the doctor so worried?"

Rachel's lips pressed together. "I don't know."

Sarah remembered Darcie's letter, her warning about Carmichael. "Did the Reverend give me something he shouldn't have?"

"Of course not." Rachel's expression was fierce.

The other memory came into focus. "Who was that woman in the clinic?"

Rachel snapped her head sideways to glare at Sarah. "What are you talking about?"

"The woman in the labor room. I didn't recognize her."

"It's none of your business." Rachel turned back to watch the road.

Suddenly, Sarah knew what she had to do. "I'm starving. Can we stop for food?"

"I don't have much money, but we can stop at a store and get something."

"Thanks, Rachel." Sarah leaned over and kissed her cheek. She felt guilty for what she was about to do. "Thanks for getting me out of there."

They slowed and turned left, pulling into a small parking lot in front of a convenience store. "Do you feel like coming in?" Rachel reached over and caressed her hair. "I know it's your first time in town, and you must be curious."

"I am, but my legs are pretty shaky. I'll just wait here."

"I'll be right back." Rachel smiled, and Sarah was so charged with guilt she almost chickened out. She couldn't go back to the compound just yet. She didn't feel strong enough. She had to see Darcie and discover the truth. She wasn't going back until she could resist the pressure to have another hormone injection. *What about the woman in the clinic?* a voice in her head whispered. *What if she needs help?* Sarah scoffed at the silly thought. Why would anyone in the church need help?

As Rachel moved toward the back of the store, Sarah slipped out of the vehicle. She felt wobbly at first, then started to jog up the sidewalk. It wouldn't take Rachel long to buy an apple.

Dozens of cars rushed past. Sarah remembered Darcie talking about hitchhiking. Could she do it? She had to get away from the store before Rachel came looking for her. Sarah's heart felt like it would explode. She was in Eugene. On her own! About to see her best friend in the whole world!

In a few minutes, she was offered a ride from a sweet boy named Isaac. Sarah wanted to ask a million questions about everything she saw, but she didn't want him to think she was an idiot. Darcie would take her everywhere and explain everything. The movies, the mall, roller-skating. It would be the greatest adventure. Sarah was almost glad for the illness that had brought her to the hospital. A blessing in disguise, as her mother would say.

Guilt brought her spirits down for a moment. Tamara would be worried, and Delilah would miss her terribly. She would write them a letter, first thing, Sarah decided. Once they knew she was all right, they would be happy for her.

She gave Isaac Darcie's address, and he took her to a big brown building with different-colored doors. The apartments were surrounded by small old houses that seemed uncared for. Sarah remembered Darcie's room was number six, so she climbed the stairs. The door was bright orange. Sarah considered that a good sign, since orange was her favorite color. She knocked loudly.

"Who is it?" Darcie sounded grumpy and far away.

"You'll never guess." Sarah was so excited, she laughed out loud.

"Sarah?" Darcie opened the door and they stared at each other. Darcie's belly was enormous!

"You said you were pregnant, but—" Sarah stared, not knowing what to say.

"God, it's good to see you." Darcie threw her arms around Sarah as best she could. In a moment they were both fighting back tears and grinning wildly.

"Come in, come in. It's freezing out there." Darcie tugged on her arm. "How did you get here?"

"I hitchhiked."

"No!"

Sarah burst out laughing as Darcie's mouth fell open. "It's true, but only from Franklin Boulevard. Before that, it's a long story."

"Sit down and tell me, girl. I can tell by the look on your face that this is gonna be good."

Chapter 25

Eric snatched up the phone as it was ringing. "Yes?"

"It's Jackson. They're expecting you at the prison this afternoon."

"This afternoon?" It was too good to be true.

"That's what I said."

"You're the best, Jackson. I owe you. You can name the favor. Anything."

His friend laughed. "This will be fun. I'll let you know."

"Thanks, pal. I'm on my way."

Eric looked around for his keys. He was ready, even though he hadn't expected to get the visitation approved until Monday at the earliest. Apparently Jackson had more clout with the women's correctional director than Eric realized. He'd have to ask him about that later.

The prison visitors' room was pale-green, cold, and quiet. Eric felt slightly queasy, as he had since he'd heard the doors lock behind him. The hour drive north had been unpleasant—hard rain the whole way and plenty of traffic. Twice he'd almost turned around with the sure knowledge that this trip would be a waste of time. Sitting and waiting for Buster's ex-girlfriend to be brought in hadn't relieved his doubt. What would he be doing if not this? Pacing his living room, thinking about Jenna. Worrying about all the possible things that could have happened to her. Wondering if she would care about him if he did find her. She hadn't done or said one single thing to indicate she had any real feelings for him. Other than that first night together, which could have been only a moment of neediness.

"Who the hell are you?"

The woman who suddenly appeared on the other side of the plexiglas window twisted her thin, sand-colored hair around her middle finger. The finger was a random choice, Eric decided. Ellen/Rose, even at first glance, didn't seem capable of subtlety. She was gaunt, with acne scars and jumpy eyes. Eric suspected she still had a drug problem, but even cleaned up, her brain would never be the same. The whole trip had been a gamble, and now his flicker of hope died.

"Hello, Rose. I'm Eric. I'm a friend of Buster's."

"Good for you." She tried to stare at him, but her eyes wouldn't hold still.

"Will you sit down and talk to me for a minute?" Eric didn't know why he was even trying. The female guard had not left the room. She apparently didn't expect Rose to stay long.

"Who told you I was here?"

"Buster. By the way, he said to say 'Hi.'"

"Tell him I said to fuck off. Tell him he owes me two hundred dollars, and just because I'm in here doesn't mean he can stiff me for it." She spit on the floor. "The shithead."

Eric spoke gently. This woman had not had a good life, and she had no reason to help him. "I'll remind him when I see him. I hope you won't hold it against me though."

"Why not? Who the hell are you anyway? You don't look like one of Buster's friends."

"I'm a freelance reporter. Buster has helped me out in the past by providing me with information."

"He was your snitch, you mean." Rose crossed her arms and continued to stand.

Eric tried a new tactic. "A friend of mine has disappeared. A woman. You might be able to help me find her."

She rolled her eyes. "How could I possibly know anything about it?"

"Please, sit down."

Rose plopped into the tan plastic chair. "Cut the crap and tell me what you want."

Eric pulled his copies of the sketches out of a large envelope and held them up to the glass. "I want to know if you recognize either of these men." The guard nodded and stepped back out of the room.

"Nope." Rose bit what was left of her nails.

Eric continued to hold up the pictures. "Look again. Buster says you might have sold drugs to one of these guys."

"Yeah, right." Rose snorted. "Buster thinks he can remember some guy I sold coke to years ago, but he can't remember that he owes me two hundred dollars."

Eric heard the acknowledgment, but decided not to push.

"Why did Buster really send you to me?" Her voice had an edge of panic.

"He didn't, not really." Eric had to tread gently here. "I went looking for him, to see if—"

"He's working for Charlie now, isn't he? He sent you here to find out where I stashed the—" Rose clamped her hand over her mouth and jumped up. "You bastard. I almost told you." She moved to the door and pounded. "Guard! I'm ready!"

"Hey, wait." Eric tried not to shout. She was obviously paranoid, and yelling at her would only make her run. He could feel it slipping away, his one lead after all this time.

"Hey, Rose, come back, please. I don't even know Charlie." Eric hated what he was about to do. "I'll put twenty dollars on your books if you'll come sit back down."

Rose stopped pounding. Eric pulled out his wallet and showed her a twenty. The door opened. Rose looked at the guard, then glanced back at the twenty.

"Let's move." The guard's voice boomed through the open door and filled the tiny room.

Rose stepped back from the door. "Give me another minute."

When she sat down, Eric said, "Please look at the pictures again. A woman's life is at stake."

"Sure it is." Rose leaned forward, pretending to scrutinize the pictures. She focused on the man with the ponytail. "This guy looks kinda like someone who used to buy cocaine from me. But maybe not." She shook her head. "His face is too full. The hair's wrong too."

"What's his name?"

"Shit." Rose leaned back, angry again. "Like I'm supposed to remember. Guys like this never tell you their real name."

Eric could feel his blood pressure building. Why couldn't she just tell him? Was she holding out for more money? "Can you remember anything about this man?" he pressed.

"It's probably not even him." Her eyes were jumpy and Eric knew she was lying.

"I'll put down another ten if you tell me something that'll help me find this guy." Eric picked up his wallet to show her he had the cash to follow through.

"Make it twenty."

"Fine." Eric pulled out two tens, leaving himself with six bucks. He hoped he didn't need any cash on the way home. Rose made a funny little humming sound.

"Tell me."

"I think he was a doctor who delivered babies."

"What makes you think that?"

She scrunched up her face, humming a little louder. "I think he said something about it once when he saw my pregnant sister."

"Any idea where he worked?"

She laughed and slapped her leg. "That's a good one. I never asked for his résumé."

"Is that it?"

Rose pushed out of her chair. "Yep."

"Thanks very much for your help."

She was already pounding the door and calling the guard. Rose didn't look back. Eric didn't blame her. He felt like running from the room himself. It had been an unpleasant half hour. He had thought he was done with this kind of thing.

Eric put the picture of the man with the ponytail on the seat next to him during the drive home. The fact that he might be a cocaine-buying doctor seemed oddly familiar, in the way his face seemed familiar from the beginning. Eric searched his mind and came up blank. He knew where to look though. The files at the newspaper had a record of every significant thing that had happened in Eugene in the last hundred years. He suspected the doctor had once made the news.

After spending his six bucks on burgers, Eric drove out to the newspaper. He went straight to the second floor in search of Pikerton. His friend met him in the hallway, smelling like a burning cigarette.

"Hey, Eric. Surprised to still see me here?"

"No. Why?"

"When we ran that missing-persons story, I promised Hoogstad an exciting follow-up. I haven't got one yet, and they're getting ready to do another round of layoffs."

"You will. Listen to this." Eric grabbed Joe and propelled him toward the corner of the big open room.

"Where are we going?"

"To look at old files."

Joe stopped. "How long is this going to take?"

"I don't know, but I think one of our mystery men might be a doctor who was in the news a long time ago."

"I didn't recognize either of them, and I've been around forever."

"He's changed. Come on, this is your follow-up story."

Joe muttered something, then followed him.

Assuming the story was at least five years old, they started in 2003 and worked back. The last ten years were all archived on CDs in the form of PDFs. Before that, it was old-fashioned microfiche. After an hour, Eric developed a headache from staring at low-resolution images on a fourteen-inch monitor. Joe offered to go find some aspirin.

Eric continued to scroll, reading only the headlines, then the first paragraph of any story related to doctors, hospitals, or medical news of any kind. The *Willamette News* was a fairly small paper, and the editions rolled by quickly. There were lots of reports from the AP about health-related research. Vitamin A reduced cancer rates. Too much vitamin A caused fetal damage. After a while he learned to skip all the national stuff.

Joe returned with two cups of coffee, aspirin, and a new aura of smoke. "Any luck?"

"Not yet."

They worked in silence for another hour with only an occasional "Remember when…?"

They had just started on the microfiche when Joe said, "Hey, come look at this." Eric was relieved to get out of the chair.

The archived headline read, "Charges Against Doctor Dropped." It was dated March 29, 1998. Eric's queasy stomach rose up in protest as he read the story:

> *After testimony from Dr. Elizabeth Harrington, who claimed Dr. David Carmichael was sober when he left her house shortly before a fatal accident that claimed his wife and child, District Attorney Darin Harcloud dropped all charges against Carmichael.*
>
> *Last Wednesday Anne Carmichael, 34, and David Carmichael Jr., 6, were found dead at the scene after the car they were riding in plunged over an embankment into a tree. A nearby resident discovered the wreck in the early morning and notified authorities. Evidence at the scene indicated Anne Carmichael may not have been driving when the car hit the tree. Police contacted Dr. David Carmichael at his home, not far from the accident, where he was found sleeping, covered with minor cuts and bruises.*
>
> *Carmichael claimed to remember nothing of the accident and refused to submit to a blood-alcohol test. The police had charged Carmichael with reckless endangerment, but after Harrington's testimony, the grand jury failed to press charges. Carmichael was released in time to attend his wife's and son's funeral, held yesterday afternoon.*

Chapter 26

Jenna had been awake for hours, her longest period of consciousness since waking up in the gray room. Her thinking was still not clear—she had to work to stay focused—but the drug in the IV was losing its grip on her mind. The longer she was coherent, the more frightened she became. Someone had hit her in the face. She couldn't remember it clearly, but she could feel the heat of the bruise on her left cheek. Little chunks of conversation kept popping into her memory...*what this was all about before you die... your sister...a cold bitch...take one of your eggs.*

Who had said these things? And why? She didn't have a sister. Jenna believed the part about dying though. If she didn't come up with another escape plan soon, she would die in this room. She was more certain of that than anything else, including who she was. Nothing about her life seemed real. Nobody out there cared about her. Why else hadn't she been rescued by now? Her despair only thrived on the surface though. Deep down, she wanted to live. There had to be a way.

In a sudden burst of inspiration, Jenna realized there was one hope of escape. The idea was simple, and she was frustrated with herself for not thinking of it before. It would take every bit of self-discipline she had to smile at her captors, to lie and tell them what they wanted to hear, but she had to try. Especially now that she'd developed a little tolerance to the sedative. Her body felt better too. Her heart had stopped racing, and she hadn't had a hot flash since waking. Why was that? Were they giving her less sedative than before? What about the injections? Jenna couldn't remember.

No, wait. A nurse had been giving her injections, but not lately. Had something happened to the nurse? The plan wouldn't work without her. She could try it on the preacher/doctor, but—

"Feeling better, Jenna?" He was suddenly there.

Startled, Jenna's pulse raced. How had he slipped in unnoticed? Had she drifted off and not known it? Hatred for him burned through the fog of the sedative. But she remembered that the plan was to be nice, so she forced herself to give him a small smile. "Actually, I am."

"Good." He smiled back and laid a cool hand on Jenna's forehead. "You didn't ask who I am. You remember me, don't you?"

His tone frightened her. She did recognize him, but decided to conceal it. "Not really." It felt safer to pretend not to remember anything. "Are you a doctor?"

"Yes, and a man of God. Do you remember why you're here?"

Jenna shook her head. The words "borrow some tissue" floated into her brain. She was too afraid to ask what they meant. Her stomach growled, and she was aware of a wonderful aroma. "What did you bring me?"

"Chicken and dumplings. Are you ready to eat?"

"Yes." She was salivating.

"First we have business to take care of."

He did something with the IV bag, then took her pulse and blood pressure. Jenna hated his touch, his cool bony fingers, the way he acted as if he owned her. She especially hated the way he exposed her buttock before giving her an injection. He seemed to be taking his time, touching her as much as possible. Jenna's jaw ached from grinding her teeth, but she was helpless to resist. Complaining was not in the plan today. She kept silent and thought about Eric, his warm hands and gentle touch.

The preacher/doctor eased her hip down to the mattress, then lowered himself quietly onto a chair next to the bed. The same thin, cool fingers that had stroked her butt gently held the spoon to Jenna's lips.

She was too hungry to spit the food back at him. She barely paused to chew.

After wolfing down the first few bites, Jenna became aware of him watching her. For the first time, she noticed his hair, which was gray at the temples, and the skin on his forehead, which was pale and unwrinkled. He had a long, narrow nose and a small mouth with dark, almost red, lips. He wasn't wearing a surgical mask this time.

Jenna became aware of the coolness of the room, the silkiness of her nightgown, the deep silence beyond the walls. Abruptly, she lost her appetite and turned away.

"Come on, Jenna. You need to eat." His voice was gentle, coaxing.

Had she not hated him, he would have been hard to resist. "I'm full, really."

Then it came back to her. The plan. Her only hope of getting out of this crazy place. She had thought it would work best with the nurse, but the way the preacher/doctor was looking at her, she decided to try it now. Jenna forced herself to look him in the eyes. "Doctor?"

Beaming smile. "Yes, Jenna?"

"I know I'm going to die here, and I want to make peace with God. Will you help me?"

He looked stricken. "Why do you say that? I promise you, with God as my witness, you're not going to die."

"Why won't you tell me why I'm here?"

"It's for your own protection. The less you know, the better."

Jenna struggled to put together the right words, to let go of her anger. "I still want to make peace with God. I'm scared all the time. And lonely. I want what you and Rachel have. I want to feel loved and secure."

His eyes wavered, undecided. Then he responded, choosing his words carefully. "God does love you, regardless of what you believe or what you do."

"Then why do I feel abandoned?" Jenna let go of her pride and let her anguish come through. "Why do I feel so afraid?"

"You must still have doubts." His eyes searched hers intently, as if he were looking into her soul. "Do you have doubts about God, Jenna?"

She tried to swallow, but her throat was dry. "Sometimes." Jenna blinked back real tears. "Why would He let this happen to me if He really loved me?"

The preacher/doctor smiled warmly, obviously partial to the question. "It's all part of His plan. He brought us together for a reason. I think He intends for you to help me heal an old wound and for me to help you find faith."

She bit back the urge to mock him. He was so arrogant, so twisted. Jenna closed her eyes to hide her contempt. She moved her lips and pretended to pray.

"Have you ever accepted Christ as your savior?" He gently stroked her hand. Jenna ground her teeth together and reminded herself she would do almost anything to be released from the bed. To be free of the needle, even for a few hours.

"When I was eight or nine, I went to a Baptist church with a friend." The memory came back with a vividness that surprised her. "The preacher scared me so badly with the threat of burning in hell that when he called the sinners to come down and be saved, I went."

He chuckled. "A Baptist preacher first put the fear of God in my heart as well."

"Do you believe in hell?" Jenna didn't believe in hell any more than in heaven, but she wanted to know what he believed. Why he thought he could get away with what he was doing to her.

"I believe that life without faith and eternity without God are hell." His voice was hypnotizing. She could picture him in front of a congregation, waving his arms and making the women swoon.

"I want to see the light when I die," Jenna ad-libbed. "The beautiful light that people with near-death experiences talk about."

"You're not going to die." He seemed flustered by her talk about death.

"I want to be ready. Being here has made me realize that my life is meaningless. I have no family, few friends. I work all the time, but I don't really enjoy my job. I've always wanted a child but—" Jenna couldn't finish the thought. Another chunk of remembered conversation bobbed to the surface. Something about her child making it out even if she didn't.

"You want to have a child?" The doctor's eyes danced.

Jenna wanted to bite her own tongue. Did this freak plan to impregnate her? The way he was looking at her was creepy. She had to distract him. "What I really want is a family. You know, a group of people to bond with and come home to. Or a church, like you have here. I want to belong."

"You're very talkative today. Very alert." His expression changed, making her pulse quicken.

"I'm lonely and frightened. Will you pray with me?" Jenna cursed herself for talking too much. Letting him know the drug was losing its effect was not a good idea.

"Of course. Would you like to pray out loud?"

"Will you go first?"

"Of course." He closed his eyes. "Dear Lord, thank you for the many answered prayers, for keeping Jenna safe and healthy while in my care. Today my prayer for her is special. Today I ask you to fill her heart with love and joy. Give her the peace of mind that comes with faith in your eternal blessing. In Jesus' name, I pray. Amen."

Jenna had drifted off for a moment. She'd known since he fiddled with her IV that she would begin to float, then eventually be unconscious for a while. She struggled to stay with the plan. She began to pray, her words slurring slightly. "Dear God, please take away my doubts and give me peace of mind. I want you in my heart and soul." It was the best she could do. "Amen."

If the drug hadn't already started to kick in, the shock of his lips against hers would have made her shriek. In her detached state of mind, Jenna simply opened her eyes and stared incredulously.

The crazy preacher/doctor continued to kiss her, pressing his tongue between her lips. Jenna tried to twist her face away, but he grabbed her head with both hands and held her while he probed the inside of her mouth with his tongue. His chest rubbed against her breasts.

Suddenly he jerked back. Jenna heard Rachel's voice come into the room. God bless the little nurse.

"Reverend, I have to speak with you right away." Rachel sounded frightened.

"I'm with a patient now. Can't it wait a few minutes?" His voice was icy, breathless.

The darkness circled Jenna's consciousness. Just before she drifted off she heard the nurse say, "It's about Sarah."

Chapter 27 >—

Once he found Darcie's apartment, Zeke drove around the block and parked in an alley across the street. He wanted to make sure Darcie still lived at the address, and to see if anyone else, like a boyfriend, was around. After he found out a few facts, Zeke planned to move on to the critical stuff, like taking care of Troutman and lining up a buyer for the baby.

Having spent almost half his life in prison, Zeke had learned to sit patiently with his own thoughts without losing awareness of his surroundings. Even though he'd never actually lived in Eugene, he was familiar with the area. He'd been coming here once a month or so to play video poker and pick up prostitutes. He had managed to stay sober during those trips. Alcohol was trouble and would land him back in prison quicker than anything. He'd learned that lesson the hard way and wasn't going down that road again.

He watched the people on the street, knowing their stories by the way they dressed. The men bundled in layers, wearing everything they owned on their backs, homeless because of their weaknesses. The women looked worn and ratty even in their sexiest clothes. They were all weak, slaves to their need for alcohol, drugs, money, and/or attention. He understood these people, felt at home here. After a while, he'd go have a talk with the apartment manager to see if—

The door to apartment number six opened, and Darcie stepped out onto the balcony looking like she'd swallowed a pumpkin. Sarah waltzed out behind her, smiling like an excited schoolgirl. Zeke was so startled he dropped his cigarette and had to fetch it before it burned his thigh. *What the hell?* Sarah was supposed to be in the hospital or on her way back to the compound with Rachel. Were the two of them pulling a fast one on the Reverend? What a twist. Now that he had mentally separated himself from the church, Zeke found the situation amusing. Too bad he wouldn't be able to use this information to his advantage, but he had more important things to do.

He followed the girls to a nearby Taco Bell. Daylight was starting to fade, and Zeke buttoned his jacket against the chill as he sat in the truck. He was anxious to take care of business. The situation with the reporter made him very uncomfortable.

Zeke had taken a lot of money that didn't belong to him and had threatened people with guns to get what he wanted. But other than slapping a smart-mouthed woman or defending himself in a bar fight, he'd never seriously hurt anyone. Now he was thinking about killing two people. Maybe there was a way to slow down the reporter or send him in another direction.

Sometimes he still thought he should just run for it. To forget Darcie's baby and the extra money and get the hell out of town. Get as far away from Carmichael and the kidnapping as he could. Deep down, Zeke knew better. If anyone ever connected ex-con George Grafton with the picture in the paper, he was fucked.

Sooner or later the law would find him. In the meantime, he would be looking over his shoulder every step of the way.

He slammed his fist against the dashboard. A teenager walking by jumped at the sudden sound. Zeke turned his head, not wanting his face to be seen. Goddamn Carmichael for getting him involved in a stupid bullshit kidnapping. He should have refused, cleaned out his bank account, and walked away. He hadn't, and Zeke knew it was more than the promise of big money. He'd gotten juiced up just hearing Carmichael talk about the snatch. After years of living in the church, with every day the same as the next, the idea of doing a job had excited him.

If only the reporter hadn't been there that day. What a rotten break. Zeke shook his head. He'd worked hard and saved his money for years; he deserved the boat and the retirement. He had to find out what the reporter knew and put a stop to his little investigation before the cops got involved.

Zeke put the truck in gear and headed west across town, hoping to find the address while he still had some daylight.

The house was in an older subdivision off Polk Street at the end of a short cul-de-sac. The location wasn't bad, but Zeke was disturbed that it was a duplex. At first drive-by, nobody appeared to be home on either side, but the risk would be double just the same. He parked next to a baseball field at a nearby school and waited for darkness.

It was his first B&E in twenty years, and Zeke was nervous. He trotted in a circular pattern to the street behind the intended address. He counted houses until he was sure Troutman's duplex was directly behind the green house with the white trim. By his estimation, the two properties should share a back fence. The green house had lights on everywhere. Zeke could see two teenagers sitting in the living room watching TV and an older woman washing dishes in the kitchen facing the backyard. The other houses on the short street seemed quiet; no one was out and about.

Before he could change his mind, Zeke moved quickly along the side fence, hopping over a short gate that separated the front and back yards. He headed straight for the back corner, not letting himself look to see if any kids or dogs were present. No barks, no shouts. The worst was over. With a surge of confidence, he pulled himself up and over the six-foot wooden back fence and dropped into the yard on the other side.

He went to his knees for a second, sucking in air and waiting for his heart to settle down. Zeke vowed this would be the last time. He was too old for this shit.

After a quick look around the perimeter of the house, he discovered getting in would be a piece of cake. The bathroom window wasn't even locked. All he had to do was slip out the screen and push the glass open. Hauling himself up and through the window, which was five feet off the ground and only eighteen inches wide, made him grunt and sweat. He remembered why he'd quit doing houses and started robbing stores. B&E was too much work, especially with all the new alarm systems people had. Troutman apparently didn't own much of value, because no alarm had sounded. This wasn't exactly an upscale neighborhood. Nicer than any place he'd ever lived, but not somewhere Zeke would come to steal valuable jewelry.

Using a small penlight, Zeke did a routine search of the bedroom first. The most important thing he established was that Troutman didn't own a gun. Or at least he didn't keep it in the bedroom as most people did. Zeke moved into an adjacent office and turned on a small desk lamp.

Books and papers and files were everywhere. A noisy ticking clock on the wall made Zeke feel rushed. He grabbed a handful of papers from a chair and tore through them. A bunch of nonsense about men and babies. Zeke threw the papers down and moved to the desk. Sitting right on top were the composite drawings. Zeke picked up his likeness, held it under the lamp, and stared. It wasn't that good. If he let his beard grow in, no one would ever match him to the picture. The Reverend's likeness was startling. If they caught Carmichael, it would be over for Zeke too. Even if the man could keep his mouth shut, his girlfriend wouldn't. The bitter taste of panic filled his mouth. Had the cops seen these pictures? Had Troutman made a statement that would hold up in court?

Underneath the pictures, Zeke found an open notebook with short daily entries. He read the first few.

Monday: talked to Det. Jackson yesterday and again today. He thinks I'm overreacting. Filed a missing-persons report while I was at the police dept. All I know is Jenna got into a gray van with two men Saturday and hasn't been seen since. This is strange, even for my dates.

Wed: talked with Katrice (Jenna's best friend) at Geronimo's and she says Jenna has taken off before without saying anything. Still convinced something is wrong.

Thurs: had police composites done and took them to Joe at the News. He'll do a story about the disappearance, along with pics. Who knows what will come of it?

Fri: only a few freaks called about the pics, and I got myself thrown out of the hospital for good. Very depressed.

Relieved, Zeke put the notepad down. So Troutman was getting nowhere, and no one had identified his picture. That was good news. Maybe the reporter just needed a little accident, something to keep him off the streets until Zeke finished his business with Darcie and moved on.

Zeke decided it would be best to do the job somewhere else, make it look random, rather than personal. It occurred to him he had no idea what Troutman looked like. He needed to find a picture of the guy. Zeke headed across the hall into the living area. Troutman's house was clean, for a guy, but musty smelling, as if no one had been home for a while. The heavy front drapes were closed, so Zeke turned on a small table lamp and began to search.

As he rummaged through a bookcase looking for a photo album, the phone rang. Annoyed, Zeke sat back on the floor and waited for it to stop. After the fourth ring, an answering machine clicked on. "This is Eric Troutman. You know what to do."

After a beep, the caller left an exasperated message. "It's Jackson. Again. Where the hell have you been? Same message as before." The phone clicked, then Zeke heard the tape squeal forward.

Jackson. He'd just read the name in Troutman's journal. He was a cop.

Zeke hurried to the machine, which was on a low table next to an easy chair. Answering machines were still new to Zeke. He'd only been out in the world for a few months between prison and the compound and had not had many opportunities to keep up with technology. This gadget couldn't be too complicated. He needed to hear what the cop had to say. After a quick look at the black box, he pushed the button next to the blinking red light.

He heard a soft click, then the cop's voice filled the room. He had an undercurrent of excitement. "Jackson here. I think we've caught a break in the case. A parole officer in Portland saw the composites in the paper and thinks the older guy might be an ex-con. You need to come in and look at mug shots before we can move on this. I'll be at my desk all afternoon and again tomorrow morning for a few hours. Call me when you get in."

Zeke's hands clenched into tight fists. He hadn't seen his parole officer in six years, but she obviously hadn't forgotten him. Fuck and doublefuck. The one and only time he'd stepped out of line, and he was busted. Goddamn bad luck had followed him around his whole life.

He wasn't going down without a fight. If Troutman wasn't around to ID his picture or testify in court, they had nothing on him. The reporter had to go.

Zeke returned to the bookcase, grabbed a high school yearbook, and quickly scanned the pages until he found Troutman's name under a picture. Blond, beefy guy with a square face, but older now.

The rumble of an engine filled the driveway in front of the house. Zeke dropped to the floor, a burglar's instinct. His chest tightened in an agonizing squeeze. Ignoring the little shooting pains down his left arm, he crawled to the space behind where the front door would open. A car door slammed, blasting the silence of the neighborhood. Zeke listened for footsteps and heard little clicking sounds instead. High heels.

A knock at the door, followed by a woman's voice. "Eric, it's Kori. I need to talk to you."

Zeke's body uncoiled. A girlfriend or ex-girlfriend. It didn't matter as long as she didn't have a key.

The pounding got louder. "Eric, I know you're in there." Long pause. "Carl hit me again, and I need to talk to someone."

Zeke thought Carl had the right idea. This woman was a whiny pain in the ass. He hoped she would go away before he had to hurt her.

"Eric!" She was crying now, loud enough to make a spectacle of herself. Loud enough for neighbors to peek out their front windows and see what was going on over at Troutman's.

Stupid cunt. Stupid bitch. Zeke wanted to choke the noisy life out of her. He ground his teeth together to keep from cursing out loud.

After a few moments, the sobbing sounds began to move away. Zeke relaxed his grip on the knife. It seemed like an eternity before the engine started and the car backed out.

His nerves almost at a breaking point, Zeke moved from his position behind the door to check out the kitchen for a beer. *Just one beer*, he thought, *to settle his indigestion and give him a little courage.* There was nothing in the fridge but a loaf of bread and a quart of milk. Pissed and relieved at the same time, Zeke quickly closed the door and hurried from the kitchen, resisting the urge to search the cupboards for a bottle of real alcohol.

Too keyed up to sit and wait, Zeke began to explore the house. He wanted to know exactly where every corner and piece of furniture was located. The yearbook picture didn't tell him how big the guy was or how much of a fight to expect. The element of surprise would be on his side, but Zeke had never stuck a knife in someone with the intent to kill. The thought made him a little queasy.

He had no choice. He couldn't let the reporter look at his mug shot and confirm his part in the kidnapping. Once they put out a warrant, his freedom was tainted. If they caught him, it was over. He'd sooner put a gun to his own head than go back inside. In fact, Zeke decided, he needed to buy a gun. That way, if he ever got picked up, he could shoot at the cops and trigger his own death. It didn't have to get to that point. Not while he had this other plan. It was him or Troutman. One of them had to die.

Zeke walked up the hallway, counting steps, knife in hand. He could smell the stink of his own fear, but the pain in his left side had finally dulled. He wished like hell he could do the job somewhere else, but he was already in the house. Might as well wait for Troutman to come home and get it over with. Steal enough stuff to make it look like a robbery.

Zeke promised himself, with God as his witness, he would get back on the straight and narrow. After this was over, he would never hurt anyone again. Killing the reporter and his girlfriend was the worst kind of sin, but at least they'd be together. Stealing Darcie's baby was different. He would be doing the kid a favor by giving it to a rich couple instead of leaving it to a life of poverty and misery with Darcie. Zeke figured it would be an act of atonement and a good way to start his new life.

Chapter 28 ⟩——

Sarah was nervous about being back at the hospital. She was afraid someone would recognize her from that morning and want to ask her more questions about the hormone. She couldn't abandon Darcie, who, after a few hours of labor, had been wheeled into surgery for an emergency C-section. The nurses had tried to keep Sarah out of the labor room, but she had insisted on being Darcie's coach. Sarah had been with her mother during Delilah's birth and had sat with several other Sisters during the first phase of labor.

She had not been prepared for Darcie's ordeal, which had gone bad from the beginning. So much screaming. So much blood. Sarah had kept wishing, even though she knew it was ridiculous, that Reverend Carmichael would rush in and take over, making everything turn out right. Darcie and her baby were still in the operating room, and all Sarah could do was sit and pray, hoping nobody would recognize her.

After what seemed like an eternity, a tired-looking nurse came by and told Sarah that Darcie and her baby girl would both be fine, but neither was ready for visitors. Sarah cried with relief. Exhausted, she laid down on a couch in the waiting room and closed her eyes.

For a moment, Sarah was overwhelmed with homesickness. She longed for the familiarity of the compound, the warmth of her mother and sister. She told herself she would be back there soon enough. After visiting with Darcie in the morning, she would head home. She wanted to check on the strange woman in the clinic and confront Carmichael with her doubts.

Chapter 29 >—

Carmichael watched Jenna through the glass. She seemed restless for someone who had just made her peace with God. Her sudden religious conversion troubled him. It was too convenient. Yet it was typical of a nonbeliever to have a change of heart when they feared their days on earth were about to end.

What if her new faith was real? The thought excited him. She might come to worship God as he did. Perhaps even join the church. The idea of seeing Jenna, day after day, gave him great pleasure. Given enough time, he could tame her. He could make her love and admire him the way other women did. With Jenna, everything would be new and fresh. No ugly past or resentments between them. Things had changed between him and Liz. Money had become an issue with her, and she no longer cherished him the way she had in the beginning.

Liz had witnessed his alcohol and drug abuse and knew what he'd done to his family because of it. She'd been pleased with his rehabilitation but resented his faith. He couldn't talk to her about God without seeing that look in her eye. Elizabeth also disapproved of the untested fertility drugs he gave his followers, especially the young girls. As much as he hated to admit it, she was probably right on that subject. The news of Sarah's collapse had been upsetting enough, but her disappearance had him scared. He loved Sarah dearly and hated the thought of losing her from the family. The idea of her talking to someone in authority about his unusual medical practice bothered him even more. He couldn't do anything about either possibility right now. He had too many other critical situations to worry about, thanks to Liz and her need to have a genetically related child.

A small smile broke through his worries. Jenna had said she wanted to have a baby. It was sweetly ironic. He felt better now about taking her eggs to create a new life. What disturbed him was the little fantasy he'd just dreamed up about being the father. He'd been adamantly opposed to ever becoming a father again, since the night he'd seen his beloved son crushed under the car that he had wrecked in a cocaine-and-alcohol stupor. He didn't deserve to have a family. Yet suddenly, he wanted one. He wanted Jenna. He wanted their child.

Carmichael shook his head and forced himself to turn away from the window. Foolishness, he chided himself. Utter foolishness. Jenna would never join the church, never share him with another woman, never willingly let Elizabeth raise her child. She was too independent. He'd learned that much about her. Getting attached to her was extremely dangerous. He could lose everything if she ever identified him. The Versed seemed to be working, but more extreme measures might need to be taken.

* * *

Jenna's hopes wavered. The crazy preacher/doctor was too smart, too unpredictable for her plan to work on him. He'd gone along with her religious talk but hadn't really bought it, she could tell. He had sure kissed her though. What if Rachel hadn't come in when she did? Would he have molested her? More important, would he be back for more? Jenna wondered where the nurse had been, why she hadn't seen her lately. Rachel was her only hope of escape. Rachel was vulnerable and easily manipulated. If only she could get another chance with her.

To keep her mind from drifting aimlessly and sabotaging her efforts to plan her escape, Jenna had been making it work. She started simply by reciting the alphabet over and over, then moved on to multiplication tables and the names of state capitals. The more she worked her brain, the longer she could concentrate and remain conscious. Eventually she started listing all the teachers she'd ever had in school, kids she'd grown up with, jobs she'd had, and people she'd worked with. Sometimes she drifted off in the middle of a list and had to fight her way back, but it happened less and less frequently. Jenna felt more alert, more in control than she had since waking up in the gray room.

When her heart rate started to escalate again, Jenna tried to control her anxiety by contracting and relaxing her muscles one at a time. She started with her toes and worked up. When she spread and relaxed her fingers after making a fist, her left hand brushed lightly against something sharp. Groping along the edge of the mattress with outstretched fingers, Jenna could feel the outline of a hypodermic needle. Instinctively, she reached for it, thinking she could use it as a weapon. But her wrists were firmly secured and she couldn't get a finger around the needle to pull it into her hand.

Groaning with frustration, Jenna tried again and again until her hand ached with the effort. As soon as she gave up, the obvious solution popped into her head: get closer to the needle. Using her buttocks, Jenna scooted along the mattress a millimeter at a time to the left. In a few minutes, she had the needle firmly in her hand.

The door opened and the nurse walked in. Panicked, Jenna pushed the needle under the mattress, but not too far.

"Hello." Rachel's voice was subdued. As she approached the bed, Jenna was surprised by the nurse's appearance. She looked as if she hadn't slept for days, and her expression was pinched, as if she'd been crying.

"What's wrong?" The question was automatic. Even though Jenna had felt hostile to Rachel in the beginning, she had come to realize the nurse, in her own way, was also a victim of the crazy preacher/doctor.

Rachel tried to smile. "Do I look that bad?"

"No, but I can tell you're upset about something."

"Thanks for asking, but I really can't talk about it." The nurse gripped Jenna's left wrist and began to check her pulse.

Fearful that Rachel would see the needle, Jenna tried to distract her. "I'll pray with you if you like."

Startled, the nurse let go. "Do you mean that?"

"Yes. I've made peace with God and I'm prepared to die."

"You're not going to die!"

Her vehemence startled Jenna. Still desperate to know what they had planned for her, she pressed for answers. "How do you know? Look at me. My heart is racing, I'm losing weight, and my muscles are deteriorating. How long can I last? Why am I here? I have a right to know."

Rachel's expression telegraphed her struggle.

Lowering her voice, Jenna begged, "Please tell me. I won't tell him that you told me. I promise."

Rachel pushed a messy clump of dark hair from her face, then glanced over at the window. Abruptly she seemed to make up her mind. The nurse leaned in close. "Your family was afraid you would overdose on heroin, so they asked us to keep you here and take care of you until you were over the addiction. They must love you very much."

"What are you talking about?" Jenna was bewildered.

"You don't have to pretend with me." Rachel sounded hurt. "I told you the truth, and I think you should be honest too."

"But it's not the truth." Jenna didn't know whether to laugh or cry. The whole nightmare was a case of mistaken identity. "You people have the wrong woman. I am not a heroin addict. Look at me. I'm too chunky to be a drug addict, or at least I was until I got here. I don't have any track marks. Do a blood test if you don't believe me."

Rachel looked puzzled. "The Reverend wouldn't make a mistake like that."

"Somebody did."

The women stared at each other, both slowly coming to realize Rachel had been lied to. Finally Jenna said, "Whatever his reasons are, I know it's not your fault, and I'm sure God will forgive you. I've come to care about you, Rachel. I envy your faith."

Rachel smiled brightly. "You can have faith too. Just ask God to come into your heart and He will." Her exuberance quickly turned to embarrassment. "Considering your circumstances, it must be hard for you even to have faith in people, let alone God. But despite the way it seems, I know the Reverend means well. You'll be fine soon. I promise."

"I wish I could believe that." Jenna closed her eyes for effect.

"It's only a matter of time." Rachel patted her hand. "Would you like to pray now?"

"I'd like to get up and walk around before I'm too weak to stand."

Rachel shook her head. "I can't let you do that."

"Why not? I'm not going anywhere. Tie my hands if you don't trust me."

"Please don't ask me. I can't."

"You expect me to have faith that you're not going to let me die, but you can't even show me a simple act of human decency."

Rachel looked crushed. Jenna didn't let up. "Please, Rachel. You've got to realize how maddening it is lying here all the time. I just want to walk around for a few minutes, maybe see the rest of the church."

Rachel's jaw worked back and forth. She glanced at the window. "I can't let you out of this room."

"That's fine." Jenna's heart surged with joy. It was difficult to sound calm. "I just want to exercise my legs for a minute."

"All right, but only for a minute. And I will have to tie your hands together. I'll be right back."

As soon as Rachel stepped out through the door, Jenna worked the hypodermic needle out from under the mattress. She could barely conceal it in her hand. What if Rachel saw it? Her pulse pounded. She was about to escape. Could she stab Rachel with the needle to gain an advantage? Jenna had never deliberately injured anyone. Rachel was someone she would feel sorry for under different circumstances.

The nurse came back with a long, braided cord. First she knotted the cord around Jenna's right wrist, then undid the strap holding her arm to the bed.

A rush of weightless exhilaration surged through her as Jenna lifted her arm into the air. It felt great to move! The urge to push Rachel down and run from the room was overwhelming. But her left arm, with the IV needle attached, was still secured to the bed. Keeping a tight grip on the cord, Rachel walked around the end of the bed and tied Jenna's free hand to her left hand before pulling the needle and releasing the other strap.

Jenna sat up and was immediately light-headed. She waited for the dizziness to pass, then gently swung her legs down to the floor. Rachel watched nervously, gripping the cord so tightly with both hands her knuckles were white. Jenna smiled kindly at the nurse. She felt bad about having to hurt Rachel, but this was her chance and she was getting the hell out.

Jenna stood slowly, legs like jelly. Her feet tingled with a thousand pins and needles. She took a few short steps and felt her quads tighten and respond. They ached to move. A surge of confidence pushed her forward another few steps. She wanted to put herself between Rachel and the door before she acted. She manipulated the needle in her hand until the sharp end was exposed, then gripped it tightly for the attack.

Rachel was slightly to the side and one step behind when Jenna swung her tied hands up and sideways, plunging the needle into Rachel's bicep.

The nurse screamed and let go of Jenna's cord, grabbing her own arm.

Jenna bolted for the door, her legs suddenly weak and threatening to collapse. The door opened just as she reached for the knob, and the thick wood slammed into her forehead. Jenna reeled from the blow, staggering backward into Rachel. The nurse wrapped her arms tightly around Jenna's chest. Jenna struggled to free herself, feeling as if she were moving in slow motion. She managed to break Rachel's grip and lunge forward.

The preacher/doctor blocked her path.

Jenna drew in her breath and charged the way she'd seen football players do. She hit him in the chest with her right shoulder. Her effort was weak from drugs and inactivity. The impact knocked the wind out of her, but the man only took a small step backward and stood his ground in the doorway. Before Jenna could step back and gather strength for a second charge, a needle plunged into her left shoulder. She twisted away with a violent jerk.

Rachel was there, holding her captive while the preacher/ doctor pressed the plunger, releasing the drug into her system. Jenna struggled for a moment, then collapsed when her legs became too paralyzed to hold her up.

Chapter 30 >—

Eric reread the article. Something about it bothered him. Something other than the fact the doctor had failed to report or remember a fatal accident.

"You think this might be the guy?" Joe peered over Eric's shoulder.

"I need a picture of Carmichael."

"I'll check the photo file."

"There must be more about this story." Eric scrolled forward on the microfiche as Joe hustled over to the cabinet files in the corner. After twenty minutes, Eric found one other mention of the accident, but it contained little information. Both accounts had been written by a reporter who'd left the paper just before Eric came on board. He wondered if it would be worthwhile to call her. Twelve years was a long time. Police records might be a better place to look.

"Bingo!" Joe dashed back across the room. "I believe we have a match."

Despite the dimly lit room and a decade of change, Eric recognized Dr. David Carmichael as the ponytailed man he'd seen with Jenna last Saturday. He was thinner in the old photo, which emphasized his delicate cheekbones and full mouth. Eric hated him on sight. "I'll be damned."

"Now what?" Joe bounced on his feet, ready to go.

"We find him. You start calling hospitals, and I'll notify the police."

Joe frowned. "You think he's still practicing medicine? Wouldn't a scandal like that ruin a doctor's reputation?"

"He probably moved on, made a fresh start somewhere else. He wasn't even charged." Eric removed the microfiche.

"The hospital might have a record of where he went."

"It's worth a phone call, but we probably won't be able to find out anything until Monday."

"Better yet, I'll call Barb at the DMV first thing Monday morning. If Carmichael has a valid driver's license, she'll know his current address." Joe started to leave, then turned back. "Any wild guesses why he might have kidnapped your girlfriend?"

"Not one."

Eric followed Joe downstairs. He decided to call his landline and check his answering machine to see if he had any messages. He hadn't been home since he'd left for the prison that morning. He pushed the first three numbers, then stopped. What if another nutcase had left messages about the pictures in the paper? He didn't have patience for bullshit at the moment. He was too close to finding the truth.

Eric hung up, then called Jackson's number. No answer. So he left a message: "The kidnapper with the ponytail is a doctor named David Carmichael. Call me."

He headed over to Joe's cubicle. "I'll be at home if you come up with anything. You should go home too."

"Who wants to sit home on a Saturday night?" Joe made a face. He had a girlfriend but was a workaholic.

Eric laughed. "Thanks for your help. I owe you."

"I want exclusive rights to this story." Joe was serious.

Eric hesitated for half a second. "Agreed."

Too excited by his discovery of Carmichael to go straight home, Eric stopped by the corner Grocery Cart for a pint of Chunky Monkey and a six-pack of Dr Pepper. On the drive to his duplex, he worried that his obsession with finding Jenna was mentally unhealthy. Yet when he arrived, he hurried up the front steps, anxious to check his answering machine. He struggled to find his house key in the dark, failing to have left his porch light on that morning. As he opened the door, Eric sensed immediately that something was wrong. The air had a faint scent of cigarette smoke. Had someone been in his house?

He set down the sack to free both hands, then flipped on the living room light. For a second, everything seemed normal. Eric stepped into the room and turned to push the front door closed. His brain registered the form—thin man, dressed in dark brown, with a long, shiny forehead and a long, shiny knife—a second before it landed on him. The blade plunged into his right pectoral before he had a chance to react.

Eric bellowed with rage and pain, a primitive, bone-quivering sound, and lashed out at the same time. He shook the skinny man loose with a strength he didn't know he possessed. The man staggered back but didn't fall. Eyes wide with alarm, he came at Eric in a sudden burst. Eric threw up his arm to block the knife. A fiery line of pain burned down his forearm. The man began to circle him like a jackal around a wounded gazelle. Eric backed toward the kitchen, hoping to find a weapon there.

The primitive part of his brain wanted to rush the guy, throw him against the wall, and pummel him with heavy fists until he was dead. But he had been stabbed twice and was losing blood. He only had one more chance with this guy. A vague sense of who the attacker was and why he was here hovered just outside Eric's conscious thought pattern. For the moment, he could only focus on keeping space between his body and the knife, while he searched with his hands along the kitchen counter for a weapon.

He grabbed the coffeepot and threw it without thinking. The man ducked, and the glass pot crashed against the dining room table. Eric wished he'd broken it against the edge of the counter and used the jagged edge as a weapon instead. Without taking his eyes off his assailant, who continued to stalk him with methodical precision, Eric groped along the counter for the big wooden knife holder. He had a big knife of his own, sharp and shiny from lack of use. But as he fumbled with his hands behind him, the fingers on his right hand began to feel numb. His whole right arm felt weak. Eric was suddenly aware of a pattern of wet, red blood on the beige tile. His blood. The room began to spin in slow lurching twists. He had trouble keeping his eyes on the man in brown, who was only a few feet away in the narrow kitchen. Eric forced his fingers to close around the big knife handle. He pulled it loose and held it out in front of him.

Something was wrong. The end was round instead of sharp. It wasn't a knife. The room closed in, and Eric's legs went weak. The man in brown leapt at him. Eric felt the piercing tip of the knife plunge into his chest. The pain was excruciating. He dropped to his knees. The floor swam up to him. The man waited, watching, until Eric fell forward into a pool of his own blood.

His last thought was this man had probably killed Jenna too.

Chapter 31

"Jenna's temperature is 98.9 this morning."

Rachel stood in his office doorway, refusing to look at him. Carmichael realized the significance of her news, but decided to take a moment to mend their relationship. Rachel was still upset from the night before, when he'd chastised her for coming home without Sarah. Later, he'd practically screamed at her for letting Jenna out of bed.

"How's your arm?" The wound wasn't serious. In fact, her pride had been injured worse. Still, it was an opening.

"Fine." She glanced up briefly, but he couldn't read her expression. "I'll get back to work now. I just came in because you said to let you know the minute her temperature went up."

"Thank you, Rachel." Carmichael stood, opening his arms wide. "I hope you'll find it in your heart to forgive me. This has been a rough few days for both of us. I'm as worried about Sarah as you are. I shouldn't have taken it out on you."

"It's not that." Rachel kept her eyes down.

"What's wrong then?"

"Why is Jenna here?" Rachel looked up, suddenly defiant.

"I've told you. Her family wants to get her off heroin and away from her abusive boyfriend."

"Why is she getting hormone shots?"

Carmichael started to deny it, then stopped, realizing how foolish it was. Jenna's and Sarah's reactions had obviously been similar enough to alert Rachel. He couldn't afford to alienate Rachel now. She knew too much.

A plausible story came to him. "Her parents, who know of my success with in vitro pregnancies, asked me to remove and freeze some of her eggs." Rachel seemed to be buying it, so he continued. "Jenna is an only child, and they fear she'll destroy herself and their only chance of having grandchildren. They can't sit back and let the family die out because of her self-destructiveness."

He watched her think it over and decide to believe him. Relieved, Carmichael smiled. "Is there anything I can do to make you feel better?"

"I'd like permission to counsel her about her addiction. I think she'd be less desperate to escape if she knew why she was here."

"It's too soon. She'll only deny it."

Rachel was silent.

"I know you want to help her. Now that she's ovulating, we can do the retrieval and get her off the hormones. In a day or two, we'll both sit down and talk with her. All right?"

Rachel hesitated. "All right." Her voice was deliberately deadpan.

Carmichael sensed her displeasure, but whatever else was bothering her would have to wait. He had too many other things to worry about, all of which were far more serious.

Rachel turned back. "Should I test her urine for luteinizing hormones?"

"Please get it started. I'll be with you in a moment."

"Yes, Reverend." The nurse nodded and left. Carmichael rubbed his temples and wished he could have a drink. The thought frightened him as much as the fires of hell. He'd been clean and sober for eleven years, eight months, and two days.

He searched his desk for an aspirin. Thank god, this would be over soon, even if it meant never seeing Jenna again. He didn't handle stress well. That's why he'd become a drug and alcohol addict during his medical internship. After the accident, God had called him to do his work, then showed him a better way to live. The Lord had provided for him as well. His life had been stress free and nearly perfect until that moment Elizabeth called in her favor.

Carmichael cursed her and her obsession with giving birth to a genetically related child. Why couldn't she have adopted? He would have done anything to help, including marrying her. The anger faded quickly. Thousands of infertile couples felt the same way about genetic offspring. That very obsession had led to the first test-tube baby and the subsequent developments he now used to help the Sisters produce healthy female offspring. Obsessive, research-driven people like him and Elizabeth were the catalysts for medical progress.

He picked up the phone and dialed Liz's number. It rang seven times before she answered with a sleepy hello.

"Liz, did I wake you?"

"What time is it?"

"Almost nine. It's not like you to sleep this late. Are you all right?" Something about her voice worried him.

"I'm fine. I was up late, that's all."

"I have good news."

"I could use some good news."

"Jenna's temperature is up this morning. We'll undoubtedly do the retrieval sometime today. I'll let you know as soon as I have her LH levels."

"Excellent. I think I'll pack a bag and drive out. I want to assist with the retrieval."

"It's really not necessary. Rachel will be here. It's such a risk to let Jenna see you."

"I have to be there, to have some control in the whole process. You know how I am."

Carmichael sighed. "Yes, I do know. We're too much alike sometimes. I'll see you this afternoon."

He hung up the phone and headed for Jenna's room. He would spend time with her while he still could.

Chapter 32

Eric knew he was in a hospital, even though he couldn't pry his eyes open to confirm it. Sleep kept dragging him under. He struggled to the surface again and again, knowing he had something essential to do.

When he finally managed to lift his heavy eyelids, the room was empty, devoid of the efficient voices he'd been hearing all morning. Was it morning? He had no idea.

Eric tried to sit up, but a fire line of agony burned through his chest. Sucking in oxygen, he squeezed back tears. What in the hell had happened? The last thing he remembered was coming home and…Oh god…the knife. The blood. He'd been stabbed in the upper chest.

But he was still alive. Eric shuddered. He'd cheated death. His life meant something.

His mother's face, aging and vulnerable, flashed in his mind. He knew he had to see her before it was too late. His brothers too. It had been too long since he'd been home.

"Hey, Troutman, you're awake." Jackson came into the room, lacking his usual bustling energy.

"Sort of." Eric's mouth was dry, and his tongue felt puffed up like a balloon.

"How are you feeling? Or is that a stupid question?" Jackson laughed nervously.

"Stupid question. How did I get here?"

"I saved your sorry ass." Jackson grinned. "After calling you repeatedly last night, I decided at the last minute to stop by your place on my way home. Fortunately, the sleazebag who cut you didn't bother to close the door all the way. So when you didn't answer my knock, I went inside in a typical nosy-cop way and saw the blood. I found you lying on the kitchen floor bleeding like a stuck pig. What a sight." Jackson shook his head. "The docs say you're lucky to be alive. The knife missed your heart and lung, but you might have bled to death if someone hadn't come along."

"Thanks." Eric could barely speak. Fear and love and gratitude welled up in his throat.

"I'm glad you're going to make it, my friend."

"Me too. Did you get my message?"

"What message? When?" Jackson reached for his cell phone and flipped it open to check his missed calls. "There's no call from you."

"I bet I called your house number." Eric's head ached, and it was a struggle to concentrate. "This is Sunday, isn't it?"

"Yes. So what was the message?"

"A doctor named David Carmichael is the guy with the ponytail."

"Why does that name sound familiar?"

"Car wreck, twelve years ago." Eric had to stop and wait for the energy to speak again. "His wife and son died, but he didn't report the accident. Possible drug and alcohol problem."

"I think I remember." Jackson pulled up a chair and sat down. "A very slick gentleman. He had a blonde lady on the side who claimed he was sober. The DA wouldn't file charges, so we let him go and he disappeared"—Jackson snapped his fingers—"just like that."

"We have to find him."

"We will."

A nurse came into the room and glared at Jackson. "That's enough for now. He needs his rest."

"Five more minutes." Jackson grabbed a picture out of his suit pocket and held it in front of Eric's face. "We've got a lead on the other kidnapper. Do you recognize this guy?"

Eric squinted, the headache pounding behind his eyes now. It was a mug shot, jailhouse blue shirt against a white wall. The man was thin, with a large nose and a receding hairline. Eric's heart skipped a beat.

"That's the guy who stabbed me. He's older and balder now, but it's him." Eric laid back and closed his eyes. Knowing Jenna's abductor was a cold-blooded killer hit him hard. His last ounce of hope for finding her alive evaporated.

"I'll find them, Troutman. You can count on it."

"Thanks." Eric blinked back tears. The sheer joy of being alive was fading fast. He was exhausted, barely able to keep his eyes open.

"You'd better get some rest." Jackson stood to leave.

"Wait." Eric's voice was weak. "The other woman's name was Elizabeth Harrington. Maybe she knows where Carmichael is."

"I'll look into it. You rest. I'll take it from here."

Chapter 33 >—

Zeke started the truck and flipped on the heater for a few minutes. He'd been watching Darcie's apartment all morning, and the temperature was steadily dropping. It felt like snow. Just what he needed right now. Zeke muttered in disgust. Where in the hell was the girl anyway? He hadn't seen her once. Now that he had a dead body on his conscience, he was more anxious than ever to get out of town. He had to get his money together first. He needed as much cash as he could get his hands on. Florida might not be far enough away.

The heat made him sleepy. He put the truck in gear and drove three blocks to a 7-Eleven for coffee. He'd spent the night in a nearby motel, but hadn't slept much. His neighbors had vibrated the walls with salsa music and annoyed the hell out of him with their gibberish. Now his bowels were in an uproar, and he'd had to leave the alley across from Darcie's apartment twice to go to the can. The coffee would probably make it worse, but he didn't care.

A group of young thugs in front of the store eyed him as he hopped out of his truck. Punks. Zeke didn't give them a second look. He bought coffee and a maple bar and drove back to Darcie's, parking on a side street this time. He didn't want to arouse suspicion. Still, he wasn't really worried. People in this part of town weren't likely to call the cops unless they heard gunfire.

Twenty minutes later he saw Sarah come down the stairs. Where was Darcie? Zeke checked his watch: 11:25 a.m. The lazy bitch was probably still in bed. He watched Sarah head up Blair Street. He considered following her, then rejected it just as quickly. Darcie was the one with the $20,000 package in her belly. All he had to do was keep track of her until she popped—which should be any moment—then snatch the baby.

He'd already called an ex-con he knew, who'd put him in touch with a lawyer who handled not-so-legitimate adoptions. Everything was set to go. He just needed to be patient and wait for the baby. Sometimes women went over their due date. Zeke had a good feeling about the whole thing. The timing was going to be perfect, he could tell.

A few minutes later, Sarah hurried back up the street carrying a small brown sack. Zeke figured she'd been to the store. He leaned back against the seat and closed his eyes. Might as well get some shut-eye. If Sarah was still in the apartment, so was Darcie. He could use a short break.

Chapter 34 >—

Eric waited for the nurse to leave. He'd been awake for fifteen minutes and felt surprisingly coherent. The headache he'd had earlier was gone, but his upper chest felt like someone had been digging around in it.

He was determined to get up anyway. Now that he knew who Jenna's kidnappers were, it was impossible to lie still and let someone else finish the job. He had to see it through, even if there was little possibility of finding Jenna alive. He had to know why she'd been taken. He needed to confront Carmichael. It was insane to go, considering his condition, but Eric was powerless to resist the pull.

Bracing for the pain, he eased his shoulders off the bed. The white-hot tearing sensation made him want to scream. He ground his teeth together and forced himself to a sitting position. Blood rushed out of his brain, leaving him dizzy. He waited for it to pass, then gently pulled the IV needle from the crook of his arm. He pressed a tissue over the puncture to stop the bleeding and held tight. His breath was shallow and painful.

Doubts about his ability to function gave him pause. He waited for them to pass, letting his body adjust and gather strength. In a burst of determination, he swung his legs to the floor and stood up.

A mild earthquake shook the floor. Eric braced himself against the bed. In a moment the shaking subsided. He realized it had been his own legs. Never in his whole life had he felt so weak. Not even the time he'd gotten food poisoning from eating butter he'd left on the counter overnight. He took a deep breath and winced with the pain. Still determined, he looked around for his clothes. The other bed was occupied, but both televisions were silent. No flowers, magazines, or clothes anywhere. He figured the shirt was probably ruined, but the pants he could use. The breezy hospital gown wouldn't do on the outside. He could feel the cold coming through the window, the gray-white sky pregnant with snow.

He took a short, tentative step toward the bathroom. Not bad. He took another one. The room started to spin.

"Hey! What are you doing?" A tiny nurse with cropped black hair rushed into the room. She cinched her arm firmly around his waist and pulled him back to the bed. Rapidly losing consciousness, Eric didn't resist.

Chapter 35 >—

Zeke woke with a start. A scraggly looking fellow with filthy clothes stared at him through the driver's side window.

"Get away!" Zeke shouted as he jerked forward into a more upright position. The bum shuffled away while glancing over his shoulder repeatedly to check if Zeke was following.

He checked his watch. *Oh shit.* He'd been asleep for over an hour. He looked up at Darcie's apartment. The light in the window, which had been on all morning, was now out. *Damn!* Had the girls gone somewhere? He stepped out of the truck and stretched his legs. Maybe he should have a chat with the apartment manager. He'd seen the guy yesterday, and he looked like an understanding fellow, someone who would appreciate an offer of cash.

He locked the truck and sauntered a hundred yards up the street. The manager's apartment was the first one on the ground floor. He rapped sharply on the door.

A voice from inside yelled, "Just a minute." Zeke waited while the young man took his time opening the door. He was a good-looking kid, but his hair was too long and his clothes smelled musty. He smiled agreeably, though, when he saw Zeke. "We don't have any vacancies right now, but I can put you on a list."

"I'm looking for my niece. Her name's Darcie, and she's nine months pregnant. I promised her I'd be here in time for the birth, but she isn't home. I'm worried that she's already gone to the hospital."

"She went last night. I loaned her cab fare."

"Which hospital?"

"I don't know."

"Have you heard anything about the baby?"

The manager shook his head. "Any chance you've got the ten bucks she owes me? I sure could use it. If it had been anybody but Darcie, I'd never have loaned the cash."

"Sure." Zeke dug two fives out of his wallet. It wasn't much to pay for a friend in the right place. "Thanks. See you around."

He headed for the phone booth at the 7-Eleven. He called North McKenzie first and got lucky. The lady said Darcie and the baby were both fine, but would have to stay in the hospital for a few days. Zeke thanked her politely, hung up the phone, and let out a stream of profanities. He'd been patient for a long time. Now he wanted to get the hell down the road. He put another quarter in the slot and dialed the lawyer.

"Mr. Johnson? This is Zeke Brothers. Al said to call when the baby was born."

The lawyer spoke softly but with urgency. "Are you in possession of the child now?"

"Not exactly. The baby has to stay in the hospital for a few days."

"Anything serious?"

"No. Just a rough labor."

"When you have the merchandise, call me at 345-2870. I'll have the cash." The phone clicked in Zeke's ear. He repeated the number to himself while he ran inside the store to borrow a pen. He pulled out the picture of his sister he'd been carrying around for forty years, and wrote the number on the back. Elise would understand. This was important.

Exhausted and frustrated, he climbed in the truck and drove down Seventh Avenue looking for a motel. Something cheap where they didn't ask too many questions, but not the one he'd stayed in the night before. He needed sleep. His left arm and shoulder were bothering him from all the driving.

In the morning, he'd stop in the hospital and see if he could find out exactly when Darcie would be released. He wanted to be waiting, grab the kid before she ever got home.

Zeke worried about how long he would have to wait. With his picture in the paper—identified as a kidnapper—and the reporter who had seen him now dead, it wasn't a good idea to hang around town long. If the hospital said Darcie had to stay more than two days, he'd head back out to the compound, slip in and quietly smother the kidnapped woman, then take off for Florida or Mexico.

Zeke decided he would make copies of Carmichael's computer files while he was in the compound. Just in case the Reverend got worked up over Jenna's death and decided to turn against him. It never hurt to keep an edge.

Chapter 36

Using the tip of his scalpel, Carmichael made a tiny incision in the folds of Jenna's belly button and a second incision near her pubis. He pushed a hollow needle through the first opening, and pumped a small amount of carbon dioxide into the abdominal cavity to create visibility and space to maneuver. He removed the needle and inserted a narrow ultrasound probe. After locating her right ovary, Carmichael began to search for mature egg follicles, which would appear as black spheres on the monitor.

The procedure was routine for him; he'd performed at least a dozen in the last two years. Liz was nervous though, he could tell. She often extracted genetic material from embryos for testing, but had never searched ovarian fluid for mature oocytes. Carmichael would have preferred to have Rachel on hand, but Liz wouldn't allow it. She didn't want Rachel to know the eggs were for her, nor did she trust Rachel's abilities. Liz insisted on being his only assistant. This was her baby. Fortunately, the transfer, which would be done in a day or so, was a quick procedure that he could do unaided.

In a moment, Carmichael spotted his first ripe follicle. He slipped an aspiration needle through the opening he'd made near the pubis. Eyes back on the monitor, he guided the needle to the ripe follicle, pushed it in, and punctured the sphere. Quickly pressing the suction pump, he drained the follicle. Strawberry-colored fluid flowed out the connecting hose into a test tube.

"First one." He let go of the aspiration needle just long enough to grab the tube and hand it to Liz through the pass-bar. She was in the embryo lab next door, but he could see her head and shoulders through the opening. This was where Rachel would have been handy. Jenna was completely paralyzed and unconscious from the ketamine, so the risk of the patient seeing Liz was minimal.

Liz stared at the tube, transfixed. Finally she whispered, "My baby."

It was his opportunity to say what had been on his mind all morning. "It could be our baby, Liz."

She looked up at him, stunned. "I thought you never wanted to have another child."

"I've come to feel differently in the last week. Your passion to be a mother rejuvenated me. I want to be the father of your child." Jenna's child, he corrected silently, automatically turning the probe back and forth in search of another follicle.

Liz sounded panicked. "I don't see how that could work. I can't live here, and you're not planning to give up the church."

"I could still be her father." Carmichael located a second ripe follicle and penetrated it. "You could bring her out here on weekends sometimes."

"I can't." Liz had her eye pressed to the Olympus microscope and didn't look up. "I can't share this child with anyone."

"What about when she's older? When she asks about her daddy?" Carmichael siphoned the oocyte into a second tube and handed it through the opening to Liz. He gripped the needle again, then continued his search with the ultrasound probe.

After a long pause Liz said. "I'll tell her the truth."

"What truth?" Carmichael scoffed. "That her father was a sperm donor who got paid a hundred bucks to jack off in a cup?" He wished he could see Liz's expression, but he kept his eyes on the monitor. The procedure required concentrated hand-eye coordination. She was silent, so he continued. "That you don't know his name, only that his sperm was the healthiest of the bunch." Liz started to protest, but he cut her off. "Or will you tell her the other truth—that you stole her from her mother, who happens to be your sister?"

He could hear Liz sucking in air and fighting back sobs. Carmichael cursed himself. He'd gone too far. And his timing was ridiculous. Finding and separating the oocytes from the bloody ovarian fluid needed to be done quickly and correctly.

"I'm sorry. I shouldn't have said that. I just don't want your daughter to have the same anxieties about who her parents are that you've had all your life."

"She won't." Liz spit the words out. "She'll have a real mother and that's enough. Let's finish this. We only have two eggs so far."

They worked in silence for the next fifteen minutes. Carmichael located and siphoned three more follicles, in which Liz found a total of four oocytes. He'd expected more. From what he could tell with the limited probing he'd done, Jenna's reproductive system seemed remarkably free of scarring or endometriosis. He moved to the left ovary and immediately discovered a large cyst, which looked suspiciously like a teratoma.

Carmichael frowned, muttering to himself.

"What is it?" Liz had heard him.

"It looks like a teratoma on her left ovary."

"Any possibility of harvesting the follicles?"

"None."

She cursed softly.

Carmichael wondered if he should remove it. Sometimes these cysts were harmless. Sometimes they grew—causing extreme pain—until they ruptured, resulting in hemorrhaging and possibly death. He couldn't worry about that right now. The six oocytes needed his immediate attention. He gently removed the probe and needle. "Time to close up."

Liz was disappointed. "Is six going to be enough? The survival rate is never a hundred percent."

"That may be true in your clinic, but not in mine." He put two tiny dissolvable stitches in the incisions. "Remember, the first in vitro baby was conceived with a single egg produced naturally, without the aid of super-ovulatory hormones."

"I know. It's just that in the ARC, sometimes they retrieve ten to fifteen oocytes, and still the woman doesn't always get pregnant."

Carmichael wiped Jenna's incisions with rubbing alcohol and put a sterile bandage on each. He leaned through the pass-bar and grinned at Liz.

"Have faith, I'm the best."

She smiled thinly. "Why don't you come in here and take over? The sooner we get them fertilized, the sooner we can do the transfer and get her out of here."

"Are you sure you won't let me be the father?"

"I can't."

"Then get me the daddy you picked out."

Elizabeth had brought the frozen sperm in a cooler packed with dry ice. She had taken it out to thaw just before they began the egg retrieval. Carmichael wouldn't let her see how troubled he was. He didn't want to admit it to himself. He had to stop thinking about Jenna. Soon she would be gone from his life forever.

He worked quickly in the darkened lab, cleaning each egg and placing it in a drop of culture medium, then encapsulating each drop in mineral oil. The oil sealed the egg from the outside world and protected it against dust, temperature shifts, and the natural exchange of gases in the air. The six droplets were placed in a petri dish and slid into the incubator, where they were kept at ninety-eight degrees.

Carmichael normally incubated oocytes for three hours before fertilizing them, but today he would leave them only for an hour. In fact, he planned to do the entire process as quickly as possible. Whether Liz got pregnant hardly mattered to him at this point. He had tried to give her the right baby, and his debt to her was paid. All he cared about was getting Jenna out of his church before the police found her. Two hours could make a world of difference.

He wheeled Jenna back into her room. He'd given her a large dose of ketamine combined with Versed, to ensure that she didn't come out too soon, like last time. It was a dangerous combination. She might never wake up, which could be a blessing. Carmichael could hear Liz pacing nervously in the entry hall. He was worried about her. She seemed to have aged overnight and had pulsated with tension all afternoon.

Carmichael made a sudden decision. He closed and locked the door behind him.

Lifting the drape that covered Jenna's body, he ran his hands over her breasts and between her legs. He had to unzip his pants and release his erection immediately. Carmichael found a plastic cup in the nightstand next to her bed and stroked himself vigorously, ejaculating in a few minutes. He couldn't have Jenna, but he could be the father of her child.

He unlocked the door and peeked into the surgery area. Liz was still out in the hall, pacing. He could hear her muttering to herself. He moved quickly through the swinging doors into the embryo lab, spotting Elizabeth's tube of donor sperm in a rack next to the incubator. Carmichael searched a supply cupboard for an identical one.

He pulled the sterilized wrap off the tube, squeezed the plastic cup to form a funnel, and poured his semen into the new tube. He looked up to see Liz staring through the glass in the upper half of the hall doors.

Carmichael waved and smiled, praying she hadn't caught on to what he was doing. Liz didn't respond.

He turned his back to her and switched the tubes. The one she'd brought was still cool and damp from condensation. Carmichael set it in the stainless-steel refrigerator, afraid that Liz would see it later if he tossed it in the wastebasket. He turned back to the double swinging doors. Liz hadn't moved. He motioned her to come in. She seemed not to notice. Carmichael worried about her state of mind. She obviously wasn't handling the stress of the situation well at all.

It hadn't been quite an hour yet, so he killed time by sanitizing his instruments from the retrieval surgery. Liz resumed pacing the hall. Carmichael decided not to wait any longer. He pulled the petri dish from the incubator and placed it under a warming light.

Using an eyedropper, he unleashed a million or so fresh spermatozoa on the unsuspecting oocytes, then slid the petri dish under a microscope. As he'd expected, his sperm were plentiful, active, and strong. In a few seconds, the first egg was under attack, surrounded by dozens of blind warriors. Carmichael loved this part, the penetration of the zona pellucida, followed by the submission of the female genetic material. It was the miracle of life. God, in his great wisdom, had masterminded this beautiful and loving conquest of the fragile female ovum. Carmichael had witnessed the miracle dozens of times, but this time was special. It was his seed becoming one with Jenna. It was the most glorious four minutes of his life.

He watched the six newly formed zygotes until his right eye ached with the strain, then placed the petri dish back in the incubator.

Now the wait began. It would be hours before the cells started to divide, displaying their viability or weaknesses. Then Carmichael would transfer the healthy zygotes to a culture of pig fetal tissue to accelerate growth. Then they would have to wait another ten to fifteen hours for the embryos to develop to an eight-cell blastocyst stage. At that point, they could remove two of the cells, expand the genetic material with PCR, and screen for sex differentiation. Like all the Sisters, Liz wanted a girl.

Chapter 37 >—

Undaunted by his earlier collapse, Eric sat up that afternoon and buzzed for a nurse. A tall blonde woman showed up about five minutes later. Eric thought that a person with a real emergency could have died in the meantime, but he kept it to himself.

"I'm starving. Do you think I could have something to eat?"

"Sure. I'm glad you're feeling better. Be back in a bit."

She brought him a tray with green jello and a small dish of rice pudding. Eric was heartbroken. "Could I have some real food, please?"

"It's too soon. If you vomit or choke you could pull out your stitches. Tomorrow you can have a sandwich, I promise." She smiled, checked his IV line, and left him alone with the mush.

Eric hated rice pudding, but he was starving, so he gulped it down without letting it touch his taste buds. As he was savoring the lime jello, Joe waltzed in.

"Hey, you're alive."

"Damn lucky to be, so I hear."

"You were right all along about the kidnapping." Joe sat and scooted the chair in close to Eric. "I mean, why else would they try to kill you?"

"Exactly. The guy who stabbed me is an ex-con. Detective Jackson's checking him out right now. What did you find out about the doctor?"

Joe scowled. "Nothing for sure, except that he's not working at any hospitals or birth centers in Oregon, Washington, or California. Tomorrow, when the DMV opens, I'll be able to find out more.

"I've got to get out of here." Eric hurt just thinking about moving. "I need you to bring me some clothes. You still have a key to my place, right?"

"Yeah." Joe's long brow was deeply furrowed. "Are you sure about this? You're still looking rather pale and worthless."

"I feel pale and worthless, but I have to finish this. I can't lie here while you and Jackson put this story to bed. You know how it is."

Joe nodded. "Shoes and everything, right?"

"Might as well. I don't know what happened to the stuff I was wearing when I came in, and I'm afraid to ask."

"I'll bring your stuff tomorrow. Anything else you need?"

"No, tonight!"

Joe shook his head. "You can't leave tonight. You were stabbed in the chest yesterday. You have to wait at least another day."

"Fine, but bring the clothes tonight anyway. I'll leave first thing in the morning."

"Promise you won't leave tonight."

"I promise." Eric was relieved. His body wasn't ready. "Thanks, Joe."

"See you in a while." The reporter headed for the door.

"Hey, bring me something to eat, would you?" Eric didn't care what the nurse said. He needed to get his strength back. "All I got for dinner was some lousy jello."

"Whopper with cheese?"

"Make it two."

At the moment, a little cholesterol was the least of his worries.

Chapter 38 >—

Elizabeth slid the glass dish under the microscope. Only four of the embryos had been viable. Two of them had never begun to divide. David claimed the oocytes had not been mature enough. But the remaining four were doing great. She'd been skeptical about the pig fetal tissue at first, but David had reassured her it would speed the process, and he'd been right, as usual. The embryo under the microscope had already reached the six-cell stage. She decided to go ahead and test it.

David was in the next room taking a short nap. He'd been up all night checking the embryos every hour and would be irritated at her for proceeding without him. This was his lab and sex selection was his specialty. But slurping embryo cells for genetic testing was a newly acquired technique for Elizabeth. She'd recently done two pre-implantation diagnoses at the ARC and was anxious to repeat her success.

Elizabeth rotated her neck, trying to snap herself out of a mental fog. She'd gone up to David's room after dinner and collapsed, sleeping straight through until morning, a very unusual occurrence for her. She could only assume it was her way of dealing with the stress of being cooped up in the compound without cigarettes. She'd left them at home after deciding to go cold turkey. The cutting-down program wasn't working, and she had to quit. Pregnant women who smoked were weak and selfish.

David had bookshelves full of medical texts and a moderately well-equipped lab, but neither held much interest for her. She hated the compound and nothing could calm her nerves. The lack of windows, the brick walls and threadbare rugs, the constant chill, even David's little clinic gave her the creeps.

On top of that, her stepfather's voice had been slipping into her head, making snide little comments about her lack of maternal instinct. Elizabeth had never cared what Ralph thought about her. Why she would be tormented by him now was inconceivable. It was as though he was reaching out from the grave to destroy her one chance at happiness.

Now she was rushing the testing, doing it at six cells instead of eight, because she couldn't wait to have the embryos transferred and get away from the compound.

Using the micromanipulator, which David had spent almost half her inheritance on, she gently pushed a flame-polished holding pipette up against the embryo to immobilize it. With the other hand, she slid the sampling pipette through the hole she'd drilled in the zona pellucida and captured a single cell. Then she repeated the process with a second pipette, leaving the embryo with only four cells and a large hole in its protective membrane.

Elizabeth wasn't worried. The hole would work to her advantage later, by allowing the growing embryo to escape the shell, which had become toughened by exposure and handling. At the ARC, zona-drilled embryos had a greater pregnancy rate than those left on their own.

Elizabeth carefully transferred the cells to a tiny beaker and added a drop of specialized bacteria, which would make hundreds of thousands of copies of the genes within an hour.

Even an hour seemed like an eternity. Elizabeth stepped out into the hall and began to pace. Her entire body ached with the craving for nicotine. The pacing had been soothing to her yesterday while waiting for David to fertilize and separate the embryos. She'd thought about her early childhood when her mother was still alive, and had experienced a long, dreamlike trance while she walked.

Today she was more wound up and unable to focus on something pleasant. Elizabeth kept pacing, hoping for the best, but Ralph's voice kept popping into her head. He was soon joined by John, her ex-husband, who told her she was unfit to be a mother, that her ovaries failed to produce eggs because she was cold and unfeeling. Terrified it could be true, Elizabeth yelled back, calling him a misogynist and a cheat.

The sound of her own shrill voice snapped her out of it. She heard footsteps pounding down the clinic stairs and hurried back into the lab. She sat down at the micromanipulator, chest heaving, and pretended to be busy.

Rachel burst into the room. "Are you all right?"

"I'm fine. Please leave me alone, this is delicate work."

"I heard yelling. I thought—"

"I'm not interested in what you thought. Please leave."

Rachel gave her an indignant look and left without comment.

The nurse would probably head straight to David's room, wake him up, and tell him, Elizabeth thought bitterly. Rachel was like a well-trained pet dog, unconditionally loving, loyal, and stupid.

Working rapidly but carefully, Elizabeth applied a sex-differentiation probe to the enhanced DNA. David did not come down. She soon discovered a Y chromosome. Fists clenched, she pushed back from the microscope and rushed to the incubator. She grabbed the petri dish she'd marked and dumped the embryo in the trash.

Worthless male.

Chapter 39

Sarah thanked the fat man and hopped out of his huge white car. She waved as he drove off down a side street, then she turned back to the main road heading out of Springfield toward Blue River. She stuck out her thumb and started walking. Her next ride, hopefully, would take her all the way to Deercreek Road. After that, she might have to walk the last fifteen miles. The roads to the compound weren't well traveled, but that was fine. She'd gotten an early start, and the day was mostly sunny and not too cold. She'd be home in time for supper. The thought made her smile.

Sarah had wanted to leave yesterday, but she'd slept until almost noon, after being up half the night at the hospital with Darcie. She'd called to make sure Darcie and the baby were all right, then decided it was too late to start out for the compound. Yesterday had been cold and the sky had looked like snow. Sarah had been afraid she wouldn't reach the compound before dark.

The idea of hitchhiking still frightened her, but she had no choice. She would trust the Lord to keep her safe. She had to get back. There were too many things nagging at her brain. Especially the woman in the clinic. Sarah worried about her more and more. If the Reverend was capable of injecting the Sisters with dangerous hormones and impregnating Darcie against her will, then…

Then what? Sarah didn't know what to think. If Darcie's claims were true, then her little sister Delilah wasn't safe growing up in the church and she had to get her out. Maybe none of the women were as safe as they thought. Sarah felt sick to her stomach. Reverend Carmichael was like a father. She prayed she was wrong.

Chapter 40 ⟩—

A hospital was the worst place to get any rest, Eric thought irritably. The night before, he'd been awakened every two hours by a nurse taking his blood pressure, pulse, and temperature. Now he was so tired he couldn't tell if he felt better or not. He planned to leave anyway. Joe had brought his clothes the night before, along with the cheeseburgers, as promised. All Eric had to do was get up and get dressed. He was working up the courage to try again. Yesterday's collapse had him worried. Thinking of Jenna, Eric clamped his teeth together and swung his legs to the floor.

The pain was bad, but not like before. Encouraged, he stood up. The room dipped and swayed for a moment, then stabilized. Eric padded into the bathroom to take his second stand-up piss in two days. It felt good to be on his feet. The agony in his chest would take some getting used to though. Getting dressed turned into a ten-minute exercise in self-control. Every movement was excruciating. Lifting his arms to slide into a shirt, bending over to put on socks and shoes. He fought to keep from moaning out loud.

"Where do you think you're going?" An attractive, gray-haired nurse in a bright yellow smock stood in the doorway, arms folded, looking more amused than upset.

"Home."

"Then you won't be needing your pain medication?"

Eric bit his lip. "That's right." He would regret it, he knew, but his pride had a mind of its own.

"Please stay another day." She came into the room, her voice serious now.

"I can't."

"Someone tried to kill you. What if they try again?"

Eric landed back on the bed with a thud. He hadn't thought about the possibility of a second attack. He was in no condition to defend himself, but he would be even more vulnerable if he stayed in the hospital, drugged and accessible. Eric changed his mind about going home. Maybe he could stay with Joe for a few days. Or with Jackson, who carried a gun.

Ashamed of his fear, Eric forced himself to stop thinking about his attacker. The police would pick up the guy soon.

He stood. "Do I need to sign anything before I go?"

"Your doctor will want you to sign papers saying you checked out against medical advice, and I need to find a wheelchair for you. Hospital policy."

Eric slipped out as soon as she was gone. He took the elevator to the first floor, trying to look normal instead of like the walking wounded. He turned left when he exited the elevator and walked about a hundred feet before he realized he was headed in the wrong direction. Frustrated, he headed back, picking up his pace in spite of the pain.

On the other side of the building, the hallway opened into a large main lobby that was busy with people going in and out through automatic doors and crowding around a three-sided admitting desk. Eric reached for his cell phone, but realized he didn't have it. Was it with his bloody clothes? He headed for the pay phone in the lobby and called a cab.

He glanced up at the clock behind the desk. A man at the opposite end of the counter caught his eye. *Holy shit!* It was the guy who stabbed him. Eric's heart beat like a jackhammer. The man nodded at the clerk and moved away.

Eric tried to follow, but a large group of people had gathered in front of the counter. They looked like an extended family with unhappy business. He sidestepped them, then hurried toward the automatic doors. The man was already outside, jogging toward the end of the parking lot. Eric followed as fast as he could, his wound screaming with every long stride. He slowed his steps when the man jumped into an old black truck and fired it up.

What now?

For a fleeting second, he pictured himself leaping into the back of the truck as it sped out of the parking lot. In reality, he knew he'd never make it. The best he could do was get the license-plate number.

A flash of yellow caught his eye. His cab! Eric shuffled back to the hospital entrance where the cab had come to a stop. He climbed in. The cabbie was fifty, fat, and had a strictly no-nonsense look. Eric grinned at him. "I know this is going to sound silly, but I want you to follow that black truck."

The cabdriver looked back over the seat with one eyebrow lifted skeptically. "Say what?"

"Follow that guy in the black truck, please. I'll give you twenty bucks." Eric reached for his wallet, which he'd found in the night-stand next to his hospital bed.

"If this is about drugs or any other crime, forget it." The cabbie twisted around to get a better look at him.

Eric started to tell him the truth, then changed his mind. "I think he's screwing my wife and I have to know for sure."

"You poor bastard. I'll try." The man turned back around and gunned the cab out of the parking lot.

"It would be best if he didn't know we were back here," Eric said.

"Is he the violent type?" The driver stared at him through the rearview mirror. "Maybe packing a gun? Tell me now if I'm about to get my ass shot off."

"I don't think so." It didn't sound convincing, even to him. Eric sincerely hoped he wasn't putting the cabdriver in any danger. "What's your name?"

"Rich Bonavatti."

"I'm Eric Troutman."

It occurred to Eric that he should call Jackson for help. Again, he reached for his cell phone, but still didn't have it.

"Do you have a cell phone?" he asked the driver.

"My battery is dead. I've got it charging now. We can check it in a few minutes."

Eric considered his options. If the killer headed out of town or changed vehicles while he stopped at a pay phone—if he could find one—they might lose the guy. It was best to stay with the truck until he had a license number at least. This guy could lead him to Jenna.

Up ahead, the truck made a left turn on Eleventh Avenue. Rich eased into the left lane. "Any idea where this guy's going?"

"No." Eric didn't feel like chatting. His chest hurt like hell, and his bowels were tied up in knots. "You don't happen to have any aspirin, do you?"

"Sure." Rich dug around in the glove box, tossing papers on the floor until he came up with a small bottle. "It's generic." He tossed it over the seat.

"Thanks."

Eric worked up a good spit and swallowed two. They stuck in his throat for a moment while he worked up another spit. He would have killed for a cup of coffee.

Rich was surprisingly good at maneuvering through the heavy traffic and keeping the truck in sight. After twelve blocks, the black rig turned right on Polk. Rich followed a minute later.

"This is kinda fun." The cabbie grinned into the rearview mirror. "Beats taking little old ladies to church."

Eric tried to grin back but couldn't muster it. Rich was being a good sport, but Eric just wanted it to be over. He felt like he'd aged ten years in the last week.

Polk was narrow and bumpy, with a stop sign at every cross street. The truck never got far ahead, but a red Volkswagen turned in front of them off Tenth Avenue, and a white Neon wedged between them and the Volkswagen at Ninth. Eric started to worry. He rolled down his window and leaned out.

The sky was dark with the threat of rain. Cool, moist air whipped past his face. Eric watched the black truck pull into a bank at the corner of Seventh and Polk.

"He's at the bank." Eric shivered and rolled up the window. His body felt depleted, unable to generate heat or strength.

Rich grunted. "Should I pull in or circle around?"

"Pull into the alley next to the drive-up windows."

They waited for what seemed like ten minutes before the traffic cleared enough to make a left turn. Rich finally screeched across in front of an old couple in a mint-green sedan, hitting the gravel alley at a dangerous speed. They bounced through a foot-deep pothole, throwing mud and water in all directions. When the cab stopped lurching, Eric spotted the truck in the bank parking lot. He didn't see the driver. Rich kept going.

"Turn around." Eric wished he was driving.

"As soon as I get out of this alley." The cabbie was still excited by the chase. "You noticed they put up a barrier?"

Eric looked back, barely seeing the short cement blocks. The ex-con had come out of the bank and was striding toward his truck.

"Stop!"

Eric's face smashed into the front seat as Rich slammed the brakes. Pain radiated from his chest to his fingertips. Fifty feet away, the truck roared to life. Eric strained to see the back license plate. He didn't get a good look at all six characters until the truck backed out. SQR-354.

"Let's go! He's headed out the Seventh Avenue exit."

Rich hit the gas, bouncing through the alley toward the cross street a block away. When he hit the pavement he turned hard to the left.

"No! The other way!" Panicked, Eric shouted at the top of his voice.

"I thought you wanted to turn around." Rich slammed the brakes and shot him a look.

"Go around the block." Eric ground his teeth.

Rich jammed the cab in reverse, tires squealing, and backed into the alley. Eric was trying not to panic, but the truck was getting away. The cab sent gravel flying as Rich hauled ass to the right. They screeched to a stop at the corner of Seventh and waited for a break before they could join the flow of traffic. The wide, one-way street was heavily congested. Rich accelerated, weaving back and forth across the four lanes, passing everyone. Eric watched the side streets and parking lots but didn't see the truck.

Damn! He couldn't have gotten very far. He had to have turned off somewhere. Eric started to sweat.

"He could have gone back down Polk," Rich offered.

"I looked." Eric was so upset he could barely speak. He had come so close.

"Sorry I lost him."

"It's all right. Not your fault."

"I hope things work out with your wife."

"I'm not optimistic." Eric's chest tightened. A person could only take so much abuse and disappointment.

After the cab driver dropped Eric at home, he called Jackson, who actually answered for a change. "I saw our ex-con when I was leaving the hospital a while ago. He's driving a black truck with the license-plate number SQR-354. I lost him at the corner of Seventh and Polk."

"You left the hospital?" Jackson seemed not to have heard anything else.

Eric closed his eyes. The left side of his chest hurt like hell. "Did you get that license number?" he asked. "The sooner you get it to the dispatcher, the more likely we are to catch this guy."

"Still doing my job for me?" Jackson sounded a little amused and a little irritated.

"What did you find out about the doctor?"

"Stop playing detective and get back to the hospital. I know I was skeptical at first, but I'm on it now."

"Fine, but I want to know about the doctor anyway. I've earned the right."

"I guess you have." Jackson paused, as if to consult his notes. "After Carmichael quit the hospital, he found God and started his own church, which has a mailing address in Blue River. The church itself is in an old survivalist compound off Deercreek Road, out in the middle of nowhere. The members, who seem to be mostly women and children, live there commune-style and rarely come into town."

Jackson paused, probably to drink some coffee, then continued. "Federal agents raided the place back in 1994 when the survivalists were stockpiling weapons, so someone at the Bureau knows how to get there. I'm still working on that end. The FBI doesn't always like to share."

The news that Carmichael was a religious nutcase sent a chill down Eric's spine. "I know how to get to Deercreek Road."

"Don't even think about it, Troutman. I've already got an arrest warrant for the doctor, and as soon as I have a more specific location, I'll get a warrant to search the compound."

"What about the ex-con?"

"His name's George Grafton. He did thirteen years at Pendleton for armed robbery. He's kept himself clean since he got out. His address is the same as the church, which by the way is called the Church of the Reborn. Patrol officers are on the lookout for Grafton now."

"Any idea why they would kidnap Jenna?" Eric could picture a sacrificial altar stained with blood.

"None. The church has been quietly collecting donations and minding its own business for nine years. Or so we think. Who knows how many missing women might turn up out there?"

"That's a frightening thought. You'd better get that license number to the dispatcher."

"I already did. Either go back to the hospital or at least sit in your recliner and don't move."

"Keep me informed, okay? I want to know as soon as you pick up either of these guys."

"Take care of yourself." Jackson hung up.

Eric was amused by Jackson's concern but had no intention of giving up now. He called the newspaper, but Joe wasn't at his desk. He left a message asking him to investigate the Church of the Reborn and find its location if he could.

Eric got in the Firebird and headed to Sheri's on Eleventh Avenue for food and coffee. He couldn't bear to stay in the house. It no longer seemed safe. The hope that Jenna might still be alive had rekindled with a flare. Carmichael might be grabbing women and brainwashing them into joining his church or, hard as it was to imagine, enslaving them for other purposes. Either way, Eric couldn't rest until he knew for sure.

Chapter 41 ⟩—

"Another girl!" Elizabeth was jubilant. Of the three remaining embryos, one had begun to malfunction, dividing into irregular cells. Thankfully, the last two were both females. She'd been scared since she'd thrown the male in the trash, leaving herself with only three. The outburst had been rash and inexplicable, so unlike her usual controlled self. Elizabeth had blamed it on the nicotine withdrawals, then had helped herself to a Valium from David's drug cabinet. By the time he came down after his nap, she was feeling more relaxed.

"Two is perfect." David's smile was patronizing. "It doubles your chance of becoming pregnant without really risking a multiple birth. I always transfer two."

"You're still angry at me."

"No, Liz." David sighed. "I admit I was. With only four embryos to work with, it seemed foolish to go ahead without me. But it's your baby, your decision."

"Are the embryos ready for transfer?"

"Definitely. Are you ready?" He gazed at her strangely.

"Of course." The Valium had helped. Elizabeth was no longer trembling, but she still had a bad feeling. "What if I don't get pregnant this time? What if we have to wait through another cycle?"

"We can't!" David looked at her as if she'd lost her mind. "Did you forget that a reporter witnessed the abduction and my picture was in the paper? Sooner or later someone will recognize me, and the police will come to the compound. We have to get Jenna out of here as soon as possible."

"This is my only chance." Elizabeth whispered to herself. David was right about the risk of keeping Jenna. Even though she trusted him to keep quiet about her part in this if he were arrested, she had no such faith in Zeke. He was the type to testify against them to save himself.

"Are you still planning to drop her off in front of the mission in Portland?" Considering recent developments, Elizabeth thought that might be too risky. Portland wasn't far enough away. In light of what Jenna had been through, Elizabeth would feel better if they left her in front of a hospital. Dumping her sister like unwanted trash would be the most shameful thing she'd ever do, but there was no other way. Except for missing a week of her life, no harm would come to Jenna.

David hesitated, apparently having second thoughts of his own. "I was thinking a mental hospital might be more appropriate."

"Is the ketamine causing brain damage?" Elizabeth was horrified by the thought.

"I don't think so." David looked grim. "The abduction and confinement could be traumatic for her, even without a conscious memory of it. I want to make sure she gets the psychological help she needs."

"You're a good man, David."

He shook his head. "I'm not so sure."

"We'll talk about it more later. Let's do the transfer now."

"All right. Do you want a tranquilizer?"

"I already took a Valium. I'm fine. Is Rachel going to assist?"

"Not unless I need her."

David moved into action, gently but deftly placing the embryos into a large drop of culture medium, then transferring the fluid into a very small catheter tube. Elizabeth undressed from the waist down. David had seen her naked hundreds of times, yet today she felt exposed and vulnerable. *It was the damn gray brick walls*, she thought.

Elizabeth climbed up on the examining table and wedged her feet into the stirrups. Even after dozens of pap smears and a series of pelvic exams by fertility specialists, she still hated having her private parts so openly displayed. The fact that it was David wielding the speculum made little difference.

Elizabeth took long, slow breaths. The Valium was wearing off, she realized, because the voices were back. Faint, cool whispers, like wind sifting through the cracks. *Whore slut bitch whore.* Ralph's harsh voice dominated John's gentle taunts. *Cold frigid thief…*

The pinch of the catheter tube against her cervix distracted her for a moment. Some women would call it painful, but not Elizabeth. She counted slowly to thirty, expecting David to tell her any moment that the tube was in. Instead, he began to press against her uterus from the outside with his free hand.

"What's wrong?" Elizabeth sat forward, alarmed. The chatter in her head picked up volume. *Barren whore thief barren slut thief…*

"Your uterus is tipped. I think I need a more flexible catheter." He pulled the speculum out, and Elizabeth felt her muscles relax.

"How long will this take? Should I put my feet down?"

"I'll just be a minute, but go ahead. I want you to be comfortable."

"Bring me another Valium." Elizabeth put her feet down and closed her legs, feeling instantly better. She told herself not to worry. David was a uterus man. The transfer would turn out fine. An embryo would implant. The overwhelming need for a cigarette would diminish. The voices would go away when her life got back to normal.

David returned with the Valium and a glass of water. Elizabeth swallowed just enough of the water to wash down the pills. The well water at the compound tasted metallic to her. Her stomach growled in response to the meager offering. Elizabeth realized she hadn't eaten anything that day. *Unfit mother unfit whore.* David was right. She'd have to start eating better when she was pregnant.

To keep the voices at bay, she focused on what David was doing. First he selected a different catheter and gently transferred the embryos to the new tube. Then he inserted a new syringe into the catheter. Elizabeth put her feet back in the stirrups. This was it. In a matter of minutes, the babies would be in her body. She would be almost pregnant.

Twenty minutes later, after a fair amount of cursing and sweating, David exclaimed, "It's in place. Are you ready?"

"Yes."

"Here goes." He gently pushed on the syringe, expelling the embryos from the tube into the top part of her uterus. Elizabeth blinked back tears. Slowly, David removed the catheter, then the speculum. He immediately took the tube to a microscope, examining it carefully to be certain both embryos had been dislodged into her uterus.

"Well?"

"I hope you're ready for twins."

Elizabeth laughed with relief. Twins she could handle. "Come over here." She wished she could get up and throw her arms around David. Not yet. It was important to stay still as long as possible, giving the embryos a chance to implant.

Chapter 42 >—

Jenna struggled to consciousness through a thick fog. She felt desperate to be awake but didn't know why. Her eyelids were heavy and wouldn't stay open for more than a few seconds at a time. Gradually she became aware of being in a hospital room, of pain in her abdomen. Had she had her appendix removed? She didn't remember coming to a hospital. She didn't remember being sick or hurt. Her mind was blank.

Frightened, Jenna tried to sit up. Restraints kept her down. What was going on? She forced her groggy brain to think. The last thing she remembered clearly was the night Geronimo's had been robbed.

No. She remembered talking with Eric at the café. But who was Eric? More important, why was she in restraints? Was she dangerous to others? Or suicidal? It all seemed so unreal. Even the room didn't seem real. Small, with plain gray tile and no windows.

An image of a dark-haired man in a surgical mask pushed its way through the fog. The crazy preacher/doctor. Who was he, and why did she call him that? Jenna's head pounded with the strain of remembering.

This was not a hospital. The understanding came out of nowhere, but Jenna was as certain of the fact as she was of her own name: Jenna Lynn McClure. With the understanding came terror. She was a prisoner. Someone had operated on her, and it was unlikely they had removed her appendix. The pain was centrally located around her uterus.

What had been done? Why her uterus? It wasn't terribly painful, just tender. Then it hit her. Jenna squeezed her eyes shut in horror. Had he planted something in her uterus? An embryo, she corrected herself. Another woman's child.

Even in her drugged condition, the irony of it wasn't lost on Jenna. Her desire to have a child was painfully fresh. It had been part of her everyday thoughts for years. Now it could be happening. But why her? Why like this? None of it made sense.

It meant that she might be kept alive for a while. The thought of spending nine months strapped in that sterile room was horrifying. Reflexively, Jenna tugged on her bindings. They seemed to give a little. She pulled harder.

And met resistance.

She tried the leather foot straps, pulling up, then sideways. As with her wrists, there was a little more slack, but not enough to make a difference. Jenna worked at it until she was exhausted.

She lay spent, tears sliding off her face, listening to the steady rhythm of her heart.

"Hello." A pretty blonde girl stood in the doorway, looking timid.

"Hello." Jenna felt strangely nervous. Who was she? The woman she was carrying a child for? She seemed so young.

The girl moved into the room, closing the door without a sound. She had the most beautiful blue eyes and pale, unblemished skin. She seemed to move without sound or effort. Until she spoke, Jenna thought she might be an angel.

"What's your name?" Her voice was as light as her presence.

"Jenna McClure. Who are you?"

"Sarah Roberts. But nobody around here uses last names."

Jenna felt a glimmer of hope. There were other people here. "Where exactly am I?"

"You're not one of the Sisters, are you?" Sarah lowered her voice to a whisper.

"Who are the Sisters?"

"We belong to the Church of the Reborn. If you're not a Sister, why are you here?" The girl's expression went from confusion to concern.

"How should I know? Look at me!" Jenna lifted her wrists as much as she could, displaying the thick leather straps. "I'm a prisoner. I've been operated on without my consent."

Sarah closed her eyes and her lips began to move. It took Jenna a moment to realize the girl was praying. "You don't believe me? Lift my nightgown and look at my lower abdomen. They did something to me. Made an incision, I think. Why? Tell me, do you know why?"

Sarah opened her eyes and blinked back tears.

"Go ahead, look at it."

Gently, Sarah pulled off Jenna's blanket and rolled her nightgown up. "Who did this?" she whispered, glancing over at the little window.

"The crazy—" Jenna stopped, not wanting to alienate the girl. The guy could be her father...or husband. "I don't know. I can't remember anything."

"It looks like a laparoscopy."

"What's that?" Jenna had to know, though part of her wanted to scream, *Just untie me and get me out of here!* This girl was her last chance, and she didn't want to blow it.

"It allows a doctor to see inside your reproductive system. It's used for cyst removal and egg retrievals." Sarah spoke calmly but looked quite upset. "None of this makes sense, but if you don't want to be here, then no one should keep you against your will." She reached for the strap on Jenna's left wrist.

Jenna bit her tongue to keep from shouting with joy.

A minute later she was standing, waiting for the dizziness to pass before she could move. Her legs felt weak and threatened to buckle. She experienced a sense of déjà vu, as if she'd tried this recently. Yet it seemed dreamlike and unreal. "I need your help, Sarah."

"What should I do?" The girl kept glancing at the door, but her expression was confident, at peace with the decision she'd made.

"Put your arm around me and get me out of here." Jenna felt like a baby, standing on her own for the first time, excited, yet frightened and wanting to grab the nearest thing for support.

Sarah moved quickly to Jenna's side and threw an arm around her shoulders. Jenna slipped her arm around Sarah's waist and together they moved toward the door. Jenna's pulse raced. She expected the preacher/doctor to block her path any second.

They stepped out of the little gray room into a larger clinic area. Voices, a man and a woman's, came from the next room. Sarah put her finger against her lips, indicating Jenna should be quiet. A swinging door with a small window separated the rooms. Sarah moved quickly toward a set of double doors to the left. Jenna struggled to stay with her. She was disoriented, and her heart hammered so hard she thought it would explode.

As they scurried down the hall, the euphoria of escaping was overshadowed by the fear that a strong hand was about to grab her shoulder from behind and drag her down. Sucking air in short frantic breaths, Jenna climbed the rough stone steps at the end of the hall, supported by Sarah, the angel who'd come to rescue her. The journey seemed unreal, a frantic ending to a long nightmare.

With each step, her legs grew stronger, responding with the conditioning of dozens of miles of roadwork. At the top of the stairs, Jenna let go of Sarah's waist. They entered an open area, also made of gray stone, with a circular tower in the center. Two women in long, drab skirts sat on a wooden bench talking, while a baby crawled on the floor at their feet. They glanced up, startled, as Jenna and Sarah burst into the room.

"This way." Sarah tugged at Jenna's shoulder, leading her down the narrow corridor before she could look around. Curious, but terrified of being caught, Jenna didn't look back.

Sarah led her into a large kitchen, bright and warm and cozy with the smell of baking bread. Sarah didn't even slow down, but Jenna was hit with a wave of homesickness so powerful it felt like a physical blow. She would have given anything to be home in her own kitchen baking low-fat apple cobbler and sipping Italian coffee. The group of women seated at the table peeling potatoes looked up in surprise.

"Sarah? What's going on?" An older woman called out as they hurried past.

"Pretend you didn't see us," Sarah yelled without turning back.

They pushed into a small mudroom filled with boots, jackets, gloves, and hats. Moving through another swinging door, they entered the largest greenhouse Jenna had ever seen.

The brightness made her blink. Beyond the sheets of translucent plastic fifteen feet above her head, the sun was a fireball in the sky. Jenna wondered how long she'd been underground. The tangy smell of tomatoes and basil filled her senses and made her stomach growl.

She promptly vomited a small stream of clear liquid. Sarah looked back and motioned for her to keep moving. Jenna forced herself to continue through the rows of plants, past a group of giggling young girls, and finally out into the open air, where a pale sky stretched to the horizon.

Sarah stopped and turned to Jenna. "Are you all right?"

She was aware of pain in her lower abdomen, upper legs, and right shoulder. Her whole body felt weak, as if she'd just recovered from the flu. But she was free!

"I'm fine." Jenna quickly scanned the area. Beyond the plowed fields was dense forest. "Where are we?"

"About twenty-five miles from Blue River." Sarah grabbed her arm, and they started running toward a harvested cornfield, the earth hard and cold under Jenna's bare feet. The sweet mountain air was cool against her legs, and tiny pebbles bruised her feet. The discomfort was strangely wonderful. With each deep inhale, Jenna's brain sharpened a little more. She had never felt more alive.

"I'll show you a path to the main road, but then I have to go back." Sarah kept running, glancing over her shoulder, and speaking in short bursts. "I'm sure he knows you're gone already, but I think I can slow him down. Turn left when you reach the road, then keep going for about ten miles until you hit Deercreek, then go left again. Eventually you will come to Blue River."

"Can you call the police from here?" Jenna was scared to be on her own, scared of being picked up by the crazy man before she got very far.

"I'll try. He has a satellite phone, but his office may be locked." At the edge of the field, Sarah stopped and pointed. "There's a path beyond that first clump of trees. It's rugged, but it'll keep you off the road for now and save some time. Good luck."

Her angel turned and ran before Jenna had a chance to thank her. Jenna headed for the clump of trees, running for her life.

Chapter 43

Eric stopped at a Texaco Star Mart to buy a bottle of ibuprofen. From the waist up, he was a walking, pulsating wound. Just hanging on to the steering wheel hurt his upper chest. He also picked up a jumbo-sized coffee, two Snickers, and a tank of gas. He had a feeling this would be a long day. Especially without his cell phone, which he had not been able to find amid the blood and breakage in his house. It had to be in the hospital somewhere.

A few blocks later, he scooted onto the expressway that would connect him with Springfield and 126 East. He had to find Carmichael's hideaway. Jenna could be at the compound, imprisoned, drugged, and/or brainwashed. The police were waiting for directions and a subpoena, but he wasn't. Eric had to find Jenna. In a way, he'd looked for this woman all his life. He wasn't giving up now.

Subconsciously, he kept looking for the black truck. Not knowing exactly where he was going, he halfheartedly hoped he might run into Grafton, the ex-con, who would lead him to the secluded church. Eric knew it was wishful thinking. Just as finding Jenna was not likely. Yet he couldn't stop trying any more that he could cease to breathe. Letting go of things had never been easy for him.

He pulled off the road in the tiny town of Leaburg to call Joe, but got his message service again. He started to call Jackson, then changed his mind. What was the point? Even if Jackson learned the location of the church, he wouldn't share it with Eric. The police were like that. Moving stiffly, Eric climbed into the Firebird and continued west.

The sky had cleared to a pale gray, and the temperature was dropping. He had the heat turned up high but couldn't seem to get warm. Eric ate one of the Snickers, thinking it would help his blood sugar, but the trembling continued. He wished he'd bought and installed a new radio, as he'd planned. Music, or even the sound of someone's voice, would help keep his spirits up.

After a while, he felt light-headed. Eric opened the window to take in extra oxygen and kept going. He was determined to make it to Deercreek Road before he pulled off to rest. As the day wore on, traffic increased in both directions. He worried about drifting out of his lane and causing an accident. Eric quit watching for the black truck, downed most of the coffee, and fought to stay alert.

Half an hour later, he rounded the sharp curve that came before the turnoff to Deercreek. Eric slowed and watched carefully to the right. The gravel road was about seven miles this side of Blue River, and unmarked by anything other than an old sign that had fallen down years ago. The only reason Eric knew the location was that he'd ridden out here once with an environmentalist who wanted to show him a particularly heinous clear-cut.

The narrow gravel road twisted its way slowly uphill into the cool, dark pines. Relieved to be away from traffic, Eric relaxed his grip on the wheel. The heat in his car was stifling, yet he continued to shiver. His chest wound throbbed with a steady, hot rhythm. Eric broke into a cold sweat.

He knew he needed to stop and sleep for a while, but he pushed ahead, navigating each curve as cautiously as an old woman. Eric kept going until his head lolled from side to side. He braked to a stop, shut the car off, and promptly dozed off.

Chapter 44 〉—

Once the embryos were transferred, Carmichael felt a tremendous relief. He whistled softy as he moved around the lab, sterilizing equipment and listening to Liz talk about pregnancy. As soon as he put everything in order, he could load Jenna into the van and get her out of his church. He wished Zeke were here to help him. Liz wouldn't be able to get up for hours. He chuckled softly to himself. Liz wouldn't be much help anyway.

Rachel burst into the room. "Jenna's gone!"

"What?" Carmichael spun around.

"I just went to check on her, and she's gone." Rachel seemed more nervous than frightened. "Her restraints had been undone. Someone let her go."

Carmichael couldn't believe what he was hearing. "You let her go, didn't you?"

"Of course not!" Rachel shouted back. She was obviously distressed and Carmichael believed her.

Minutes! He'd been minutes away from transporting Jenna out of here. God damn it to hell anyway. Carmichael turned to Liz. "Don't get up or you'll lose the embryos. I'll find her."

He grabbed a syringe and dashed from the room before she could respond. A thunderous roar filled his ears, and he didn't trust himself not to hurt anyone who stepped into his path. Fueled by panic, he sprinted up the stairs. Carmichael could feel it all sliding away, the church, his clinic, his chance to be a father again.

He couldn't let it happen. He couldn't let Jenna see the compound or be found anywhere near his property. She needed another hearty dose of ketamine and a long trip north before she started talking to anyone.

Carmichael reached the central tower room. Danielle, a young, timid woman with a horrible scar on her face, was coming down from the platform.

"Reverend Carmichael! I just saw the strangest thing. Sarah and a woman I've never seen before just ran across the south field to the edge of the woods."

Stunned, Carmichael thought he must have misunderstood. "Tamara's Sarah?"

Danielle nodded. "I'm as surprised as you are, but I'm sure of it."

Carmichael shook his head. What was going on? "Thank you, Danielle." He touched her on the shoulder. "Now get back up and keep a sharp eye out."

"Yes, sir." She scurried up the circular steps.

Rachel came panting up from the clinic, calling out to him. Carmichael ignored her and ran toward the kitchen, the most direct route to the south field. Sarah's involvement was such a mystery. The last he'd heard, Sarah had ditched Rachel in Eugene after they left the hospital. How had she gotten back to the compound and into the clinic? Had he left the labor-room door unlocked after Jenna's oocyte retrieval?

Carmichael wished Zeke was by his side. Zeke would track Jenna down like a hunting dog after a fox. Why hadn't he heard from him?

He charged through the kitchen, oblivious to the women who called after him, their voices shrill with confusion and drama. Their tranquil lives had been subject to more commotion in the last few days than they usually saw in a year. Lungs aching, Carmichael burst through the mudroom into the greenhouse. He ran straight into Sarah, knocking her to the ground. Concerned that he'd injured the girl, he stopped and turned.

"Are you all right?" He reached out to offer help. Eyes blazing with anger, Sarah grasped his hand in a painful grip and pulled herself up.

"Answer me, Sarah, are you all right?"

"No, I'm not. I need to talk to you."

Exasperated, Carmichael jerked his hand free. "Not now. If you're hurt, see Rachel. She should be coming along any second." He turned and started to jog away.

"Why did you make Darcie pregnant?"

Carmichael froze. When had she talked to Darcie? And for God's sake, why was everything coming apart now? He turned to face her. "I didn't! Darcie is confused and untrustworthy. Now, please, I have to go. We'll talk about this later."

The look of disbelief on Sarah's face hurt him deeply. Carmichael wanted to reach out, draw her back into the fold. It would have to wait. He turned and trotted into the field. Jenna had to be found and brought back, at least for now. It shouldn't be too difficult, he told himself. After nine days in bed, she would be weak and disoriented from the drugs. She wouldn't get far.

Carmichael heard Sarah running after him, and he silently cursed her. If she didn't back off, he would be forced to use the syringe he'd brought for Jenna on Sarah instead. In a few moments, the girl caught up to him and grabbed his arm.

"Why was Jenna being kept here?" Sarah shouted and pulled against him, trying to slow him down. Her strength surprised him. "What kind of man are you, Reverend?"

Carmichael stopped and shook free. He took a moment to speak as gently as he could, considering the magnitude of his stress. "I am the same man you have always known. Jenna is a drug addict and her family asked me to keep her here until she was free of her addiction. Now I must find her before she hurts herself or becomes lost and dies of exposure."

Sarah's expression progressed from relief to confusion to disbelief. "Why did you do a laparoscopy on her?"

Carmichael started to give her the same story he'd told Rachel, then decided he didn't have time. Sarah was working against him and needed to be put on hold. Carmichael grabbed her shoulder and plunged the needle into her deltoid, giving her only half the dose. Sarah started to protest, but muted squawking sounds came out instead. She staggered backward and collapsed.

Carmichael left her prone in the barren cornfield. The sun was warm and she would be fine. She would wake in a few hours and not remember a thing, maybe not even how she'd helped Jenna escape. He would deal with Sarah later. Carmichael turned back to the compound. Jenna had too great a head start on him now. He needed to get the van and cut her off where the trail reached the road. Jogging, he headed east across the field to where he kept the van, outside his office. He noticed several women watching him from just inside the greenhouse.

Had they seen him with Sarah? *Of course they had*, he thought bitterly. He would have a lot of explaining to do, but the

Sisters loved him and would take it in stride. Once Jenna was safely transferred, he could put his church and daily routine back together. *Damn Elizabeth! Damn her selfishness.* She had made it seem so simple, so harmless. Just grab the woman, pump her full of hormones, then harvest and transfer a few eggs. Throw in a few memory-repressing drugs and drop her a hundred miles from home, and she would never know what happened.

They hadn't counted on the reporter witnessing the kidnapping. Or Sarah getting nosy. Carmichael still couldn't figure out how she'd become involved. He remembered at the last moment to dash down to the clinic for another syringe of ketamine and Versed. He ignored Elizabeth's questions and pleas to be careful. He knew it must be killing her to stay on the examining table and depend on him to get the situation under control, but he couldn't take time to reassure her.

Carmichael rushed up the stairs. At first he ignored the women and children who'd come out of their sewing circles and classrooms to whisper and stare. But they had been loyal, and he owed them something.

"Pray for me," he called out as he ran through the foyer and into the chapel. He ducked into his office to grab his keys, then out his private entrance to the van.

Chapter 45 >—

The path wasn't really a path at all, but a barely discernible trail. The pinecones cut her feet and Jenna kept stubbing her toes on rocky inclines. But she kept running, breathing in a slow, steady rhythm that was very familiar. She checked over her shoulder a few times, but no one was back there.

She was free. She was free. She was free. The words kept playing in her brain like a mantra. As she moved farther and farther from the prison, her fear gave way to exhilaration. She wasn't even sure what she'd escaped from. Her mind was still a mess of foggy images and long dark blanks, but it didn't matter at the moment. She was free.

She hurt everywhere, but she was alive. Jenna's legs stayed strong, despite the pain, all those miles of jogging paying off. She was cold and hungry and didn't know where she would find sanctuary, but she was free.

The sun was up beyond the shade of the trees, still high in the sky. Jenna guessed it was early afternoon. Sarah had said Blue River was twenty-five miles away. It felt wonderful to know her actual time and place, after being in a black hole, drugged and disoriented, for God only knew how long.

Jenna pushed herself, trying to keep up her pace even when the trail went uphill. Her feet eventually grew numb to the stinging pine needles and cold rocks. She planned to run until she hit the first road Sarah mentioned. After that she would run and walk in intervals as long as she could. Twenty-five miles to Blue River. She could do that in five hours.

Maybe.

By the time Jenna reached the dirt track, she was ready to collapse. She sank to a bed of pine needles and leaned her head against a tree. Her heart worked overtime and her legs trembled with exhaustion. She had never felt so vulnerable. Wearing only a nightgown, weak and disoriented, she was stuck in the middle of nowhere. The silence itself was frightening.

Jenna drifted off, her brain visiting the dark place to rest.

She woke to the rumble of a truck engine. Someone was coming! She would be saved! Jenna struggled to clear her mind again. She had to be coherent when the truck came by. The way she looked, they might think she was a mental patient or a lunatic. She had to sound rational if she expected someone to give her a ride.

Slowly she stood and brushed herself off. The truck sounded close now, but the trees were so thick and the road so curvy, she couldn't see it. The sound was coming from the right. Sarah had said to turn right at the dirt road and follow it to…Jenna couldn't remember the name of the second road. The vehicle was going the wrong way to give her a ride.

A black truck rounded the curve and stopped in front of her.

Or had Sarah said turn left? Jenna was confused and frightened.

The man at the wheel rolled down his window.

Jenna thought he looked familiar. It didn't matter, she realized too late. He was headed in the direction of the prison.

He called her name.

Jenna bolted. But she was exhausted, and the man overcame her in seconds. He grabbed her by the hair, jerking her to a painful stop. A gun pressed into her rib cage. For a second, Jenna wished he would shoot her and this horrible nightmare would end. It would be better to die than return to the gray room and mind fog of the prison. She was breathing too hard to taunt him. She twisted to face him. The man lifted the gun as if to strike her. The air filled with dust and the rumble of an engine. They both turned to see a white van thunder to a stop two feet away.

"Zeke! No!" the preacher/doctor shouted, just as Jenna's head exploded in pain.

* * *

When Zeke had seen the woman sitting by the road, he'd decided to drag her into the woods, put a bullet in her head, and be done with it. No one would ever find her out here. But fucking Carmichael had to show up. Now the Reverend was kneeling next to Jenna, trying to stop her bleeding.

"How the hell did she get loose?" Zeke demanded. He had no intention of taking any shit from the Reverend.

"Sarah untied her and led her out of the church."

"I thought Sarah was still in town."

"I don't understand either. Right now it hardly matters. Help me get her in the van." Carmichael was gently pressing his hands against the unconscious woman's head where Zeke had struck her with the gun.

Zeke's brain raced, trying to form a new plan. He was tempted to shoot both Carmichael and Jenna, then get in the truck and hightail it for the border. That would leave Elizabeth to blame him for the kidnapping. He wondered if Liz was at the compound.

"Did you do the transfer thing already?" Zeke bent down and grabbed Jenna by the legs.

"Yes." Carmichael lifted Jenna's torso.

"Is Liz at the compound?"

"Yes, why?"

"Just curious." They started toward the van, Jenna between them. Zeke felt a stab of pain on the upper left side of his chest. *He must have strained a pectoral picking her up*, he thought with disgust. He needed to start working out again.

"Were you planning to take her out of here today?" It took him a while to say it, he was breathing so hard. Maybe he ought to quit smoking too.

"I have to. I was hoping you'd show up to help me." Carmichael gave him a look, questioning where Zeke had been. Zeke ignored it. Carmichael opened the side doors and they laid Jenna on the floor. The Reverend pulled the syringe from his pocket and gave her an injection.

"We have to go back to the compound first," Carmichael announced, pulling the needle out. "To get some restraints and a blanket to cover her. This is going to be a long trip."

A quick stop at the compound was fine with Zeke. All he needed was five minutes to grab the Reverend's financial files from the church office. And maybe the cash Carmichael kept stashed.

"Where are you taking her?"

"North. To a little town just across the Washington border."

Beautiful. Zeke would convince Carmichael to bring Liz along, then he would shoot all three of them when they reached their destination. Or somewhere along the way. It hardly mattered as long as there were no witnesses and the bodies were left in a different jurisdiction with no IDs. The confusion would buy him time.

"I'll ride with you and keep an eye on her."

Zeke was proud of himself for thinking it through. He never planned for any of it to turn out this way and didn't like to think of himself as a killer. Carmichael and his girlfriend had started this shit, and he didn't feel sorry for them. He felt bad about Jenna though. She seemed much worse for the wear, and who knew what Carmichael had done to her mind with all those drugs. She'd be better off dead.

It was a relief to know he wouldn't leave any loose ends or people to point a finger at him. He could start his new life without looking over his shoulder, wondering when the law would catch up with him. Zeke leaned back against the seat and massaged the pain in his left shoulder.

Chapter 46 >—

Eric woke with his face in a puddle of drool. He had no idea where he was or how he got there. After a moment of confusion, he recognized the interior of his car. He tried to sit up, but his chest hurt. Eric pushed with his elbows and gritted his teeth against the pain. Blood rushed from his head and he felt dizzy. He remembered driving and feeling his head spin. When the grogginess cleared, Eric looked around. All he saw were tall pine trees and a narrow gravel road.

It came back to him slowly. Being stabbed, seeing his attacker in the hospital, searching for Carmichael's church. Eric opened his blue denim shirt to check his wound. The bandage was soaked with blood but still intact. He left it in place. He must have pulled some stitches out. No wonder he'd been dizzy. The blood on the bandage was dark and congealed, no longer flowing freely. He felt weak but decided he'd be all right. He'd come too far to turn back now.

Pressure in his bladder forced him out of the car, as the jumbo coffee demanded release. Eric discovered the Firebird was parked in the middle of the road. He walked to an opening in the trees, then shuffled another twenty feet into the woods before relieving himself. He didn't expect company; it was a privacy thing.

With that distraction out of the way, he took in his surroundings and realized he was standing in the middle of an old dirt logging road with ruts so deep it was barely discernible as a path for vehicles. The road didn't look as if it was used often, but it did look as if it had been used recently.

Earlier, someone had splashed through the deep chuckhole where the two roads met, leaving a trail of wet tire marks that gradually disappeared into the forest. The black truck. Eric could picture it bouncing through an hour before. He hurried back to the Firebird and turned it around.

Adrenaline rushed through his system, giving Eric new strength. He bounced along the rough road wishing he had four-wheel drive—with a shotgun mounted in the cab. Approaching the hideout alone and unarmed was dangerous. Eric was scared, but he couldn't stop or turn back. He remembered that he had softball stuff in the trunk, including a bat. The knot in his stomach relaxed a little. A bat could be useful.

The road twisted and dipped and climbed. Eric kept his foot off the gas, not willing to risk tearing out his suspension. He felt himself getting weak again, so he ate the other Snickers. After driving for an hour, he noticed the trees began to thin and the mountain seemed to rise straight up around him. In a moment, Eric got his first sight of the structure that had been the home of gun-loving survivalists and now was the Church of the Reborn. It was huge and gray and had a cluster of smaller buildings connected by covered walkways. It reminded Eric of the prison he'd visited two days before.

Why would a religious commune be out here in the middle of nowhere? What were they hiding?

A cold, prickly sensation ran up his back. Eric eased off the road and shut the engine down. He could see a gray van, a dark-blue Lexus, and an old white truck parked under a long carport on the left side of the main building. Where was the black truck? Was Grafton not here? Eric wished he knew what he was up against. The thought of running into either Carmichael or the ex-con chilled the sweat on his chest. If he could maintain the element of surprise, Eric thought he might have a chance of finding Jenna—and coming out alive.

Chapter 47

Elizabeth heard double footsteps thumping down David's private stairs from his office above. She lifted her head and glanced through the windows in the lab doors in time to see the men set Jenna down on the surgery table. Her face and head were covered with blood. No! Oh, please, no. She couldn't be dead. Elizabeth's insides went cold. Ralph's voice came back. *Killer liar whore killer.* No! How could this have happened?

Zeke! Of course. The bastard. Why hadn't David stopped him? Elizabeth heard David and Zeke's muted voices, then the sound of Zeke clomping into the hallway and up the main stairs. What was going on now? Why didn't David come in and talk to her? He knew she couldn't get up. She started to call out to him, then stopped when she heard David's voice. Was he talking to Jenna?

Was her sister still alive or had David lost his mind? His voice was so gentle and loving. Elizabeth slid off the gurney bed and hurried to the connecting door.

She watched through the plexiglas as David meticulously cleaned her sister's wounds, making soothing noises as he worked. Jenna was alive! Relief washed over Elizabeth. She would have never been able to live with herself if Jenna had died. What kind of mother could she be with her sister's death on her conscience? How would she ever look her daughter in the eye?

The embryos!

Elizabeth clutched her abdomen. What was she doing standing here?

She hurried back to the hospital bed. Was it too late? The survival rate for IVF embryos was less than fifty percent. Had she blown the whole cycle with one thoughtless moment? Ralph's voice gently mocked her. *Barren barren barren barren.*

David pushed through the doors as she eased into a reclining position. "Zeke wants us all to drive to Washington with Jenna."

"Why?" Elizabeth sat up. She wasn't going anywhere yet. "What happened to Jenna? Is she all right?"

"She's fine. Zeke thinks the police could raid the church at any moment and that we should get her out of here right now." David moved toward the bed. New wrinkles had worked their way into the skin around his mouth. "I think he's right."

"Because of the reporter?" Sharp spikes of tension streaked up Elizabeth's neck. She wondered if it was too soon to take another Valium. "Because of those pictures in the paper?"

"There's more, but we don't have time to talk right now. I need to pack both of us a small bag and get Jenna ready to travel."

"I want to keep one of her ovaries."

"What?" David was stunned.

"We should harvest one ovary and sustain it with fetal tissue and hormones. It's been done." Elizabeth spoke rapidly, remembering the article she'd read recently. "A team of researchers in Australia—"

"But why?" David cut her off.

"In case these embryos don't survive." Elizabeth felt the hot pressure of tears build behind her eyes. She clenched her fists. Why was she getting emotional now? "I've been under a lot of stress these last few days." She stopped and swallowed hard. "Then these last few hours of waiting and not knowing what was going on have been pure hell. What baby would implant itself in this negative environment?"

"Your embryos will be fine. Stop worrying." David stroked her hair and made soothing noises.

Despite his many weaknesses, he was a kind man, Elizabeth thought. "Will you do the surgery? Keep an ovary for me?" She felt better already, her emotions fading as quickly as they came.

"There isn't time, Liz." David looked weary, older than she'd ever seen him.

"It would only take an hour. Or less. You shouldn't take her out of here until after dark anyway." Elizabeth grabbed his pale, delicate hands. "Please, David. Think of the research possibilities. You could make medical history."

"But no one would ever know," David mumbled, but his eyes danced with intrigue.

"What have you got to lose?"

"Everything, if the police get here while I'm operating."

Elizabeth was silent. She didn't believe the police were on their way. Nobody even knew where the damn church was. It was just Zeke's way of trying to control the situation.

"There isn't time, Liz. We all need to get out of here."

"I'm not going unless we do the harvest."

David shrugged. "We'll go without you. If you stay and the police come, you'll be arrested and questioned."

"I'll tell them everything. You and Zeke will be picked up before you drop her off." It was a bluff, but Elizabeth was determined to have one more chance. She had a bad feeling about today's transfer. Jenna only needed one ovary for herself. If they could keep the other one alive and harvest more oocytes, she could have that chance.

"Elizabeth." David collapsed in a chair, unable to finish his plea.

"Less than an hour, David." Elizabeth felt animated, suddenly realizing the full possibilities of what she had planned. "Just think. We can create and freeze as many embryos as we can produce for as long as we keep the ovary alive."

"Which Australian doctors and where did you read this article?" David pretended to be skeptical, but Elizabeth could tell he was intrigued by the challenge.

"Jochian and Weber, last month's *Journal of Embryonic Medicine*."

"You said fetal tissue?"

"Monkeys and pigs, they claim, but you know researchers are using aborted fetuses for various types of gene therapy."

David nodded. "Pig fetal tissue has proven to be a great culture medium."

"Then you'll do it?"

"You'll have to assist."

She should have expected it. David always struck a bargain if he could. He was testing her to see how badly she wanted the ovary. "Do you think it's safe for me to get up?"

"Of course. It's been a couple of hours."

Damn him. He knew she wanted to stay down as long as possible. "You get her shaved and prepped and ready first."

"No, you get her ready. I have to prepare a culture for the ovary."

Elizabeth got to her feet. After an embryo transfer in the ARC, the women went home after a few hours. She would just have to take her chances like everyone else.

She pushed through the double doors into the surgery area, seeing her sister for the first time since that day in the clinic. She was so pretty, even with the abrasion on her temple. Jenna was pale now. Her outdoor glow and robust look were gone. She would recover quickly, though, Elizabeth told herself.

She unbuttoned Jenna's nightgown to expose her torso. She stared at the paralyzed woman, so similar to herself. A long shiver rippled down her spine. Jenna had the same round, high breasts, long torso, and wide hips. Did they have their mother's body? Did they look like her?

Elizabeth's hands trembled as she shaved Jenna's flat lower abdomen. It wasn't fair. Her sister had two working ovaries, while her own insides were a mess of dysfunctional scar tissue. Jenna was a good person. She wouldn't mind sharing. If the situation had been reversed, Elizabeth would have donated oocytes to Jenna. She was sure of it.

She applied a topical disinfectant, stroking Jenna's abdomen absentmindedly. Why had their mother abandoned them? Did she have any idea what she'd done? The selfish woman had caused all of this with her irresponsible behavior. How different their lives would have been if she'd kept them together. She and Jenna might have been sitting in a restaurant, having lunch, and talking about their children.

Liar thief barren whore. Jenna's voice joined the others in her head.

Elizabeth jumped back from the table.

"Ready to scrub in?" David was watching from across the room, an unreadable expression on his face.

Elizabeth nodded and they moved together toward the sink. After a minute of ritual hand washing, David cleared his throat. "This clears my debt, Liz. All of it. Even the money."

"You feel differently about me now, don't you?"

"I don't know what I feel right now except stress. I want this woman out of my life as soon as possible."

"You're attracted to her, aren't you? I saw the way you looked at her." Elizabeth was surprised by how much it bothered her. David had always had other lovers. Her sister was different.

David picked up a pair of latex gloves and grinned. "She looks so much like you, how can I not be?"

Liar thief whore. Jenna's voice grew strong.

Elizabeth bit back her anger as she pulled on gloves. David was such a charmer. That's why the checks poured into the church every month. Little old ladies who'd heard him speak once at a garden meeting would send him money forever. He would probably even weasel more money out of her in the future. Maybe not. Once she had a child, everything would be different. She would be different. She wouldn't need David in the same way.

They stood on either side of the operating table, and David verbally walked her through the procedure. Elizabeth felt nervous. This was different from sucking a few oocytes through a tiny incision. David was going to cut through muscle and tissue to remove an ovary. Elizabeth hadn't done any cutting since her intern days. The scalpel glinted under the bright fluorescent lighting. David pressed it hard against Jenna's pale flesh.

As a thin line of blood began to show, Danielle burst through the double doors. "Reverend! There's a stranger outside the church. He's carrying a bat and sneaking around! I saw him from the tower."

Chapter 48

Eric worked his way around to the side of the huge stone building. Going in through the front door did not seem like a good idea. He could hear children on the far side, laughing and shouting as if on a playground despite the chill in the air. Three women had come out through the double front doors while he hid behind a tractor and planned his approach. The women had chatted and carried Bibles as if on their way to church. This was a church, he reminded himself. He had no proof that his attacker or the elusive Dr. Carmichael—or Jenna for that matter—was even here. He could only hope.

He moved along the outside of the building, staying as close to the wall as he could. Low-growing shrubs and thick patches of weeds created a natural barrier. Eric struggled through the brush, searching for an opening, even a small ventilation hole, but the wall was solid. His chest wound throbbed, and it hurt to breathe deeply. Eric moved along low to the ground, panting like a dog in hot weather. When the shrubs cleared in a small patch, he took the opportunity to lean against the stone to rest.

The wall gave way and Eric stumbled through the opening, slamming into an interior wall, which was, fortunately, made of sheetrock instead of brick. It took his eyes a minute to adjust to the shadowy darkness of his surroundings before he noted a narrow slit of light from a spot a few feet away. The dim whiteness illuminated a row of pants, sweaters, and light-colored shirts hanging from an overhead rod.

He was in a closet.

He moved cautiously through the doorway, bat poised and ready. The room was narrow, like dorms at a university, with only a bed, nightstand, and large chest of drawers. Cautiously, Eric moved past the foot of the bed to the wooden door. It was locked.

From the inside. All he had to do was turn the dead bolt. The next room was slightly larger, containing desks, file cabinets, and a computer setup complete with printer and modem. Eric wanted to snoop around, especially in the computer, but his sense of urgency had grown. The idea that Jenna was here and needed his help compelled him forward. The place was strangely quiet, the voices of women and children no longer present. A deep sense of dread weighted his legs, slowing him down. Ever so slowly, Eric edged the next door open and peered through a crack into what appeared to be the pulpit of a small, crude chapel.

A middle-aged woman and a young girl sat in the second pew, heads bowed in prayer. Beyond them, the room was empty. Eric stepped into the foyer and lowered the bat to his side. He didn't want to frighten the innocent, didn't want their screams to alert the bastards who ran the place. The two became aware of him as he passed, but only stared, frightened and silent. Eric kept his own silence. He wished Jackson were with him. Jackson and his Sig Sauer.

The chapel opened into a wide central room with a spiral staircase in the center. Eric realized it led to the watchtower he'd seen from the car. A group of women were gathered around the base of the stairs, talking excitedly. They were all different ages but dressed similarly in long skirts and sweaters. A silence fell over the cluster as he approached.

"Who are you?" a thin, dark-haired woman asked, voice trembling.

"Eric Troutman." What else should he say? Would the truth put Jenna at risk?

"Why are you here?"

"I'm looking for someone. A woman named Jenna. Is she here?"

The whispered, excited conversation resumed in full force, with many glances in his direction. Eric waited nervously, watching for Grafton or Carmichael.

The dark-haired woman came forward and spoke in a whisper. "Are you her husband?"

"No. Just a good friend."

"Why are you carrying the bat?"

"Self-protection. I don't want to hurt anyone. I just want to get Jenna and leave."

"You should leave her in the church until she's better. It's the best place for her right now."

"Better?" Eric's stomach flip-flopped. "What's wrong with her?"

"She has a drug—" The woman stopped and her eyes and mouth popped open in disbelief. Eric turned, hearing the voice and seeing the man at the same time.

"Shut up, Rachel!" The man who'd stabbed him two nights earlier in his own kitchen was here now, holding a small gun and looking extremely annoyed. The women's chatter stopped.

"Why do you have a gun, Zeke?" Rachel asked bravely.

"I said, shut up!" He pointed the gun at Eric's head. "Put the bat down and move slowly toward the back stairs."

Eric laid the bat on the floor, never taking his eyes off Grafton. The man was muscular but skinny and looked to be in his early fifties. Eric had at least forty pounds on him. Without the gun, he should have been able to take him down easily. But this man had almost killed him before. Eric's knees felt weak and his heart pounded against his chest wound. He stepped to the left, hands out from his sides.

"Go about your business, all of you!" Grafton thundered. The women scattered like frightened squirrels. Only Rachel stood her ground. The ex-con ignored her, eyeballing Eric and waving the gun at a dark opening in the wall.

Eric went where he was told, the stink of his own sweat permeating the narrow hallway. In front of him were descending stairs. What in God's name was down there? Would Grafton shoot him in the back now that they were alone? Or would he find out what had become of Jenna before they killed him? His death seemed certain. The fact that he hadn't already been killed seemed like a small miracle, and it was only due to the presence of the church women.

"Move." The gun poked him in the back.

Eric moved.

At the bottom of the stairs, a long hallway stretched out, with a series of rooms off to the left. The first area was open and looked like an examining room in a medical clinic. Eric heard voices from deep inside, a man and a woman shouting at each other. The presence of a woman gave him hope. Maybe he would survive. Eric stopped. The woman sounded familiar. Grafton prodded him in the back with the gun. "In there."

Eric pushed through the double swinging doors into a large room lined with stainless-steel counters and overhead fluorescent lights. It appeared to be a crowded medical lab. A wide swinging door to the right led to another area, from which Eric again heard shouting. He assumed that was where they were going. He moved slowly forward, scanning the counters for something that could be used as a weapon. Microscopes, glass tubes, a small refrigerator. Nothing sharp or handy.

The gun still pressed against his back, Eric pushed through the single swinging door. The third area was bright, spare, and clearly being used as an operating room. The man and woman, one on each side of a narrow table, stopped shouting and turned to stare. A white sheet covered what was obviously a patient lying between them.

Eric recognized Carmichael immediately. He'd seen him get into the van with Jenna the day she disappeared, then he'd seen a picture of him just days ago. It took a moment longer to realize the woman was Dr. Demauer, whom he'd met briefly in the hospital.

"Damn it, Zeke! Why did you bring him in here?" Except for the blush of anger in his cheeks, Carmichael's pale skin seemed almost blue under the fluorescent lights.

What kind of illegal medical practice were they running down here? And what had they done to Jenna? Eric felt sick.

Zeke stepped out from behind him, keeping the gun aimed at his head. "What else should I have done with him? There's a church full of women and children upstairs."

"I know we have to deal with him, but not here in my clinic." Carmichael seemed to be fighting for control.

"What in the hell are you guys doing?" Zeke finally noticed their activity. "You're supposed to be getting ready for a road trip!"

Eric inched forward, straining to see the patient.

"Give him a shot of ketamine!" Demauer screeched at Carmichael.

"Good idea." Carmichael moved away from the operating table and stepped briskly toward what looked like a small office in back.

The patient's face was turned away from him, but Eric's eyes widened when he saw her long, honey-colored braid. It was Jenna! And she was alive! She must be; he could see a steady breathing movement under the sheet.

Ignoring his wounds, Eric threw himself sideways, knocking Grafton into a wall. The man's head smacked against the tile-over-stone wall with a dull ringing sound and he slid to the floor. The gun dropped from the ex-con's hand and skidded under the operating table. Before Eric could dive for it, Demauer bent down and picked up the weapon. She pointed it at Eric, her hands shaking so badly the gun seemed to be alive.

"Don't make me hurt you. Let David give you the ketamine and everyone will be all right. You won't even remember what happened." Demauer's eyes glistened with unshed tears.

Oh shit. He heard Carmichael moving behind him, but Eric didn't take his eyes off Demauer. He couldn't just stand there and let Carmichael drug him. The lady doctor had obviously lost touch with reality, but did she have the nerve to shoot him? Would he and Jenna die anyway?

He felt the needle press against the knife wound in his bicep. Eric reacted blindly to the pain, jerking his arm upward and smashing his fist into Carmichael's face. The doctor dropped the syringe and screamed like a child as blood poured from his nose.

Eric spun back toward Demauer. She hadn't moved during the brief fight and her eyes held a faraway look. Maybe he could take the gun from her. She seemed to be fading in and out. Maybe not. If she was that far gone, she might kill him without hesitation. Where was the syringe? Eric looked around, not seeing it.

"Hey, tough guy." Grafton was on his feet with a scalpel poised above Jenna's throat. "Any more bullshit from you and this woman dies. Now lie down on the floor and let the doctor give you a shot."

Eric couldn't move.

"You think I won't kill her?" Grafton drew the scalpel lightly across Jenna's throat, and a thin line of blood appeared.

"Don't you dare hurt my sister!" Demauer swung the gun toward Grafton. They faced each other on opposite sides of the table, Jenna between them, silent under the white sheet.

Sister? Was the woman completely insane? Eric searched desperately for the syringe out of the corner of his eye.

"Liz, give me the gun." Carmichael moved toward Demauer while keeping his distance from Eric. He still had one hand pressed to his nose, trying to stem the flow of blood.

"Get the syringe and give him the shot." Grafton tried to bark out the words, but there was no strength to his voice. Carmichael hesitated, shifting his focus between Demauer and the ex-con.

"We have to get moving, for Christ's sake!" The ex-con grimaced. He now sounded like he was in pain.

Carmichael spoke rapidly to Demauer. "It's over, Liz. We're not going to take Jenna's ovary. You're not going to shoot anyone. Give the gun to Zeke. We might still get out of here, but only if we leave now." He turned and began to search the floor for the syringe.

At the mention of the ovary, Eric got his first glimmer of what was going on.

"But what if I don't get pregnant?" Demauer's voice was childlike, pathetic in its selfishness.

"Oh, shut up!" Carmichael bellowed without even looking up.

They spotted the syringe at the same time. *Oh shit.* It was now or never.

Eric lunged for the syringe, but lost his balance and fell. Adrenaline and willpower brought him to his feet again. Carmichael was there, waiting to wrestle the syringe from his hands. Eric threw himself forward, aiming for the doctor's left shoulder. Carmichael's eyes widened in fright and he stepped sideways.

Not fast enough. The needle penetrated a muscle just below Carmichael's clavicle. Eric pressed the plunger, then jumped back, taking the syringe with him. The drug was mostly spent, but it was the only weapon he had. Carmichael tried to speak, but no words came out. A moment later, he collapsed.

Eric whirled back to the operating table. Demauer still had the gun and Grafton was coming at him with the scalpel. *Oh god, not again.* Eric's heart pounded in his ears.

Grafton stumbled, then clutched at his chest. "Oh fuck." The man staggered forward, making a clumsy effort to stab at Eric. He missed and fell to his knees. "Doublefuck." Grafton pitched forward, hugging himself in obvious agony before passing out.

Eric didn't have time to rejoice. He turned back to Demauer, who now had the gun pointed at his chest.

"It's over," he pleaded. "The police are on their way."

The woman seemed not to hear him. She turned to the operating table. Eric stepped forward. Jenna's eyes were open.

"Put the gun down." He tried to sound friendly. "I know you don't want to hurt anyone. You're a doctor, not a killer."

Demauer didn't hear him. She was talking to Jenna, begging to be understood. "I just wanted to have a baby of my own. All I needed from you was a couple of mature eggs. I know I should have asked, but I was afraid you'd say no."

Jenna sat partway up, the sheet falling away. She seemed to be coming back from a far-off place and was unaware of her own nakedness. Eric resisted the urge to rush toward her. Demauer was unpredictable, too close to the edge to be trusted.

"Who are you?" Jenna asked softly, looking up at Demauer.

"Can't you see the resemblance?" The doctor smiled warmly, leaning toward Jenna as if they were good friends. "I know my hair is a lot shorter than yours, but we have similar faces. We have the same mother." She touched Jenna's hair. "If you can find a way to forgive me, we can be a family."

"What do you mean we have the same mother? Don't you work at the ARC?"

Eric watched Jenna struggle to comprehend. His heart went out to her. He now had a pretty good idea of what was going on, but she would probably never fully understand her sister's actions.

"We're twins." Demauer smiled. "Not identical, but born at the same time and adopted by different people." She shook her head. "I can't believe your mother never told you. It's so selfish." The gun was down at her side now.

Eric moved cautiously toward the two women. Jenna saw him for the first time. "Eric?"

"Get back!" Demauer swung around, pointing the gun at his head. "This is between us. I may never have another chance with my sister, and if I have to shoot you, I will. Your life doesn't mean anything to me right now, but Jenna's forgiveness does."

"All right." Eric spoke softly, letting her know he wasn't a threat. At this point, he really wasn't. He didn't know how much longer he could hold up, but he had the feeling Jenna was no longer in danger. His own safety was another matter.

"Are you the reason I'm here?" Jenna's eyes darted from Demauer's face to the gun.

"I won't hurt you." Demauer started to sob. "Not any more than I already have."

"But why?"

"I wanted to have a baby. Just like you wanted to have a baby." The doctor continued to cry. "But my ovaries don't produce eggs, and I didn't want to adopt." She fought for control, wiping at her eyes with one hand. "I knew I was adopted, and my childhood was hell. Adoption wasn't even an option for me. With all the advances in fertility treatments, I knew somehow there had to be a way for me to have a child from my own genes." Demauer smiled softly. "Then you walked into the clinic."

Jenna leaned forward, mesmerized. "How did you know we were sisters?"

"You looked so much like me, I compared our DNA."

"And decided to help yourself to it?"

"It was selfish, I know." Demauer bit her lip. "Can you forgive me?"

"Why should I? Do you have any idea what it's been like for me here?" Jenna's voice escalated, emotion pouring out in audible sound waves. "What is this place anyway? And who is that creepy preacher guy?"

Demauer started to speak, then stopped suddenly. Her focus shifted to the wall behind Eric. He heard the door swing open.

Jackson, Schakowski, and two other officers burst into the room, guns drawn.

"Nobody move!" Jackson's voice boomed against the stone walls. Eric sagged with relief.

There was a moment of silence, then Demauer's gun went off, a booming explosion that shook the room. Eric dropped to his knees. Gunfire filled the room, a deafening cacophony of metal thunder. Demauer's body flew back, her blood splattering the white walls.

Chapter 49

Jenna refused to be admitted to the hospital. She had already been in the emergency room for hours, and a dozen different doctors had examined her. Nurses had taken her blood, checked her vital signs, and cleaned her various wounds. The clearer her mind felt, the more desperate she was to leave.

"We need to run more tests, do a CAT scan. It's important that you stay overnight for observation. You've had a combination of powerful drugs pumped through your system. There could be serious side effects."

This particular doctor—Jenna couldn't remember his name— was older and more intimidating than the others. She still had no intention of spending the night in the hospital.

"What would you do if you did discover a side effect?"

"We'd give you something to counteract it."

"More drugs? No thanks."

Jenna was worried about the long-term effects of what had been done to her, but she couldn't bring herself to lie down in a hospital bed and let them stick an IV in her arm. They'd already determined her ovaries were fine except for a large cyst, which would be removed at a later date. That was all she needed to know for now. In the meantime, she wanted to get away from the hospital, away from the doctors and their poking and prodding.

"Run the tests if you have to, but don't expect me to lie down for it. I may even sleep sitting up for a few weeks." She laughed at her own intensity. Even though it felt good, she stopped herself, afraid the laughter would abruptly turn to tears. She didn't trust her emotions, didn't trust the doctors, wouldn't trust her own mother if she walked into the room.

"I realize you've been through a lot but—"

"Forget it. Just do what you have to do and make it fast. I want to go home."

"That's what I keep telling them, but they won't let me go either." Eric rolled into the little room in a wheelchair. Jenna's heart leapt into her throat. It was like seeing someone from another lifetime, someone she'd loved and thought she'd never see again. His smile was beautiful. A little less carefree than she remembered, but totally heartwarming. She wanted to throw herself into his arms but didn't dare. He'd been seriously injured because of his determination to find her.

She forced herself to sound casual. "I hear you escaped from here once already, fortunately for me." She had heard most of Eric's story from the cops who brought her in and one of the doctors who examined her.

"Obviously, I didn't get very far." His expression was suddenly serious. "How are you, Jenna?"

"I feel like an alcoholic who has just sobered up from a two-week blackout. I'm weak, dazed, shaky, blank, and vulnerable." Jenna shrugged. "But fine other than that."

"Do you remember anything of the time you spent at the compound?"

Jenna remembered the crazy preacher/doctor's eyes. She would never forget those piercing gray eyes. She remembered, fairly clearly, her conversation with Dr. Demauer, which seemed distinct and separate from the rest of her time in the basement. "I remember running through a field with a pretty blonde girl, but not much else. Who was she, by the way?"

"One of Carmichael's followers." Dr. Rubison cut in with the information. "Actually, she's the daughter of one of his followers. Her name is Sarah, and she's here in the hospital. He hit her with a dose of ketamine right after she helped you escape."

"Is she all right?"

"She's fine. They'll release her soon. But this conversation can wait." Dr. Rubison tapped the back of the wheelchair he'd opened for her. "Jenna needs to go upstairs for a CAT scan now."

Jenna ignored the doctor and kept her eyes on Eric. Before she had a chance to ask him how he ever found her, a tall, dark-haired man in a dark suit was escorted into the room by a nurse.

Eric grinned. "Hey, Jackson. Just the man I wanted to see."

"Don't even talk to me, Troutman. You went way over the line between brave and stupid."

Jenna sensed these men were good friends.

"I know." Unaffected by the harsh words, Eric turned to her. "This is Detective Jackson. He's the man who saved us both."

"Thank you." Jenna had a million questions, but Eric beat her to the big one.

"So what does Carmichael have to say?

The detective shook his head. "What you'd expect. That it was Demauer's idea. That she and Grafton forced him to go along, threatening to expose Carmichael's medical practices to his major contributors if he didn't do the egg-transfer thing, whatever it's called." Jackson made a scoffing sound. "Carmichael claims they planned to let Jenna go. He says he would never hurt anyone."

Jenna didn't believe it for a minute. She would have died in that basement if Eric hadn't shown up.

"Carmichael has been running a little test-tube baby clinic out at the compound for years. The plan, according to Carmichael, was to let Jenna go after messing up her memory with drugs." Jackson turned to Eric. "But you saw them grab her that day by the park and you put those composite drawings in the paper."

Eric groaned.

"Grafton apparently got scared and decided to kill you. Carmichael claims he didn't know anything about that action. He says he tried to keep Demauer from killing both of you." The detective rolled his eyes.

"It's true." Eric looked grim. "I hate to admit it, but he did try to get Demauer to put down the gun."

Jackson was suddenly all business. "I'll need a detailed statement from both of you whenever you're feeling up to it."

"I can't believe that woman was my sister." Jenna still couldn't get over it. She'd been thinking about Demauer nonstop since she'd left the compound. What terrible things had happened to her sister to make her so desperate? Why had their real mother given them up? There were so many questions she might never have answers to.

"Did anyone call my mother? To let her know I'm all right?"

A dark look passed across Eric's face. Jenna braced herself for bad news.

"I don't think she ever knew you were missing."

There was a long silence. Jenna's mother had always been a mystery to her. At least now she knew why. She let go of the hurt and laughed out loud for the first time in ages.

"It's probably a good thing. If she and Eric had both been looking for me, I would have been killed for sure."

Eric's cheeks blazed. "Hey, I meant well."

The doctor cleared his throat. "I hate to rush this, but I was scheduled to go home hours ago. Let's get this CAT scan done now."

Jenna slid off the narrow hospital bed into the wheelchair. Might as well get it over with. Find out all the bad news at once. Then she would put her life back together, one step at a time.

"When are you getting out of here?" She looked back at Eric's beautiful blue eyes.

"Tomorrow."

"Would you like to have dinner with me tomorrow night?"

"I don't know." He grinned like a kid trying to keep a secret. "You stood me up last time we made a date."

"Give me another chance."

"All right. Where do you want to go?"

"Geronimo's. I have some unfinished business there."

"Pick you up at six?"

"Can you drive with your injuries?"

Dr. Rubison lost his patience and started pushing her wheelchair out of the room.

"I'll hire a limo." Eric beamed at her as she rolled by. "We have a lot to celebrate."

Jenna had to agree. "It's a date."

Chapter 50

"Do you think she'll look like me?" Jenna asked out of the blue.

"You mean, will you look like her?" Eric knew he shouldn't give her a hard time. In less than an hour, Jenna would be meeting her biological mother for the first time. He couldn't help it though. Jenna was so serious, and he had such fun teasing her.

"Whatever." She gave him a phony piercing look.

"I think you're lucky to have found her after all these years. Who cares what she looks like?"

"I don't, really." Jenna laughed. "I'm just nervous."

Eric loved it when she laughed. Her whole face brightened, and he could forget for a moment what she'd been through.

"Hey, I'm nervous too." He reached over and stroked her hair. They were driving west through Colorado to the town of Pueblo. After spending a day or so with Jenna's birth mother, they would head for various parts of Illinois to see his family.

"Not only am I about to meet my future mother-in-law," Eric paused and grinned. "I'm going to see my own mom for the first time in twenty years."

"I haven't agreed to marry you yet."

"Once everyone finds out you're pregnant, you will."

She shot him a worried look. "Promise me you won't say anything yet."

None of their friends back in Eugene knew, but they didn't have much of a social circle. Jenna had moved in with him after their third date, then started working out of their home as a fund-raiser for an environmental group. They rarely went out.

"If that's what you want." Eric didn't understand her reluctance. He wanted to shout the news from the rooftops. He'd waited a long time to become a father.

"I keep thinking something will go wrong." Jenna chewed the inside of her cheek. "Like my brain will start to malfunction, or I'll have a miscarriage. Who knows what the long-term effects of those drugs are? Right now my life seems too good to be true. I'm afraid if I talk about this baby, I'll jinx myself."

"Eventually you won't have to say anything. You're starting to show a little already."

"I am not." She sucked in her stomach. Even with the baggy T-shirt and cutoff sweatpants, Eric could still see the tiny bulge that was their child. His heart wanted to burst with happiness.

"Let's bring your mom with us to Illinois and get married while we're there. Save them all a trip out to Oregon later. My family will love it."

"You're crazy." Jenna smiled. "I love you anyway."

"Is that a yes?"

"I'll think about it."

About the Author

L.J. Sellers is a native of Eugene, Oregon, the setting of her thrillers. She's an award-winning journalist and bestselling novelist, as well as a cyclist, social networker, and thrill-seeking fanatic. A long-standing fan of police procedurals, she counts John Sandford, Michael Connelly, Ridley Pearson, and Lawrence Sanders among her favorites. Her own novels, featuring Detective Jackson, include *The Sex Club*, *Secrets to Die For*, *Thrilled to Death*, *Passions of the Dead*, *Dying for Justice*, *Liars, Cheaters, & Thieves*, and *Rules of Crime*. In addition, she's penned three standalone thrillers: *The Baby Thief*, *The Gauntlet Assassin*, and *The Lethal Effect*. When not plotting crime, she's also been known to perform standup comedy and occasionally jump out of airplanes.

18177736R00202

Made in the USA
Charleston, SC
20 March 2013